OH, SUGAR

Longlisted for the Santa Fé Writers' Project Literary Prize 2022

Jane Labous is the author of three novels, including *Past Participle* (Afsana Press), longlisted for the Bath Novel Awards 2022, and *The Chameleon Girl,* published in Nigeria by Farafina Books. Jane is also an award-winning journalist known for her frontline coverage of human rights, humanitarian and gender issues, always telling the powerful human stories behind the headlines, with credits ranging from the BBC – including regular slots on BBC Radio 4's *From Our Own Correspondent* – to other radio, magazines, newspapers, and the UN. She has won the BBC Radio 4 and Royal Geographical Society Journey of a Lifetime Award; a European Journalism Centre Development Reporting Grant, and a Guardian Development Prize, while her Senegal-based documentary, *Angels,* won the Merck More than a Mother Media Recognition & Film Award for Francophone African Countries 2019, and Best Documentary at the Southampton Film Festival 2019. Jane lives in Dorset with her daughter.

For more information: www.janelabous.com

OH, SUGAR

Jane Labous

Afsana Press
London

First published in 2024

by Afsana Press Ltd, London

www.afsana-press.com

Typeset by Afsana Press Ltd

Printed and bound in Great Britain by Clays Ltd, Elcograf S.p.A.

A CIP catalogue record for this book is available from the British Library

ISBN paperback: 978-1-7385552-1-5

ISBN hardback: 978-1-7385552-8-4

ISBN e-book: 978-1-7385552-2-2

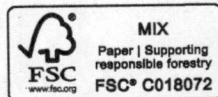

MIX
Paper | Supporting
responsible forestry
FSC www.fsc.org   FSC® C018072

PROLOGUE

Gloria Fontaine

Extract from tape six, taken from Gloria's diary

Sugar, I needed to get rid of the car, right away. My watch said four a.m. According to my mission schedule, I was exactly on time. There in the guts of the forest, I stood listening to the shrieks and scratches of a thousand nocturnal creatures, as my heart thudded in my chest, my skin poured with sweat. I was shivering slightly. Lourenco's men would be here soon, but I told myself there was nothing to be afraid of. After all, wasn't this once my world? Trying not to panic, I groped for my flask through the rear window of the Land Rover and took a long swig of lukewarm water.

Think, I told myself, think.

It was just getting light; luminous gold streaks slashed the deep indigo of dawn. I could see a dense tangle of vegetation organised in tiers, from a towering canopy of mahogany and teak trees through to the lower palms and fruits – paw paws, mangoes and sops, bananas and bread fruit – to the fungi and rotting leaves of the forest floor. A little way ahead, through the trees, I thought I could make out a small dip, and, as the sun rose further, I made out a meandering stream, then a hill sloping downwards to a deep ravine.

From the passenger seat of the car, I grabbed the rest of my belongings: the map and torch, my gun, and the leather travelling bag containing the deeds and the photographed blueprints. I wound down the window of the driver's side and leaned in, releasing the hand brake, then shoved the car as hard as I could in the direction of the ravine. But the wretched thing was large and heavy, and the more I pushed, the more the tyres caught. I looked down to see a creeping, red-blossomed orchid, metres wide, whose tendrils were entwined vice-like around the chassis. I drank more water and set about cutting it away with my pocketknife. I'd been ambushed by a damn plant.

Then, mustering all my strength, I pushed and rocked, pushed and rocked, until at last the car caught the momentum of my movements, and with a final heave, began to roll in silence across the dip, towards the ravine. I watched it teeter on the edge, then jackknife theatrically downwards, generating a commotion of breaking branches and a flock of parrots which took off with a great deal of noise, flapping and shrieking as the car crashed to the ground.

Amid the pandemonium, I could have sworn I heard the thud of footsteps through the trees, and voices calling over and over, the voices – or so I imagined – of all the men who'd ever pursued me. Oh, Sugar, it must have been my paranoia speaking! Even so, I understood with a flash of fear that I was only hours away from being captured, and from nowhere Sunstar's voice came echoing: *Don't get caught, Gloria. For God's sake, don't get caught.*

CHAPTER ONE

Dolly Fontaine

London, late March 2011

It was difficult to put a finger on when, precisely, everything began to go wrong, but it was most likely that Tuesday afternoon, three weeks before Dolly Fontaine discovered her mother's tapes, when Shaun Kingsley turned up in her kitchen again, big, glowering, and horny. When they kissed, Shaun tasted of Digestive biscuits and breath mints, and after a moment or two Dolly pulled away, mumbling something about putting the kettle on, telling him about her newest lead on Lusenka and the rumours she'd heard of the UK's shady dealings with rebel groups targeting the Balaika people.

'What's the lead?' Shaun looked interested.

'As if I'm going to tell *you*.' She laughed to disguise her irritation at the question, her mind wandering to the rumours she'd heard about a genocide, or so they said, happening under the radar, and no one was taking a blind bit of notice – neither the UK nor the UN. 'You could be a government mole,' she added with a playful smile.

'Oh, come on now.' He leant closer to her. 'You know I'd make a terrible mole.' She could feel the warmth of his breath against her cheek. 'I just can't get enough of your journo adventures,' he murmured, kissing her ear.

'Nope, I'm not spilling,' she insisted. 'Sorry.'

But for some reason, talk of Dolly's work only seemed to excite Shaun, and they ended up in bed again, despite her mixed feelings and a thought, nagging and uneasy, that he seemed more interested in her work than her, sometimes.

Later, they lay still in each other's arms while it began to rain; the bedroom a warm cocoon behind storm-lashed windows. Dolly stared at a spot on the ceiling, trying not to feel anything, when all she really wanted to ask Shaun was, where's this going? Is this real? Do you care at all? But somehow, she couldn't find the right words, so instead she closed her eyes and breathed quietly, listening to the sound of the rain pattering on the glass, imagining how it would feel to be Shaun's girlfriend or his wife; to go to the supermarket together, to cook meals and do *life*. At the idea, at its impossibility, she felt a strange, lingering sadness.

'Your mum was in *The Telegraph* yesterday,' Shaun remarked eventually, reaching over to his side of the bed and rifling in his bag. 'Did you happen to see it?'

Dolly opened her eyes and frowned. 'Nope.' She leant up on an elbow, remembering how the kitsch, silhouetted credits of Sundowners used to invade her dreams when she was a child with their menacing, monster-like shapes. 'But Gloria's all over the papers at the moment,' she added. 'It's thirty-five years since the film came out. I can't get away from her.'

Shaun threw a copy of *The Telegraph*, open at the features section, onto the bed. 'Well-written, I thought. Anyway, I saved it for you.'

'Why, thank you,' Dolly retorted jokily, recognising a black and white portrait of Gloria on the double page spread. She shook her head at the somewhat absurd, passion-killing introduction of her mother into the bedroom. 'Seriously, you do pick your moments don't you, Shaun.'

She put the newspaper on a side table, got out of bed, and stooped to pick up a towel, heading for the shower as she knotted it around her chest. At the dressing table she paused to gaze at a pocket-size portrait of Gloria in a small, gilded frame. In the familiar photograph, her mother was tall and statuesque, lanky as a model, her face lit by a dazzling smile, though as always, her expression held a hint of mystery; sunlight through a dense forest. Her emerald-green diamanté ballgown twinkled in the lights. Her afro hairstyle was held in place by a gaudy, tiara-type affair that made her look like Wonder Woman. She always was so good at that look, Dolly thought; the epitome of seventies cool.

She straightened the photograph and went into the bathroom, still thinking about Gloria. It had been only a year since her mother passed away, and she felt a pang every time she caught sight of that picture, with Gloria's signature scrawled across the bottom corner in her unmistakable lopsided cursive: *Gloria Fontaine, BAFTAs, May 1976.*

When Dolly returned from the shower, Shaun was lounging against the pillows, sheet bunched at his crotch. He appeared to be re-reading the article.

'Did she ever get involved in politics?' he said, looking up. 'Gloria, I mean?'

'Politics?' Dolly stopped in her tracks, mulling this over. 'Not that I know of.'

'I heard something about her being mixed up with something in Lusenka.'

'My mother lived in the wilds of Cornwall, so I doubt it. Or are you talking about back in the seventies?'

'Exactly. Someone mentioned it, can't remember who. Anyway, you don't remember—'

'No.' Dolly shook her head emphatically, recalling Gloria's peculiar aversion to discussions of her home country. Besides, why was Shaun, of all people, suddenly so interested in her *mother*? 'Mum left Lusenka as a teenager and never went back,' she added, musingly. 'She refused to talk about her past.'

'I see.'

Shaun appeared to ponder this as Dolly pottered naked around the bedroom, applying a moisturiser she'd picked up for a quid in last week's newsroom beauty sale. For some reason, the fact that the cream was worth more than her entire weekly food budget made her skin feel amazing.

'You should take me down to Cornwall sometime,' Shaun remarked suddenly. 'Show me your roots. I know a few people down there.'

'Seriously?'

'Our first dirty weekend.' He flashed her a smile, his eyes on hers, and Dolly felt her heart skip a beat. She couldn't help feeling pleasantly surprised at this unexpected development in their complicated relationship. 'I'll always try to do the right thing, you know.'

When Dolly turned to look at him, Shaun was observing her with a newfound seriousness.

'I mean,' he added, 'I'll help you get that scoop before anyone else. It excites me, you being a journo. You're a forbidden fruit.'

She cringed and turned away to cover up a frown. *Forbidden fruit.* She didn't want to be a temptress, or indeed anything relating to fruit, forbidden or otherwise. Ordinary, run-of-the-mill love would suit her just fine, though she would never in a million years admit that to Shaun.

He reached over with a smile, pulling her by the hand back to bed. 'I've never felt this sort of connection before,' he murmured, tracing small circles with his tongue over her right nipple, and she moaned softly to herself, unable to resist the allure of this man who could never bring her any real happiness – only a temporary escape for a few reckless hours away from the cut-throat chaos of the newsroom. The situation was futile, yet aggravatingly addictive.

More than a week went by. One evening after work, while she was trudging home on foot across Clapham Common because the tube was down, Dolly was surprised to receive a text message from Shaun, inviting her to visit his offices at Portcullis House. She was flattered and intrigued, mainly because the invitation seemed a step forward, signalling a willingness on Shaun's part to show her more of his world. She allowed herself to hope that his new reserve was officially dropped. On the day itself, he texted to say he'd booked a private hour for them to talk, and she chose to ignore the emojis – a beating heart, a burning fire – hinting that he derived only a sexual thrill from the thought of her visiting his workplace.

As it turned out, Shaun was interested in one thing, and one thing only, which meant that Dolly refused to feel guilty for embracing the transactional aspect of their meeting. It was all too easy to snoop around Shaun's office while he was called away, too easy to note the memo half-written on his email account, left open after the impromptu sex they'd had on the same desk, minutes before. Too easy to open the attachment, a 550-word dossier summing up the prime minister's supposed errors relating to the defence budget and Lusenka during his two-year tenure. She took screenshots and saved them to her phone. It wasn't the story she was after, but it was still a big scoop, one that could build her case for investigating the contentious Balaika issue further, and the rumoured genocide, for the foreign pages.

'Did you leave that open on purpose?' she asked when Shaun returned. Jesus, she wasn't that underhand!

Shaun smiled. 'You mean just in case my favourite journo happened to see?'

'You're leaking it?'

'No way.' He kissed her neck. 'Don't know what you're talking about.'

She pulled away slightly. 'Still, I need to be careful, Shaun.'

'Careful about what?'

'People have been burned before. I can't afford to make a mistake.'

'You worry too much.' His fingers traced gentle patterns on her back. 'We both want Pickering out, and besides, I'd never screw with you, Dolly.' He moved back slightly to look into her eyes. 'You must know that.'

He kissed her again, gently at first and then more passionately, and she found herself kissing him back, closing her eyes. Shaun was helping her, just as he promised he would. Perhaps their fling would go somewhere, after all...

CHAPTER TWO

Dolly

Cloud News HQ
A fortnight later

Dolly arrived at work, breathless from the cold, raindrops glistening on her coat, to find her colleagues guzzling wine out of Cloud News kitchen mugs at a quarter past twelve on a weekday lunchtime. Everyone was talking about the leaked memo, the allegations accusing the prime minister of recklessly overspending the UK defence budget in Lusenka and the fact that Westminster was, as they spoke, scrabbling for a statement. In the excitement, Dolly found herself being clapped on the back and shaken by the hand. People stood up, applauding as she walked past the rows of desks. *Great scoop! Bravo! Outstanding work, Dolly, outstanding...*

'Bloody fabulous,' called Angus Cunningham, chief news editor of Cloud News, appearing in the door of his office, quoting at Dolly from a copy of *The Daily Mail* brandished in one hand. 'The prime minister's fucked!'

'There's more to come, I promise,' Dolly replied with a smile, declining Angus' offer of bubbly with a raised hand, though secretly she was loving the buzz of universal praise, and the sense that her work was making a difference, finally. As a young girl she'd dreamed of becoming a reporter like the foreign correspondents she saw on the news – Kate Adie in Iraq, Michael Buerk in Ethiopia – influencing world affairs for the better. She'd worked hard over the years to gain a place on the foreign desk covering human rights and humanitarian news, issues that *mattered* on the wider political stage. The Lusenka story was her first real break, and it hit her now that her childhood dream was coming true. She was at the heart of the biggest foreign news story that year, though exactly *how* big was only just beginning to sink in.

Even Gloria might have been impressed, she reflected as she nodded her thanks, with a small smile, to another colleague who raised a thumbs-up as she walked past. Miracles and all that. But she pushed the thought away, refusing to accept the idea that her ongoing investigations into Lusenka should be reduced to some morbid homage to her secretive late mother. No way. If her pursuit of this story was inspired by personal matters, it was purely for professional gains.

'Not too personal, I hope?' Angus had enquired anxiously when, earlier in the year, she pitched an investigation into human rights violations against Lusenka's indigenous Balaika people. 'I'm not convinced anyone cares about some God-forsaken backwater in the back end of a foreign continent,' the editor added, still dubious. 'But prove me wrong. Just make sure this isn't about your mum, okay?'

And Dolly shook her head, eager to reassure him, suggesting she could pull strings via close contacts like Shaun Kingsley. 'Look, Angus,' she corrected herself. 'Lusenka is hot. And Kingsley – well, he's putty in my hands.'

Dolly went straight to her desk and placed her bag underneath, running her eyes over a pile of newspapers someone had helpfully stacked up near the keyboard. The red-tops' sensational headlines were unequivocal: 'Leaked memo shows Pickering's screw up on Lusenka'; 'Government in a Pickering.' Excitedly, she noted that every single major news source was quoting the piece she'd broken live to camera that morning, followed by a pre-recorded package running at the top of every hour. For all this she'd risen at four am and slogged home on the tube afterwards for a quick cat nap, before heading back to Cloud News headquarters in time for an afternoon news conference. Talk about dedication.

She turned on her computer and watched her inbox fill with requests for insights from other TV channels. Of course, Westminster would be furious, would question her sources and her integrity, but, as with all of her assignments, she'd checked and double-checked the facts. This was a scoop, by all accounts, *her* scoop, and given that the memo represented a more or less unrecoverable position for the British Government, Angus was probably right: Pickering *was* fucked.

In haste, she answered the email messages one by one: *Yes, sure thing, what time, live or down-the-line?* Afterwards, she shot out a couple of tweets, ignoring the trolls lurking in the background, though she couldn't help replying to one particularly rude message. *It's my job to ask difficult questions!* she typed out briskly with loud taps of the keyboard. *For goodness sake, this is real journalism!* As far as she was concerned, though, this story was only the beginning. There was a lot more to say on the Lusenka story, and she was determined to be the one to say it.

'Well, well, congratulations.' It was a freelance sub-editor from the hot desk opposite – Oliver something? Late fifties, cynical as hell, always ready with a sarky comment – an old-school hack Dolly wasn't keen on. He raised a mug and bowed his head in mock deference, and Dolly breathed in wafts of stale breath and dampish laundry. 'Quite the glorious success, comrade.'

'Thank you,' she replied cheerfully.

'Reckon you'll get that press award you missed out on last year...'

'I don't know about awards,' she said, choosing not to rise to the barb beneath the compliment, 'but I'll be mightily glad of a day off.'

'You having a drink? The boss bought Cava, Co-op's finest.'

She smiled, giving in. 'Go on then. Might as well make the most of our esteemed leader's generosity.'

Oliver or whatever-his-name-was went over to the kitchen and came back with a mug and a bottle, which he gripped by the neck in a vaguely obscene way while he poured. Dolly watched the pale gold fizz glug into the china cup, where it sparkled and settled. After taking only a single mouthful, she felt the alcohol go straight to her head, the fizzing bubbles amplifying her own frothy sense of intoxication.

'I think it's marvellous when these diversity drives for recruitment actually pay off. Don't let anyone tell you this was about anything other than decent reporting.'

'Excuse me?' Dolly rolled her eyes, choosing not to let the sub-editor know what she thought of his comment.

'Only a joke, love. Drink up.'

Love? She couldn't win. She drank up.

It was nearly three o'clock. She took more sips of the Cava, swirling the cup in her fingers as the bubbles fizzed playfully, contemplating the day's events. If she were honest with herself, she had Shaun to thank for all this, didn't she? Technically he'd helped her, though she was loath to give him all the credit just when it was finally her time to shine.

Let's face it, why should she, when Shaun was never going to leave his wife; that much was painfully clear. She was being utterly foolish, repeating the same screwed-up, destructive old patterns, searching for the dad she never had in the arms of older lovers. Avoidance, a counsellor had called it once during a periodic effort to sort out her ailing love life: 'You're seeking a relationship with someone impossible, Dolly. Do you understand that?'

Because what would she have told people if they asked? That the troubling presence of the wedding ring on Shaun Kingsley's left finger belied the reality of the way he looked at her? That she was in too deep? That this was love, whatever anyone thought?

Shaun Kingsley, Junior Minister for Defence Procurement for the UK government, charismatic, square-jawed, a consummate smooth operator, who the year before had made a beeline for her at a government press briefing about the MOD's Lusenka response efforts. Of course – *of course!* – there existed between the two of them an instant, inescapable chemistry: he with his big shoulders and dry humour, a boyish twinkle in his eye. The first time they talked it felt like an electric shock. They couldn't seem to take their eyes off each other. Those first weeks had been intense. Eagerly, Shaun had offered leads and introductions, all of them useful, and, eventually, their so-called 'work chats' turned into long, spellbound meetings in coffee shops and low-lit restaurants where they would sit opposite each other with their laptops pushed aside, the air charged with a peculiar intensity. She remembered the first time they kissed, sitting in his car, and the guilty, heart-fluttering knowledge that they would end up in bed, and that this was no longer just a flirtation but a full-blown affair.

After that, they met whenever they could. Sometimes all they did was touch each other. She felt giddy and consumed, drunk with lust in a way she'd never experienced before, as if nothing else mattered but those few short hours spent tangled in each other's arms, erotic and blissful and addictive. She found herself thinking of Heathcliff and Catherine, of Antony and Cleopatra, of star-crossed lovers doomed by fate never to be together properly – and somehow, that made everything okay.

Months passed; things changed. Shaun became emphatic that they *must* be careful, and his view of their weekly rendezvous for coffee or bed – whichever they could wangle between the demands of their busy schedules – became depressingly transactional. More and more, Shaun seemed determined to frame her as a sex object, all body and no brains; as if, outside the fucking, she didn't exist at all. When she tried to bring up her feelings – God forbid! – Shaun urged her to compartmentalise. She was starting to understand what it meant to be objectified, to be *reduced,* and it filled her with dismay. She ought to break it off, and would have, if it wasn't for the enduring memories of those first enchanted weeks, the pull of their connection, and the rare moments when Shaun was loving again, declaring that he missed her, hinting at deeper feelings. So she clung on, hoping that things might go back to the way they were, hoping that in the end, she would be loved.

She took the lift downstairs and bought a green smoothie in the Cloud News HQ canteen, wishing she hadn't accepted the cheap Cava, because a daytime hangover was beginning to hammer above her left eye. She headed outside and stood near the smokers loitering by the revolving doors, enjoying the clean sensation of ginger and apple on her tongue through the straw, though she felt, suddenly, overwhelmed with exhaustion. The job had taken its toll over the past weeks. She wasn't sleeping well; it was days since she'd cooked herself a proper meal. She eyed the smokers with envy. How she'd love to join them for a cigarette.

But there was no way she was giving in. She was just tired, possibly burnt out after all the hard work and excitement, in need of a holiday where she could rest and get her head together. A shepherd's cabin on a Greek island, an isolated cottage in deepest Devon, or some sort of glorious villa on the southern edge of Italy where she would wander through hills of scented rosemary to get to the sea. Somewhere warm, peaceful, and *away* – away, if she were honest, from this complicated entanglement with Shaun.

Occasionally, a new habit, she liked to play with the idea of doing something completely different from journalism, something physical requiring her hands not her brains, like lavender farming or beekeeping, or she would move to the country and write a novel, a thriller or a detective story; something zappy and adventurous that captured the current zeitgeist. Except such daydreams were all nonsense, she knew. She loved her job, the buzz of finding meaningful stories that changed lives. A holiday, she decided there and then, was out of the question.

CHAPTER THREE

Dolly

Back at her desk, feeling somewhat rejuvenated, Dolly found the editor's secretary, Margaret, scribbling a Post-it note.

'Not *another* interview?' Dolly remarked with mock despair.

'Sorry, Doll.' Margaret straightened up with a neutral expression, balling the small yellow piece of paper between her fingers. 'Channel 4 just cancelled your slot.'

'Oh? Any idea why?' Dolly felt a lurch in her stomach, recalling a scandal a few years ago, a rape story, when Alexander Bennett in features was fired after it turned out his source had fabricated her account. If she remembered rightly, it had all started to unravel when his TV slots were cancelled.

'No clue,' said Margaret. 'They just said they don't need you anymore.'

Barely a minute later, the desk phone rang.

'This is Dolly Fontaine,' Dolly answered. On the other end of the line, the producer from *Question Time* sounded harassed, cancelling Dolly's evening commentary appearance without apology.

'I see,' she replied. 'May I ask why?'

'We can't corroborate your statements from our own reports, and Kingsley's issued a denial. In light of this, do you stand by what you published?'

'You mean *Shaun* Kingsley?' Dolly's words caught in her throat. There was a plummeting sensation in her stomach. 'Yes, I stand by it, of course I stand by it.' Tight-lipped, she resisted slamming the receiver down and turned to Margaret, to anyone who'd listen. 'What the hell is going on?!'

But the secretary was already walking away across the newsroom.

Googling hastily, Dolly found Shaun's statement all over the internet headlines: 'The dossier in question is unpublished and unvalidated,' said a quote from an hour or two ago beneath a headshot of Shaun looking smart, suave, and serious. 'I would have thought Miss Fontaine would know better than to peddle fake news.'

Dolly swore under her breath, he must literally have just spoken to the press.

Seconds later, an email flashed into her inbox abruptly titled: CHAT. *Dolly, can you come in,* it said with ominous brevity, followed by the automated signature: *Best wishes, Angus.*

Panicking, she mentally ran over the wording of the dossier she'd photographed in Shaun's office, which had been straightforward, hadn't it, its meaning clear as day? Or had she let her guard down, blinded by her attraction to Shaun, by the fact it was Lusenka and all too personal? She caught herself. Presumably she could fix this. Certainly, it was fixable, like most things. With an audible sigh, she pressed reply and typed a message back to Angus: *Sure. Give me five.*

Gathering her bag, she made her way to the loo, considering the implications of the word 'chat' as she peed. Nowadays that passive-aggressive little phrase seemed to imply anything from a job offer to a dumping. Afterwards she checked her appearance in the mirror, tucking an errant curl into her low ponytail and retouching her lips with a fresh coat of lipstick, another bargain from the beauty sale – Brave Red, it was called, Jesus, talk about pathetic fallacy! She leaned towards her reflection, grimacing at her mirror-self, who looked a damn sight more composed than she felt.

'Oh, come on, Doll,' she whispered out loud, smacking her lips together and making a kissing expression at the other Dolly, the better Dolly. 'You got this, girl.' She straightened her polo neck and corrected her posture, heading for the door. If there really *was* something wrong with the story, she must put it right, at all costs.

Angus was in his glass-fronted office, issuing a loud stream of swear words into the phone. 'No, no,' he bellowed, 'we are not going to bow down to fucking Westminster, for fuck's sake.'

There were no traces of the early afternoon's Cava-infused euphoria, and Dolly felt her stomach knot with dread as she sat down on the sofa, trying to breathe normally, running her gaze instead over the framed National Press Awards adorning Angus's windowsill, which dated back to the beginning of the millennium by the looks of it, and the floor-to-ceiling bookshelves where photographs of the Cunningham family were strategically placed to catch the eye. He was a tall, very thin man, in suit trousers and a check shirt, one sleeve fraying, reading glasses hooked over his shirt collar. He was known as an industry legend, so much so that when he first offered her a junior role at Cloud News, Dolly was elated, more than elated. She considered herself thick-skinned – you had to be in this job – but the idea of letting him down pained her far more than any public humiliation.

'Bloody hell!' Angus's voice on the phone cut into her thoughts. 'For Christ's sake, kill it!' He slammed the phone down on the table and took a noisy slurp of tea before looking up at her with a neutral but penetrating stare. 'Fontaine,' he said, flatly. 'You're here.'

'What's going on, Angus?' She folded her hands on crossed knees, trying to disguise her growing panic. 'My interviews have all been ditched?'

But as soon as the words left her mouth, she felt a creeping sense of unease, as if the words were coming to life right then and there, spectres lingering in the air, too stark, too real. Angus rose from the desk and began pacing back and forth, hands on hips.

'What the fuck were you doing? This is an *almighty* cock-up.'

'But Angus, the dossier is a hundred per cent kosher.' She was all too aware that she was speaking too fast. 'You've seen it with your own eyes. I checked it with four other close sources.'

Angus went to the desk and picked up a print-out of an email, which he threw at her. 'Kingsley says you're unreliable, says the dossier is unvalidated, not accurate. His cronies – your bloody *other sources* – are backing him to the hilt. For Christ's sake, Fontaine, what the fuck is going on?'

Dolly felt dizzy, overcome, suddenly, by the sense that she was falling from a precipice, and there was no one at the bottom to catch her.

'Kingsley was eating out of my hand,' she said with puzzlement in her voice. 'I was careful and thorough – it was watertight. I wouldn't have gone with the story if I wasn't comfortable, you know that, Angus. Shaun gave me his blessing to leak it.'

'I bet he bloody well did! Christ Almighty, you played right into his hands, whatever he's up to. I thought better of you, Fontaine.'

'Look, if Shaun Kingsley wants to gaslight the general public, that's fine, but it's our job to bring them the truth. I'm close to something big, Angus – something even bigger than this.'

'I thought you had fucking Kingsley on fucking speed dial? And now it's your word against his?'

'Jesus Christ.' Dolly got to her feet, horrified, and stood facing Angus. She balled her fists as an idea began to form. 'Look, what if he's deliberately set me up, from the beginning, when he let me read that email? He must have known I'd be on it like a rash.'

She gripped and ungripped her fingers, feeling a wave of nausea rise in her throat as she followed the thought. Why the hell would Shaun do such a thing, and why the hell was she stupid enough to fall for it, if so?

'Look, there's more to this,' she offered desperately. 'There must be. Give me a few hours, let me investigate—'

Angus shook his head. 'We can't just issue a fucking retraction, Fontaine. That's not how it works.'

Through the window, the sky darkened with rain. Half a second later, the lights of the building opposite sprang to life, theatrically, revealing hundreds of silhouetted figures hunched over lines of desks. Dolly stared out at the view, overcome with self-doubt. Had Shaun been screwing with her this whole time, then? Yet he was one of her closest confidants, she had shared things with him that she'd never told anyone else. For God's sake, she'd *slept with him*. She shuddered to herself. Keeping it classy, Doll.

'God Almighty, Jesus fuck.' Angus arched his hands, tapping his fingers together with a frazzled expression, as if he had finally run out of appropriate expletives. 'I can't take the risk of you creating even more of a fucking shambles. It's a shame, you had such great promise. I liked having you on my team.'

'Please, I swear I can fix this. Give me a few hours, and I'll—'

'Clear your desk, will you? HR will sort out the rest.'

'Angus, please, I'm so sorry—'

'Sorry won't bloody well hack it, Fontaine.' But Angus's gaze softened, and he sighed deeply, shaking his head. 'Look, Dolly, I suspect there's more to this. It might not be your fault, but someone's got to take the rap, and that person is you, I'm afraid.'

Outside the editor's office, Dolly fled, heading for the exit. A few people turned their heads, staring, and she hastily dropped her gaze, feeling her face flush. They *know*, she thought with horror. Already she was the rogue reporter, the one who screwed up the scoop of the year. She passed the sub-editor from earlier, who shot her a smug look.

'Bloody hell, Dolly,' he murmured. 'Looks like the bubbly'll have to stay corked.'

'No, that'll be your sex life,' she countered quietly, and she could feel the man gawking after her as her bravado dissipated with the noisy backswing of the exit doors.

Downstairs she swiped her card through the turnstiles, bypassing programme guests, celebrities, and eager teenage schoolchildren on guided tours of the building, all smart clothes and backpacks. They were strolling in and out with a nonchalance that seemed altogether irreconcilable with what had just happened to her. Down the street, at the newsagents next to the tube station, she bought a packet of Marlboro Lights and stood smoking by the edge of the tube's concrete steps, staring at the shoppers browsing the neon-lit windows of H&M opposite. Beside her a man piled *Evening Standards* into metal trays for passers-by to help themselves, and she registered the headline. 'Leaked memo proves a fake,' it declared in heavy black type, 'after government source found dodgy.'

Frowning, she drew deeply on the cigarette. There was more to this, she was certain. What if, as she had suggested to Angus, it was all a big distraction, and someone – Shaun? Shaun's cronies in Whitehall who were now steadfastly backing up his lies? – didn't want her anywhere near the Lusenka story, because, as she'd pointed out to Angus right at the beginning, Lusenka was hot?

She exhaled a curl of smoke, visualising for a second the dark brown stain of tobacco seeping into her body, a slow poison. That memo leaked by Shaun was always bound to go off like a grenade, but what if she'd been incredibly naïve? What if that email was actually designed as a smokescreen to keep her nose out of the real story – because the UK *was* involved with something dodgy in Lusenka, of that she was absolutely certain, even if she couldn't prove it yet.

When had she told Shaun about her possible lead into shady British involvement in Lusenka's rebel movement? Wasn't it that afternoon at her flat, *the sex afternoon*, as she couldn't help thinking of it, like something out of Judy Blume, for fuck's sake – ten days, maybe a week before he leaked her the memo about the prime minister? The timing seemed fishy now. Had Shaun realised she was close, too close? To what? To something.

And then, wham… Shaun had orchestrated the dossier on purpose to put her off the scent, publicly discrediting her in the process? And she, idiot of idiots, had fallen for it. But why? What could Shaun possibly have to do with Lusenka other than a usual professional interest via the MOD? What could he possibly have to hide?

Dolly closed her eyes, the cigarette still smouldering between her fingers, contemplating the fact that she'd have to go back to the office to collect the rest of her belongings – to face the music, to run the gauntlet. The thought made her stomach churn with apprehension. She groaned under her breath and threw the fag on the ground, stubbing it out with her toe. An injustice had been done, and she didn't have a clue how to fix it.

She dug in her pocket for her mobile phone and typed a text message to Shaun Kingsley – *we need to talk!* – adding a cluster of exclamation marks to the end. She pressed send. All she could do now, she told herself, was hope for the best, hope for the whole thing to be a mistake, a mix-up, a simple and solvable misunderstanding. She checked her watch. Four-thirty. If she were quick, she could make it in and out of the office to pick up her things before the rush hour, stealthy as a ghost.

At the shelter of her desk, she set about clearing up with a self-conscious industriousness, glad of an opportunity to look busy, telling herself to concentrate on the task and not the feeling that people were staring over with curious looks, devouring the juicy details of her downfall just as, later on, they would set upon the cakes and treats piled up on the office filing cabinet to celebrate an occasion of some sort: a birthday, a wedding, a new hire, perhaps. For the last fifteen years she'd worked in this building, first as an intern straight out of university, then, after a handful of junior and middle-level journalist positions on features and elsewhere, as senior correspondent on the foreign desk. Cloud News was her work, her social life, the source of two long-term relationships and a couple of flings. She'd grown up here. Determinedly, she bit her lip to contain any tears that might dare escape. How could she possibly leave here in such disgrace?

Any minute now, Angus would appear. She needed to get out of the office. She checked the drawers and under the desk, cramming the last of the notepads and a few other belongings into her rucksack: a Dictaphone, a quantity of random notes, biros, a stapler. Maybe she should have brought in an offering for the filing cabinet too, she specu-lated, like those divorce cakes popular in America: *Congratulations on being sacked!* The cake could display a sugar replica of her with a dagger through the heart. She grimaced to herself, conducting a final sweep, wanting to tell someone the grim joke, but there was no one to tell – and how could she blame them? Given today's drama, she could well imagine the titillating sort of pleasure of watching from the side-lines as your once high-flying colleague cleared her desk, the sweet melodrama of wondering what you'd do in her place.

To add insult to injury, her computer was already locked, password invalid. In a gesture that seemed to stab at some distant past normality,

Margaret had stacked the afternoon's post on the desk, and there were a few press releases, some review copies of new books piled up, and a largish brown-paper-wrapped parcel marked 'Special Delivery'. In tight, spidery handwriting that reminded Dolly of something out of a Victorian novel – *Bleak House* or *Great Expectations* – her name and work address were handwritten on the front.

She picked up the parcel with mild curiosity. It was not unusual to receive fancy gifts or random freebies from big brands whose marketing teams imagined, wrongly, that she might promote their product on TV. The beauty sale almost entirely consisted of free cosmetics sent to the weekend supplements' beauty editors. Odd though, that she should receive a gift today of all days, a last hurrah in the dying days of Rome.

She broke open the seal of the parcel and drew out a miniature pink can of gin fizz which she set aside on the desk, then a plain-looking jewellery box with no insignia – just a small silver line marking the edges. Inside, two diamond earrings nestled on sapphire blue cloth. They were pretty and vintage-looking, expensive enough, and under normal circumstances she would have been thrilled to receive them, but of course whoever had sent them would be expecting her to wear them to an awards event, which was out of the question now.

It struck her that the package was odd – significant, somehow, arriving out of the blue at this singularly catastrophic moment, though she couldn't pinpoint why. She would take a good look later, she decided, chucking the can of booze in the bin and stashing the earrings back in the envelope. This she placed in the rucksack, before hoisting the bag onto her back.

As she stepped away from her desk for the last time and walked towards the exit, someone on features began to bang a desk, the customary Cloud News tradition to bid farewell to long-standing colleagues, but to Dolly's mortification, no one else joined in, and the noise quickly petered out. Jesus, could this day get any worse? With hurried steps, eyes down, without a word to anyone, she ran the gauntlet of her former colleagues, and left the office.

CHAPTER FOUR

Dolly

Straight away, Dolly spotted Shaun Kingsley through the window of the coffee shop, sitting at a table near the back, typing quickly on a laptop, wearing glasses and a pale blue shirt. She could already tell the shirt would match his eyes. For a man in his late forties, early fifties perhaps – she wasn't sure of his exact age – he was very attractive. Too attractive for her own good. She smoothed down her hair and fished a mint from her bag to disguise the smell of cigarettes. Breathe, she told herself, chewing the sweet as she pushed open the door. Perhaps this was all some kind of hideous mistake.

When she approached the table, Shaun stood up, and she felt suddenly, acutely aware of his body close to hers, of the kiss that lingered too long on her cheek. Against her skin his face was smooth-shaven, his aftershave expensive and vanilla-traced, a little bit smoky, a little bit spicy. Dior probably, or Gucci, a scent that tugged at something inside she was unable to control.

'Hello, Dolly.'

'Yo, Shaun,' she said, bundling her bag under the chair. 'What's popping?'

But despite her weak attempt at humour, she was unable to muster a smile. It was her habit to tease Shaun a little, mainly because he was so strait-laced, so *establishment* – to the point of stuffiness, she sometimes secretly thought. God knows why she even liked him…

'You look beautiful,' said Shaun. 'And quite stressed. What's the matter?'

He had a public schoolboy's flawless received pronunciation; cut-glass words that were somehow not cool these days, not hip. Cloud

News encouraged regional accents for all its broadcast correspondents: Geordie, Welsh, the anchoring lilt of anything but posh. *Diverse voices*, they called them. They liked – *had* liked, anyway – Dolly's own regional accent, which was well-spoken West Country, with an occasional trace of Lusenkan patois picked up from her mother if she felt like drawing attention to herself.

In the warmth, her cheeks began to glow. She reached for a cocktail stick, fiddled with it until it broke in two, scattering two jagged ends on the tabletop. Shaun hailed the waitress and ordered tea. As the woman walked away, he fixed Dolly with an intense stare that, as usual, made her feel like she was the only person in the room – his trick, Dolly knew, to make people like him, to seduce colleagues, lovers, the public. She wouldn't be surprised if he'd been unfaithful to his wife before. He was certainly a player, and she was likely not to be his first extra-marital conquest. She frowned, pushing away the fragments of cocktail stick and choosing another from the pot. I thought I was special, she desperately wanted to say. We were friends, weren't we? More than friends.

But she said nothing.

Snapping the laptop closed, Shaun leant smiling across the table, feigning innocence, or so it seemed, his big hands folding near to hers. Unbidden came a recollection of those same hands on her skin, on her breasts and nipples, and she pushed the thought away.

'Is something wrong?'

'I've been sacked,' she announced without preamble. 'Just like that, gone…' She clicked her fingers in the air. 'What the actual fuck, Shaun?'

Shaun moved back in his chair with a strange expression, the smile snapping from his face. Dolly's eyes wandered to the wedding ring of shiny white gold on his left hand, a ring he usually took off when they were in bed together. He was one of those men who had it all: glamorous wife, big house, big job, big car, a clutch of step-kids at private schools, a wardrobe full of premium cotton pastel shirts, all carefully ironed, or so she imagined – and a medium-sized yacht moored off the south coast. Jesus, even the way the guy walked screamed luxury.

On the table, Shaun's phone buzzed. 'Excuse me a minute,' he said and pushed back his chair, hurrying out of the café. Dolly watched him stand outside on the pavement, phone pressed to his ear, talking intently with a serious expression. Her heart was hammering unpleasantly. For God's sake, was this really happening? Presumably the phone call was something to do with the news headlines, or his wife: either was possible. Dolly shook her head and took small sips of her tea, fighting back tears. Shaun Kingsley – her lover and her downfall.

She didn't usually care to dwell on Shaun's home life, especially when it came to his wife, Arabella – Abs, as he referred to her with a matey sort of jocularity which puzzled Dolly for reasons she didn't quite understand. Somehow the nickname was far too jolly-hockey-sticks, bordering on dismissive, as if poor Abs were just one of the boys, a cheerful pint-swigging mate who was up for anything, but not a wife, not a woman.

In her mind, Dolly imagined Abs as well-spoken and possibly blonde, sporty and well-organised, though from there the image became indistinct, deliberately perhaps, as if Dolly's brain refused to venture down that particular path. Even so, Dolly couldn't help piecing together a picture from Shaun's occasional comments and her own imagination, to the point that she could envision his home: a mock-Tudor five bed tucked on a residential street near the Hurlingham Club in Parson Green where Shaun could watch the river and his Ferrari 458 Italia – another of his indulgences – from enormous bifold windows.

Dolly had the impression that everything in Shaun's life was carefully curated, all fashionable Scandinavian neutrals and neatly organised socks. She recalled a selfie he'd sent once, of himself holding up a cut-crystal wine glass of the sort you might acquire in the home department of John Lewis, evidently expensive, but run-of-the-mill, borderline ugly. To Dolly's mind the glass signified a life of careful order, of functional, luxurious convention in which possessions were bought without effort, money-no-object, but not sought out or treasured. She couldn't imagine Shaun scouring a flea market for a second-hand object of beauty, an antique lampshade, a beautiful vase, or a second-hand novel. Indeed, she seemed to recall him calling her 'pikey' for mentioning a vintage coat she had purchased.

Besides, Abs didn't like books around the house, he'd told her once. They cluttered up the place and gathered dust. To Dolly, this spoke volumes.

Minutes later, Shaun returned. 'Well,' he said briskly as he sat down, dropping his phone into his bag. 'Where were we?'

Dolly swallowed. 'I got sacked. Just now, by Angus.'

'I'm sorry that happened, Dolly. This whole thing's a bit of a shit show if you ask me.'

'Jesus.' She paused, tongue-tied. How could he be so blasé about something so important? 'I trusted you, Shaun, and you betrayed me.'

The words came out differently to how she intended. *Betrayed*, for fuck's sake, like some tragic Shakespearean protagonist. What the heck was wrong with her? Perhaps her judgement *was* impaired. Perhaps she was too in love with Shaun Kingsley to have noticed he'd been fobbing her off all along.

Shaun lifted his coffee cup, sipped from it slowly. A tiny flush of rosacea was blooming on the skin of his left cheek. Dolly could sense his brain working as he stared at her, doubtless calculating his next move, until after a second, he let out an avuncular sigh, as if she was some adorable little lady who'd gone and made a foolish little mistake: *silly you.*

'Do you mean this blasted memo you've gone and published?'

'You know very well I mean that.'

'Okay,' Shaun said carefully. 'Look, you must have misunderstood my little joke. I should have told you to go through the press office on everything to do with Lusenka.' He gave a little laugh, held up his hands in defence. 'My sincerest apologies.' There was a long pause while Dolly waited for him to continue, and he did. 'It was a misjudgment on my part.'

'Little joke?' Dolly shook her head in disbelief. 'Misjudgment? I'm baffled, Shaun. I assumed I had your blessing to leak that dossier, and that certainly wasn't a joke. You put it right in front of me, on purpose. Are you telling me now that it was deliberately a fake, to set me up?'

'Indeed. It was a draft, of sorts, something I'm working on.' He drummed his fingers on the table. 'Unfinished.'

Speechless, Dolly took a breath, unable to contain a quiver in her voice. 'You told me a while ago that you wanted to *further my career*? I mean, you don't give a shit about the prime minister, you've told me that, so why protect him? We both know the government *is* a shambles, and that Pickering *has* been misspending the defence budget. So why would you trash my story?' She frowned, scrutinising Shaun, wanting a reaction. 'I could tell your wife, for God's sake, about us.'

Shaun stared back, emotionless, as she held his gaze.

'I'm beginning to think that this is all just a big distraction by you and your mates to stop me and anyone else sniffing around. Is there more to this, Shaun, something you're not telling me?'

If she wasn't imagining things, an infinitesimal recoil. Shaun's eyes shifted about, scanning the coffee shop, before his gaze returned to meet hers. He cleared his throat.

'Look, I like you, Dolly, you're an exceedingly intelligent woman, and your political discussion is very arousing.' He paused for half a second and gave a lazy, insinuating smile. 'But your emotional manipulation won't wash with me. As for my wife, perhaps I never mentioned, but Abs is a very tolerant woman.'

'For God's sake!'

The truth, Dolly suspected, was more complicated, although so far, she was unsure of the whys and wherefores. Had Shaun been coerced into this? Was someone blackmailing him about their affair? Was his deception the all-too predictable misjudgment of a middle-aged man governed by his balls not his brain? In that case she almost felt sorry for him. On the other hand, rather than messing up his career, he had messed up hers, and she should have been more careful. Why the hell had she let her guard down?

'Isn't there anything you can do,' she asked, 'to make this right?'

More blotches of colour were appearing above Shaun's shirt collar, on his neck and cheekbones. For a few seconds he fiddled with the empty coffee cup, rearranging the spoon then the saucer. Behind him, to the right, a male customer stood at the counter, eyeing the pastries on display as the barista took an order. Dolly could hear the whoosh of the espresso machine, and a faint thread of a Beyoncé song coming from the radio, and snippets of other people's conversations. Everyone was having a very ordinary day, everyone but her.

Shaun looked across at her, conciliatory, vaguely panicked-looking as he reached an arm down for his laptop bag. 'What sort of thing do you mean?' he said, hoisting the bag onto his knees.

'We both know,' Dolly bluffed, 'that the UK *is* doing shady dealings over in Lusenka, even if we can't back it with that particular memo, but only you or your MOD colleagues can make that clear, and at least I might get my job back.' She broke another cocktail stick apart, and fiddled with the pieces. 'You could talk to Angus.'

'Bloody hell, Dolly, I can't possibly do that.'

'Surely it's the very least—'

Shaun shook his head. She watched him take the laptop and pack it into the bag, all coolness now, all matter-of-fact decorum.

'If you want my opinion, you need to stop all this digging around on Lusenka. Forgive me. My feelings for you are real and complicated, but I can't get more mixed up in this God-almighty mess. How about we zero-in on a coffee date next week?'

Shaun's manner contained an imperceptible touch of the old flirtation, as if he thought they could go back to dirty texts and sexy coffees, Dolly registered with a feeling of astonishment, and everything would be okay. *Jesus.* What the hell was Shaun up to, washing his hands of the issue when he was the cause?

'Look, Dolly, I'm sure we can get this all squared away, okay.'

Dolly wanted to laugh out loud. *You actually think you can square this away,* she wanted to say. She'd learned during the course of their relationship that Shaun was fond of corporate metaphors – circle back, ducks in a row, peel the onion, low hanging fruit – phrases to trivialise real emotions, real life, one way or another. Then there was 'compart-mentalise', that other favourite saying of his, as if her romantic feelings could be neatly shoo-shooed into a drawer and locked down tight.

'Alright,' she answered dully, hating herself, unable to fight the manipulative pull of this man's charm which lured her weak soul, despite everything. Fool, she admonished herself inwardly, adding, despite her better judgement, 'if you like.'

'Smashing.' He leaned over and kissed her lingeringly on the mouth, the first time he'd ever embraced her in public. 'Text me, okay?'

'Sure,' she said, disentangling herself and giving him a sad smile. 'Bye, Shaun.'

Numb, she watched him go. Why had she allowed herself to be fooled by his flattery and attention? She was usually so level-headed, prioritising her career above everything else, yet here she was with her professional life in tatters and the man she loved – or thought she loved, she corrected herself – walking away without a hint of regret for his role in her downfall.

'Shit, shit, shit,' she muttered to herself, closing her eyes momentarily, downing the last dregs of her tea. 'What a hellish mess.'

At five o'clock exactly, Dolly made her way through the riverside gardens towards Parliament, where other walkers were headed for the underground, shoes tapping quickly on the lamplit concrete paths. The sensible thing, Dolly told herself, would be to attend this evening's parliamentary debate, try to get the lowdown on the Foreign Office's revised European Union Act. The other reporters would consider it too deadly dull to attend, so maybe she could redeem the situation with a breaking story about an amendment to the protocol – Jesus, she must be desperate! – and impress Angus enough to allow her back. Surely, this wasn't too much to ask? Yet she felt shivery, numb, and slightly floaty, as if she wasn't quite there. In the pit of her stomach a hollow sort of despair was forming. What *was* she, after all, without her job?

In the lobby, she feigned confidence and reached for her electronic press pass, making a pretence of cheerfulness as she waved to the familiar security guard and passed her rucksack through the machines, but when she came to the turnstiles, the light flashed red instead of green. Her heart sank. She held up the plastic card with a questioning look, but the guard shook his head, and called her over. A few passing MPs eyed her with a mixture of curiosity and amusement. She recognised Esther Bell, one of the senior whips, and Muhammed Ba Singh, the much-anticipated new communications director for the Labour Party, of all people. Dolly lowered her eyes, mortified, smarting beneath their stares. They were people she knew and worked with. Was everyone aware, by now, of her disgrace?

'I'm very sorry, Miss Fontaine,' the guard said in his lilting francophone accent. 'Your ID card's coming up as invalid.'

'There must be a mistake?'

'No.' He frowned in puzzlement. *'Je ne crois pas.'*

She stood next to the guard while he checked the system. His name was Amadou, from Dakar in Senegal. In the past she'd helped him on occasion, translating school paperwork into French for his wife and teenage son, Ibou, who now attended an outstanding-rated London comprehensive, and was predicted four A stars and a place at a top-tier university. She remembered Amadou telling her the news, his face lit with happiness.

'Looks like your card was cancelled earlier today.' Amadou's expression registered genuine dismay. 'I don't know why, Miss.'

Dolly looked at the guard, frowning. 'By who? Who has the power to do that?'

'I'm sorry, Miss, I can't...'

'Si'il te plaît?' she said with a pleading expression, and he must have sensed her despair because he leant down, consulting his computer.

'A Monsieur Kingsley sent through the request,' he announced, glancing up. 'Via the security manager. *Je suis vraiment désolé,* Miss Fontaine.'

Oh, Shaun, you asshole.

With a sorrowful expression, Amadou escorted her to the exit, where a small gaggle of reporters was converging. A camera flashed, then another, and Dolly hastily averted her eyes, pushing through the burgeoning crowd, fumbling for her cigarettes in her pocket.

'Dolly, do you have any comment?' one called. 'For the *Westminster*

Times.' A microphone was thrust in her face, and she batted it away. 'Do you want to make a statement?!'

'No,' she said angrily. 'I stand by the story.'

They circled like baying wolves around fresh prey, sniffing scandal on the breeze, gathering for the kill.

CHAPTER FIVE

Dolly

The next morning, Dolly waited for the kettle to boil as the sound of the radio's early morning shipping forecast filled the kitchen of her flat with a soothing monotone: Northwest Hebrides, Bailey, southwesterly four, drizzle for a time, becoming poor for a time, gales at first. She switched on her mobile phone, only for it to buzz manically for a few seconds with a trail of missed messages and calls, then a pile-up of social media notifications. Without bothering to check them, she made a cup of tea and went outside to the balcony, where rain clouds were slowly rolling in across the greyish Vauxhall cityscape.

She lit a cigarette, sipping the tea, and wiped away a stray tear. At the looming prospect of the day to come, she felt uneasy – more than uneasy. The sheer reality of the situation was beginning to hit home, a creeping fear of the future. She took a long drag on the cigarette, enjoying the rush of nicotine. Jesus, a whole year of resisting, and now she was right back to chain-smoking… *Well, what you gonna do about it, Sugar?* So Gloria would have said, but Dolly didn't want to think about her mother right now.

She sighed, tapping the cigarette on the side of the ashtray. For a start, she would have to leave this flat. Though she had savings from the inheritance, the money would run out soon enough, and without a job she couldn't possibly afford the nine-hundred-and-fifty pounds a month rent, plus bills, not to mention the cleaner. There was nothing for it but to pay two months upfront, she decided, then give notice on the lease. Perhaps she could go down to Cornwall, stay at Genévrier if it wasn't let? She didn't relish the thought, but what other choice was there? She rubbed her temples wearily, aware that she ought to be fighting, kicking up a stink and proving Shaun's skullduggery. What had Shaun said? *You need to stop digging around on Lusenka.* This, as well as yesterday's desperate bid to block her from Westminster at all costs, told her there was more to Shaun's actions than met the eye. But... and it was a big but. Without her official job title, without her press pass or her professional reputation intact, who was going to talk to her? She hadn't a hope in hell of going up against the government.

In the living room she flicked on the television, where a news ticker ran across the screen of the morning breakfast show: *Leaked documents discredited, government memo proves a fake.* A video clip flashed up, showing her standing on the north steps of Parliament yesterday evening. She was pushing the microphone away, grimacing with a freakish expression at the camera. Cringing, she turned the volume up.

'Pickering's government is once more facing unwanted scrutiny after an unverified document claimed to prove overspending on defence in Lusenka,' the presenter was saying. 'The Junior Minister for Defence Procurement, Shaun Kingsley, denies the claims, which were wrongfully leaked by a reporter at Cloud News. Matt, can you give us more?'

The correspondent appeared on screen, followed by a shot of Shaun Kingsley's talking head. 'I cannot possibly comment on an unpublished and unvalidated dossier,' he told the camera, all charm, all suave certainty. 'If you ask me, the whole thing's a bit of a circus.'

'For fuck's sake,' Dolly swore under her breath, hastily flicking the TV off with a sick feeling in her throat, but not before she glimpsed her own mugshot photograph flash up, the one from ten years ago that was still used in some places, next to her by-lines. In the picture she looked fresh and young, her hair longer then, braided into a neat side ponytail. She groaned out loud, remembering the day that photograph was taken in the lobby of Cloud News headquarters, and the giddy feeling of triumph she felt at finally reaching the ranks of journalists who required a professionally shot by-line picture. But not anymore, Dolly thought. *The past is another country.*

At the window she stared out again, noticing a pair of reporters staked out below on the opposite pavement, doing exactly what she'd done herself so many times in the past. It must be a slow news day. Not that there was anything to see here. They'd be better off shadowing Shaun's mock-Tudor five bed in Parson Green. The thought brought a fleeting surge of dismay at becoming the watched, when once she was the watcher.

She sighed and rubbed a temple, easing the beginnings of a headache. She should, she knew, be doing something constructive – exactly what, she wasn't quite sure yet – but instead she stood still, contemplating a layer of fluffy white clouds rippling the sky – a mackerel sky, or was that something quite different? – and considering how little she enjoyed the sensation of being the subject of a story. She hated the idea that she might join the other side, as she tended to think of the powerful people, men mostly, businessmen and politicians with questionable morals and even more questionable reputations, whom journalists like her were supposed to hold to account. No, she was supposed to be on the right side of justice and truth, but now her reputation was in tatters. She was destined to be broke in a month or so, and it looked like she would never work again.

Down below, one of the reporters stared up, too far off to meet her gaze, yet Dolly had the distinct impression the man was smiling directly at her, crudely, no doubt, in the way of male news desk hacks, probably loving a little bit of voyeurism. She was always taken aback by the coarseness of her male colleagues' banter about the women they staked out, the innuendo and the rape jokes, as if by stepping out of the newsroom these sons and husbands left the boundaries of decency behind.

'Ugh.' She grimaced, flipped the man two fingers and turned away from the window.

Half an hour later, in her bedroom, she threw clothes, underwear, toiletries and other bits and pieces into a large suitcase. As she collected items from the wardrobe, she stopped to stare at the photograph of her mother on the chest of drawers, imagining Gloria looking out with an admonishing expression in her eyes, as if she knew exactly what was going on beyond the boundaries of her picture frame. Dolly was, she had to admit, very glad that Gloria wasn't around to see her sacked from her job. Her mother would surely have been more horrified than sympathetic at the scandal– and she was never a woman you wanted to lock horns with.

With a sigh, Dolly packed the portrait on top of her other belongings, her mind turning to the work paraphernalia from yesterday. She needed to go to the Post Office to return those earrings, promptly, otherwise – now that she was *persona non grata* – the press office might end up charging her for them. From her rucksack, she retrieved the mysterious parcel, only to search in vain for an accompanying press release. Instead she took a closer look at the jewels, which were exquisite, tiny white diamond halos set around sparkling blue centres the colour of pale sky. Delving further inside the package, she pulled out a thick, cream envelope, plain, with no addressee at all.

It contained a white notelet handwritten in the same elegant cursive as on the front of the parcel, with a few small blotches indicating a cartridge pen had been used – and who on earth, Dolly wondered, used a cartridge pen these days? Attached to the note by a rubber band was a mini cassette. The note said: *Get out of London. Find the Lusenka tapes.*

The Lusenka tapes? She scrutinised the note more closely, turning the tape over in her fingers, trying to puzzle out its meaning, but there was no correspondence address, no hint as to the sender's identity whatsoever.

Gripped by curiosity, she inserted the mini cassette into her Dictaphone, put on her headphones, and pressed play, her pulse quickening with anticipation.

The next time I saw Sunstar, it was a Saturday, I remember well, because news of the latest American space shuttle programme was all over the headlines that morning.

Mum?

Dolly's mind was reeling. Her mother's voice was unmistakable, a marvellous voice, like warm honey, or palm shadows on a summer afternoon, or a length of velvet rippling in the sunlight, with that famously seductive accent – the sexiest voice on earth, as one film critic had once described it. The breathy BBC vowels, precise and decidedly seventies, were infused with the melodious Lusenkan lilt that was Gloria's stage trademark. Drifting from the tape, her voice seemed shockingly voluptuous, shockingly alive:

The next time I saw Sunstar was a Saturday, I remember well, because news of the latest American space shuttle programme was all over the headlines that morning. I recall listening to the wireless while I fiddled with the coffee grinder, experiencing that sense of wonder we humans always feel, don't you think, Sugar, at the thought of mankind reaching for the moon. What a marvel, I pondered as the newsreader offered details of the new space exploration plans. I understand how difficult it must be for you, with all your new-fangled technology, to imagine how exciting it was back then to witness the beginning of the space age. We were glimpsing a new future, a new frontier, and ever since '69 we'd all had a feeling that uncharted worlds were opening up; distant, dazzling moons and galaxies just waiting to be explored.

It was six a.m., a cold morning, just getting light. Through the windows of my flat I could see the first hints of dawn streaked across the sky, pink, blue and lavender, signalling the start of a new day. Frost sugared the pavements, and the cars parked along the kerbs were decorated with glistening patterns of ice that the girl in me – the Lusenkan girl who'd grown up beneath the baking sun – still found marvellous, a small miracle of the cold, even after years of living in England.

I had rehearsals, so I put on a rose-pink dress with platform heels and a warm woollen coat. Around my hair, I tied a scarf the colour of sunset. After a hasty breakfast of boiled eggs, toast with butter and a few cups of strong Ugandan coffee, I set off downstairs just as the clock said ten to seven, but the minute I stepped outside, I had a shock.

The recording stopped abruptly. Mystified, Dolly pressed play a few more times, hoping for some continuation of the narrative, but found nothing. She turned the envelope over in her fingers, searching for a clue, an explanation, but the note ended with no further comment. So, what on earth *was* this, and who on earth would send such a thing, now of all times?

She left the bedroom, needing a strong cup of tea, but stopped in her tracks as a sudden memory crashed into her mind: of Gloria, one hot day last summer. Was it late July or August? She could vividly remember the clear, pure, boiling heat, the barometer hitting thirty-nine, the way the heavy air sapped her of will and energy. Or maybe it was just that Gloria was dying and the house seemed pervaded by the heavy stench of illness, sweet and violet, as if life itself were decaying there.

'Honestly, Mum, what *are* you doing?'

Reluctantly, Dolly had followed her mother up into the airless roof, where Gloria commenced rummaging in boxes with the over-zealous air of a woman possessed. Five minutes later, she held up a tatty-looking cardboard shoe box.

'I'm going to die soon, Sugar. When I do, I'll leave you this, here, in the attic. Think of it as a treasure hunt.'

'What *is* it?'

'A box of secrets.' Gloria cheerfully swiped dust off the lid of the shoe box. 'For your eyes only – well, for your ears, anyway.'

'Oh, so very cloak and dagger.'

Dolly had felt a surge of irritation at her mother's bizarre melodramas, her callous indifference to her own demise, always so bloody theatrical, as if she expected everyone to jump to cater to her secretive ways and sudden caprices. Nonetheless, she couldn't resist peering over to glimpse inside the box, which contained a number of shabby cassette tapes in plastic cases labelled with felt tip pen. She tried to read the labels, but

Gloria was already placing the lid back on the shoebox, pressing it down with her fingers with a furtive expression.

'We all have secrets, Sugar. Just because I'm your mother, doesn't mean I haven't had a life of my own. I hope one day you'll understand.'

Nothing more was said, leaving Dolly feeling exasperated and a little intrigued, if only momentarily. After a few hours she dismissed her mother's teasing, her secret box and her treasure hunt fantasies as just another strange whim, and quickly forgot about the matter.

Still, Dolly reflected now, going through from the hall to the kitchen, it was curious that Gloria should have shown her a box of tapes that day, of all things, and now here was this mysterious note with all the earmarks of a treasure hunt clue: *find the Lusenka Tapes.*

Deep in thought, Dolly boiled the kettle and poured water on a tea bag, smashing it against the side of the mug, adding a dash of milk before returning to the bedroom. Come to think of it, where *was* that box of old cassettes? Still in Gloria's attic in Genévrier?

From somewhere outside, a car horn jarred in the still afternoon. Dolly finished packing the suitcase, still brooding over her discoveries. For as long as she could remember, she'd purposefully kept herself from getting to know Gloria, never bothering to learn about Lusenka – at least, not enough to understand her own foreign roots. As for her father, his identity remained shrouded in secrecy.

'Why did he leave?' Dolly used to ask sometimes. 'Why doesn't he visit us?'

'It's not possible,' Gloria would say with a closed-off expression. 'That's all.'

'Was he kind, handsome, a good man? Did you love him?'

'Leave it, Sugar,' Gloria would say. 'The past is the past.'

All Dolly knew for sure was that her father was white – that much was evident from her own pale skin. And that Gloria had been madly in love with him, if the expression in her eyes whenever Dolly brought it up was anything to go by. Dolly could only surmise that her parents had some kind of illicit affair. When she turned eighteen, she took matters into her own hands and tried to find out about her father, but he was a phantom, absent from her birth certificate, absent from all records of her mother's life. Despite her best efforts, the search led only to dead ends, as though he'd slipped through the cracks, leaving nothing but unanswered questions. Eventually, Dolly gave up hope of ever finding this seemingly invisible man, although she occasionally allowed herself to imagine his return one day, a long-lost hero galloping in on a white horse to sweep her off her feet. Something like that, anyway.

With a sigh, she zipped up the suitcase and stood it upright on the floor. Was it possible that these mysterious tapes the note talked about contained information about her father? If so, perhaps now *was* the time to ask those long-avoided questions?

On her laptop, Dolly logged into Twitter and scanned the comments, thousands now, accumulating by the second under the hashtag #rogue-journo. As always, the trolls were having a field day, but it was the unexpectedly scathing backtalk of her thousands of previously adoring fans which made Dolly's stomach lurch with shame. *@jlevin83 What a total fucking disgrace! @856russianfirefly These journalists are so full of shit @mastermindUK Fucking foreigner.*

Her followers were dropping off by the second. In haste, trying her best not to get sucked in by the heckling mob of virtual commentators, Dolly deleted her Twitter account, then did the same for Facebook and LinkedIn. Via email, she cancelled her internet, landline, weekly cleaner, and next week's waxing appointment at an extortionate salon in Notting Hill she'd been toying with ditching anyway. Finally, she emailed her landlord to give notice on the flat, offering assurances that she was happy – not that she was, but she felt obliged to be diplomatic – to pay an early release penalty.

Half an hour later, with a cathartic sense of relief that left her almost breathless, she fetched her mobile phone and called Rich.

CHAPTER SIX

Dolly

The following afternoon, Dolly arrived in Truro on the 12.23 stopping train from Paddington, feeling inordinately relieved to have escaped the press scrum who'd trailed her all the way to the railway station, via the Tube, shouting questions. She waved when she spotted Rich through the carriage window, waiting on the southbound platform, wearing faded jeans and an AC/DC sweatshirt, no coat, and flip flops. It was still late April but her little brother never seemed to feel the cold. He had buzz-cut hair and dark-framed spectacles, a fairly fly guy in his thirties, Dolly thought, glimpsing him for a split second as a stranger might.

The train doors clicked open and she clambered down onto the platform, laden with luggage – and feeling terribly nervous, all of a sudden. It was months since they'd last seen each other. To her relief, Rich came forward with a fist bump and a smile – 'Yo, Sis' – and a hug in large arms, and she breathed in his familiar smell of washing powder, cocoa butter and a gingery aftershave he'd worn ever since he was about fourteen, hoping to impress the girls. Smiling, she kissed him on the cheek and hugged him back, though still between the two of them hung a gossamer cloud of unease. He would hold back, she knew, and so would she.

'Shit, you look awful, Doll,' Rich said, tucking her other bags under his shoulder, dragging the second suitcase behind him. 'You're too thin.'

'Better than being fat, right?' Dolly raised an eyebrow.

Her brother shook his head, laughing quietly. 'Long time no see.'

'Sorry about that.'

A trace of what? Hostility? Anger? Still the trailing remnants of their bitter arguments.

'I guess you needed a reason,' Rich said with a shrug.

Dolly followed her brother through the ticket turnstiles. Outside the station, taxis were pulling up, dropping passengers. Doors slammed shut. People clustered outside the entrance to Costa Coffee, laden with bags.

'Are you sure this is okay?' she said as they crossed the road, hoisting her laptop bag higher onto her shoulder. 'To stay at the house, I mean?'

'It's your house too – you can crash there as long as you want. I mean, we won't get the rent money, but...' Rich glanced over with a half-smile, changing the subject, but Dolly felt the sting anyway. She was in the way, her brother seemed to say. She was *disrupting* things. 'Gracie and the girls cooked dinner,' he added. 'We need to feed you up.'

'What, like a Mauritanian bride?' she said, archly.

'A what?'

'In Mauritania, some parents still force-feed girls ready for marriage. It's called *le gavage*. I did a story on it once.'

Rich chuckled. 'Crazy as ever, then.'

'True though.'

'Whatever, Doll.'

Still, these bitter remnants in the gaps of their small talk. Their sibling relationship had never recovered, Dolly was thinking, from what she'd done all those years ago. It had happened when Rich worked in the police. One day he'd let something slip about a harassment case he was investigating – Dolly could barely even remember the details now, but it was something internal to do with a Chief Inspector in the force – and she, under pressure to get new stories, leaked it to Cloud News. Another of her terrible decisions. Rich was angry, too angry. She was promoted. Now she was always on edge around him, trying to make up for the past.

But after a moment he seemed to soften. When they stopped to wait at the traffic lights, he put an arm around her shoulder and brusquely pulled her in.

'Hey, Doll. It's going to be okay, you know.'

'If you say so.'

She shrugged and pushed her brother away, play-fighting, pulling her scarf tighter against the chilly noonday sun as they reached the station car park. He flicked his key at a big Citroën Aircross which flashed once, then twice, and Dolly clambered into the front. In silence, they made their way through the slow traffic out of town, until Rich indicated off the main roundabout down a winding coastal road through open countryside, the sea in the distance, via St Agnes, to Penrennie. A mist hung over the coast, blurring sea with sky. Still, Dolly felt a lift at the sight of the miles of arable fields, the jagged grass cliffs that even in early spring were edged with a smattering of heather and gorse.

After a short while, Rich switched on the car radio and Maroon 5 floated from the speakers. Dolly hummed along. Casually, her brother turned the volume up and they sat in companionable silence as they passed through Porthlowe, where Rich lived. Dolly took in the sight of The Crab and Bottle pub where a sign advertised two for one Sunday roasts. The sloping dunes and the children's playground. The surf shop with children's wetsuits hanging outside and the tiny Spotted Cow ice cream parlour, closed now in midweek.

'Same old, same old,' she remarked, half-enjoying the normality of it all, quiet and strangely comforting.

'Always,' said Rich with a chuckle.

A smart new sign adorned the curly wrought-iron gate of their mother's former home: *Genévrier*. So-called because it was, apparently, the word for 'juniper' in Lusenkan patois, though Dolly had never really understood why Gloria chose that word, of all possible, random words. Yet how that name took Dolly back, and how this place, this beloved childhood place, was fixed in her heart…

Rich parked, turned the engine off, and for a second or two, they sat without talking, looking out. The lime-washed farmhouse stood squarely against a backdrop of rolling fields and vast skies, weathered but unchanged, a throwback to their childhoods. In the porch, a Wellington boot rack stood empty. A seashell hung from the door knocker. Opposite, a ramshackle mud-walled barn housed garden tools, an ancient lawnmower and – way back in the distant past anyway – Gloria's annual onion crop from her vegetable garden, which she used to lay out to dry in the hayloft over winter. Unmistakably, her presence lingered here.

'Isn't that Mum's?' Dolly asked in surprise as they got out of the car, nodding at a navy-blue Morris Thousand parked outside the barn.

'I fixed it up for you to drive. Thought you might need some wheels.'

'Thanks, that was nice.' Dolly smiled, genuinely pleased. 'I always forget how lovely it is here,' she added. 'The air's so different.'

Rich slammed the boot, observing her with a look somewhere between amusement and annoyance. 'Sea air. Best in the UK. If you actually bothered to visit, you'd get to enjoy it.'

'I'm sorry about that.' She shot him an apologetic smile, finding she *was* sorry. 'After Mum died, well—'

'At least you're here now.'

'Yeah.'

Over the phone, Dolly had told Rich what had happened. Now she had the sudden sense that she was a prodigal daughter returning to the fold – presumably that was how her brother saw this scenario, anyway, and his wife too – much as she liked Gracie. Were the two of them crowing secretly, she wondered, glad for once to have the upper hand? Unfair, but possibly true. After all, everyone here must know what happened in London. It was all over the news, they'd only have to join the dots.

Rich handed her a large bunch of keys. 'Look, you must be knackered, I'll leave you to it. Dinner's at six, over at our place. You do remember where that is? Gracie wants to give you a proper welcome.'

They stood facing each other as Dolly thanked him, wanting, quite suddenly, to cry. Rich furrowed his brow, as if sensing how she felt, and opened his arms in a bear hug which she willingly stepped into, feeling something inside her chest give way as she pressed her cheek to the soft cotton fabric of his t-shirt smelling of aftershave and soap.

He squeezed her tightly. 'Everything will be okay, Sis, I promise.'

'Do you fancy a quick drink,' Dolly asked tentatively as the hug ended. 'It's been a rough couple of days.'

'Better not. We don't really drink during the week. It's not London down here, you know.'

The moment was gone. He drove away, raising a hand out of the window.

Inside, Dolly took her boots off and carried her bags upstairs to her old bedroom. Through the window, she could just make out the blue-green sea, dreaming in the distance. Apart from a large bed, there was a pine wardrobe, a chest of drawers, a small wooden desk. On it, a vase of bright spring daffodils bloomed cheerfully, one of Gracie's little touches, she was sure. Leant against the vase was a handwritten note from her nieces: *Welcome back Auntie Dolly!* She smiled to herself. She was looking forward to spending time with them.

She changed into tracksuit bottoms, a sweatshirt, and comfortable socks, before unpacking her belongings. The portrait of Gloria, she placed face down in the empty drawer of the bedside table, putting the mysterious parcel containing the note and the earrings beside it. Downstairs, she made a cup of tea and wandered the rooms, admiring the new holiday-let furnishings, and feeling glad that, by some barely expressed agreement, neither she nor Rich had wanted to sell the place after Gloria died. Dolly recalled their lengthy telephone discussions over a number of days about what to do with the inherited property, after which it was decided that Rich and Gracie would refurbish Genévrier into a holiday rental, and the three of them would split the rent money. Rich and Gracie had certainly gone to town, she thought now.

The kitchen had pale cupboards above marble counter-tops and a stainless-steel extraction hood, all shiny, pristine newness. In the living room there were wool carpets in place of the tiled floors and the lingering damp smell that used to pervade the house, particularly during the winter months. There were pretty, pastel walls and puffy cushions on a comfortable-looking settee, and a rustic pine table set with an empty vase. Dolly stared around, running a finger along a trendy silk throw bearing the motif of a peacock. She couldn't shake the feeling that her mother was somehow present, watching her every move.

On a sideboard near the fireplace, she was surprised to see Gloria's old record player, along with a handful of seventies and eighties pop records mysteriously scattered on the floor in the otherwise immaculate room, as if someone had been rummaging through them. The mess struck her as odd. Quickly, she texted Rich: *Has anyone been here today?*

Just the cleaners, he replied, before calling her back seconds later, sounding worried.

'Why? What's happened?'

'Chill, everything's fine, it's just that Mum's records are all over the floor.'

'That's weird.' He paused. 'Come to think of it, I thought the cleaners were a bit shady this morning.'

'Really? Did you give them the keys to the attic? I thought you kept it locked?'

'I was running in and out like a madman, didn't notice the mess. They were itching for the attic keys. I told them cleaning the loft might be a step too far.'

They both laughed, and he rang off, but still Dolly felt puzzled as she knelt down and stacked the records back into a pile. She plugged the record player in and lifted the stylus, but paused, considering whether to put a record on, deciding against it. Music, at the moment, was peculiarly painful, raising emotions she had no interest in confronting right now.

Besides, she had more pressing matters to attend to. She thought of the mysterious note – *find the tapes* – and the peculiar fatefulness of her arrival here. Here she was in her mother's house, as if destiny were pulling her back. She was glad, suddenly, of the distraction, which felt like a buttress against the traumatic events of the past week. She stared reflectively at the clock on the wall, which said half past three. Plenty of time to go up in the attic.

Upstairs, she unfolded the ceiling ladder and teetered cautiously up the steps, where she craned upwards to test the small key that, in her mother's time, used to unlock the trap door to the roof. Predictably, it jammed and failed. She swore out loud, trying each of the other keys, but none worked. Just as she was about to give up, the original key crunched, resisted and, after a small amount of pushing and fiddling, turned in the lock. Triumphantly, she pushed open the trap door and climbed through.

CHAPTER SEVEN

Dolly

The vast roof space was stale-smelling, deep silent, clouded with cobwebs. Looking around, Dolly had a sense of opening the past, of ghosts rising from the dust. She shook the feeling away and began investigating a pile of stacked-up cardboard boxes containing old-fashioned tennis racquets in hatched wooden frames, and a quantity of novels and non-fiction: Jilly Coopers; a few art manuals; a large volume entitled *Romanticism, an Anthology*. In a third box, old computer keyboards, plug sockets, a Walkman, and some pairs of retro-looking headphones. A plastic bag contained more of Gloria's vinyl records. Dolly filed through them with curiosity, exclaiming in surprise at the vintage titles. With a treasure-seeker's thrill, she lugged the bag to the top of the ladder ready to take downstairs.

Towards the back of the roof space, a battered-looking pine chest looked vaguely familiar – perhaps it used to sit in one of the bedrooms, Dolly wondered, or in the study? One after another, she pulled open the drawers, finding most empty apart from a few floral paper liners, their patterns almost entirely worn away, and a couple of ancient lavender bags which released a faint whiff of dried herbs. Dolly ran her fingers over the dusty fabric, overcome with a sudden feeling of nostalgia at the smell of home, of childhood, of safety.

She sighed, casting her eyes around. Another cardboard box was filled with documents: visa forms, cheque stubs, pay slips dating from the seventies and early eighties, and a series of expired passports, Lusenkan, then British. A black and white picture of Gloria stared out from the back page of one, looking young and serious with a short, neatly trimmed Afro. Delving further, Dolly pulled out another photograph, of the three of them this time – Dolly, Rich and Gloria – one summer, it must have been, when she and Rich were teenagers. The sun was out, the sky a deep azure blue. There was Dolly in a swimming costume, tanned and smiling, stretched on a rug beneath a candy-striped parasol, while Rich turned sausages on a grill, grinning through clouds of smoke. Next to him, Gloria held a tray, the sun in her eyes, laughing as she raised a hand to the camera set to automatic. Half-smiling, Dolly picked up the photograph and stared at it for a moment, feeling nostalgic, then put it back in its place with a sigh.

In the far corner of the attic, a collection of hats and leather handbags, crinkled from damp, stacked along with several other boxes containing clothes and shoes. Platform heels and leather boots, flared jeans, silk scarfs and hot pants spilled out. A bell-bottomed Karl Lagerfeld power suit patterned with crocodiles. A pair of cream hot pants with a sleeveless buttoned top, and flares to match. Several boho-looking day-dresses, and dozens of retro evening gowns which, by the looks of the labels – Biba, Chloé, Vivienne Westwood, Mary Quant, Bruce Oldfield, Laura Ashley – were worth a fortune.

Dolly shook out the garments, filled with excitement, then stopped herself. She'd have loved to spend a few hours rifling through Gloria's vintage clothes, but she ought to find the tapes. She put a couple of things by the trap door – a fashionable Chloé jumpsuit of muted green, a cashmere cardigan with pretty cap sleeves – and continued her search. She was on the point of giving up when her fingers grazed something hard beneath a long, tailored, wax cotton dress with a geometric design of bold lime and black concentric circles, rather the worse for wear – the only Lusenkan-looking outfit in the collection. Pulling it aside, Dolly reached for a tatty-looking shoebox which released a musty smell of dampish cardboard lingering in the air.

'The box of secrets,' she murmured, biting down a smile.

At pains not to break the already torn lid, she swiped away the dust and slowly opened the box. Inside were a few carefully preserved launch invitations from the seventies, then a faded film photograph dated August 1975, showing Gloria with the entire cast of Mirrorball, the cast forming a long, crescent shape in front of the Odeon in Piccadilly Circus. With a dreamlike feeling, Dolly held the photograph in her fingers, lost suddenly in her mother's world, with all its unknown faces, and all its small mysteries.

She put the memorabilia aside and examined a bundle of tattered hardback notebooks with worn covers, musty smelling, faded with age, secured with a rubber band. She hesitated, her fingers lightly tracing the bindings as it flashed through her mind that she could put them right back and let the dust gather again. Only she had the strangest sensation, an excitement welling inside her, as if she was about to enter a story unfolding for her alone. For so long, her questions about the past had lain dormant, but now they jostled through her mind, noisy as a crowd of reporters, impossible to ignore.

'For fuck's sake, Mum,' she whispered aloud. 'Why are you doing this to me...'

The pages of the first notebook were half nibbled away – by mice, by silverfish? Other pages were welded together with damp, the ink blurred and distorted as though by falling rain. The rest of the notebooks were the same, containing just a few pages intact, these filled with lines and lines of Gloria's unmistakable handwriting. Scruffy and haphazard, there were crossings-out and notes scribbled in the margins. Dolly brushed her fingertips across the ink-stained pages. Was Gloria deliberately weaving a mystery, then, a sort of long-drawn out exposé of her own past – but why, if it wasn't simply an attention-seeking tactic?

Quickly she scanned one of the only undamaged diary entries:

10th August 1972

I saw a boy, yesterday, as I walked from my flat over to the tube station. He must have been ten or eleven, playing football in the park. The sight of him made me stop in my tracks, overwhelmed by a terrible, aching loss. You see, the boy looked just like my little brother, Chilembé, and for a moment I stood there helpless, longing for my beloved sibling, for my country, for home. The unknown boy must have sensed my gaze because he turned, laughing with big white teeth at something his friend had said, just as Chilembé would have done, and all I could do was stand and stare like a lemon, wishing I could turn back time, wishing that boy was my brother. My God, I miss him more than anything else in the world.

A fly buzzing near the rafter broke the spell of Gloria's words, and Dolly closed her eyes with a new tightness in her chest, remembering how Gloria never, ever spoke about her little brother – Dolly's Uncle Chilembé – out loud. Uncle Chilembé had died before Dolly was born, and it felt strange to read this passage now, so raw and so private, an outpouring of grief and homesickness.

With a renewed sense of determination, Dolly put the notebooks aside, fished underneath them until she found two full-size, old-fashioned cassettes in plastic cases, each marked with a number, a date – 1979 – and a title. The first was labelled: 'The Beginning'. The second: 'Mission Plans'.

'Oh man,' Dolly exclaimed out loud. These, undoubtedly, were what Gloria had meant that sweltering afternoon last summer, though there appeared to be fewer tapes here than her mother had suggested. What could they mean, with these mysterious titles?

Dolly snapped open the cases and turned the cassettes over in her hands, looking for clues, wondering if there might be any more in the box – but there were none.

Oh, Mum.

For how long had Gloria been hiding this secret collection of diaries? It seemed hard to believe that she was so closed off, yet all the time she was engaged in recording her thoughts in private. The idea that she might have wanted to talk, but for some reason couldn't bring herself to, made Dolly want to cry. She took a deep breath and closed her eyes, trying to calm herself as best she could, and remembering Gloria's words. *You must listen to them after I'm gone.*

But still, contained in this box were secrets she didn't know if she wanted to confront, secrets that might, she suspected, help her unlock the mystery of the note – if not other mysteries, too. Her mother. Her father, even. As yet, she didn't understand anything.

Dolly cast her eyes around the attic and reached for the vintage Walkman. Had her mother left it there on purpose, she wondered, to make it easier to listen? With her various discoveries stacked in her arms, she staggered to her feet and teetered carefully back down the ladder.

Downstairs, she stacked the old LPs next to the others in the living room, fancying she could hear her mother's nagging: *Come on, Sugar, listen, for goodness sake!*

'Okay, okay, I give in,' Dolly grumbled to herself. 'You win, Mum.'

Tentatively, she opened the shoebox again. Fingering one of the tapes, she hesitated, finding she wasn't quite ready. She put it aside and turned instead to one of the notebooks, leafing gingerly through the damp-damaged pages to a section that was just about legible, dated 11th January 1974, and then another from 1975.

11th January 1974

I often think of something my mother said to me back in Lusenka more than a decade ago. "One day you'll do this instead of me." We were standing on the roadside of our village, Cap Bleu, while she sold kola nuts to the passing cart drivers. "It's your destiny," she declared, "like everything in life. Even if you put your hand on your cheek, God has willed it."

I clung on to the print fabric of her wrap, pondering this as I watched the cars and carts go by, pulled by donkeys and weary-looking mules trotting through the hazy dust. Sometimes, a driver stopped to buy a packet of kola nuts from the tray my mother carried on her head. She was a village woman, a devout Catholic whose only horizon was the shining blue Atlantic rolling onto the beach near the line of tin-roofed shacks where we lived. Beyond that, well – I don't think she'd ever bothered to imagine what lay beyond.

Whereas I wanted to be different. I wanted to see outside the limits of our village. There was something out there waiting for me,

I was sure – though I didn't know what.

"Ma, I want to go to school," I said.

She leant into a car window to speak to a driver, ignoring me, exchanging a small plastic bag of nuts for a coin. When she emerged, she pocketed the silver coin and smiled a faraway smile.

"Nothing will teach you as well as God and life," she said. "You're a girl, and girls must be good wives and mothers. Stop your daydreaming, child, and help me sell."

My head ached in the hot sun. Obediently, I fell into step beside her, but I was cross. I felt as much frustration as a girl of ten can feel when her dreams are dashed, and she's told that, because she's a girl, the future is closed with a prison lock. There and then, I decided I would teach myself to read and write, and over the next two years, I did.

5th November, 1978

A sunny Saturday afternoon, with the promise of a party lingering in the air. I wandered along the Embankment enjoying a cigarette and some time to myself, away from prying eyes. A chill breeze whipped off the river, slicing across the pavement. I was wrapped, incognito, in a dark brown wool coat, a floppy hat, and a long, woollen scarf in shades of autumn – orange, yellow and gold. Still, I wasn't warm enough. I don't think I'll ever get used to the cold of this northern country, or its unpredictable seasons, the way the air reaches out with icy fingers into my heat-starved bones. How I long to bask in the scorching Lusenkan sun. But it's a distant memory, now, fading in the cool English wind.

The party was at seven. I went home to change into a gown delivered that morning by Bruce Oldfield's people. The dress was lovely, plunging and sapphire blue, with a fishtail skirt and silver threadwork. Still, I'd far rather have stayed at home. I'd begun to loathe the falseness of the London theatre crowd, with their absurd pretensions and relentless ambition, always striving to climb upwards, like hundreds of Jacks on hundreds of beanstalks.

At the Savoy, there was no chance of remaining anonymous, as I'd have preferred. Instead, I found myself air-kissing what seemed like hundreds of guests, though I said very little. Despite the ebullient atmosphere, I felt lonelier than ever. After an age, I managed to escape, and wandered to the fringes of the crowd, where I watched the ebb and flow of people until Sidney came over to interrupt. I tried to fend off his offers of champagne, but he wouldn't have it. The man's becoming more and more of a nuisance, forever trying to persuade me to sleep with him. Now that Mirrorball is such a success, I think he feels I owe him something.

It happened just as the dancing began. Someone tapped me on the shoulder. 'Miss Fontaine, a call for you at reception.'

On the other end of the receiver, a man's voice came on: 'Miss Fontaine. This is the British High Commissioner in Lusenka. I'm afraid I have some bad news. It's about your brother.'

I felt a rushing in my ears. Chilembé, Chilembé, Chilembé.

Stunned, Dolly sat with the notebook in her lap, imagining her mother listening to that terrible stranger's voice on the other end of the telephone, bringing the news that her beloved brother, Chilembé, was dead.

Wanting more, she flicked to the next entry, but there was only a lengthy description of Gloria's plane ride to Lusenka, and nothing about the funeral that followed, or her grief, which seemed strange, though fairly unsurprising. In real life, too, Gloria never discussed the important things, and now it struck Dolly that perhaps her mother thought silence could somehow erase all her pain.

She found some batteries and inserted them into the back of the Walkman, then placed the cassette marked, ONE, LONDON 'The Beginning' into the flip-out holder. Linking it to her mini speaker, she pressed play and held her breath, willing the old-fashioned tape machine to work.

At first, the audio crackled with white noise, fading in and out with the spool of tape grinding against the heads of the player. Dolly turned up the sound, straining her ears to listen. Through the hissing of the tape she could make out some very faint background noises against the static. Was that the high trill of a blackbird, and the rumble of a lawnmower, or a tractor? Garden sounds. Had Gloria recorded this here then, at Genévrier in Cornwall, and if so, when, and why?

She felt another rush of excitement as she recalled Gloria's words: *Everyone has secrets, Sugar.*

After a short while there came the heavy bump of a microphone, then a muttered exclamation, 'Oh, blast and dammit! How does this wretched thing work...'

Gloria.

Dolly sat rooted to the chair, riveted by her mother's voice, a strange lullaby rising from the tape machine. She felt like a child again, listening to her mother on the radio or television. She always loved her accent, its rolling 'r's and soothing foreign cadence, the ordinary words gently spiced with Gloria's own very distinctive intonation.

'Testing, one, two, three.'

Mum.

How on earth could these tapes have stayed forgotten here for so long? She'd had no idea they even existed, let alone held her mother's diaries, and now she wanted to know why they were recorded, what secrets lay in Gloria's past, the truth behind all the puzzles.

CHAPTER EIGHT

Dolly

Dolly arrived in Porthlowe at six o'clock, her mind still on the tapes, and her investigations. She was greeted by her sister-in-law, Gracie, standing in the frame of the front door, smiling warmly, her long hair hidden in a ruby-coloured wrap, wearing jeans and a hoodie that suited her slender limbs and impish smile. Flora and Fern, five and seven, seemed ridiculously tall, suddenly, and long-legged, way more grown-up-looking since Dolly last saw them. The sight of their small, upturned faces tugged at her heart, because in them, unmistakably, was Gloria.

'Auntie Doll!'

Dolly fought back a sudden urge to cry. She'd forgotten how much she loved these people, *her* people – and now it hit her in a rush. Why hadn't she come back sooner?

'Look at you two.' Smiling, laughing, Dolly caught the children in her arms. 'You've grown so much.' She hugged them tightly and turned to Gracie, a little awkwardly, but her sister-in-law drew her in, murmuring a welcome, patting her on the back.

'Hey there, love. You good? Really great to see you.'

At the big kitchen table, Gracie served baked fish with a spicy sauce, mashed potatoes and black beans, then a warm sponge made with tinned cherries. Making a pretence, Dolly pushed the fish around the plate and sampled the sponge, which turned out to be tasty, more than tasty. It occurred to her that she hadn't eaten a hot meal for two days, had been surviving on cups of tea, the occasional cream cracker, dozens of cigarettes. She left the table to go to the loo, only to hear, as she descended the stairs, one of her nieces talking in the kitchen.

'What's happened to Auntie Doll, Mummy?'

Dolly felt her face flush. She paused mid-stair, giving the family time to conclude the conversation about her without the embarrassment of their subject bursting in. With a vague sense of despair, it dawned on her that in this self-satisfied family cocoon she was very much the outsider, someone to be cared for, a patient to be fed up.

Back at the table, the kids ran out, squabbling in the lounge. Though Dolly hadn't finished the first portion, her sister-in-law spooned more sponge into her dish, and she ate it slowly while her brother and Gracie discussed the logistics of school run drop-offs, pick-up times, and homework with a trace of tension in the air.

Dolly got up to get a glass of water from the tap, thinking how the two of them – she and Rich – were so different nowadays, though growing up they'd been close, undertaking lengthy adventures in the outdoors, surfing and picnics, expeditions across the fields and heather-clad cliffs surrounding Genévrier, always accompanied by Gloria. If their mother was emotionally distant, she was always watchful when it came to their safety – strangely so, Dolly had sometimes thought, considering Gloria's seeming lack of interest in other matters, in matters of the heart, in anything that didn't revolve around herself.

Rich grew up to be a keen surfer, then turned down numerous university offers to go into the police straight from sixth form. After a few successful years in London as a detective inspector with the Metropolitan Police, he met Gracie, who at the time was something high up in Human Rights Watch – Head of Advocacy, Dolly seemed to think. Her sister-in-law was influential, as she remembered, a high-flyer working on influencing human rights policy change. But Rich missed the sea, and Gracie loved him. The couple moved back to Porthlowe to set up a small but lucrative property management business.

As for Dolly, the older sibling by a couple of years, she was the fucked-up one, the *car-crash* one, trailing a string of unsuitable lovers and questionable life decisions in her wake. Let's face it, she was always far more like Gloria, and as full of paradoxes. Head girl at school, except she listened to rap music and smoked weed in her spare time. An Oxford scholar who nearly got sent down because of an unfortunate incident in the second year involving weed and lime-flavoured vodka jelly. If she'd made a success of anything it was her professional life, but her personal life – forget it. Whereas Rich was forever top at school, then found a stable job and a stable marriage to his first steady girlfriend. Rich always had it all together, the saint to Dolly's sinner.

Flora burst into the room and clambered onto Dolly's lap, begging her to play. The little girl smelled of soap and biscuits and childhood. Dolly wrapped her arms around her and kissed her on the cheek. 'Give me two minutes, darling.'

She watched her niece run back into the lounge. 'I don't want to be a pain, hanging around here, I mean,' she remarked, sipping at the water, looking over the table at Gracie and Rich. 'I hope I'm not interrupting.'

Her brother spooned sponge into his mouth. 'Don't be ridiculous. You're family. You'd do the same for me.'

'If I wasn't homeless and unemployed,' she joked awkwardly.

'We like having you around, love,' Gracie said. 'The girls are thrilled.'

'If you're sure.'

'We're sure,' Rich agreed, finishing his pudding. He got up and flicked the kettle on, adding, more inquisitively, 'Sounds like it was rough up there.'

Dolly sighed, sensing that Rich wanted more juicy details, more fucked-upness. 'I screwed up,' she said in a low voice. 'I thought I could trust my contact, but I guess you can't trust your so-called friends these days.'

She paused, on the brink of tears. When she said the words out loud, it hit her how true they were, and her thoughts drifted to Shaun, and their relationship that now seemed a lie.

'I'm a crap journalist,' she added despondently. 'And a crap person. Everyone can see it.'

'We all make mistakes.' Her brother squeezed her shoulder and took a seat beside her. 'I know things didn't go as planned with your story, but you were brave to take a risk. Sometimes things just don't work out.'

She gave a weary smile. 'The trouble is that London's cut-throat. If you fall, you get trodden on. There's always someone waiting in the wings to take your place.'

'Well, perhaps that's not a world you want to be part of,' Gracie's measured voice cut in. 'Everything has a reason. Take a break, get some fresh air, recuperate, and find your zen. Forget about work for a bit.' Twinkle-eyed, Gracie shot her a smile. 'Look on the bright side, it's Fern's birthday at the weekend. You'll be our guest of honour. Imagine, from the bright lights of London to an eighth birthday party in Porthlowe. The glamour!'

Dolly couldn't help smiling at her sister-in-law's dry humour. 'Sounds amazing, honestly.'

'And stop smoking,' added Gracie gently, 'maybe?'

'You noticed?'

'I can smell it on you, love.' Gracie placed a mug of tea in front of her and patted her arm. 'I thought you gave up…'

'Fuck it.' Dolly leant her head on her hands with a groan. 'Everything's falling apart.'

In the lounge, Dolly sat on the floor, cross-legged, playing Connect Four with her nieces, slotting yellow discs into a blue plastic grid as the two girls beat her hands-down, one after the other, before twirling around the room waving their arms, singing *We Are the Champions*. Amid the hilarity, Gracie brought her another cup of tea. Rich dropped into an armchair and turned on the television, resting his feet on the coffee table.

Opposite, Dolly sank into the sofa with a niece snuggled under each arm for a round of Junior Scrabble. Together they composed words: owl, house, pretty, sounding out the letters before placing them on the board. Rich glanced over, smiling. Dolly couldn't remember when she'd last felt this relaxed. Certainly not for weeks, possibly months. It was a quiet sort of happiness, comfortable and effortless, and free from worry, like flinging off a heavy coat after a long winter. It felt nice just to be herself.

There was a knock on the door. It was Morgan Smith, an old friend from secondary school, dropping off a Tupperware container. She looked fresh and summery, expensive in a way Dolly didn't remember, in a well-cut dress and cardigan that accentuated the bump rising from her stomach. To Dolly's dismay, Gracie asked Morgan in, offering tea and crumble, and momentarily, Dolly panicked. The comfortable feeling disappeared. It was years since she last saw Morgan, and she wasn't sure what they would have to talk about. She wondered how soon it would be polite to make her excuses and go home – already she thought of Genévrier as home – to continue listening to the tapes.

'Doll,' Morgan exclaimed, her eyes seeming to widen as Gracie put a dish of crumble in her hands, covered in cream. 'I didn't know you were here. My God, after all these years.'

'You look amazingly well,' said Dolly, trying to be nice.

'And you're even tinier than ever, babes.' Morgan said, spooning the crumble into her mouth, explaining that her daughter went to the same school as Fern; that was how she knew Gracie. 'Fellow mums, you know. It's all birthday parties and the school run and feeling too bloody exhausted.'

For a few minutes the two of them chit-chatted about Morgan's pregnancy, which was seven months in, *I'm about to pop,* and a boy. Hunter, they planned to call him. Morgan no longer worked, she told Dolly, drifting between old memories and new plans. She was relieved to be able to relax into motherhood and the new pregnancy without the worry of a job.

'So, what happened in London, then, babes?' Morgan asked eventually, finishing off the last of the pudding. 'I mean, you had to come back down here?'

'Does everybody know? I mean, everyone's gossiping, aren't they?'

'I seen it on the telly.' Morgan brushed a crumb from her chin, looking apologetic. 'Guess you're pretty famous.'

'More infamous.' Dolly couldn't quite muster a proper laugh yet found herself curious to know what Morgan actually thought. 'My career's all over.'

Morgan shrugged. 'Don't matter down here, does it? No one really cares in Kernow, do they?'

Later, Dolly drove home feeling tired – shaken by Morgan's unexpected appearance, the incessant explaining of herself and all that had happened in London. Back at the house, she parked the car and rushed inside, hastily boiling the kettle. Once she was settled in her bedroom, pyjamas on, mug of tea in hand, she reached for the Walkman – which still had the tape inside – and pressed play. At once, Gloria's low, husky, accented voice filled the room.

CHAPTER NINE

Gloria

Tape one
The beginning, 1979, London

Sugar, it began with a man, as it so often does.

It was the last week of January, and utterly freezing weather. I'd been rehearsing all day at the Madeira Theatre for *The Shadow Hour*, in which I was playing the lead, Agatha Cake. At three o'clock, our usual home time, David and I were still on stage – David Madderley Shaw, that is. You might have heard of him, he won an Oscar in '77.

I vividly remember what I was wearing: a V-neck jumpsuit of deepest night-blue velvet with fabulous bell sleeves, a favourite of mine, and leopard-print platforms from a shop on Portobello. And a rather lovely coat of deepest chartreuse green, with a swinging silhouette that caught the light. On stage, I always preferred my own clothes over outfits chosen by the costume directors. I didn't like people telling me what to wear. Fashion was my armour against the world, you see. If something looked good on me, everyone wanted it...

Sorry, darling. I digress.

The scene wasn't going all that well. David and I were both exhausted and crotchety. God knows, he was a marvellous actor but a very difficult man – no time for anyone but himself, if you ask me – and I was struggling to find any sort of chemistry between us. Eventually, the director suggested we take a break.

I went backstage to get my things, lit a cigarette and strolled up through the circle to go outside for a breath of air. That's when I spotted a dusky figure sitting alone in the back row of the theatre seats, observing me silently. He was in his late thirties, early forties perhaps, in a dark overcoat and trilby hat.

As I passed, the stranger nodded wordlessly, so I nodded back, thinking nothing of it. I made my way out of the auditorium and stood on the pavement in the cold, smoking and shivering slightly as I watched people hurrying past, and enjoying the biting sensation of fresh air on my skin after the warm, mildewy atmosphere of the theatre.

Across the road, a teenage busker in denim flares and a red woollen hat was playing the Spanish guitar, a song about love and time passing. Beneath the sunless sky, I listened to the melody float over the street, thinking how the wisdom of its lyrics far surpassed the girl's age and experience. How on earth could this child know of such things?

Oh Sugar, it never fails to surprise me how our emotions rise at certain harmonies, like petals opening to the light. The music was too much. It spoke to me of my home country and my beloved brother, and there on the side of that cold, damp street, I suddenly wanted to cry. I pushed the feelings back down, unwelcome as they were, raw and completely disorientating. With the toe of my shoe, I extinguished my cigarette on the pavement and made my way back inside the theatre.

The following day was a Wednesday. The director let us go early with his usual plea, 'Drink water, please Gloria darling, gallons of water!'

In my dressing room, I changed into a pair of casual slacks, dabbed on lipstick, and put on my coat, feeling listless. Daily rehearsals were intense, but it wasn't just that. Ever since Chilembé's funeral, I was unable to sleep. Every night, I would lie awake until three or four a.m., my mind forming complicated puzzles about the whys and hows of my brother's death. Just the night before, I'd sat for hours on the windowsill of my bedroom, gin and tonic in hand, hidden by the dark, peering down through the curtains at the gaggle of reporters gathered on the pavement below. Dozens of them lurked down there in the shadows, waiting to see if I'd appear.

Eventually I left the window, but as I prepared for bed, I could sense those eerie shadow men with flashbulbs prowling the pavement below, a constant reminder that no matter where I went, the real price of fame was my privacy, and my happiness. Chilembé was gone, dead, and I blamed myself for leaving him behind. As it was, there was only emptiness. I was trapped in a prison cell, hoping for a reprieve. Perhaps my punishment was to be constantly pursued – by the fans, by the cameras, by the hacks and the beastly paparazzi. Sometimes during those years, it felt as if the whole world was hungry for Gloria Fontaine. I swear they'd have devoured me piece by piece, if only I'd let them.

I brushed my teeth, brooding about my situation as I stared at my reflection in the bathroom mirror. My eyes were big, my face thin and chalky from lack of real sunlight. I was a hunted girl, lost and sad, lonely and hopelessly grief-stricken. Without Chilembé, I had no family, no soul in the world who loved me, and no true friends, either – despite my numerous fawning admirers.

I felt no consolation that my name was up in lights. I was more and more aware that I detested my job, my life, the way I was just a songbird trapped in a gold cage, and no amount of fame or money could make me feel better. I wanted to hide away and shed my tears in private, yet I had to keep up appearances. Fame was fickle. The attention wouldn't last forever, and I was pragmatic enough, *Lusenkan* enough, to know I needed to make the most of my time in the sun.

CHAPTER TEN

Dolly

Dolly turned the tape off and sat staring into space, tears in her eyes. She couldn't help it. When her mother called her that familiar pet name, Sugar, pronounced in her distinctive accent – rich and low like a piece of chocolate being unwrapped, the thick syrupy shushing of the 's' – Dolly found her mind drifting back to when she and Rich were children. To the times, the rare, good times when her mother would ruffle her hair affectionately, and whisper an endearment: *Oh Sugar, be careful today.* Always a warning, *take care, be safe,* as if Gloria were forever worried that by walking out of the front door, something was going to happen to them. And she remembered quite clearly that showstopping suede coat her mother used to wear, how it glistened deep jade in the sunlight, always far too glamorous, too showy for rainy, rural Cornwall.

But then there was the other Gloria and all her complexities, so many it was hard to pin down her true character, because her moods shifted with the ever-changing Cornish weather, tempestuous and stormy, unsettled and full of contradictions. Gloria Fontaine, at once charming and reclusive, fragile yet tough as nails, a barefoot hippie and an ambitious taskmaster. At times, secretive and critical and cagey, often distant, sometimes ignoring her children for hours, days or weeks, and disinclined to talk with any sort of openness about anything, even her favourite foods. Unpredictable, so that often she was overtaken by a manic energy, and the house would be filled with music and cooking smells. At other times, her light snuffed out. A self-professed feminist who, in her own love affairs, appeared to let men push her around.

'Shit,' Dolly whispered out loud, pulling the duvet up to her chin, burying herself deeper under the cover as she recalled all her mother's small betrayals. The time she had first confided her dream of becoming a journalist, age twelve, only to be met with her mother's cold silence. The day she returned from her second term at Oxford; Gloria accusing her of *being too good for them now*. And once, when Dolly mentioned wanting children one day, Gloria's scoffing dismissal: *You? You couldn't raise a child!*

There were countless other instances when Gloria had let Dolly down. Afterwards Dolly would feel lost and anxious, as if she'd done something wrong, though what it was, she wasn't clear. Now, she wondered, should she feel grateful to Gloria for recording her thoughts, or deeply, blazingly upset that for so many years, decades even, her mother felt it was okay to keep her secrets locked up inside these taped diaries? Surely a proper conversation would have been far more useful…

She wound the tape back a little and closed her eyes, compelled to listen to Gloria's voice caught on the shiny ribbon of brown reel, peculiarly intimate, like the whisper of the sea caught within a landlocked shell. There followed a blip on the cassette reel for a second or two, causing the words to rush out, as if Gloria were in a hurry. Dolly ran the tape back again, and the voice went back to normal.

She had so many questions – but no answers yet.

She rose from her bed and retrieved the framed photograph of Gloria hidden amongst her things. Slowly, she brushed it off and set it upright on the top of the chest of drawers. She stood very still, staring into Gloria's face as a sharp, silver burst of grief ran through her, like the tip of a knife. What on earth was her mother trying to tell her, and what on earth might lie behind that cryptic film star smile?

There was a sigh as the tape ground on, and then, after a short moment, Gloria spoke again.

CHAPTER ELEVEN

Gloria

When I emerged from the stage entrance, the stranger from the day before was standing on the pavement outside, smoking a Gold Leaf Virginia, and apparently watching the door. It was another dingy afternoon, drizzling with rain. The man was a good head and shoulders taller than me – I estimated his height to be around six foot three – with a pleasant face and well-built shoulders that drew my attention. He wore a long, dark overcoat, and that silly trilby hat again, which gave him the look of a television detective, Colombo, or Kojak. The thought made me want to smile.

Oddly, there were no snappers waiting to hound me for the following morning's gossip columns, as they usually did. The street was deserted. I felt a fleeting – but only fleeting – sense of liberation.

'You've been following me,' I said sternly, extending my red umbrella, which caught a gust of wind and billowed upwards like a sail. 'Are you a journalist?'

The stranger removed his hat and produced a weathered gold cigarette tin from his pocket. 'Forgive me, Miss Fontaine, for the intrusion. Would you care for a cigarette?'

'I don't even know your name?' I said, helping myself to one.

'You can call me Sunstar.'

'Is that some sort of code name?'

Deadly serious, he nodded his assent.

We went to Locketts on Drummond Street, where he bought me a gin fizz and ordered a double whisky for himself. It was the sort of bar where the staff didn't particularly care when I walked in, because, at that time, the place was a hotspot for famous faces who came there to flirt and socialise with other movers and shakers. If they noticed me, they gave no sign of it. Perhaps Sunstar knew this. In fact, I'm sure now, in hindsight, that the place had been meticulously selected, many weeks before, for this very attribute.

Moreover, the bar was almost empty that afternoon, at four o'clock on a wintry Wednesday. Only a few other shadowy figures occupied the leather sofas and lamp lit booths, hunched over their drinks, and a solitary waiter rearranged spirits bottles behind the bar. The place buzzed softly with murmured conversation, and food smells mixed with tobacco.

'I must apologise again,' this Sunstar said, 'for ambushing you so unexpectedly.'

'I rather think you're not all that sorry.'

'Perhaps you're right.' He gave me a broad smile. 'Apologies aside, would you do me the honour of dining with me?'

'Of course.' I relaxed a little.

'Splendid.'

My companion's voice was remarkably distinctive, deep and hearty, with a trace of Scots and a rather attractive shh-ing around the consonants. I suppose I have the natural instincts of a performer, which meant that by that time, after years of living and performing in England – not to mention dozens of elocution lessons – my ear was well-attuned to my adopted country's regional accents. This peculiarity elongated everything the man said, giving his speech a soothing sort of burr that was extremely pleasant to my ear. Sugar, I've always had a thing about voices, and I could have listened to that man for hours.

Sunstar took the drinks from the waitress and extended an arm, gesturing towards a booth tucked away in a faraway corner. As he ushered me onto a bench and offered me another cigarette from the same gold tin drawn out of the upper pocket of his suit jacket, I remarked his tired-looking green-grey eyes, his darkish brown hair going grey at the sides, and his wide forehead dented by three prominent lines. Traces, I wondered to myself, of life's troubles, or just fatigue, like me. His suit was traditional, three-piece, wool, navy blue and rather impressively cut. I've always had a soft spot for a man in a well-tailored suit. It struck me with a rush of some unidentifiable emotion that this Sunstar person was really rather handsome.

With a slight flourish he lit my cigarette, then his own, and leant back in his seat, puffing on the cigarette. He crossed his legs and exhaled out of the side of his mouth.

'I'm sorry about Chilembé,' he said.

'Chilembé?' I took a sip of the gin, shocked and vaguely affronted by such a surprising statement by this curious stranger. What in heaven's name could this man know about my brother?

'What do you mean?' I asked carefully.

'Your brother worked for me.' Sunstar spoke with a smile and an encouraging nod, drawing me out, drawing me in. 'Do you know what Chilembé was doing when he was killed?'

'I really don't want to talk about that.'

'There's a chance for retribution, you know.'

'Retribution?'

'Your brother was a spy, Miss Fontaine, a covert operative for the British Government. He would have wanted you to seek out the people responsible for his death.'

A spy? I couldn't believe what I was hearing. I drank some more gin and drew on my cigarette, trying to stem my alarm at the turn the conversation was taking.

'I don't understand? My brother was a lawyer. He never came to England.'

'I understand this might be perplexing, Miss Fontaine, but when you arrived here, our people identified your brother Chilembé as a

67

valuable asset, given his ties to you, and his hatred of the Lourenco regime. Coupled with his impressive education, he proved to be an exceptional agent, one of my finest. He was not only adept at his job, but a man of integrity, and he was aware of my intentions to rendezvous with you.'

I took a long sip of my drink. Perhaps it was the effects of the alcohol, but in spite of myself, a memory rose of Chilembé's infectious smile, of my brother making me snort with laughter at some hilarious sibling joke only we two ever understood. Of when he was little, and we used to lie down on our sleeping mats at night, his baby voice whispering my name, *Gl-or-ia*. And that last time we were together, the deep painful red of the sky as night fell, and his darling smile, precious as the sun burning gold across the rooftops.

My God, how I missed him.

'You don't have to tell me he was a good man,' I managed to say. But despite my best efforts to the contrary, tears pricked at my eyes. I excused myself and headed for the ladies' room, where I sat on the loo and sobbed, dabbing at my eyes, wishing with all my heart that I could turn back the clock – and wondering what on earth this handsome stranger could want with me.

CHAPTER TWELVE

Dolly

About nine, Dolly grabbed a quick breakfast. She was due in Porthlowe later, to help set up the birthday party, because Rich was in London for work, he'd informed her over the phone earlier, and Gracie could do with a hand before he returned that afternoon.

She ate eggs on toast, still pondering the tape of the night before, which she'd sat listening to again and again well past midnight. She could just see her mother holding a Dictaphone to her mouth, full of excitement at what she'd have doubtless considered a new adventure, as well as an interesting extension of her acting skills. If Dolly remembered rightly, Gloria had worked on radio dramas for the BBC at one point, hence the elocution lessons, which would have meant she was well used to making recordings of this kind. And she was certainly a good actress, bringing Sunstar alive with her deliberate inflection, her subtle rendering of the man's voice. Listening, Dolly could almost smell the leathery tobacco smoke of the London bar, see the wintry sun filtering onto rainswept streets.

A memory rose unbidden, of a darkening afternoon, of sleety snow falling in heavy flakes outside. A Sunday, perhaps – it must have been a weekend, though she couldn't remember exactly when. Was she ten years old, or thereabouts, and Rich six or seven? At the table the two of them were doing homework while their mother cooked tea. There was the drifting smell of grilling sausages and the sound of Gloria's curses coming from the warm kitchen as she negotiated the grill pan, and the never-ending tedium of schoolwork, maths, perhaps, or science. Dolly was always better with words than numbers, whereas Rich was the opposite, a maths geek through and through.

Hungry, anticipating the food, Dolly wasn't particularly interested in the fact that her mother had a visitor, a man, though she couldn't remember any details about him. Back then it had not seemed important. Perhaps, she wondered now, this memory was always there, and she had suppressed it?

With the realisation of its new significance, Dolly delved deeper, imagining herself a fisherwoman drawing in her nets, coaxing the elusive childhood remembrance from the outer reaches of her consciousness. But the distant past remained elusive and unsatisfying, slipping through the net. A tall figure in the armchair. The smell of cooking meat. A rising tendril of Gloria's laughter. Had the two adults talked into the evening? Had the man joined them to eat, then spent the evening with their mother? He must have been there some time…

Dolly sighed. Was that man Sunstar, then?

She loaded the dishwasher and hastily wrapped Fern's birthday present – a glittery unicorn pencil case set she'd bought in London months before, complete with scented pens and an assortment of unicorn-shaped rubbers – in a length of colourful paper she found in a cupboard upstairs. As she was putting the roll back, she found herself sidetracked by half a dozen old photograph albums stacked on a lower shelf, suffused with a musty smell that made her want to sneeze.

She peered at the pictures of a barely remembered past, of endless summers when she and Rich were children, in which she recognised the beach head at Porthlowe and the dazzling, silver-light dunes of Godrevy, and herself as a toddler in a stripy swimming costume, holding out a handful of seashells glistening like the pearls of a necklace. There was Rich in a pram, then a pushchair. As a small boy, chubby-legged, full of exuberant smiles. Then holding a rugby ball, a surfboard, a school trophy. The two of them, rangy teenagers in winter coats and bobble hats, making peace signs on top of the hill at Pigeon Bay. There was a pink-striped beach tent staked into the sand; ice creams and storm waves; barbecues, bicycles, hiking trips, sunshine. She scanned for the mysterious man of her memory, but found only Rich and herself, never Gloria – who was always, presumably, behind the camera. Still, it seemed odd, almost as if she were hiding. And of course, there was no sign of their father, whoever he was.

Dolly turned the pages, feeling sad. The photographs were happy, happier than she remembered. She missed those carefree days when she and her brother were inseparable. Rich making her laugh until her sides hurt. Long afternoons after school when they explored the woods, built camps, invented stories. They climbed trees in the garden, daring each other to go higher, and hunted for washed-up treasures at the beach. One of the pictures showed Rich sitting on the rocks at Porthlowe in shorts and t-shirt, grinning at the camera, putting his trainers on. Dolly chuckled at the memory, recalling how, when Rich was ten or eleven or so, he would insist on meticulously brushing off every speck of sand before he could bear to put his shoes back on. She'd be waiting for ages, in fits of laughter at her brother's absurd war against the entire beach, one grain of sand at a time.

A final album showed Gloria in a series of film and stage portraits, professionally shot, with the name of the photographer printed on the sides. There was Gloria outside a West End theatre wearing a beautiful silver-blue gown with a silk headscarf and sheeny heels. Gloria in the basement of a bar somewhere, sipping a tequila sunrise in an A-line mini dress swirled with bright, psychedelic patterns, and leather platform boots. Gloria framed by a blue-grey sea, wearing a straw hat, looking out over the wall of a seaside pier, in denim hot pants and a tie-dye shirt knotted above her belly button. And Gloria on stage in ballerina chiffon, accepting a gigantic bouquet of pink roses. Another in which she was dressed head to toe in silvery cashmere, with violet eyeshadow and eighties shoulder pads. In the last, she looked older, slighter and more subdued than in the other photos, with a tired, world-weary expression in her eyes – though still ethereally beautiful, thought Dolly – all long legs and cut-glass cheekbones.

At the end of the album was a single picture, unlike all the rest, that made Dolly stop and look more closely. A faded photograph of

Gloria sitting on the edge of a bed, smiling radiantly, cradling a baby in her arms. When Dolly turned over the picture, she saw her mother's handwriting on the back. *Sugar, 26 weeks old,* it said, followed by two kisses, and a small heart loosely drawn in ink.

Dolly put the photograph back. She was going to be late. Hurriedly she packed a bag with Fern's present and – on a sudden impulse – the clothes, Gloria's clothes, which she'd found upstairs the other day, the jumpsuit and cardigan. By the time she let herself out of the house, it was nearly half past nine.

Dolly drove out of Genévrier, still thinking about the photographs, and took a right turn on the roundabout. She carried on up the narrow coast road flowing north, where the sloping land met the sea in a patchwork of earth and blue, melting into the sky beyond. Thick hawthorn hedgerows lined the sides of the road, a flower garland bursting into blossom. For some reason, they made her remember how much she loved growing up here, and the Larkin poem they'd learned at school, once, for spring festival, a poem about the blossoming of new life, about loss and renewal and fresh beginnings.

A tractor loomed around a corner, snapping Dolly from her reverie. Swearing, she tucked the Morris Thousand tight against the hedge, suddenly overcome by déjà vu of her childhood – rekindled by the photographs, perhaps. There came a memory of Gloria behaving with hair-raising bravado when negotiating the local traffic, as if her Lusenkan side was awakened by the act of driving. In the Morris Thousand, Gloria would hare through the lanes, shaking her fist and pummelling the steering wheel, making prodigious use of the horn, as if in her head she saw not the gentle roads of southern Cornwall, but the busy streets of Port Salé. By the time they were teenagers, Dolly and Rich were well-accustomed to the terror of the school run. Every time Gloria met another vehicle on a too-narrow bend, Rich would shout: 'Brace! Brace!' and they'd both assume a crash position in the back seat, joking around, muttering audible prayers to live.

Outside Porthlowe, Dolly came to a halt at a traffic light, following a construction lorry with her eyes as it turned left onto a steep dirt track edged by brambles. In the hedge, an impaled sign: *Peverell Greyson Developments Ltd: renowned for quality and value.* Beyond the sign was a car park. Greyson, Greyson. Why did that name ring a bell? Something to do with work...

She peered through the windscreen and drew a breath. Wasn't that Rich up on the hill, walking away from his parked car? There was no mistaking her brother's well-built gait, his familiar shirt of blue plaid too trendy for words, not to mention the hulking black Citroën. But what on earth was he doing here? Shouldn't he be in London?

Dolly indicated left onto the track, hovering on the gears as she bumped the car across potholes and puddles. If she remembered rightly, there was once a disused quarry up here, and a cluster of ill-maintained houses rented by junior doctors working at the hospital in town. In those days the doctors were cliquey, almost a commune, known for their wild, drug-fuelled parties. But at the top of the hill, the houses were gone. In their place, an unpaved car park and a length of high chipboard fencing with another sign nailed up beneath an area of sloping pines: Greyson Developments. Rich was nowhere to be seen, but the car was certainly his – she recognised the colourful surf sticker on the back window.

The sky darkened; it was beginning to rain. She got out of the car, strolled along the fence boundary line until she came to a door locked with a small metal code box. She fiddled with the buttons, rain pattering on her fingertips, and gave the door a nudge with her trainer, but it wouldn't budge. More signs were nailed onto the fence: KEEP OUT, PRIVATE PROPERTY, DANGER OF DEATH, KEEP OUT. She could hear the low rumble of a machine's engine and the heavy sound of the same machine lifting and falling. Somewhere in the distance, a dog barked. She yanked off her sweater and tied it around her waist, wiping the sweat off her forehead with her arm.

The ground was steep, slippery with pine needles. Dolly scrambled up the bank, using her hands to pull herself up, digging her trainers into the mud. Earth gathered under her fingernails. Where the fence ended, she slipped on a patch of wet mud and grazed her knee on a sharp stone before steadying herself with a pine branch, releasing a shower of raindrops. Eventually she managed to pull herself up onto the steep bank and scrambled up. At the top, she found herself staring down into an old quarry.

Directly below, she could see a low building that looked like some sort of warehouse. There were trucks parked and moving about, and figures in fluorescent jackets working at the trucks or driving heavy loaders back and forth between the lorries and the building. The scene was busy and organised without much sound, at this distance, just the faint rumble of engines and the shifting, sliding, clattering noises of objects being moved, which gave the site a surreal, eerie, slightly otherworldly atmosphere. From somewhere down below came the far-off melody of a worker whistling along to a radio.

Squatting, Dolly balanced precariously on her ankles, wishing she had binoculars, trying to make out what the workers were moving, contained in large crates. Perhaps she could gain access another way, she told herself, because there was no point trying to get down from here. The incline was too steep, too dangerous on the quarry side, and how would she get back up? Instead, she turned and began to slide down the incline on the forest side.

'Dolly?! What the!'

A pace away, her brother stood, arms crossed. He was wearing jeans and wellington boots with steel toecaps. For a second, because Rich was meant to be in London, because he was meant to be *elsewhere*, Dolly couldn't put the two together. The place and the person weren't meant to be a pair, and something was off, she knew at once.

'Rich? What are you doing here?'

Her brother narrowed his eyes, lips pressed flat. 'More to the point, what the heck are you doing here?'

'Looking around, I guess.' Dolly shrugged, her pulse quickening. 'I thought you weren't back until later. Gracie'll kill you if she catches you.'

Rich frowned. He leaned forward and roughly grabbed her wrist, marching her back along the fence line. 'Come on.'

74

She shook her arm free. 'Hey, let go of me!'

They grappled for a second or two, a couple of wild dogs in the dirt, Dolly thought breathlessly, stepping back with her hands on her hips, rubbing her wrist and glaring furiously at her brother as drizzling rain fell on his face, sprinkling his cheeks, his forehead and eyelashes with a glistening veil of droplets.

'What *the fuck* are you doing, Rich?'

He pressed his lips into a thin line. A vein in his cheek twitched. She'd never seen him so spooked.

'Dolly, you have to leave. You're trespassing.'

'Oh, *come on*.'

Drops of rain slanted against her eyes. She blinked them away, her stomach knotting. Rich's behaviour was baffling and out of character, yet it seemed now was not the time for an argument. After a second or two, her brother took a breath as if to calm himself, running a hand over his face to wipe away the rain.

'You *cannot* be here, Doll,' he said in a new, controlled voice. 'You just. Can't. Be here.'

'I don't get it. How come you're supposed to be on the way back from London and you're here? Does Gracie know you're back?'

Rich looked as if he was going to say something, then changed his mind and mumbled a swear word. It would have been better if she hadn't come, Dolly realised – talk about making things worse! – yet she was filled with a need to know more. There was something both clandestine and anxious about her brother today that she hadn't seen before, probably ever. It dawned on her that Rich – *perfect Rich!* – might be in hot water, and she felt a protective flash of apprehension.

'You need to go.'

'Are you in trouble?' she asked, looking at him quizzically.

'My work trip finished early.' He averted his eyes, scanning the site before giving her an awkward smile. 'I do some property management for Peverell Greyson if you have to know. It's a well-paid side hustle. This site is on my watch at the moment.'

Dolly raised her eyebrows. 'You didn't say anything.'

75

'Why would I?'

'I saw his name on the sign. Peverell Greyson, I mean.'

'It's his site.' Rich frowned. 'And he's not someone you want to piss off, believe me. Now let's go.'

Dolly fell into step beside him, her trainers squelching in the wet mud. 'Are you allowed to tell me what's being built here?'

'No.'

'But I'm your wonderful sweet sister.'

'No.'

'Honestly, for goodness sake! Who's this Greyson guy then?'

'None of your business.'

Dolly sighed. The conversation seemed strange and out of context away from Rich's comfortable carpeted house down in the valley, where the family coexisted according to the circadian rhythm of the household: meals, work, life. Now this was a completely different brother – and who was he, actually? Rich, the shady businessman? Rich, the quick cash on the side guy? The characterisation did not suit him.

At the car she unlocked the door, slid into the driving seat. She switched on the engine and wound down the window, peering up at Rich. Raindrops raced down the glass of the windscreen, anxiously, like dozens of hurried white rabbits from a Wonderland garden. *I'm late!*

'Be careful, won't you?' she said.

'I can look after myself.'

'You're okay, though?'

Another pause. Rich leant into the tiny window, one arm on the car roof. 'Look, I can't talk about it, Doll,' he said. 'I can't so much as *breathe* about it. Please try to understand.'

Dolly gave an exasperated shake of her head and clicked the seatbelt into the holder. She went to wind the window up, but then stopped on an afterthought. 'Listen, Rich,' she said with sincerity, peering up at him with an anxious look, 'we have our differences, but the last thing I want to do is get you into trouble.'

'Just stop being such a bloody busybody.' But her brother's eyes softened. 'It really doesn't help when you're going around playing Miss Marple.'

'I always did love an Agatha C.' Dolly smiled, giving him a wink. 'Do you remember how Mum used to chain watch Poirot?' She flicked on the windscreen wipers. 'See you back at the house.'

CHAPTER THIRTEEN

Gloria

The day Ma and Papa died it was hot, too hot. As far as I can remember, we were all carrying on with life as usual. My brother Chilembé was ten and I was thirteen, just a little village girl who'd never been to school, with no idea about politics at all. For the most part, I was blissfully unaware of the turmoil brewing in my country, though every now and then I'd catch snippets of Ma and Papa's hushed conversations about villages set ablaze, and instinctively I'd cover my ears to block out their words, and the fear and uncertainty that crept into their voices. This must have seeped into my consciousness somehow, though, because some nights my dreams would be dark and terrifying, filled with fire and men with guns, casting a shadow of dread over my innocent young mind – only for these spectres of unseen horrors to disappear with the daylight. In hindsight, I think my childish brain chose not to dwell on the unseen dangers looming beyond the confines of our tranquil village.

I know now that six months before, President Jean-Marie Balfour's plane had been shot down by a group of renegade Balaika extremists. A new left wing president, Baptiste Lourenco, was spreading propaganda that all Balaika civilians were a threat. First there were assassinations of moderate Balaika leaders, then massacres of ordinary Balaika people – my own village people, slaughtered in their homes. Meanwhile, Russia's President Volkov was cosying up to Lourenco by arming our country's militia with modern weaponry, and the violence was worsening. Many hundreds had died.

As I say, that particular day was unusually hot, windless and stagnant beneath an ash-blue sky, the kind of day that made me long for the shade of the forest lying just east of our village. It had been weeks since Ma and Papa talked together in hushed whispers, and my own worries seemed far off too – mere figments of my imagination. So when Ma asked us to go and look for firewood, Chilembé and I set off willingly, eager to escape the scorching heat.

The forest was cool and quiet, slashed through with sunlight, colonised here and there by small armies of ants crackling across the forest floor. Birds called through the treetops; parrots and macaws, the whistle of a kingfisher; the childlike cries of the sunbirds who occasionally took off from the shadows and soared across the high canopy of trees. We searched for firewood, but were distracted by other treasures; flowers, seed pods, and fallen fruit; over-ripe mangoes and guavas which we scooped out with our hands, and ate until our bellies were full.

When Chilembé and I returned home, it was nearly noon. The sun burned the tops of our heads. Everything was quiet. We stood staring at the blackened ruins of our family's burnt-out hut, our limbs heavy, our minds spinning, unable to accept what our eyes were seeing. Ma and Papa's blood-smeared bodies were blanketed with a swarm of flies. Their mouths gaped. Their eyes stared upwards at a sky they would never see again.

I was too scared to cry, too afraid to move.

I knew the killers must be the group of militias I'd heard our parents talking about, cruel gunmen who were systematically raiding villages and banana plantations along the coast. That morning, while we were out in the forest, they must have come to our village, hacked the cattle with machetes, thrown grenades at the church and killed the villagers in their homes, including our parents and our other brothers and sisters, our uncles and aunts and elders who lived nearby.

More flies, thousands now, a buzzing, blue-black swarm. A smell of death and fire. Chilembé quietly took my hand. As we stood there, still and silent and tearless, I don't remember feeling anything at all, other than registering the heavy smell of blood that made me retch and fall to my knees, vomiting onto the blood-stained earth.

In a daze, we stumbled away, only to hear a sound, men's voices somewhere in the distance. I turned to look at Chilembé, whose face was pale with fright. Together, we ran for our lives.

For what seemed like hours, we hid on the far side of the village, holding hands, listening to the militia searching through the belongings of people they'd killed. I found myself remembering with a new clarity Ma and Papa's whispered conversations – how they talked of children like us being killed or captured or beaten, forced to work as spies, slaves, or messengers. With terror, I recalled Ma's descriptions of these dead-eyed, kidnapped children, with guns bigger than their own bodies slung around their waists, high on drugs and alcohol.

'Hey,' we heard one of the armed men say to another in a low, raspy voice. 'I've found something.'

We waited and waited while the men looted our relatives' bodies. By some twist of fate, by some outlandish miracle, they didn't spot us. As soon as they had gone, we fled east through the forest, headed for Port Salé, where I had to assume we Balaika were safer, at least for now.

During those long days and nights, we walked by day and slept hidden in the thick forest undergrowth. We ate fruit to survive, and drank water from springs and streams. Finally we reached a road, then a village, where a bus happened to be passing. We persuaded the bus driver to take us the rest of the way to the capital. We were dirty, sad, frightened, and alone. We had nothing. No money. No relatives to take care of us. I was far from sure that we'd survive, but somehow

I knew I just had to carry on, for my brother's sake, however difficult the challenges to come.

A week later, I found work as a dancer at a Port Salé nightclub called Le Tropico, while Chilembé went begging for scraps and coins on the city streets. We rented a run-down room in the slums from an Imam who took pity on us, though I think he simply coveted the meagre collection of cash we offered up every week as rent. It's hard to imagine what poor little waifs and strays we must have seemed to him.

In my dizzy, delirious grief, in the panic and intensity of that time, I went all at once from child to adult, from sister to parent. I understood that there was no longer a chance to make something of myself, and I let go of my dreams forever. Every day, I remembered my mother's words, 'even if you put your hand on your cheek, God has willed it,' which were wise for reasons she herself could never have anticipated, and, as it turned out, portentous. I told myself that whatever happened, everything would make sense in the end. In the meantime, Chilembé and I needed to survive, at all costs.

CHAPTER FOURTEEN

Dolly

For the time of year, it seemed optimistic to hold the birthday party outside, though the weather was clearing for the afternoon, the sky a pearlescent blue, a watery sun emerging from behind thin layers of clouds. Dolly found Gracie in the garden, setting a trestle table with paper plates and cups decorated with flower fairies. Amid a sea of balloons, Flora and Fern chattered excitedly, flitting around the garden in chilly-looking party dresses. Dolly pulled her sweater closer around her and walked over to help, calling out a greeting.

'Are you looking forward to the party, Auntie Doll?' Fern came running up, flushed with excitement.

Dolly dropped a kiss on the top of her head. 'Happy birthday, birthday girl. Absolutely! I can't wait.'

'Did you get me a present?'

Dolly laughed. 'Maybe.'

'That means yes!'

'Flora, you're not meant to ask that, it's rude.' Gracie handed Dolly a cup of tea and grimaced. 'Don't worry, it'll be over by tonight. I'm truly ashamed that my child is so materialistic.'

'It's nice to be appreciated,' said Dolly, handing the present to her niece. 'Here, you can open it if you like, sweetheart.'

Dolly sipped her tea and watched Fern tear open the present. Fragments of wrapping paper floated to the ground as the little girl unzipped the pencil case with a cry of delight, pulling out the pens one by one. A synthetic smell of strawberries filled the air.

'I love it, Auntie Doll.' Fern wafted a peach-coloured scented felt tip in front of Dolly's nose. 'Thank you.'

'It's a pleasure, darling.'

'Well, you got that spot on,' said Gracie admiringly when Fern ran off to show the pencil case to her sister.

Dolly grinned, feeling pleased with herself. 'Thanks.' She sipped the tea, adding casually after a pause. 'You heard from Rich? I thought he'd be here.'

'He called to say he's on his way back.'

'Does he often go up to town? To London, I mean, overnight?'

Gracie darted Dolly an embarrassed look. 'He does a bit of work on the side, but he doesn't tell me much. The mortgage on this place is so high. We need the extra cash.' She gave a frustrated little sigh. 'Though to be honest he never seems to get paid much – we're living on fresh air.'

'Strange,' Dolly pushed, recalling Rich's puzzling behaviour that morning – so furtive and guilty. 'He always used to say side hustles were a conflict of interest.'

'Yeah.' Gracie stretched out her back with a circular reach of her arms. 'He's strait-laced like that.' She laughed. 'But clearly not that strait-laced.'

'Men…'

'Exactly.'

After lunch, Dolly went upstairs to change into Gloria's jumpsuit, which was beautiful – cotton crêpe de chine, nipped at the waist, delicate sage green with tiny gold sequins across the neckline. Then the cardigan, soft cloud blue with pearl buttons. As it turned out, both garments fitted Dolly perfectly, and it felt strange and bittersweet to slip her arms into the sleeves – comforting, like slipping into her mother's skin. Dolly added a touch of lipstick – when had she last worn lipstick? – and whirled in front of the mirror on the landing, smiling to herself. Her mother's clothes suited her.

In the bathroom cabinet she found a pot of coconut oil, sweet and tropical-smelling, and decided on a whim to change her hair. Shaking out her usual low ponytail, she spent some time in front of the mirror, finger-twisting and backcombing her curls into a neat, seventies-style do. As she worked handfuls of the oil into her hair, she let her mind run back over Gloria's story so far, which she'd been trying to push from her mind all morning, because the latest instalment brought an undefined anger that was almost physical.

Now she allowed herself to picture her mother and little Chilembé fleeing from the gunmen, imagining their panicked footsteps. Two children running for their lives. The thought of their fear, their desperation, made her breathless. How could anyone bear such unspeakable atrocities? She was beginning to understand why Gloria never talked about the years before she came to England.

Dolly paused her hair curling and let her mind spool backwards. Only rarely had Gloria mentioned Lusenka, she recalled, sometimes pronouncing Lusenka's current president – Lourenco's successor, Florian Kilomi – a scoundrel. And, just the once, being visibly reduced to tears at a report about the Balaika people on the six o'clock news. But if ever Dolly or her brother dared to ask a question – who's Kilomi? Why are the Balaika being persecuted, Mummy? – Gloria would shake her head and walk away, stony silent.

This was just another of her mother's enigmas. Dolly's own life at that time was filled with school and homework and the intricate entanglements of her teenage friendships. Gloria seemed to exist in quite another world, untouchable and far away. She was a film star, after all, and strangers sometimes recognised her face in public, gushing her name in awe. 'Is that the actress? Is she the one in Mirrorball?' Her stardom made a great impression on Dolly's friends, bringing a sparkle of Hollywood to the school gates, yet deep down Dolly secretly yearned for the reassuring softness of the other, more pedestrian mothers, around whom she didn't always feel she had to prove herself.

In later years came the depression, the alcohol, the silences and nit-picking, the withdrawn, discontented attitude that frazzled Dolly's brain because nothing was ever good enough. The empty wine bottles in the bin. Gloria drunkenly stumbling up the stairs, fumbling for the light switch, half cut. Countless times, Dolly read bedtime stories to Rich because Gloria was too pissed to care. Then the obsessive cleaning that followed these bouts of alcoholism, when Dolly had the impression that her mother was trying to scrub away much more than household dirt or dust. And there were afternoons when Dolly would find her mother in the bedroom, sitting on the edge of the bed, staring dreamily out the window or simply sketching in a notebook, seemingly lost in a world of her own.

Had Dolly caused her mother's unhappiness? Deep down she always assumed so. Certainly, it never occurred to her until now that Gloria's oddities might have sprung from her own past, from memories of a childhood which she kept hidden because of shame, of trauma even. It seemed peculiar now that in her occasional therapy sessions over the years, Dolly had never explored this possibility. With the counsellor she had discussed her errant love life and her absent father, but never her mother, never Gloria, and it struck her now that all along, she was subconsciously avoiding the biggest issue of all.

Dolly stepped back from the mirror, a pleasant scent of coconut lingering in the air. The vintage clothes looked gorgeous, she decided. Not since she was a teenager had she worn her hair in an Afro, and now the effect – a tight halo of cute curlicues framing her face – pleased her immensely. A new start, she told herself. A new beginning. She remembered the portrait of Gloria on the dressing table at Genévrier, her mother's hairstyle in the photo. Who'd have thought they could look so alike…

'Oh my God,' exclaimed Gracie in excitement, coming upstairs. 'What on earth are you wearing? It's absolutely gorgeous.'

Dolly giggled. 'You think? It was Mum's. I found it in the attic.'

'I *adore* it.' Gracie squealed, giving her a hug. 'And the hair. You go, girl. You look just like her.'

Downstairs, Rich was back, but he paid no attention to the clothes, or to Dolly's new hair for that matter, which was fairly typical, Dolly told herself – men were usually oblivious to such things.

Feeling awkward, she went outside and lit a cigarette. Her brother followed her out, carrying a cup of tea, but his unease radiated from him, and from his warning look, she gathered she was not to mention the encounter earlier at the building site. She stood up, still smoking, and pretended to examine a sun-faded rose in one of Gracie's borders, crushing a petal between the fingers of her free hand, noticing the petal's softness, its fragility.

'Do you remember that time we did art, with Mum?' she said eventually, trying to lighten the mood, thinking of the painting in the bedroom at Genévrier that she'd been meaning to ask Rich if she could have.

'Art?'

'In the garden? You painted a seagull.'

It was a summer weekend, Dolly reminded him. They'd spent an afternoon painting the sea and the trees, then other pleasing shapes of their imaginations, a pineapple, a rose, a cycad palm.

'I remember now,' said Rich with a half-smile. 'Shirley Bassey, and a picnic on the rug.'

'Mum getting down to Aretha,' re-joined Dolly, grinning, dancing her arms in a swimming motion. She could still remember the sun on her face, the paint smudged on her hands, the music in her ears. Most of all, the happiness. 'And Luther...'

'Good old Luth.'

Rich grinned and the two of them laughed, then fell silent. Somehow Dolly knew her brother was thinking the same thing, that the memory was pleasant until its jarring aftermath. How could they forget that a few hours later, darkness fell and it began to rain, a gigantic summer storm. From their beds, they heard Gloria drinking and dancing alone downstairs to the sound of the record player, amid rolls of thunder coming in from the sea, in the distance.

In the morning, Dolly discovered their precious paintings outside on the gravel, a sodden mess of Prussian blue and scarlet on water-logged canvas. She blamed herself for leaving them outside. Alone, she threw the ruins away while Rich burst into tears, and Dolly avoided Gloria and her hangover while she waited for her anger to subside, for calmness to return.

'Did you know Mum left me some stuff?' Dolly said, changing the subject. 'Some tapes, actually.' She crushed more petals in her fingers, breathing in the soft, floral perfume. Presumably Rich didn't know about the tapes, and she wondered why, and whether he might know where the missing ones were. 'Was there anything else in the will? Maybe something given to you to keep for me?'

'I don't think so.' He seemed disinterested.

'Can you have a think?'

'Anything to distract you, Miss Marple.' He gave a mirthless little smile. 'Greyson and Shaun Kingsley are nothing to do with you, you know.'

A pause. Dolly stared at Rich with the uneasy feeling that her brother had just let something slip, but he hurriedly averted his eyes. He cleared his throat and seemed to busy himself, suddenly, with stirring his tea.

'I don't understand' she said sharply. 'What's Shaun Kingsley got to do with any of this?'

Silence.

'Rich? Why did you just mention Shaun Kingsley?'

'It's nothing.' Rich took an exaggerated slurp of tea – or so it seemed to Dolly – tipping his head back as he swallowed. 'Kingsley's been all over the news, and I was just thinking about what happened to you, how much of an asshole he is. I don't know why I said anything, a brain slip or something. Stupid.' Rich trailed off.

But she wasn't going to let him go that easily: 'Do you mean this extra work you're doing is somehow tied up with Pev *and* Shaun?' she insisted. 'What's going on in the quarry, Rich – what were those blokes loading into those lorries?'

'Back off, I said.' Rich got to his feet with a furious expression, shaking his head, waving a finger. 'For fuck's sake, Dolly, no joke, you're going to land yourself in deep shit.'

'I'm already knee deep in it. I've nothing to lose.'

'Please yourself.' Rich shrugged, pouring the dregs of the tea on the ground beneath the rose bush 'And stop trying to look like Mum. It won't bring her back, you know.'

'Oh, so you noticed then,' Dolly snapped sarcastically, as Rich stalked inside the house.

CHAPTER FIFTEEN

Gloria

Le Tropico was nothing but a tin shack with a stained dirt floor, halfway down the main city drag near Independence Square. The place reeked of cigarette smoke, stale beer, and the stench of male sweat. A small man called Elvis was in charge of the bar. His job, as I recall, was to stack beer crates, pour drinks, and act as a go-between between the customers and us girls, ferrying cash and alcohol back and forth.

We all came in from the slums every night to dance on stage beneath the lights to the rhythms and cross-rhythms of Lusenka's music, calypso mostly, popping with the *balafon* and the talking drum, the steel guitar, the gourd rattle and the *shekere* made of shells, from six pm until midnight, seven days a week. There must have been a dozen of us, all underage, you might say now, though most of us didn't know our actual birthdays. The eldest, a tall girl called Destine, thought she was about seventeen. As for me, I was barely a teenager, with buds for breasts and a thin, gangling body like a boy.

Still, the men didn't care. They were businessmen, mostly, except for a few white foreigners and Lusenkan officials, important government figures and civil servants who drifted in after work from the city centre offices and embassies. In truth, I think they came to the club because we *were* so young – that or companionship, I always suspected, for there was a longing in their eyes when they gazed at us on stage, as if all they really wanted was for someone to love them for real. Nevertheless, I soon learned I could make more money if I allowed them to touch my legs or fondle my chest with their groping hands.

There was one man, Mr Adalao, who visited the club every Thursday. He was well-dressed and obviously rich, with a gleaming round face and big pot belly. People said he held a high up position in the government.

Mr Adalao soon began harassing me to go with him to a room at the back reserved by the club owner for what we girls called 'private sessions'. I'd never done a private session before, but I'd watched Destine going into the room with various men in tow, young and old, thin and fat, tall and short. Some of the other girls went in there, too, with a resigned demeanour, prisoners being marched to a cell. I didn't dare ask Destine what a private session really was, though I suspected and dreaded the answer.

One day, Mr Adalao held out fifty francs, which seemed like riches to me, and I agreed to go with him. After that I let him take me into the back room once a week, and told Chilembé he could stop begging, and enrol in a local school. Of Mr Adalao, I don't remember much, just the way his hands sweated when he removed my underwear, greasy spiders crawling over my body, and his big tongue pushing and thrusting like a wriggling eel in my mouth. The rest, I don't care to recall.

Every night, when I returned to our shack, Chilembé would wake up, snuggle close on our floor mat, and quickly fall asleep again, his head heavy against my shoulder. I'd put my arms around his warm little body, listening to his childish breaths slowing to match mine, a tiny snoring bear. Huddled together we slept like that, my only hours of peace.

I've long blanked all that out, Sugar. There's no need to go back to those years, and I don't believe any good comes from dwelling on sections of the past that conjure only pain. You might have noticed that I'm no fan of my homeland's music, and when you've asked me about it, I've avoided your questioning. Now you know why.

One night out of the blue, close on midnight, a European man came strolling into Le Tropico. He wore an expensive-looking tailored shirt and loose, beige, cotton trousers, and by my estimations – bearing in mind I was only young, and everyone looked old to me – he was in his late thirties, with poufy hair receding at the forehead, and a long, thin nose. For some reason he didn't look like the other white men who came to the club. Whether it was his clothes or his seeming disinterest in touching us girls, or his distinctly European air, I couldn't quite put my finger on.

That first evening he sat at a table in the corner drinking bottles of beer, one after the other, and staring at me in a strange way, neither sleazy nor avaricious. Rather, I had the sensation that he was studying me, trying to work something out. I suppose I expected him to come over sooner or later, but after a while he got up and left the club.

Every night for a fortnight he came in, drank a couple of beers, stared, and left again. Plainly, I should probably have approached him and offered to dance – the club owner encouraged us to proposition the customers – but I held back, for the man seemed different to the others who visited the club and deep down, I didn't want him to be like the rest.

A Friday came, and the European man appeared as usual, just as it was turning midnight. Looking over, I soon spotted him chatting with the barman. To my surprise, he strolled over, called me down from the stage and invited me to join him for a drink at his table. I knotted a wrap around my waist with a tremor of disappointment that this man would indeed turn out to be just like the others.

He sat down opposite me, legs crossed, and ordered drinks from Elvis, who was hovering nearby. Then he leaned over the table, scrutinising my face. His eyes were a peculiar shade of light brown flecked with black, and not unkind. Close to, without the elevation of the stage, he was bigger than I'd imagined, taller and more thickset in the shoulders. His pale forearms were covered in thick, dark, gorilla hairs. I felt intimidated all of a sudden, and found myself hoping he wasn't going to suggest we went into the private room together.

'You're so young.' He reached out and touched my cheek. 'How long have you been dancing here?'

'A few months,' I replied without looking at him. Instead, I stared straight ahead at the other girls cavorting up on the platform beneath the disco lights, a blur of naked limbs and garish makeup.

Elvis brought over a bottle of Coca Cola for me, with a straw poking out, and a beer for the man, who took a long swig, and plonked the bottle on the table. He explained that he was English, here on holiday, which sounded dubious to me, because what sort of place was Lusenka for a holiday? He'd spotted me the first time he came to the club, he said, and recognised my potential, my *stage presence*, as he described it.

'I could make you a star,' he concluded mildly. 'You've got the looks, the figure. There's something about you that draws the eye; the camera would love you. Have you heard of England?'

'Of course,' I said, telling him what I knew of that country; its green hills, its queen.

He took another swig of his whisky. 'Would you like to go there?'

'Sure.' I shrugged, acting nonchalant, unsure of the right answer. I sucked at the Coca Cola through the straw, savouring the unfamiliar fizzing sweetness on my tongue.

'I could get you work, dancing, acting.'

'Acting?'

'You're beautiful, and you're a natural on stage. They'd snap you up.'

'Who's they?' I said, raising an eyebrow.

He reached into his pocket and brought out a small rectangular card, which he pushed across the table at me. *Sidney Dunn, Talent Agent*, I read. *1, Bloomsfield Square, London.*

'Think about it,' said Sidney. 'I'll come tomorrow night, but soon I'm going home, to England.' He shot me a smile. 'This is your way out, love.'

I took the card and stashed it in my wrapper. That night, when I returned to Chilembé, I lay staring into the dark, my thoughts chasing tails in my mind. When the sun came up at five, I was still awake. If this man Sidney Dunn was serious, I knew I had no choice but to go. With the money I could make in England, Chilembé would be able to go to secondary school, maybe even university, something we could never afford with just the money from Mr Adalao. No Lusenkan worth their salt would turn that offer down. It was my responsibility to go, and exactly what my dead parents would have wished for us. I fell into a fitful sleep, hugging my brother close.

The following evening, Sidney turned up at Le Tropico, just as he'd said he would. After some small-talk, I launched into my request: 'I'll do it, but only if you pay for my brother to go to Port Salé Academy.'

As the only private school in Lusenka, Port Salé Academy was attended by the children of wealthy ex-pats and politicians. I'd seen a huge advert for it on a billboard near the The Tropico. The slogan was written in big, blue letters: *your child's path to success*. There, I knew, my brother would be safe and well cared-for, and his future would be secured.

Looking back, I don't know why I didn't just ask Sidney if my brother could come to England with me. It seems ridiculous now, but I have come to understand that in my young mind, I didn't think I was going away for long. In a few months, I planned to return, rich, successful, and free. Besides, you can imagine how intimidating Sidney was – I couldn't upset him and lose the opportunity. A couple of months and I'd be back, I told myself, so that Chilembé and I could lead a decent life with enough money beneath our belts to be happy and comfortable.

'Alright,' said Sidney, and though I acted unsurprised, I was a little taken aback at the ease of his agreement to put my brother into school. He proceeded to regale me with a blur of logistical details that were seemingly planned out already: flight tickets, visas and pre-departure health checks, of which I had little to no understanding. I decided that, however frightening-sounding, everything was worth the sacrifice – for Chilembé.

Oh, Sugar, what would have happened if I'd said no to Sidney that day? If I'd been honest and told him that the idea of going to England filled me with horror and dread. Worse, that leaving my little brother, my only living relative, was so appalling it made me feel physically sick. What if I'd admitted that I felt pushed by Sidney to go against my better instincts, pushed by the shroud of responsibility hanging over my head. There I stood, a naïve young teenager, agreeing to something that would change my life and Chilembé's forever – and I did it blindly, a moth batting about in the dark.

A week later, the day of my departure loomed. That final night, neither of us slept. We clung together, our arms wrapped around each other, our heads close. Eventually my little brother cried himself to sleep.

In the morning, I helped Chilembé put on his pristine new school uniform, both of us in a daze. Sidney rolled up outside in a ghost-silver car, sleek and purring, of a sort we'd never seen in our lives, and instructed the driver to take us to the academy, which turned out to be a magnificent colonial house on the outskirts of Port Salé, surrounded by acres of manicured lawns stretching towards the edges of the forest. The sight was breathtaking, but I didn't care. My heart was being wrenched from my insides. I longed to grab my brother by the hand and run away.

On the stone steps, Chilembé clung to me, sobbing. Fighting my own tears, I turned to tell Sidney that I couldn't go, I couldn't do it. Not for all the money in the world would I leave my little brother here in this strange place, without his big sister to look after him. But Sidney took my arm and frogmarched me back to the car.

When I turned around, my brother was being dragged the other way by a suited receptionist in high heels, wielding a clipboard.

Chilembé turned his face back towards me, sobbing loudly, imploring me not to go. I've never forgotten that look, nor the gigantic tears rolling down his cheeks, nor the sound of his voice, crying out my name. Even now, decades later and a world away, I still hear him sometimes in my dreams, a lost child, my lost brother. 'Sis! Don't leave me! Please!'

I managed to visit him, just once, years later in 1978, with the practical aim of filing his permanent visa application for England. By that time, I had enough money to bring him over to London once the paperwork was filed. Chilembé was a qualified solicitor by then, hailed as one of the bright lights of his generation. I knew he'd easily find a job in London.

It was just after Christmas. I'd saved up my wages from Mirrorball to buy a ticket to Port Salé, and I packed my suitcase feeling deliriously excited, because I'd dreamt of returning for so long. When I emerged into the arrivals hall of Port Salé airport, I saw a man in place of the boy I'd left, tall and handsome with his clipped afro, his fashionable bell-bottom jeans and leather sandals. Chilembé flung his arms around me and we danced around together, laughing with happiness. I could hardly believe how much he'd changed, but he was still my darling baby brother.

Shortly afterwards, he drove me back to his apartment in a battered old Volkswagen – which he'd picked up for a song, he told me cheerfully, on the black market. So much had changed. His apartment building was a tallish, ochre-painted confection with jutting, circular balconies, overlooking a soft blue stretch of sea lying beyond the nearby rooftops. Inside, as we talked excitedly, sharing our news, he put Miriam Makeba on the record player, fetched a bottle of gin, and fashioned two bright cocktails out of *sirop de grenadine*, dropping slices of orange into the tall glasses.

'Cheers, Sis,' he said, lifting his glass. 'You and I, we're survivors, we're the lucky ones.' And he shot me one of his smiles, dazzling as the sun.

Evening fell. We sat on his balcony, woozy with alcohol, watching the sky turn gold, and for the first time in years, I felt like I was home.

Later that year, back in England, I was at a promo party for Sundowners at the Savoy in London when I got a call, out of the blue, from the British Embassy in Port Salé. Chilembé was dead, a male voice told me coolly, down the line; shot at point blank range in his apartment by an unknown hitman – an opportunistic thief, they thought, scavenging in the rich districts. Nothing unusual, the voice said – not in one of the most violent cities in the world, where car-jackings happened several times a day and armed break-ins were commonplace. Nothing out of the ordinary about a wealthy young man being killed in his own home.

'Just one of the many,' the voice said.

We were weeks away from Chilembé's visa coming through. His words echoed in my head, *we're the lucky ones, Sis*. And all of a sudden, we weren't.

The next day, I returned to Lusenka for the funeral. I forget exactly what went on, but I remember the soil falling from the gravedigger's spade onto my little brother's coffin, pip pip pip like red-stained rain on the dark wood, covering his lifeless body until it disappeared into the ground. I felt both shocked and bewildered, angry at his killers, angry at myself, unable to accept the idea that Chilembé was gone forever, or that inside that wooden box, my own darling brother lay dead.

When the diggers were gone, I stood alone, giddy with grief, gazing down at the plot of freshly turned soil, wishing I were dead too. Part of my own heart was buried there now - there with Chilembé deep in the blood-red earth. Broken-hearted, I knelt down beside his grave and wept.

CHAPTER SIXTEEN

Dolly

Dolly circulated the garden with a tray of drinks, easing her way through the clusters of children racing around the garden. Someone put music on as parents dropped gifts like religious offerings on a nearby table and gathered eagerly near the refreshments. Dolly observed them with interest: frazzled-looking, armed with bags, keeping a watchful eye on their kids and eying up the alcohol – but happy. She recalled the look on Fern's face when she opened her birthday present and smiled to herself. Her own upbringing had never been like this. For some reason, Gloria had never hosted birthday parties in the garden, or for that matter, any other celebrations at home. The Fontaines were known for keeping themselves to themselves.

Someone caught Dolly's arm from behind: 'Hey babes!'. It was Morgan, looking genuinely pleased to see her. Amid the crowd of children, Morgan pointed out her daughter, tiny, blonde and noisy.

Moments later, a man approached carrying a wine glass and a tumbler of water. Tall and slim, at least six foot five, and peculiarly handsome – not attractive but *beautiful,* with longish blond curls, narrow red jeans, a tightish shirt. A cashmere jumper slung around his shoulders, and moccasins. *Moccasins.* To Dolly's surprise he came over and stood next to Morgan, handing her the glass of water.

'You must be the esteemed Auntie Dolly,' the man said. 'Guest of honour, I'm told.'

There was something of the military about the man, thought Dolly; the formal way he spoke, perhaps, and his manners and posture, bullet-straight and tense, reminding her of a sergeant major.

'My husband,' Morgan said, taking the drink, and Dolly hid her surprise as Morgan's husband extended a handshake, vice-firm, uncomfortably so. On closer inspection his eyes were extraordinary, the sea on a clear day, though in them she glimpsed a certain piercing callousness. All at once she didn't quite like the man, though she couldn't put her finger on why, a feeling in her gut that made her hackles rise.

'Dolly Fontaine,' she introduced herself. 'And yes, indeed. Aunties are all the rage these days, aren't they?'

Morgan's husband seemed amused, all smiles, all charm. 'Name's Pev. Nice to meet you.'

'You too.'

'Christ, children's parties, eh.' Pev gave a colourless laugh. 'Thank God there's alcohol to get us through it. Guess we've got all this to come a second time, haven't we, Morg. Anyway, what brings you down here to the wondrous beach haven that is the sticks?'

'Babes,' Morgan cut in. 'Dolly's a journalist, remember? She's the one I went to school with.'

'My question stands.' Her husband's eyes scanned the garden as he slugged his wine. 'What in God's name brings a gorgeous journo like you to this place? I mean, Christ, talk about cut off.'

'I *was* a journalist. But now… well, now I'm back.'

He raised his eyebrows. 'Was? Oh, go on, the suspense is killing me.'

'She *is* a journalist!' Morgan interjected with enthusiasm. 'She's basically a celebrity—'

Dolly felt embarrassed by Morgan's fizzy certainty. 'I'm not anymore. I'm pretty much unemployed these days.'

'Unemployed?'

'Yeah.' She took a breath, returning his gaze without a smile. 'On the dole,' she added, feeling rebellious, 'or about to be.'

'Oh, she'll be back,' insisted Morgan. 'You'll see her on TV again soon enough.'

'Nope. You won't.'

'Sure.' Morgan reached for a second croissant and turned to Dolly. 'Babes, we should get together, have a proper catch-up, drinks or something.'

Morgan trailed off, glancing at her husband, who was raising his eyebrows at the pastry in his wife's hand, casting her a dubious look. Dolly sensed a meanness, a steely inquisition beneath the man's good humour that confirmed her earlier dislike.

'Well,' he said, ignoring his wife, 'it's nice to meet you, Dolly.'

With that, Morgan's husband sauntered down the garden towards the children clustered in front of an entertainer, a short, loud, tubby man who was frenetically engaged in pulling fake flowers out of a top hat to the loud, syncopated beat of disco music. The children's faces were rapt, eyes wide as they sat transfixed by the show.

Dolly stared too, surprised to find that Morgan's husband had stirred a deep-rooted infuriation, perhaps because he reminded her of other men she'd come across in the course of her work, powerful men with lots to hide, businessmen, politicians, the odd Russian oligarch. Of Shaun, too. You're my treat, my indulgence, he used to say. As if this married man believed he was entitled to the extra privilege of sleeping with another woman. With sudden distaste she realised Shaun hadn't been in touch, even to say sorry. She hated herself now for being enchanted by his empty flattery.

Morgan followed her gaze. 'He works so hard, bless.' She spoke in an apologetic tone, as if sensing Dolly's curiosity about her husband. 'He's really investing in the community with his building work. God knows we need it round here.'

Dolly noticed that Morgan had abandoned the croissant and was sipping water instead. Beneath the pretty clothes and surface cheerfulness, there was something different about Morgan, she decided, a vulnerability that she didn't remember from when they were teenagers. Aged sixteen her friend had been ambitious, into the sort of Girl Power advocated by the Spice Girls, the idea that women should be independent, that men were a luxury and not a necessity. Now she seemed changed, the fire gone.

Dolly refilled Morgan's glass with water and served herself with a gin and tonic. Side by side they sauntered towards the group of kids.

'Actually, I'm learning to shoot,' said Morgan. 'There's this new adventure place where they do clay pigeon shooting. I'm going in a couple of days if you want to come. Shotguns can be quite therapeutic – angry pregnant lady and all that.'

Dolly was about to refuse the invitation when Morgan gave a long belly laugh, linking her arm into hers, and she found her old friend's mood lifting her own, too. Maybe she'd been too hasty to judge her.

'Sure. I'd like that,' she said instead.

Morgan reached into her pocket and handed Dolly a booking slip with her own name on it: *Morgan Greyson*. With a rush of understanding, Dolly put two and two together. Of course, Morgan's husband was the Peverell Greyson of the sign at the building site earlier. Pev was Peverell, and so this Peverell Greyson was the man Rich didn't want to upset.

But why was that name so familiar? The Peverell part rang a bell now. Had she come across him somewhere before, for work or socially?

'Do you happen to know,' she ventured cautiously, 'what your husband is building down in the valley, outside the village?'

'Nada.' Morgan looked sheepish. 'He won't tell me, it's all a big secret for some reason.'

'A secret?'

'I'm just little wifey, you know; he doesn't tell me anything. Hey, I can't wait for our shooting date. It's nice to see you, babes.'

'You too.'

Morgan grinned, and Dolly couldn't help thinking that her school friend had just changed the subject rather too abruptly.

'I'll text you later with some dates,' said Morgan, wandering off.

Later in the afternoon, Dolly went back and forth between the house and the garden helping Gracie clear up leftovers, their conversation falling into an easy rhythm. An R and B album drifted out of the sound system. On the lawn, in the quiet, blue-gold shadows, Rich was folding up trestle tables, and Flora and Fern ran around, playing with balloons. They were all a little high after the party.

Dolly stood for a moment, humming along to the music, watching her family. To her surprise, despite the contretemps with Rich earlier, she found she didn't miss London. In fact, she was beginning to think she never wanted to go back to that stressful life, so fast-paced and impersonal. Perhaps she didn't need that anymore.

'Penny for them.' Gracie took her hands and spun her into a dance. Dolly laughed and joined in, caught up in her sister-in-law's carefree mood.

'I don't know how you do it,' she said when the music changed, stooping to pick up a balloon, then another. She clutched the balloons to her chest, glancing around to make sure her brother was out of earshot. 'Gracie, I didn't realise that Morgan was married to that man called Peverell Greyson, from the party. Do you know much about him?'

Gracie tossed a deflated balloon into a dustbin bag. 'Pev Greyson?'

'He's married to Morgan. He seemed—'

'Annoying?'

'Yeah. I thought he was a bit of a prick.'

'*And* some.' Gracie shot her an amused look and popped another balloon with her fingernail. 'Though apparently he's a *pillar* of the community.'

While Gracie went upstairs, Dolly poured two glasses of wine for her brother and his wife, and took a can of tonic water from the fridge for herself, adding two fingers of gin from the alcohol cupboard, then ice cubes, watching the ice crackle and split in the cool liquid. She stirred the drink, sliced a lemon into eighths and added the small wedges before topping up again with tonic, just like the gin fizzes her mother used to enjoy, every afternoon, without fail.

In the stillness of the kitchen, Dolly exclaimed out loud, 'Oh!'

Carefully she examined the can of tonic, recognising the font and vibrant colours of a trendy tonic brand. Hadn't there been a can of gin fizz in the parcel with the earrings and the note with the tape? Hadn't everything in that parcel held a key to her mother's distant secrets so far? So why not the seemingly random can of gin fizz, too? How stupid to have chucked it out so carelessly! What if it could lead her to the other significant person in her mother's story so far – Sunstar? In fact, what if Sunstar himself had sent that parcel? It would be just the sort of thing an ex-spy might do – send a nameless parcel full of mysterious clues…

'What's the matter, love?' said Gracie, coming back in.

'Nothing,' Dolly replied hastily. 'Nothing at all.'

Offhandedly, she'd dismissed the canned drink in the parcel without a thought, presuming it a whim of whoever sent the jewellery. But now here was gin fizz again, popping up again in the *present day* and the past – Gloria's favourite drink. Was it a coincidence, or something more? Holding the gin and tonic and the glasses of wine, Dolly stepped out into the hot garden.

CHAPTER SEVENTEEN

Dolly

It was nearly sunset by the time Dolly got the chance to drive home. On arrival, she went straight up to the attic, moving slowly through the boiling hot space, exploring hidden corners she hadn't bothered with before, looking for a clue.

Behind the battered wooden chest, her eye was drawn to a stack of canvas portraits painted by Gloria years ago. Dolly knelt down, feeling a wave of sadness at a rendition of herself as a child, pastel-hued, the sweet turn of her chubby cheek beneath long, dark eyelashes, and her big smile lit as the sun. In the brushstrokes there was nothing but love, Dolly realised now as she touched her fingers lightly to the painted child's cheek.

She must have been very young then; five or six years old, flopped out on the grass in the shade of the tree, reading a book. She thought she could remember the feeling of the grass against her bare skin, baked hard and yellow from the sun and salt air, hatched with fallen leaves. Rich was still a baby, pottering nearby with little gurgling sounds. Near the patio, Gloria stood barefoot at an easel in a lurid one-piece swimsuit, high at the hip, eighties style, a scarf tied around her hair, humming along to a record playing from the house and tinkling the ice in her aperitif, and the sea was shimmering in the distance, and there was the bright, sharp smell of the sea and the rhythmic humming of the bees.

The paintings were leaning against a forgotten box of ageing papers – old film scripts, as it turned out, as well as a great quantity of yellowing Christmas cards and birthday cards dating back to the sixties and seventies. Dolly filed through them, mildly fascinated at these scraps of Gloria's past, of no use to anyone now, surely – yet she couldn't bear to chuck them out. One day, she resolved, she would take the time to read everything and make an archive, but for now, there was no time.

Instead, she scanned the dark corners of the attic, unsure what she was searching for. After a moment, she pulled out an ancient-looking address book, her interest piqued by the names, famous stars and interesting people, all of them: Diana Rigg, Honor Blackman, George Lazenby. Jesus, an archive journalist would have a field day!

Evidently, her mother had used the book for many years, and it was a curious thing to examine, filled with a jumble of addresses, phone numbers and hastily scrawled notes. Rather than write details in the correct sections, Gloria had slipped random pieces of paper between the pages: a scribbled address, a half-torn receipt, a postcard from a long-forgotten trip, a handwritten letter from a friend. Still, there was nothing that seemed like a clue.

It was getting dark; Dolly had the beginnings of a headache. Through the skylight, the sky was turning pink and violet. Red sky at night, shepherd's delight, she thought for no reason. Feeling defeated, she was about to climb down the ladder when she was suddenly struck by a new possibility. She picked up the address book again and examined Gloria's scrawls more closely in the half-light, looking for some clue that might lead to an entry about Sunstar, the mysterious spy.

Tattered from age and use, some of the pages were dislodged from the spine. Quickly, Dolly turned the pages, pulling out each scrap of paper, reading the entries in haste. Minutes later she came to a small, unprepossessing scrap of paper bearing two words instead of a name: gin fizz. The sloping cursive was unmistakably her mother's, and there was an address: 22, The Laurels, Lyton Minster, Devon.

'There you are,' Dolly exclaimed out loud.

Triumphantly, she tucked the book and the scrap of paper into her pocket, but not before she'd taken a picture of the address with her phone. It was ten to seven, too late now to drive up all that way, so she would go tomorrow, she decided with a small thrill of excitement, and find out what gin fizz meant to Gloria, and why it was important enough to keep hidden in the depths of an old address book.

In the kitchen, Dolly set about making a casserole, adding carrots, turnip and sprigs of rosemary from the garden, allowing her mind to turn over the events of the past days and weeks: Shaun's betrayal, as she still couldn't help thinking of it; Gloria's tapes, and this strange new notion she had about the gin fizz, about Sunstar. Plus, what to make of her brother's peculiar behaviour, and this arrogant Peverell Greyson person, Morgan's husband, whom she was sure was up to something shady at the building site? There was something about that name, but for the life of her, she couldn't think what it was.

She poured a tin of tomatoes into the stew, added a slosh of red wine, and turned the gas up. While the casserole came to the boil, she opened her laptop, clicked on the document folder where she kept her old research on Lusenka. 'You can't be too careful,' Angus used to say, and she took him at his word, making a habit of doubling up all her important work stuff at home, too, even though it was totally against all of Cloud's copious confidentiality clauses.

Now she scrolled to the folder containing screenshots of the memo she'd photographed in Shaun's office, and clicked on the image, peering in closely at the jpeg.

In a rush, fragments of memory shifted and settled into place. She hadn't realised at the time, but the screenshot had also captured the side panel of Shaun's inbox, listing his emails from that day. Dolly whooped out loud as she zoomed in and saw that there, in the left panel, third from the top, was an email labelled: Re: [EXTERNAL] Confidential.

The sender's name was Greyson, Peverell.

Hurriedly, Dolly googled the Companies House website, where she typed in Peverell Greyson's name. But apart from Greyson Enterprises – *registered Suite 22, The Globe Centre, Truro. Company status: active. Nature of business: property development* – there was only a list of defunct businesses named after creatures of the sea, mythical or otherwise: Mermaid Developments, Seahorse Construction Ltd, and one other, Dolphin Technical Solutions. Company status, it said after each of them: Dissolved.

Methodically, she entered Greyson into the search box of each document from her work notes, then the names of the dissolved companies, one by one. Finally, on a document from a few years back, the system brought up a match amid a list of other partners. It was a contract awarded by the Ministry of Defence to a Dolphin Technical Solutions; in 2018, it seemed, though the explanatory paragraph was imprecise, and no more details were specified as to the nature of the contract, or its length, or what exactly Dolphin Technical Solutions was contracted to do.

Dolly stared at the screen, all too aware of her own breathing. Back when she was working on the story for Cloud News, the document hadn't seemed significant, just a list of government partners, nothing unusual, nothing to warrant suspicion.

'Damn,' she whispered under her breath, mentally kicking herself. What kind of a crap journalist *was* she?! Why hadn't she questioned this at the time? As she remembered, she'd been so focused on the government's links with Lusenkan officials, blindsided by her conviction that the British were in cahoots with corrupt ministers abroad, and convinced the memo proved it.

Now the facts were triangulated, however, this match seemed interesting, because if Dolphin Technical Solutions belonged to Peverell Greyson, then it would seem her brother's slip up, mentioning Shaun Kingsley out of the blue, hadn't been a mistake. All this time, she'd been diving down completely the wrong rabbit hole.

The casserole was bubbling noisily. Dolly turned back to the cooker, lifted the dish into the oven and set the dial to a low heat. For a minute she stood deep in thought, turning over the new strands of information in her mind. As far as she knew, Shaun's only link with Lusenka was the memo he leaked, though there was every possibility that via his job at the MOD he could pull some pretty influential strings, wasn't there?

And evidently Peverell knew Shaun, if he was sending him

confidential emails, but why and how were the two connected? Had Shaun, in his capacity as Junior Minister for Defence Procurement, awarded Pev an MOD contract, and if so, for what? Then, to complicate matters, there were Gloria's conundrums too.

Could it be possible, wondered Dolly, that tomorrow she might find the mysterious Sunstar? For some reason it felt as if everything might be connected, though as yet she'd no idea why. Yet she was almost certain now that the common denominator was Lusenka, and Gloria – as preposterous as that seemed. Somehow the mysteries were intertwined, and she just had to follow the clues.

She shook her head, forcing the thoughts out of her mind as she set the oven timer for just under an hour; she really ought to stop speculating.

In the living room, she rifled through the old box of records until she found Shirley Bassey's *Yesterday I Heard the Rain*. She put it on the turntable, watched the arm drop and the vinyl disc begin to spin until the halting touch of the needle brought the familiar voice that her mother loved so much. Dolly turned the music up, only for an unexpected jolt of grief to run through her, sharp as needles in her chest. She recalled Gloria in her all-too familiar pose, outside in the garden chair next to the French window, where she was in the habit of sitting most summer evenings.

'Time for an aperitif, darlings!'

Dolly could recall the scene quite clearly. It would have been four o' clock, or five, the sky gradually fading into evening, the light across the fields glowing orange to blue black. Gloria would drink one gin fizz after another, tonic sloshing over ice, thin fingers fiddling nervously with the cigarette lighter.

Dolly remembered her mother's red-painted nails, her slim wrists emerging from the sleeve of her kaftan. In those moments, Gloria seemed to forget entirely the presence of her children. There was an absence in her and a trace of sadness, as if she wished to be somewhere else, with someone else. Over the years this so-called aperitif began to happen earlier and earlier, until it would barely be mid-afternoon, and

Gloria would be hitting the drinks tray.

Another memory followed on the back of the first, of Dolly as a girl of ten playing with a water pistol someone had given her for Christmas; of accidentally spraying her mother while she poured a gin; of Gloria's burst of fury as the water pistol was ripped out of her hands. Of her sadness as she watched Gloria stomp inside with the toy, which was never seen again. For years, Dolly had avoided these dark memories, assuming the hardness in Gloria was somehow her own fault – that her mother's distance was her own doing, because as a daughter she had failed. Never had it occurred to her that Gloria might have considered the situation to be the other way around.

'Oh, Mum,' she murmured. 'What are you trying to tell me?'

She went over to the window and stared out through the glass, thinking of Gloria, then of Pev and Shaun and the inexplicable connection between them, unable to shake off the feeling that, just earlier, she'd discovered something important. She closed her eyes, letting her mind follow the lyrics of the song until the record finished, but she didn't play another. Sometime later, she ate alone while the same unanswerable question circled in her mind: if Peverell Greyson and Shaun Kingsley knew each other, how did that change things, and what did it mean for her?

CHAPTER EIGHTEEN

Gloria

Tape two
Mission plans, 1979, London

The next time I saw Sunstar was a Saturday, I remember well, because news of the latest American space shuttle programme was all over the headlines that morning. I recall listening to the wireless while I fiddled with the coffee grinder, experiencing that sense of wonder we humans always feel, don't you think, Sugar, at the thought of mankind reaching for the moon. What a marvel, I pondered as the newsreader offered details of the new space exploration plans. I understand how difficult it must be for you, with all your new-fangled technology, to imagine how exciting it was back then to witness the beginning of the space age. We were glimpsing a new future, a new frontier, and ever since '69 we'd all had a feeling that uncharted worlds were opening up; distant, dazzling moons and galaxies just waiting to be explored.

It was six a.m., a cold morning, just getting light. Through the windows of my flat I could see the first hints of dawn streaked across the sky, pink, blue and lavender, signalling the start of a new day. Frost sugared the pavements, and the cars parked along the kerbs were decorated with glistening patterns of ice that the girl in me – the Lusenkan girl who'd grown up beneath the baking sun – still found marvellous, a small miracle of the cold, even after years of living in England.

I had rehearsals, so I put on a rose-pink dress with platform heels and a warm woollen coat. Around my hair, I tied a scarf the colour of sunset. After a hasty breakfast of boiled eggs, toast with butter and a few cups of strong Ugandan coffee, I set off downstairs just as the clock said ten to seven, but the minute I stepped outside, I had a shock. Sunstar stood smoking beneath the larch tree opposite my flat, smoke curling into the freezing air. His dowdy figure cut an odd presence on those residential London streets, and it struck me that like me, he wasn't from this world. I sensed that the two of us couldn't have been more different to the moneyed crowd who inhabited that quietly genteel district of gated gardens and mansion flats.

I crossed the street, puzzling about the fact that, as usual, there were no reporters around. It seemed to me that this new phenomenon always coincided with the arrival of this mysterious spy.

'Good morning.'

'Good morning to you, Miss Fontaine.'

Sunstar was smiling in a friendly way, and stepped forward to greet me, as if we were friends rather than near strangers. I could tell he wasn't going to leave me alone.

'I suppose you'd like a coffee?'

'That would be delightful, thank you.'

Inside my flat, he settled on one of the stools at the kitchen counter without waiting for an invitation.

'Do you mind if I smoke?' he enquired.

'Of course not.'

He lit up, watching me fiddle about with the coffee machine. I set a new triangular paper in the filter and spooned in the remainder of the ground coffee grains from earlier, rich and nutty, filling the kitchen with a pleasant aroma of coffee and caramel. Turning the machine on, I left it spluttering in the background and helped myself to a cigarette from Sunstar's gold tin. I leaned over for him to light it and stood back, waving smoke away from my face.

'So what is it you want, Mr Sunstar?'

He took a puff of his cigarette. 'If you were called upon to deceive your friends for an important cause, would you be willing to do so?'

I arched an eyebrow. 'I don't have many friends, but yes, naturally.'

'And you were tasked with risking your life for your country?'

'Which country do you mean?' I countered. 'I'm Lusenkan and British now, and this country has treated me well.'

'Both?'

'Well then, yes, I suppose.'

His eyes were fixed on mine, and again I noticed their muted green-grey colour around dark irises, the colour of the sea on a rainy day. Clever eyes, tired eyes.

'Relations between London and Moscow have been worsening for months,' said Sunstar, smoking and proceeding to give me the rundown on the political situation in Lusenka. Russia's Vladimir Volkov was supplying Lusenka with arms, he explained, funding militia training centres so that Baptiste Lourenco could crack down on the Balaika people. The country was teetering on the edge of civil war.

'Which begs the question,' Sunstar concluded, exhaling smoke, 'what do the Russians want in return?'

'Oil,' I answered firmly, 'and diamonds. Lusenka has both in abundance.'

Sunstar nodded thoughtfully. 'A fringe benefit for British and American involvement, obviously.'

'But how can you persuade Lourenco out of Volkov's clutches?' I asked. 'It sounds like you need a diplomatic miracle.'

'Which is precisely why,' Sunstar said, extinguishing his cigarette in the ashtray, 'we need you to go to Lusenka on our behalf.'

'Who is we?'

'President Lourenco is, as you're aware, an exceedingly tricky character,' Sunstar continued, sidestepping my question. 'A narcissist, by all accounts. Charming, clever, and absolutely without a soul. And let's not forget, quite the ladies' man.'

'You don't say.'

I kept my tone of cool composure, though my heart was racing madly, and I felt sure this man could hear it, a spring bouncing from my chest. After all, we were talking about President Lourenco the dictator, the heartless animal whose regime had killed first my parents, then my darling little brother. A man who fed his enemies to his pet crocodiles, or so people said. If there was anyone I hated on earth, it was Baptiste Lourenco.

I looked away, trying to disguise my feelings as best I could. Dragging at my cigarette, I conjured my single memory of Lourenco, whom I'd had the misfortune to meet a few years back, when he attended the opening of one of my films in London. I recalled a charming man with a peculiar, encyclopaedic intelligence. A man who could speak six languages and discuss world politics or eighteenth-century art as articulately as the most erudite Oxford scholars. A charismatic man who filled a room with his presence.

Our fleeting conversation had been so short, I was sure Lourenco wouldn't remember it. *I* did though, very well indeed. That evening, I'd detected something unbalanced beneath the president's charm, as if his good humour teetered on a cliff edge, poised to fall into the dark at any moment. For not the first time in my life, I realised, with a keen sense of dismay, if not much surprise, that monsters don't always appear in monstrous form.

'Miss Fontaine?' said Sunstar quietly. 'Are you alright?'

I took another drag of my cigarette and met Sunstar's gaze, knowing there and then, with a new, crystal-clear kind of certainty, that I'd do anything – anything – to help orchestrate Lourenco's downfall.

'Yes, thank you,' I said. 'I'm perfectly fine.'

The coffee was ready. I poured out two cups of the hot, dark liquid, adding sugar and a dash of milk, and set each cup on its saucer, pushing one cup towards Sunstar across the counter. I took a sip of the other.

'What do you need me to do?'

Sunstar nodded. 'We require intelligence on Lourenco and his association with the Soviets, and we're counting on you to get it.'

I stirred my coffee, tinkling the spoon against the china. 'And what makes you think I'm capable of such a thing?'

Sunstar chuckled softly. 'You're quite the well-known actress, Miss Fontaine. Men are drawn to you like moths to a flame. You have beauty, eloquence, and the unique status of being both Lusenkan and British. Lourenco admires all those qualities, as our sources confirm. You're a prize in his eyes, and there's no need for elaborate pretences. You have the perfect cover, just as you are.'

I tipped my head back and exhaled a plume of smoke, taken aback to hear that Lourenco remembered me. After a moment's pause, I replied, 'You want me to lure him in, a honeytrap?'

Sunstar met my gaze steadily. 'I learned long ago that to outmanoeuvre the Russians, one mustn't *be* the Russians. Honeytraps are a Soviet game, Miss Fontaine. You don't have to sleep with Lourenco – quite frankly, I'd much rather you didn't. Instead, you'll operate as an agent in plain sight.' He extinguished his cigarette in the dish. 'The mission demands ingenuity and acting talent, all of which you have in abundance. You simply need to be yourself.'

'So you're counting on our adversaries being so starstruck they won't kill me?'

'Absolutely.'

'Sounds like a foolhardy plan,' I said, with a low laugh.

Sunstar got up and wandered to the large window, where he stared out for quite a few minutes without speaking. I glanced beyond his head to see what he was looking at, but there was nothing of note down in the street, just the blank, white faces of the mansion flats opposite, and the leafless trees lined up against a greyish February sky. Perhaps a reporter turned up though, trying to stake out my flat, because all of a sudden Sunstar turned sharply and made his way over to the drinks tray, where he helped himself to one of the crystal tumblers and poured a large whisky. In the quiet flat, the liquid sloshed noisily into the glass. The whole thing was strangely intimate, yet I found I didn't mind. There was nothing arrogant about Sunstar, you see. Everything he did was measured and sensible, backed up by a methodical thought process of one sort or another.

'You might as well have ice,' I said. From the ice bucket I served Sunstar two cubes that went rattling down into the glass, crackling noisily, and he nodded his thanks. Then he sat down on the settee and took a sip, swirling the drink, tinkling the ice.

'But how will this help?' I blurted out. 'Retribution, you called it, the first time we met. I just don't see how that's possible.'

'Now that the Americans, our allies, are withdrawing from Vietnam, their sights are set on other countries, other conflicts. If they and the British can get eyes on what Lourenco is up to with Volkov, together we can influence the political stage, destabilise the military systems, stop the brutality and try to put another president in power. Subtle, but effective.'

'You can't possibly guarantee that.'

'Nothing in life is guaranteed. But many things are worth a shot. And you, Gloria, represent our best shot.' Sunstar sent me a slow smile. 'Moreover,' he added. 'Your brother Chilembé believed in you. He believed you were capable of anything if you put your mind to it.'

I went and stood with my back to the window, facing Sunstar as it dawned on me that we were acting a scene, he and I, slow dancing with each other in that age-old theatre of humans and their wishes. Ours was the theatre of the Greeks, of Sophocles and Euripides, guided by our primal human desires for love, for money, power, and pleasure – desires that would propel us to act. For a moment or two I stared at Sunstar, imagining a director prompting me from stage left. *Why does your character make this choice, Gloria? What is her ultimate desire?*

I thought of my baby brother Chilembé swimming in the bay on sunny weekend days, the way he used to float in the clear blue ocean, water glistening on his face, laughing and calling me in. 'Come on, Gloria, don't be a wimp, come on!' I thought of Chilembé's body lying abandoned, bloodied and limp, on the floor of his home. My brother, my precious boy, once so alive, was gone.

I felt Sunstar's eyes on me. He was frowning slightly, his brows knitted as if he were keeping his emotions in check, but he didn't utter a word.

What did he see, I wondered then, when he looked at me? A lost soul with her heart in shreds, easy to manipulate? Or was he imagining a pretty, plucky girl bravely luring the tyrant who killed her family to his downfall with her wit and beauty? What a part to play, I thought. How unreal it all was, just like a film. I turned away and sipped the last dregs of my coffee, craving the privacy of my own thoughts.

'Do you really think Chilembé would have wanted me to do this?' I said eventually, hesitantly, turning back to look at Sunstar.

'He told me himself.' Sunstar leant forward, observing me with a thoughtful expression. Once again, I couldn't help noticing his eyes, how their colour in the half-light matched the rain-washed sky through the windows. 'Chilembé spoke of you often,' he continued. 'Many times, how you kept you both alive, and how unflappable you are. You see, Gloria, good intelligence agents possess a unique ability to detach, to compartmentalise emotions and maintain a careful grip on what's happening. It seems you have precisely these qualities, in spades.'

Chilembé.

I stood in silence as a plume of anger rose in my chest, a flash of profound fury like an explosion. A dormant volcano of all my grief, suddenly awakened. I remembered Chilembé sobbing as I left him that awful morning in Port Salé, a little boy huddled in his too-big uniform, tears pouring down his cheeks. What I wouldn't give to turn back time.

But that was impossible, now. My brother was dead, and only one thing could give me relief. Only one thing could exorcise my misery. Retribution.

I paced the room, careful to show nothing of my emotions. I poured myself a large gin and tonic, even though it was barely eight o'clock in the morning. Adding ice, I stirred the drink, sloshing it around, and took a large swig.

Together we sat in silence, Sunstar and I, watching the window. On the branch of a tree, a bird, a starling I think it was, caught my eye. It sat swaying in the wind, small against the great width of the tree, ruffling its feathers for warmth and turning its head this way and that.

Presently, I swivelled to face Sunstar, looked him straight in the eyes, and told him what I'd known half an hour ago:

'Alright,' I said. 'I'll do it.'

CHAPTER NINETEEN

Dolly

Dolly got up promptly before dawn, stopping at a service station outside Truro to refill with petrol. It was only just getting light, and the weather was mild, the radio forecast predicting a storm then sunshine all week. As she was coming out of the kiosk carrying a takeaway latte, a voice made her jump.

'Fontaine! Fancy seeing you here.'

She turned to find Peverell Greyson in red jeans and a polo shirt, sunglasses hanging from a buttonhole. He seemed to have appeared from nowhere. He was holding a slightly wilted bunch of red roses from the flower stand, and his smile made her skin crawl. There was something frightening about him, she decided, feeling utterly disconcerted; something bad and brutal lurking beneath the well-dressed surface.

'You're up early,' she said, for want of anything better to say.

'Up with the larks and all that.' He caught her gazing at the drooping flowers and gave a quiet laugh. 'For the wifey. Who says I'm not romantic.' He plucked a rose from the bunch and held it out to Dolly with a small bow. 'For you, Fontaine. Call it a moving-in present.'

'No, thanks.' She shook her head as a few petals drifted to the ground. 'I don't know what you mean, anyway.'

With a shrug, he slotted the rose back into the bunch. 'You're living at your mater's house, aren't you? How idyllic. When's the housewarming?'

'Did Morgan tell you that?'

He laughed. 'Oh, I like to keep abreast of what's going on in the local community. It pays, you know. *Anyhoo...*' He paused, keeping his eyes on her. 'Nice party the other day. Very sweet. Your bro was on good form. Must be happy families all round...'

'I hope you're not getting him into trouble?'

'Oh.' Pev feigned a babyish voice, his smile fading. 'I didn't realise your precious brother needed a babysitter.'

'Since he met you, it seems he does.' Dolly paused, deciding to take a risk. 'You and Shaun Kingsley.'

'Ohhhh.' A suggestive smile played on his lips. 'The lovely Shaun? I was under the impression it was *you* and Shaun Kingsley, actually. What makes you think I know him?'

'Just a gut feeling.'

'That's one way of putting it, I suppose. But Lobster's nothing to do with anything.'

'Lobster?'

'Nickname, on account of the fact he loves the fancy life, fancy fuck.' Peverell laughed roughly, that hint of something harsher again beneath the careful charm, as if he'd forgotten he was talking to a stranger.

'Do you know him well?'

Pev tutted under his breath. 'All these questions, Fontaine. They're going to get you into trouble one day. Oh wait.' He put a finger to his chin, mockingly. 'They already have? Best not to meddle anymore, then, or things might get difficult.'

Dolly could feel her fingers burning on the coffee cup. She took a small step back.

'What are you talking about?'

'You know, Fontaine, you should be careful living at that big, old house all alone. Who knows what sort of dangers lurk down here.' He gave a twisted smirk. 'It's deepest, darkest Cornwall after all.'

'Jesus, are you threatening me?'

But Pev was already hauling open the heavy door as another customer, a woman, approached from the petrol pumps.

'After you, Fontaine darling.' Pev turned with a sweeping bow, holding the door open.

Dolly swore under her breath and watched him saunter away, laughing raucously to himself, the bunch of roses held in one hand like some sort of weapon, bright scarlet against the greyish dawn. When he reached a big, silver Mercedes, he turned with another dazzling smile and slowly pointed a V sign with two fingers first at his own eyes, then at her. He blew her a kiss and Dolly's heart flipped over. It was a smiling, silent promise. *I'm watching you.*

Rattled, Dolly climbed back in the Morris Thousand, still shaking slightly. She tried to calm down, gulping a few big mouthfuls of coffee, but as she pulled out of the garage and drove slowly up the A30 into Devon, she couldn't stop thinking about Pev and his veiled threat, and the undisguisable menace shadowing his pale, beautiful features. How dare he threaten her! The man was dangerous, that much was clear, and she suspected his words were not to be taken lightly. And then there were his insinuations about Shaun... She winced inwardly, imagining what lurid details Shaun may have shared with him, and what he might know about their affair.

It wasn't until noon, and her arrival in the village of Lyton Minster, that she felt a little calmer. The place was deserted and tiny, consisting of a dozen or so well-groomed houses arranged around a neatly mown green, and a country pub with beer-branded parasols outside. Glad to have found it successfully; glad, too, for a distraction, she pushed all thoughts of Peverell Greyson aside, and got out of the car.

Behind a shapely yew hedge, 22 The Laurels was a pretty, detached cottage with a thatched roof. A beautiful, burgundy-coloured classic car was parked outside. Tentatively, Dolly opened the garden gate and went to knock on the front door, only to notice a scribbled handwritten note sellotaped to the letterbox: *I'll be in the garden.* She followed a path leading around the side of the house past low shrubs and herbs, lavender, and rosemary, then a line of tomato plants clambering up a sunny wall. In the back, the garden was resplendent with summer annuals. She gazed at the neat borders edged with upturned bricks containing squash plants flowering with giant orange trumpets. Two sheared sheep grazed beneath an apple tree in a field to the rear. The barn door of the kitchen was half open at the top. It was just coming up to half past eleven.

A man appeared, wearing khaki Bermuda shorts and a weather-beaten cricket hat, with an elderly border collie following on his heels. In the man's hands was a rusty instrument with spikes that looked vaguely dangerous. Was it a garden tool, Dolly wondered, feeling alarmed, or a weapon to fend off intruders?

'Hello?' The man approached with a wary look, then stopped in his tracks, looking taken aback. For a moment he stared at her with a perplexed expression, then seemed to recover himself. 'Can I help you?' he said.

'I'm sorry to disturb you. Your address was in an old notebook of my mother's, and I wondered if we could talk?'

'Your mother?' The collie fussed around Dolly's ankles, but the man called it sharply back, 'Lucy!'

'Yes. My name is Dolly Fontaine. My mother was Gloria Fontaine.'

The man drew an almost imperceptible breath and narrowed his eyes, then gave a very slight smile.

'Well, well, Dolly Fontaine. I've been expecting you.'

He stepped closer, scrutinising her, though his own face was inscrutable. Other than this slight change of expression, he betrayed no emotion whatsoever.

'You have?' she said. 'I mean, you knew Gloria?'

'Indeed, I knew your mother very well.'

Dolly noted his voice, well-spoken, with a mildest lilt of Scottish around the consonants, a very nice voice – more than nice, a voice that made her want to close her eyes and listen.

'Could we talk?' she asked. 'I've so many questions. Someone sent me a note, and I've been listening to some diaries…'

She was unsure now, what she was asking for. Information? Answers or a plan of action? Was this Sunstar, then?

The man frowned and wiped his thumb and forefinger wearily across his eyes. He appeared to be thinking something over. Then he glanced past Dolly's head at the garden beyond, at the sky and the trees. She waited for him to speak or decide to chuck her out, whichever it was to be. In the end though, it was she who broke the silence.

'Sunstar? Is that your name? My mother called you Sunstar, didn't she?'

The man didn't react, yet there was the slightest movement of his body, a new, almost imperceptible alertness. Dolly could almost feel his mind working. From inside the house, she heard a telephone ringing: four rings then silence, and for some reason the sound made her shiver despite the intensity of the noonday sun, scorching now, beating fiercely down on the top of her head. Without looking at her, Sunstar walked over to the house, and Dolly followed. With slow movements, he slid the bolt across to open the lower half of the kitchen door.

'You'd better come in,' he said. 'I'll put the kettle on.'

CHAPTER TWENTY

Gloria

The days passed. There was nothing to do but wait, but I found myself in turmoil. For months I'd banned myself from crying, but the conversation with Sunstar had somehow unlocked all my grief, and I found myself weeping uncontrollably whenever I was alone. At night, if I eventually managed to sleep, I'd wake with my cheeks wet with tears, remembering my brother's warm little body sleeping next to me, snoring gently, his head on my shoulder, sweet as a bear cub. The memories induced a longing that tightened my chest and brought more tears – loud sobs I stifled with a pillow. When dawn came, I was exhausted, only relieved to escape the night. And despite my usual self-control, I couldn't seem to stop these troubled dreams emerging from the deepest, most diabolical chasms of my mind.

In hindsight, I wish I'd turned to painting, just as I did later, after you were born, Sugar. For me, the act of putting paint to canvas was always peaceful, soothing, escapist. Healing, even. Do you remember when we painted in the garden sometimes; you, me, and your brother? It was always summer, warm and blue as delphiniums, the smell of roses and turpentine in the air. I would set up an easel in the shade and put on music, and we'd paint for hours, just the three of us, as the shadows stretched like long sighs across the fading afternoon.

I regret not doing more of that, don't you? In recent years, I've come to understand that I made a mistake, thinking that opportunities for you two – school, books, money, everything I could lay at your feet – could replace a loving touch, a loving word of encouragement.

I purposefully avoided your grandmother's mistakes – my Ma's – but made my own. I shut myself off. I drank. I wallowed. I did not behave as a mother should.

Every now and then, I find myself upstairs, God knows how I get there, staring at those paintings of you and your brother with a heavy feeling in my chest. Every brushstroke seems to hold a love I couldn't express when you were children. Can you imagine what it's like, wishing for time to reverse itself? I don't think I understood then how I sought to capture you both just as you were, as a photograph crystallises a single, cherished moment in time.

If only I'd known how quickly you'd grow up. Your childhoods were over in a wink. All that time, I didn't realise how difficult it would be to let you fly.

In daylight hours, I threw myself into rehearsals, and, in the brighter moments, found myself intrigued by the thought of a mission to Lusenka for the British Secret Services, though I wondered how a prolonged absence would go down with my fearsome director, Jefferson Hunt. By that time, we were in the middle of filming Mirrorball 3, and any sort of mission would surely last several weeks. Jefferson was known in the business as a bit of a bulldog, not to mention a creep. So far, I'd been lucky enough to escape his groping advances, but numerous stories were circulating at that time about his antics with rookie actresses, young women just out of drama college, desperate for a break. Though Jefferson liked my work, I knew he wouldn't hesitate to replace me with one of his underage squeezes if I didn't come up to scratch.

As it turns out, I needn't have worried. One freezing Wednesday evening, just as the darkness was settling over London, I was walking down the road to my flat when a beige Ford Grenada pulled up beside me. The door opened, and a harassed-looking driver got out, very portly and grey-faced, in a creased suit and tie. He looked like a weary civil servant with rather too much on his plate.

'Miss Fontaine,' the driver said. 'You're to come with me. It's about Sunstar.'

'Sunstar?'

The man gave a small nod, opened the passenger door, and gestured to the back seat with a vague air of dismissal.

'Yes, Yes. Please, make yourself comfortable. We mustn't waste time, what.'

I felt a brimming sense of excitement as we drove through the centre of London and out again to Richmond Park, where the car came to a halt outside a pair of high, wrought-iron gates, and the driver came around to open the door for me, ushering me out with a deep frown before sloping across the road for a cigarette.

According to my wristwatch, it was five-thirty exactly, just before the park's closing time, and no one was around. The temperature had already dropped so low that a layer of powdered frost glistened on the tarmac. A street lamp pooled cold yellow light onto the pavement, and a biting cold stung my cheeks. If Sunstar intended to give our rendezvous a hint of cloak-and-dagger, he'd certainly succeeded. I got out of the car, hugging my coat around me and taking care not to slip in my heels.

Sunstar sat on a bench, cigarette in hand, flicking through a newspaper. The smoke from his cigarette fogged around him in opaque clouds. Wrapped in his overcoat and that ridiculous trilby hat of his, he cast a shadowy figure, every inch a spy. I found myself enjoying the illicit nature of our meeting, which felt deliciously melodramatic.

I pulled my coat closer around me and sat down a small distance away on the same bench, aware that the two of us must not be seen talking. I took a cigarette from my own packet and cupped my hands to light it, breathing in gratefully, enjoying the warmth of the tobacco and the feeling that somehow, this moment marked the beginning of something new, something that might very well change my life.

'You wanted to see me?'

'Yes.'

Sunstar folded the newspaper, still looking ahead, cigarette balanced between his fingers. I followed his gaze to the silhouettes of the poplar trees rising tall and slim against the moonless sky.

'I've received the details of your mission.'

'I see,' I replied, exhaling smoke. 'I'm going then?'

'You leave next month.'

'To Lusenka,' I said, dubiously, 'Port Salé?'

'Yes. But before that to South Devon, for training.'

'Training?'

'You'll have six weeks to learn as much as you can. It won't be perfect, but time is of the essence.'

I inhaled slowly at the cigarette, and, for the first time, felt a rush of fear. I'd spent all those years acting plucky heroines on the silver screen, but I really had no idea how to play them in real life. Here I was, without stage lights or clapperboards, without retakes or a script. This wasn't the damn flicks. The odds were stacked against me, and I suspected there would be no one to save my bacon if everything went wrong. But whether it was my grief making me numb and reckless, or simply my past – the trauma of everything that had happened in my life up until that point – I found I didn't care. I'd no idea what on earth I was getting into, but now that Sunstar wanted me to work for him, I couldn't hesitate. God knows, if a way existed to somehow revenge my brother's death, however dangerous or foolhardy, I'd do anything Sunstar asked.

In any case, what had I got to lose?

On the bench beside me, Sunstar remained silent, exhaling against the lamplight as cigarette smoke fogged around his profile. I stole a glance at his Roman nose and strong jaw, which reminded me of an actor or a politician. He was so serious and intelligent, so *intense*, this enigmatic spy who'd come into my life so suddenly, and on whom, now, everything seemed staked.

'I wonder what your real name is,' I said, teasing him in spite of myself, flirting perhaps. 'John, William?'

'I can't tell you that. I'm sorry. You must only use Sunstar.'

He scanned the park with his gaze – searching, I suppose, for watching eyes.

'I have another question,' I said. He turned and our eyes met, and I recognised something in those darkened pupils that I couldn't quite put my finger on. Was it amusement, or fondness, even?

'What is it, Gloria?' he said.

'Do you *really* think I can do this?'

All of a sudden, the distance on the bench seemed to gape between us. I found myself wondering what it would be like to kiss Sunstar, and unexpectedly remembering something a fellow actress, an American girl from New York, had once told me, recounting some romantic adventure or another: 'I tilted my head, Honey, and closed my eyes, it's the universal sign for kiss me.' I shook off the thought and crushed my cigarette on the ground, focusing my mind.

Sunstar gave a smile. 'No one but you can do this, Gloria,' he said, softly. 'You have no idea how important this is.'

'Alright then.'

He produced his gold tin and extracted another cigarette. Without a word, he reached across, extending the tin, and we both lit up in silence, the smoke weaving patterns between us on the bench as we sat apart, side by side. But when I casually flicked the stub of the second cigarette to the ground, this time he caught me up.

'An agent never throws her cigarette on the ground,' he said firmly. 'There's a wealth of information the enemy can glean from that simple act.'

'Such as?'

'Consider this. The lipstick stain indicates you're a woman, and the brand, Gold Virginia, suggests either American or British origins. Furthermore, the mere possession of a cigarette suggests a certain level of morale and confidence.'

'I wouldn't have thought about it.'

'Don't worry. You'll be taught everything.'

In the silence that followed, Sunstar tore off the filter of his cigarette and stowed it in the gold tin, along with a quantity of other small filters – from previous smokes that day, I supposed. I followed his example, putting the filter of my own cigarette discreetly in my pocket before dropping the remaining ash on the ground, feeling – ludicrously so – as if I'd just taken my first step into the world of undercover espionage.

Presently Sunstar spoke again, more matter of fact this time. My training, he informed me, would take place under the guise of preparing for my latest Mirrorball role – adding that there would be someone in Lusenka to give me further instructions when I got there. It was too dangerous, he pointed out, to give me the details of my mission all at once, but the intelligence I'd be gathering would be central to Lourenco's eventual downfall.

'A driver from the High Commission will meet you in Port Salé,' Sunstar finished up. 'You'll be taken to the Sheraton, where there'll be a suite booked under your name. There'll be a party on the Saturday where you'll have the chance to mingle.'

'And then?'

'And then you're largely on your own, I'm afraid. At the party, Lourenco will be easy to access. Your mission is to secure another invite, a private one, after which you'll receive further instructions.'

I considered this for a moment. If someone had offered me the role in a film, I'd have accepted without hesitation. Sunstar was right; I had more than enough acting skills to persuade corrupt, capricious Baptiste Lourenco to trust me. I could take care of myself just fine. There and then, I made up my mind to give my everything to Sunstar's

126

risky spy games.

'What about my filming?' I said presently.

'Jefferson has given you two months off.'

'You spoke to Jefferson?'

Sunstar chuckled. 'We have ways and means.' He stood up, slipping the newspaper under his arm and adjusting his hat. 'Pack everything you might take for a two-week holiday in the sun.'

I raised an eyebrow, and he ventured a smile. 'It's not Moscow, you know.'

'You could have fooled me.'

Sunstar held out his hand, and I took it. Like that we stood gazing at each other, his hand lingering a moment too long on mine.

'Good luck, Gloria,' he said, still holding my hand.

'Goodbye, Sunstar.'

Out of nowhere the big Mercedes appeared by the park gates, its engine barely making a sound. Without turning around, I walked to the car and climbed into the cushiony, leather back seat, letting the driver slam the door shut. Through the window, as we drove off, I watched Sunstar walk the other way, his shoulders hunched against the cold, roaming off into the darkness to God knows where. He didn't turn around, either.

CHAPTER TWENTY-ONE

Dolly

By Dolly's calculations, Sunstar must have been in his late sixties, yet he was still slim and muscular, with traces of past athleticism in his neck and broad shoulders, his arms sun-browned beneath the shirt. There was the unmistakably strong jaw, Dolly noted, and striking Roman nose, and grey-green eyes the colour of a rainy sky, just as Gloria had described.

'Just tell Lucy to get down if she bothers you.'

'It's okay – I like dogs.'

'Good.' He cast her another curious glance, shaking his head. 'Dolly Fontaine, good gracious.' He turned, filling the kettle at the tap. 'So, my dear, how did you find me?'

'I got your parcel. At least, I think it was from you. And then I found the tapes in the attic of my mother's house.'

'Very good.'

'There was an address in an old notebook up there. It mentioned gin fizz. I've been listening to the tapes. You must have meant me to piece things together?'

Sunstar chuckled, collecting teacups. 'Like mother, like daughter.' He fetched a biscuit jar from a shelf, setting everything on a metal tray. 'I told Gloria it was risky to record those damn things. It's classified information, after all. Eyes only. But she wouldn't have it.' He gave another wry chuckle. 'She was hell bent on setting you a trail, and while I can usually outmanoeuvre the British security services, I was no match for your mother when she set her mind to something.'

Dolly laughed. 'Tell me about it. But there were only two tapes in the box. I've listened to them both but I'm sure there must be more to her story.'

'Indeed, indeed. Come, let's go back into the garden.'

Dolly followed Sunstar outside as he exclaimed, 'Good gracious, it's hot!' and set out the tea things on the patio table. He pottered about, erecting the parasol, pouring out the tea. Everyday tasks, Dolly thought, just like any other warm afternoon in any other English country garden, except he was a spy. A bee hummed around the tea tray. From somewhere came the low burr of a lawnmower.

'So it *was* you who sent me the note, wasn't it?' she said. 'Why? Did you know I'd just been sacked?'

'I caught wind of your story on the news when it broke, and the ensuing scandal.' Sunstar settled into his seat, crossing one leg over the other before taking a leisurely sip of tea. 'I thought I should lend a hand in some way, and I'll admit I was curious – part of me wanted to see what Dolly Fontaine was made of, so I set you a little breadcrumb trail of my own, couriered that package to your desk. I have my ways and means...' He paused, a faint crease forming between his brows. 'Then, well, I started to second guess myself. Delving into the past is not a risk I'd typically undertake, you understand? What's the use, after all, when everything's said and done?'

He cast a look around, across the garden and the path again, as if scanning for onlookers, and Dolly had the impression he was checking for something, but for what, for whom? Old habits, she decided. Perhaps he imagined they were being listened to by the Russians or the Chinese. She thought of Pev turning up in the service station that morning. Perhaps they were.

'What are you looking for?' she asked, wondering if that could be the source of his anxiety, resolving to watch Sunstar carefully despite his apparent amiability, and read between the lines, whatever he said.

'Nothing,' he replied in a cheerful voice, 'just making sure we're alone.' He offered a half-smile, but a hint of worry remained in his eyes. 'Your mother always did have a way of getting under my skin...' He sighed. 'You've come to ask for my assistance, have you?'

Dolly frowned. 'I don't know. I don't really know why I'm here. I

129

just thought I needed to find you.'

'Go on. You'd better tell me everything.'

'Firstly, are there more tapes from Gloria? She called it a treasure hunt before she died.'

'Indeed.' His look was spry and scrutinising. 'Ah, so you really are your mother's daughter.'

'I *think* that's a compliment?'

'Hang on there.' Placing the cup on the saucer, he held up a hand. 'Gloria was too daring by half.' He gave a small laugh. 'But first, the story you broke, it involved one Shaun Kingsley, the Conservatives' Junior Minister for Defence Procurement, yes?'

'Yes. I believe Kingsley set me up, but I don't know why.' Dolly observed the spy quizzically. 'You seem to know a lot about me already.'

A nod of assent. 'I've followed your career from a distance, yes.'

'Which is all ruined,' she replied grimly without pausing, without asking why.

'All men make mistakes, but only wise men *learn* from their mistakes. Churchill.'

'That's nice of you.'

'Good God, it's not about being nice, it's quite simply about the truth. People's memories are short, my dear. Give it a year and they'll have moved onto the next juicy nugget of scandal. You're young, and so very talented. Don't lose hope just yet.'

She shrugged. 'Okay.'

Sunstar nodded with a matter-of-fact expression. 'Now. Let's see. Let's deal with the present, first. You were following a story, before this rather unfortunate spanner in the works about Lusenka?'

She looked at him in silence.

'You suspect,' he continued, his voice steady, 'that the British Government is somehow entangled in some underhand affair there, am I right? And the involvement of Lusenka raises all sorts of questions that you're eager to unravel, because you care about principles. And you miss your mother, who in my experience was always somewhat evasive about personal matters. You believe that by delving into this, it will

130

bring you closer to her, and to the elusive truth, whatever that may be.'

Dolly stayed silent, feeling suddenly emotional, though she wasn't sure exactly why. 'Initially, yes,' she agreed. 'I was following a lead about Lusenka. There are rumours about the British supporting rebel factions, possibly supplying arms to commit human rights atrocities against the Balaika, and I was gathering evidence. I made the mistake of telling Shaun Kingsley.'

'A common mistake, placing trust in others,' Sunstar remarked, observing her with a gentle look. 'Go on,' he urged softly.

'I believe now that the minute Kingsley knew I was getting close to the truth, he set out to distract me, and the general public, by getting me to publish a different story, and then discrediting me.'

'I think you may be right, my dear. Now, what exactly do you have so far?'

'That's the trouble, nothing concrete.'

Dolly showed Sunstar a screenshot of the controversial memo, telling him of her new suspicion that Shaun Kingsley was linked to Peverell Greyson, but deciding to hold back her original notes on her own Lusenka investigation, her brother's furtive behaviour, and the lorries being loaded at the building site in Porthlowe.

She didn't tell Sunstar, either, about her encounter with Pev earlier that morning. After all, she'd only just met this enigmatic spy – was she really sensible to trust him?

'I know it probably sounds preposterous,' she concluded, 'but what if Peverell Greyson and Shaun are in league somehow?'

'Not preposterous in the slightest.' Sunstar adjusted his reading glasses and scrutinised the memo with his undivided attention for a minute or two. Eventually, he looked up, removed his spectacles and dangled them in his right hand. 'You see, I'm retired, my dear Dolly. No longer in the game. My old connections, well, let's face it, everyone's either dead or lost their wits, and I'm just an old man tending sheep before my afternoon nap. Regretfully, the days of multiple passports and midnight runs to Moscow are long gone.' He sighed wistfully, shaking his head. 'Good gracious, even the old headquarters has been replaced by that monstrosity in Vauxhall. But I do know one thing. You mustn't jeopardise your safety. Matters like these can be very dangerous.'

'Dangerous?'

'Yes.' He uncrossed his legs, rising to his feet. 'Come, stroll with me.'

Dolly walked beside him with the sheepdog doodling at her heels, past the flower borders along the path into a meadow, where a river ran along a bank of weeping willow trees. Chickens scratched the ground in the long purplish grass. Near a wooden shelter containing bags of animal feed, two thick woollen fleeces and the ancient-looking shearing tool from earlier were abandoned on a wooden pallet, next to an ageing camping chair.

She watched Sunstar take a scoop of feed and call the sheep – 'Hilda! Marigold!' – scattering the nuts in the long grass. It was coming up to midday. Out of the shade of the parasol the sun was high, the shadows hard-edged, the heat oppressive. She squinted in the light, feeling tired suddenly, and a little bit defeated.

'I only came here because of the tapes, and my mother...' She raised a hand to shield her eyes from the sun. 'But are you saying you can help with the Lusenka story, that it's all connected?'

'It's entirely possible. Your mother's tapes are merely scratching the surface, but you must understand, Dolly, my dear, these are dangerous people. If they catch wind of what you know... Well, as I say, they're not small fry, and I can attest, from bitter experience, that governments can be just as corrupt as these individuals. If the powers-that-be are obstructing this story, it means there's something suspicious at play. There always is. As for you being mixed up in it, my dear... Well, you could be in grave danger.'

'I know.' She paused, following Sunstar into the shade of the apple tree. 'But you must still have contacts?'

Together they watched the sheep in the dappled leaf shadows. Beside them, the sheepdog settled on the ground in the pool of shadow, nose on paws. Sunstar handed Dolly the metal scoop.

'Here, throw some for the girls.'

132

The two sheep wandered up, nosing the ground. Dolly scattered feed, putting out a hand to touch the coat of the nearest animal. She breathed in its grassy, lanolin scent, the shorn fleece stubbly and soft between her fingers.

'You must go to Lusenka,' Sunstar said. 'Conduct some thorough investigations at the heart of things and you have your story.'

Dolly's expression mirrored her surprise. 'You think I should go to Lusenka?'

'If you wish to do this properly, then yes, undoubtedly.' Sunstar frowned. 'I've an old acquaintance there, an amiable fellow. Trustworthy. Relies a little too much on the calming effects of marijuana and alcohol, but on the whole, a good egg. I'll see what arrangements I can make.' He patted the sheep. 'Now, my dear, let's get you a cold drink.'

So that was it, Dolly was thinking, the plan of action she'd come for? She felt strangely anti-climactic as she followed the ex-spy back to the kitchen.

'Isn't there anyone else I can talk to?'

In the cool interior, Sunstar took a glass from the cupboard, poured water from a filter jug, handed it to her. She drank it gratefully.

'There's a man here in the UK called Abimbola, Lionel Abimbola. His father, Hervé, was a rebel during Lourenco's time.' Sunstar rose from his seat, leaving the room as Dolly petted the dog, who had settled in a ball next to her.

At last, Sunstar came back with an ancient-looking address book. Flipping through its pages, he scribbled a number on a piece of paper, and handed it to Dolly. 'Don't mention my name, just say you have a contact.'

Afterwards, Sunstar walked her outside. As Dolly opened the gate, she turned back to him. 'Before I go,' she said, 'I've a question.'

'Yes?'

'What's your name? Your real name, I mean?'

There was a brief pause, before Sunstar gave a small smile. 'Your mother asked me that, the second time we met, and at the time I couldn't tell her. My name is Montgomery, Robert John Montgomery.

133

Your mother occasionally used to call me Robert, but only when she was cross with me,' he added, with a wink.

'Robert.' Dolly paused. 'You said there was more to the story. Do you have the other tapes?'

'Of course.' He inclined his head. 'Here.' He reached into a supermarket carrier bag he had brought outside with him, retrieving a small plastic zip bag containing some cassettes. 'Forgive me,' he continued, handing them to her. 'The gin fizz in that parcel was a little jest of mine, a nod to my old spy days. I knew Gloria would have liked that clue – and as I said, I wanted to see what her daughter was made of. But the earrings were Gloria's. I always thought them charming and assumed you might like to have them.'

'I do,' Dolly replied with a smile. 'Very much.'

'Gloria gave them to me for safe keeping. I believe she harboured a hope that one day you'd find me.' Sunstar balled the empty plastic bag in his right hand. 'However, I suspect there may be one or two tapes still to be discovered. Your mother and her penchant for treasure hunts, you understand.'

'I do.' Dolly laughed. 'Thank you. For everything.'

As she began to pull away, Sunstar approached the window, so she rolled it down.

'You might also try the newspaper archive in Truro,' he suggested. 'Just a thought. You might find something of interest. The editor's a decent fellow.'

He stood at the gate as she drove off, raising his arm in farewell.

When Sunstar finally disappeared from the rear-view mirror, Dolly pulled the car over in a layby and scrolled her phone to the number he'd given her. *Good afternoon, Mr Abimbola,* she typed. *My name's Dolly Fontaine. Is it possible we can talk?*

Then she sat for a moment, deep in thought, thinking about Sunstar, remembering the last tape she'd listened to. How, no matter where they were, Gloria used to tear off the filters of her cigarettes and stash them in her handbag. It was a *thing*, a habit of hers which neither Dolly nor

Rich could ever understand. In point of fact, Dolly always found it vaguely repellent, especially when Gloria used to clear her handbag of all the tiny stubs accumulated there over the weeks, leaving a stale smell of old smoke behind.

Dolly leaned her head against the steering wheel. How painstakingly she'd kept her sadness in check, and how far all this seemed from her own final memories of her mother, an old woman as drained by cancer as a worn out leaf after winter. She remembered this distinctly, and the evening near the end, sitting at Gloria's bedside, when Gloria suddenly blurted out an apology.

'We wasted time, didn't we, Sugar?'

'What do you mean?'

'You and me. We should have talked more about everything, darling. I should have been more...' Gloria frowned, trailing off with watering eyes – from emotion, Dolly wondered, or just the illness? But her mother reached out a shrivelled hand, like a delicate bird skeleton in Dolly's hand.

'I should have been softer,' Gloria murmured eventually. 'Maybe.'

Dolly gently squeezed her hand, not knowing what to say, unable to bring herself to utter the words she sensed her mother wanted even after all this time: I love you. It just wasn't something they ever said to each other.

Feeling sad, Dolly slotted one of the new cassettes, labelled 'Training', into the old car tape machine fitted by Rich in the nineties, when they were teenagers, so that Gloria could listen to her audio books – Agatha Christie, Frederick Forsyth, John Le Carré. She loved anything involving detectives, spies, or renegade politicians.

But Dolly swore under her breath when she heard the sound of grinding on the spool. Hastily she turned the machine off, unwilling to risk damaging the reel. With delicate fingertips she prised the length of brown ribbon off the spool and carefully rewound it back into the cassette with an unsettling sensation that the object was somehow bewitched; that Gloria might leap from the tape any minute, smoke from a cauldron.

'Mum,' she whispered. 'I wish you could help. I wish you had answers.'

The ribbon shimmered in the light. *Don't give up, Sugar,* her mother's voice seemed to say. With a shiver, Dolly shook the ridiculous thought away. Doubtless Gloria's narrative would be distorted now. Still, it was worth a try.

She switched the tape on again, hoping for the best. After a few more glitches it began to run, and she pulled out of the layby as it started up, shifting gears, thinking about Sunstar and her mother's story. Now that she'd met Sunstar, finally, she could perfectly imagine him sitting side by side with Gloria on that park bench, cigarette smoke curling up between them in the winter dark, a pair of souls embarking on a mission for the love of country, for the greater good – but for other reasons too, not least Gloria's own salvation.

How she would have loved to tell Gloria of her own – failed – journalistic efforts to tell the truth, against the odds. She was beginning to understand that Gloria might not have judged her own mistakes as harshly as she'd always assumed.

Dolly turned onto the coast road, letting all other sounds disappear until she could hear only the low hum of her mother's voice as she drove past the cliff meadows dotted with purple heather, beneath a hazy sun.

CHAPTER TWENTY-TWO

Gloria

Tape three
Training, 1979, Gwynarthen

A week later, my train from London Paddington pulled into Newton Abbot railway station at a quarter past three on a drizzly Thursday afternoon. There, I was met on the platform by a man who introduced himself as Gregory Seal. He sported a bushy ginger moustache and a thick glass monocle over one piercing green eye, whose magnifying effect made this eye appear larger and floatier than the other one, giving him a look somewhere between a mad scientist and an eccentric university professor.

'Charmed to make your acquaintance, Miss Fontaine,' he said, shaking my hand.

'Where are we going?' I asked.

'Gwynarthen House,' he answered curtly, carrying my suitcase to the car. 'You'll see.'

Half an hour later we arrived at a three-storey Georgian townhouse tucked away behind the shopping arcade of a market town deep in the foothills of Dartmoor. With its honey-coloured stone walls and hanging baskets planted with primroses on either side of the front door, you might have thought it was a provincial set of civil service offices – a bank or a local council HQ, although naturally, it served a much more interesting purpose than that. Inside, Seal instructed me to carry my bags upstairs, directing me to a miniscule bedroom on the third floor. The room was stark, with a worn carpet and a single bed, a wardrobe, a mirror, and a small lamp with a tasselled shade on a formica side table.

'Now, Miss Fontaine,' Seal said once I returned downstairs, scrutinising me with unnerving intensity through his solitary eyeglass. 'Can you tell me if you have any skeletons in the cupboard?'

'No, Mr Seal, not that I know of.'

'Chances are we know things about you that you don't even know yourself.'

'Goodness,' I replied with a laugh, before realising that the man wasn't simply exchanging pleasantries – he was deadly serious. 'Look, I've nothing to hide, Mr Seal,' I added in a more formal tone. 'My past is an open book.'

'Jolly good,' he replied.

I couldn't help thinking he was an unlikely looking fellow to be training spies, but I soon learnt that The Colonel, as the staff called him, was a formidable operator. I found out later that in the years after World War Two, Lieutenant Colonel Gregory Seal had been responsible for interrogating the most hardened of German secret agents, and he seemed no less focused on his current job of training British ones.

'You need to be taught the basics,' Seal informed me after lunch in Gwynarthen's plain dining room. 'We'll put you through a series of field exercises. If you pass, you'll be sent on the mission. We don't have much time, so I require from you the utmost dedication and concentration. No smoking, no socialising. Here at Gwynarthen we keep ourselves to ourselves. Do you understand, Miss Fontaine?'

'God knows, I don't mind that,' I answered. 'Except the cigarettes, naturally. But as long as Sunstar thinks I'm up to it, I'm all yours, Mr Seal.'

'Jolly good.'

In the days that followed, I found myself immersed in a new and thrilling world. There was something pleasantly outlandish about attending school after all these years, albeit an exceedingly unusual one, where lessons included deciphering secret codes, reading maps, and how to shoot a gun. There was also a colourful new lexicon. 'Flaps and seals', I learned, was the tradecraft used to surreptitiously open and close letters, envelopes, or secure pouches. A 'music box' was a clandestine wireless transmitter. And the shadowy, enigmatic figures who oversaw our activities – whoever and wherever they were – were simply referred to as HQ. Compared to learning film scripts, this real-life espionage dictionary presented a whole new, enjoyable challenge.

To begin with, I was introduced to a woman called Miss Lavender Campbell, a slim, rather coquettish figure with a pronounced Scottish brogue, who smelt incongruously of violets. During the course of the following week, she appeared every morning at breakfast holding an enormous carpet bag containing all the props required for our lessons. Thanks to Lavender, I quickly became familiar with the art of dead drops, live letterboxes, invisible ink, and various inventive methods of concealment.

'As women, we're fortunate enough to have certain advantages,' she confided breathily during our lesson on the subject, as though she might be imparting some juicy nugget of gossip. 'Use them,' she added, proceeding to demonstrate the technical aspects of an array of modified hairbrushes, heels, handbags, make-up, and undergarments.

With Seal, I played countless rounds of Kim's Game, in which I had to memorise all the items he put out within a certain time limit, then recall them in exact order. Gradually the number of objects swelled from fifty to seventy to over one hundred, and my brain felt as if it might explode from the strain. But Seal was relentless. Night after night, after dinner, we engaged in this mental duel, sometimes for hours, until I could recall every single item without hesitation.

Under Seal's guidance, I became an expert in lock-picking, using bobby pins, a piece of cardboard, even paper clips. Meanwhile, the local town became our training ground. Seal taught me to blend into a crowd and drop a shadow, insisting I rehearse the method over and over before practising in the field, which in this case proved to be a question of skulking around the bustling streets in daylight, as inconspicuously as possible – not easy considering I was a Lusenkan woman, and a famous one at that. But Seal encouraged me to suspend my disbelief and focus on the task at hand.

'The main thing is, you'll know the ropes for your mission,' he told me.

'You know where I'm going, then?'

'Not the details, that's classified. Main point is, being able to sense that something's up, and that you're being watched. There's no room for mistakes, Miss Fontaine, none at all. Let's go through it again.'

Out on the open moor, a burly army man named Will Crisp – 'call me Crispy,' he grunted on the morning of our lesson, puffing on his cigarette – taught me how to handle a beaten-up old MOD Land Rover. He had a strong Northern accent and large oil-stained hands, and together we spent a jolly few hours changing wheels and rattling along the uneven moorland tracks, before he showed me how to hotwire the vehicle's ignition into action.

'Not a trick you want to necessarily put to use, mind you,' he cautioned with a wink, 'but good to know if you lose your keys.'

After that day, Crispy vanished into thin air, just as Lavender eventually did. Such was life at Gwynarthen – people came and went like fleeting shadows, their true identities shrouded in mystery. You could never be sure if the name they'd given you was the real one. Only Seal was a constant, formidable presence, his emerald eye watching and assessing my progress from dawn to dusk.

Several times a day I was called to intelligence briefings. During those hours, Seal and I scrutinised photographs of rooms and corridors and staircases in President Lourenco's palace and grounds. These I memorised before Seal quizzed me on the details. How would you get from the ballroom to the study? How many entrances are there to the garages? What objects are on Lourenco's desk?

Endlessly, I was drilled in the personalities of Lourenco's government and given endless dossiers about British Lusenkan diplomatic relations to learn by heart. These I revised in the evenings before bed, as if I were preparing for an exam, sitting upright against the pillows, repeating details aloud to myself, an anarchic compilation of facts, statistics and names that circled all night in my brain. I was all too aware that, one day, these very facts might save my life.

Every morning, before dawn, I was sent on a speed hike across the moor, armed only with a map and a compass. It was mid-March, a late spring that year. Those mornings I walked through every sort of weather; frost and wind, driving rain and sleety snow, or the occasional spring-like sun. If I made it back in time, there was a mandatory series of pushups, sit ups and skipping exercises to do before breakfast, supervised by another dour-faced instructor in army fatigues whose name I never learnt, and who, if I did well, made me repeat the circuit all over again. After a time, I began to notice new muscles in my arms. My body felt hard and strong, an unfamiliar sensation I found I liked very much.

There were other things too, knots and first aid and making an outdoor camp. How to pluck a pheasant or pigeon and snare a rabbit. Ways to light a fire; signal with smoke; extract water from the ground, and forage for wild plants and berries. It wasn't perfect. We didn't have much time. As Seal explained, I needed to learn what I could in the six weeks we had. Barely an afternoon was spent on microfilm, studying the details of the tiny sub-miniature camera shaped like a cigarette lighter I was to use on my mission. Just a few hours were taken up with hollowing out a variety of household objects – a shaving brush, the sole of a shoe – to fashion receptacles for a piece of microfilm. Another with cleaning, loading, and shooting different pocket pistols, including a close-range single-shot gun intriguingly loaded into a lipstick tube.

'Developed by the Soviets,' imparted Seal with undisguised admiration. 'Damn nifty little thing, if you ask me.'

We spent a morning going through the basics of hand-to-hand combat: how to use my fists, fingers and teeth to defend myself, and how to disarm an adversary, or knock them out using a neck hold. One evening after dinner, I returned to my bedroom to find a shadowy figure lurking in the darkness – an assailant poised to attack. Even though I knew very well that this was another of Seal's famous field exercises, I felt fearful and intimidated. I had no weapons; I was armed with only the skills Seal had taught me. 'Not by strength, by guile,' he liked to say. He meant that ideally my brains, not my fighting skills, would keep me out of trouble.

With calculated movements I advanced towards my would-be assailant and feigned a distraction by glancing sideways as if surprised. Fleetingly, the man's eyes followed mine, affording me a split second to remove the gun from his hand with a deft twist of my wrist.

After a minute or two, Seal arrived with a terse, 'Not bad, Miss Fontaine, not bad at all,' and gave me a nod of approval. I felt jubilant; I'd successfully faced an assailant with nothing but my wits, and won. Seal had taught me well, and Sugar, I'll never forget the lesson: that one's wits are sometimes more effective weapons than any amount of strength.

The days drifted into late March, and spring began to break in earnest. Out on the moor the sun contained a hint of warmth, and birds sang hopefully in the leafless trees. Suddenly, the gorse came into bloom, a riotous yellow that filled me with joy. During those weeks, I felt as if I existed in another world to the one turning outside Gwynarthen. Through my bedroom window I could see daily life playing out in the town below, people shopping and visiting the post office, but I had little in common with them, absorbed as I was in my surreal little world of secrets. Even my past belonged to Seal and his superiors.

One morning, he pulled out a chair across from me at breakfast, and sat down, buttering a slice of toast.

'Your records came back clean, no red flags whatsoever.' He looked at me, monocled eye bulging. 'You've passed the background checks.'

'Thank you,' I said. 'I'm glad to hear it.'

'Very good.' Seal rose from his chair, his expression inscrutable. 'Stay sharp, stay vigilant.'

I nodded, imagining a legion of secretaries in London, faceless civil service ladies in brown tweed sifting through the details of my past, dissecting my loves and tragedies with clinical precision, and filing them away in order. An index card for every triumph, every heartbreak. If *my* past were deemed clean, I shuddered to think what a murky one might entail.

On the last Saturday, I prepared for my final exercise alone in the wilderness. Seal talked me through the course, which involved a night on the moor, he explained, before a demanding two-mile stretch of tunnels, pools, streams, bogs, and woods to navigate, followed by a final four-mile trek back to Gwynarthen on a time limit.

'This is one of your final tests, Miss Fontaine. Remember, survival is above all a mental exercise, a basic instinct to live. If your mind is strong, your body will follow.'

By that time, well into my sixth and final week of training, I felt confident of my abilities, yet at the thought of the dark moor outside, cold and desolate, I felt nervous. A lone woman in the wilderness, for God's sake! How would I measure up?

The night of the exercise, I dressed myself in a black tracksuit, a woollen hat, and plimsolls. When I stood in front of the mirror, I almost cried out in surprise at the sight of my reflection, because in the glass I saw a straight-backed, athletic woman I hardly recognised. Her body was strong and her eyes shone with a steely determination. In that moment, possibly for the first time in my life, I understood all the past challenges I'd faced and overcome. At last, I realised how fiercely I'd fought against everyone's expectations: my mother, who envisioned me only as a wife. The gunmen wanting me dead. The lecherous men in the Port Salé nightclub, and Sidney, who saw me as a conquest. And the male directors who consistently cast me as 'the girl', the dolly bird, the sidekick – but never the heroine.

Now, dammit, I could shoot a gun with deadly accuracy. I could drive like a stuntman. I could pick a lock, read a map as well as a seasoned adventurer, run five miles, and do fifty-five press ups without breaking a sweat. My body was hard and fit and strong. I told myself I should feel nothing but confidence in who I was, and what I could achieve.

Oh, Sugar, I hope you'll hear this and look at yourself too, and recognise the strength in your own heart, your own bravery and courage. If there's one thing I'd like to say to you, it's that we women face so many unspoken barriers in life. The going is tougher for us than for men, and the climb steeper. Sometimes the biggest barrier we face is in our own heads. The more we fall, the more we must rise up.

Believe in yourself, my darling Sugar, and the mountain will not loom so large.

CHAPTER TWENTY-THREE

Dolly

The tape ended just as Dolly pulled into the grassy driveway of Genévrier. She killed the engine and sat in the car for a few minutes, reflecting on her mother's words, *believe in yourself,* only to realise with a touch of dismay that, once again, she was out of tapes.

'Damn,' she murmured under her breath, letting her eyes drift from the house across the garden where the evening sun cast elongated shadows across the lawn. So where *were* the rest of the tapes hidden? Perhaps in the depths of Gloria's chaotic attic, or perhaps in the hands of another stranger – who knew. It was so typical of Gloria never to make it easy. Secrets seemed to trail in her wake like a clattering trail of tin cans attached to a honeymoon car.

Dolly sighed, feeling a gnawing tension in her stomach at the idea of Gloria's lost story, at what seemed now, after just a fortnight, her own responsibility to unravel its secrets. But where could the other tapes be, and how should she handle all this new information she had gathered? Sunstar's suggestion of a journey to Lusenka seemed impossible. Was it really feasible, as the former spy had suggested, that she should actually go to her mother's homeland and get to the bottom of things? Jesus!

She opened the car door and swung out her legs. By now, it was five o'clock. Her phone buzzed with a text from Morgan. *Sorry babes, turns out I've got a hospital appointment tomorrow am – can you shoot alone this time? Pev might go, you could meet him.*

Dolly texted back, *sure, hope it goes well! x* – though Morgan's sudden cancellation struck her as odd. Perhaps her old school mate was cooling off their new-found friendship. Or was her horrible husband Pev at the bottom of her no-show? Dolly wouldn't put it past him to stop Morgan coming, especially after their puzzling encounter at the service station.

For a brief moment Dolly closed her eyes, allowing her self-doubt to pass. She *would* find answers, no matter what it took, though the thought of going to Lusenka alone filled her with consternation. She caught herself up. For fuck's sake. Look at what Gloria had accomplished. Of course she had the guts to do this. The answers had to be somewhere – and if that place was Lusenka, then there, it seemed, she would have to go...

The following afternoon, on the way back from the supermarket, Dolly parked along the river in Truro and walked over to the *Cornish Guardian* building that sat squarely on the riverbank. Because she'd called ahead, the editor himself was waiting for her in the reception area, a burly, rosy-cheeked man who looked like he might play rugby in his spare time, with a bushy dark-brown beard, and kind eyes behind gold-rimmed glasses.

He greeted her with a warm smile, 'Peter Lowen – Editor in Chief,' and motioned her to sit in one of the leather armchairs in the waiting area.

'After you telephoned, I took the liberty of having a look in the archive for you,' he said as he sat down in the other chair and handed her a folder. 'It seems no one realised, at the time, that we had a film star living in our midst. I'm sure everyone would have been thrilled.'

'Thank you for making such an effort,' said Dolly. 'Did you find anything interesting?'

The editor nodded and gestured towards the folder in her hands.

'A few bits here and there, collected by fans of your mother over the years, I should think. Feel free to have a read through. If you'd like to take them away, we've created a borrower card for you.' With a flourish he waved a small plastic card in the air. 'Like gold dust, these things are. With this little beauty, you can sign the folder out for three weeks.'

Dolly laughed and thanked him. As she shook hands to go, the editor plucked a business card from the top pocket of his jacket.

'I'm told you're a bit of a superstar yourself,' he said, with a twinkly look. 'We always need good journalists, you know.'

'I'm sorry,' Dolly said, rather startled. 'You must have heard wrong; I lost my job.'

The editor took off his glasses and wavied them in his right hand, rubbing a hand across his eyes. 'From what I hear, there are two sides to that story.' He put his glasses back on, pushing the card into her hand. 'If you can stand our little backwater after the bright lights of London, perhaps you'd like to write us a piece about your mother. Why don't you email me?'

Dolly grinned. 'I'd love to. I'll be in touch.'

She left the office feeling slightly giddy as she tucked the little card into her purse, and floated along the cobblestones back to the car, humming under her breath. She couldn't believe this editor was actually willing to take her seriously. In truth, it had never crossed her mind before that she could work in Cornwall as a journalist, and now it seemed possible at least. She'd be near her family, her nieces. But as she got in the car and drove away, doubts crept in, nagging fears rearing in the background, reminding her of the London scandal and her failures, dauntingly huge. She pushed the thoughts aside, resolving to focus on the mystery of her mother's tapes for now, and drove on through the late afternoon traffic.

Later, in the early evening. Dolly spread the newspaper clippings about Gloria on the table and sat down to read them. They were from *Vogue* and *Company Magazine* and *The Independent*. *A Spy's Secret Weapon*, read the headline of one. Another: *Unstoppable, Unshakeable, Unbelievable. Gentlemen prefer… Gloria. Meet The Rising Star of 1975!* The first, written by someone called Prue Carmichael, began:

> *Gloria Fontaine welcomes me to her Notting Hill flat with the offer of a gin and tonic, and a dazzling smile. It's 11 o'clock in the morning, but I gladly accept, partly because I don't want to appear un-hip in the eyes of this glamorous girl who, this flaming June day, sports a beautiful emerald- green Biba day dress that reminds me of the sort of thing that Cleopatra might wear, teamed with a silk turban and kitten heels.*

Somewhere towards the middle, Dolly found herself chuckling at the journalist's description, so seventies, and then her mother's words:

> *Fontaine is one of those sexy, liberated, slightly impudent women whom men are generally rather scared of these days. She's not coy about being sexy – she's got it, and she flaunts it.*
>
> *"I'm proud to be a woman," Fontaine says. "Being womanly, gutsy, it's fun, and to any man who thinks a woman can't have brains and beauty, I say, what utter rubbish! And to women, I say, we'll be free the moment we stop caring what men think of us."*

Near the end of the article, Gloria talked about motherhood.

> *"I am the most unlikely of single mothers," says Fontaine, "but I have given everything up for my children."*

Dolly heard the crunch of a car pulling into the drive. She got up to find Rich at the front door holding his car keys in one hand, smiling sheepishly.

'Gracie sent me to check you're okay. Sorry I was a bit off the other day.'

Dolly grinned. Good old Gracie, always the peacemaker. 'She sent you to apologise you mean?' she said, jokingly. 'Course I'm okay. Do you fancy a drink this time?' She mimicked their mother's voice: 'Time for an aperitif!'

Rich laughed. 'Just the one then. I'm driving.' He ducked his head to come through the low threshold. 'You know Mum taught me how to make a gin fizz, when I was fourteen?'

'I remember. She used to let me taste them. Jesus, I was only about ten.'

Rich snorted. 'Man, she was a nut head sometimes.' He leant against the counter. 'I wish you two could've got along better. Things were easier between us, I'm not sure why. She opened up to me more.'

Dolly shrugged. 'Mothers and daughters, I guess.'

'Yeah.'

Dolly mixed the gin with the tonic water, the bubbles fizz-popping like tiny fireworks against the ice. She handed one to Rich and clinked her own glass against his.

'To Mum,' she said.

Rich smiled, a big, warm smile that lit his face, reminding Dolly of when they were children.

'To Mum,' he echoed, taking a large gulp of his drink, and Dolly felt glad, glad that the tensions of the other day seemed to be forgotten, glad to have her brother back, though she wouldn't – couldn't – mention Sunstar, or what she'd discovered about Peverell Greyson. Not yet. She missed her brother. She didn't want another argument.

Rich tapped a rhythm on the edge of the glass. 'Gracie's got this crazy idea that we should watch one of Mum's films,' he said. 'Bonding, she calls it.'

Dolly raised her eyebrows momentarily. 'Do we *have* Mum's films?'

'In the TV cabinet, apparently. All the Mirrorballs are there, and some others.'

Dolly took a sip of the gin. 'Sure, why not.' The alcohol was going to her head. Suddenly she wanted to get drunk, really drunk, and hang out with her brother, and talk about old times, and forget about all her problems.

She topped up her glass from the bottle of gin as Rich drained his drink, pouring another, and strolled into the living room.

'We can order pizza,' he called out cheerfully. 'I'll kip in my old room.'

Dolly couldn't remember when she'd last watched one of Gloria's films, or any film, for that matter. She'd forgotten how cool they were. The familiar theme tune played and their mother's name, GLORIA FONTAINE, appeared in the opening credits in big retro letters. Cheering, Dolly and her brother sang along, full of laughter and alcohol. They whooped as their mother, half-dressed in a yellow bikini, athletically kick-boxed an evil villain named Maximilian Storm, only to set off smoke signals to guide a helicopter into land. They roared and clinked glasses as Gloria screeched through a neon-lit shopping mall in a bright red Mercury Cougar, swerving from side to side with a police car in hot pursuit. And when Gloria, in a second, even skimpier bikini, was balanced precariously on the side of a boat zooming across a stretch of turquoise sea, firing a gun, Dolly couldn't help dancing around the room, drunk and giggling, pointing an imaginary gun and purring her mother's famous line: 'I can take care of myself just fine.'

'You know Mum used to style her own outfits,' she remarked at one point, while Rich poured more drinks.

'Nope,' he said, dubiously.

'This is from *Vogue*, 1978.' From the table, Dolly picked up the article from earlier and cleared her throat: 'We sit on the settee in the lounge,"' she read out, doing her best husky newsreader voice, '"where Fontaine charmingly calls me 'darling' and smokes Pale Virginias, talking with that famously hypnotic voice, rather soothing and sexy, somewhere between a cat's purr and a Roll's Royce engine.'

'Whatever,' Rich snorted, but he was grinning. If she wasn't mistaken, his eyes were glistening.

Three Mirrorball films and three quarters of a bottle of gin later, Rich had fallen asleep with his head on the arm of the settee and was snoring gently. He looked like he used to as a small boy, drifting off during a bedtime story. She went to get a blanket and gently placed it over him, adjusting his head so he was in the recovery position.

'I'm not that drunk,' he slurred, groggily, opening an eye.

'Of course you're not.' Dolly giggled and patted his head. 'Night, night.'

'Night, Sis.' He reached up a hand to high five her and missed. 'Love you.'

'Love you too, Richie.'

Dolly woke with a start the next morning, in an extremely hungover state, to find sunlight pouring through the bedroom window. Downstairs, Rich had left a note and a box of maxi-strength paracetamol on the table downstairs: 'Great to see you, Sis x'.

Dolly smiled, groaned, downed two tablets with some water and considered having a cigarette, only to decide against it. Watching her mother on screen the night before had stirred a physical ache and a new determination. They had lost Gloria too early; life was too short to waste on bad habits. She promised herself she would quit for good this time.

Without stopping to have breakfast, she showered quickly, grabbed a cereal bar, and drove over to Godrevy just in time for half past ten. On her arrival, a burly instructor emerged from a low prefab building, a pair of ear defenders dangling from one hand, and signed her in, jotting her name in a book.

'Fontaine,' he said musingly. 'I think I know your brother, nice bloke.'

'Cool,' replied Dolly, mulling the fact that a day ago she would have said her brother's niceness was rather dubious – even though last night's 'bonding session' had been good, great even. Also, it made a change to be recognised for something other than her work scandal, for once.

Behind the office, a line of open wooden booths on an area of rough heathland were set out for clay pigeon shooting. A man with his back to them was calling 'pull!' in a loud voice, firing at a series of clays emerging steadily from a machine on the heath.

Dolly narrowed her eyes, trying to see the man's face, but it wasn't Peverell Greyson. He was too short, too fat. With each shot the man's shoulder jolted back with the pressure of the gun. The small clay discs haloed across the sky, bursting at intervals into clouds of dust. Otherwise, the booths were empty.

'Rain's coming in,' the instructor remarked in a pleasant Scottish accent, glancing at the sky as he led her into a booth. Dolly followed his gaze to the dark clouds clustering on the horizon, rolling in across the sea. The booth was narrow, close, and dark, with smells of gun oil and metal. The instructor handed her the ear defenders and demonstrated the mechanics of the shotgun with gentle movements of his big hands.

'What about the kick?' Dolly asked. 'Will it hurt?'

'Aye, you'll get used to it.' He placed the shotgun in her arms. 'Women are often better shots than men. Less testosterone, more precision.' He grinned. 'Less to prove, you might say.'

He leaned in across her shoulder, adjusting the gun, and she could smell the earthy scent of tobacco on his jumper and breath. Out of the blue, she felt flustered. 'It's okay,' she said. 'I mean, I'll work it out.'

The instructor stepped away. 'I'm sure you will.' He wandered off, pausing to pick up a piece of litter.

Dolly willed herself to concentrate as a fluorescent clay came winging across the sky. She took the shot. A bullet zinged out; the gun rebounded into her shoulder. A miss. Undeterred, she called and fired over and over as if nothing else mattered, just the gun and the inverted saucer of the target, that finest hair breadth between hitting and missing. She liked the meditative precision of the build-up, the gentle arc of the gun as she aimed, the focus required to hit the clay disc. What did it take to achieve complete accuracy, she wondered? Hand eye coordination, and a complete stillness of the mind, perhaps. Eventually, she hit a clay, and it came shattering out of the sky in a burst of limestone.

In the next booth, a group of men were chatting noisily, their well-spoken voices interspersed with bursts of laughter. They talked in the loose, insinuating way of some men when women were not around. Without meaning to, Dolly found herself picking up the drifting current of their conversation. Gently, she removed her ear defenders and listened.

'That's obvious isn't it,' one said. 'We all know what Pevvers gets up to out there.'

Pevvers? Could they mean Peverell Greyson, she wondered. They sounded like the same sort of types: posh, rich, annoying. Perhaps they were his mates. Perhaps Morgan had given one of them her ticket.

'I heard the women are stunning. Lucky bugger.'

Another of the men whistled under his breath. 'And cheap. Mate, it's a fucking paradise.'

'Is it just Lusenka he's in, or other countries?' one of the men asked.

Lusenka? Her ears pricked. She made a pretence of reloading the gun and edged closer, tuning in.

'Just Lusenka, I think. Though he wants to expand, says he's onto good shit.'

'What's the craic over there?' said another of the men, with a hint of an Irish accent. 'He must be making a killing?'

'Got it sewn up, mate.' It was the main orator of the group. 'Finger in all the fuckin' pies.'

'Literally.'

The men dispersed, laughing, and chatting. Dolly glanced sideways at the group straggling inside the main building, discussing where to find a coffee, something about the Seahorse Café in Godrevy. Moments later, she saw Peverell Greyson come out of the loo and go to join them.

She put her ear defenders back on, recalling the time, one hot summer when she was eight or nine, when she had found a tiny seahorse on the wet sand at Godrevy. Even now, she could recall the creature's jewel-bright, prism scales, glittering in the sun like a decorative brooch on a grandmother's cardigan, or the sort of gimmicky toy found in a Christmas cracker. She remembered dropping the seahorse back into the foaming waves, where it came to life and submerged like an anchor beneath the foam.

That same day, a good day, Gloria had taken them up to the café – the same café the men were talking about. There, Dolly had sat swinging her legs at a table, drawing the seahorse with her felt tip pens – flamingo pink, sapphire blue, a sparkling malachite which seemed to suit the creature of her memory. Afterwards they drank Coca Cola from cans while Gloria, in a clingy, red, halter neck bikini, swigged water from a bottle, ignoring the mesmerised waiter and curious diners who craned their necks to look. *Gloria Fontaine,* you could see them thinking excitedly, the wives glaring warningly at their men. *Is it really her*? But Gloria was oblivious. She carried on drinking and eating, as radiant as the seahorse. What had that man said in his eulogy at the funeral, someone Dolly didn't recognise? *Gloria Fontaine was the most sensational woman I've ever met.*

'You need to line it up better,' said a voice.

Dolly jumped. A man was craning around the wooden partition. At the sight of Peverell Greyson, Dolly's mouth went dry. Another man lurked behind him, the first man from earlier.

'Do you want me to show you?' Peverell stepped across the divide and Dolly lifted one ear defender up, feeling irritated.

'No thanks, I'm fine.'

The paracetamol was wearing off. A burgeoning headache nagged behind her right eye.

'Fancy seeing you here,' said Peverell.

'Weird, huh.'

He wore shooting plus-fours with a mustard-coloured shirt, a rifle pointing upwards over one shoulder. In one hand, he held a magazine of bullets. The other man stepped into the booth and extended a hand, running his gaze over Dolly's breasts with a blatant, leering stare, and she felt suddenly afraid, an instinctive urge to cover herself, as if he could see through her clothes. She stepped back slightly as he spoke.

'I've seen you around.' A London accent, a trace of estuary. 'I'm Will Brown – Browny, to my mates.' The man was short and overweight, his flushed cheeks accentuated by a pink crew neck with a crocodile logo.

'Oh, right, hi.'

With reluctance Dolly returned the handshake, feeling the unwelcome touch of Will Brown's cold, clammy hand lingering too long on her own. She wrenched her hand away. Undeterred, the man cocked his head, scrutinising her, and she could sense his interest – something in his pale watery eyes indicating, what? Suspicion, or just lust?

'In fact,' he said, 'we got the distinct impression you were eavesdropping just then?'

She stepped back, balancing the gun in her arms. 'Not at all.'

'Word is,' added Pev, his tone steady, 'you've been nosing about, acting the journo?'

'That's all in the past. I'm just a civvy now.'

He raised an eyebrow, and an unsettling silence hung in the air between the three of them.

'Well, I wouldn't get too curious, Fontaine.' Peverell leaned in, so close Dolly could hear him breathing. 'You understand what I'm saying?' he added, giving a smile that didn't reach his eyes.

'No idea,' she said in a steady voice, her face blank. 'Whatsoever.'

Slowly, carefully, Peverell loaded the magazine into the rifle and raised it to his shoulder. He pulled the bolt back, pointed the barrel into the distance, and made a little explosion sound under his breath.

'Be careful, Fontaine,' he whispered. Then he smiled coldly, handed the gun to Will Brown, and walked off, leaving his henchman staring at her with a gormless expression.

'Hey,' Dolly called after Peverell. 'What the—'

The instructor came up quickly, placing himself squarely in the entrance of the booth, staring in with a stern expression.

'Everything alright over here?' he said, and despite herself, Dolly felt relieved. She shifted back towards her own gun.

'Not harassing this lady, are we?' added the instructor, holding Will Brown's gaze until he stepped away with a grunt, and skulked back into the other booth. 'Everything's fine, mate, just fine.'

From the other booth, Dolly heard Will Brown muttering obscenities under his breath. The instructor's face darkened slightly, but he didn't say anything. Instead, he circumvented the dividing wall and said firmly, 'Pal, you're out of time.'

Dolly watched him escort Will Brown out of the booth and swiftly untucking the gun from the other man's hands. 'Can you hand in your ear defenders, please, then sign out at the desk?' The instructor bowed slightly in the man's direction. 'After you,' he added, sweeping his arm towards the main exit. 'Cheers, Pal.'

Will Brown inclined his head as he passed. 'Good day, Dolly Fontaine.'

She gave a tight-lipped nod as, together, she and the instructor watched Will Brown slope towards the exit.

'Thanks,' she said to the instructor when Brown had gone.

'No bother. You alright?'

'I'm not going to let people like that intimidate me.'

The instructor took a tin out of his pocket and began rolling a cigarette. 'You seem like the kind of woman who can more than take care of herself.'

Outside, the sky had gone dark. It was about to rain. 'It's none of my business,' he remarked. 'But from what I've heard, Greyson and his mates are dodgy as fuck.' His eyes met hers. 'If I were you, I wouldn't get mixed up.'

Dolly paid the bill and left, bumping down the stony track, cursing the Morris Thousand's ancient suspension. She had a thumping headache. A short way along, the steering wheel went slack, and she swerved and stopped: a flat tyre.

She swore, switched off the engine, and reached for her bottle of water, swigging it down with a couple more headache tablets. In the boot of the car, she rummaged for the jack, then lifted out the spare tyre and threw it onto a sandbank next to the car, where it spun and came to rest. Splotches of rain landed on her face and shoulders, light at first, then heavier. She knelt down to position the jack on the metal plate of the tyre, winding the handle. As she was about to remove the wheel bolts, she heard an engine then a shout; it was the instructor emerging from an ancient-looking Land Rover.

'You okay?' he called from a distance.

'Just a flat tyre,' she called back. 'I can handle it.'

But he was striding down the track, zipping his jacket against the rain, apparently determined to play the hero. He came up, out of breath. 'Let me give you a hand,' he panted. 'You're getting soaked.'

'I'm perfectly capable,' she said primly, 'of changing a tyre.'

She did not want to socialise with strangers, however good-looking, let alone let them save her, but it seemed the instructor was unwilling to take no for an answer. He knelt down on the rough sand and handed her a big bunch of keys.

'I've no doubt you are. I love these old girls; I learnt to drive in a Moggie. I'm a veteran of the double de-clutch. Look, I'll sort this out. There's a coat in my office. The key is the green one.'

She raised an eyebrow, feeling a spasm of irritation – another man taking over – but he didn't seem to take the hint.

'You'll catch a chill,' he insisted.

'You sound like my mother.'

'If you want to put the kettle on, feel free…'

'Okay, okay.' For some reason, she found herself relenting. 'Milk, sugar?'

'Julie Andrews, please.'

Again, she raised an eyebrow.

'White nun…' He sat back on his heels. 'Julie Andrews was a nun in *The Sound of*—'

'I see.' She fought the urge to laugh. 'Alright, then…'

She strolled the short distance back up to the centre and unlocked the door to the office, which was basic and neat with a desk and two chairs, a quantity of adventure equipment ordered neatly around the edges. Some men's coats hung from a wall hook. In the sink were well-washed mugs decorated with Scottish thistles, and a clean Scottish flag tea towel was folded neatly on the kitchen worktop.

Pocketing the keys, Dolly filled the kettle at the tap. While it came to the boil, she wandered the office aimlessly, peering up at the walls decorated with the instructor's professional certificates for firearms and first aid, others showing he was qualified to instruct surfing, climbing, and other outdoor pursuits. She paused to examine a small statuette on the desk, a pair of boots cast in bronze, with a dagger and beret mounted on a wooden base. On the far wall was a large map in a wooden frame, and she inspected its lines marking towns, forests and the ocean, its other marks and gradations in different colours and codes whose meaning was unclear. With a start, she noticed the engraving on the frame: *Lusenka, 2005, 42 Commando*. On a second look she recognised some of the names on the map: Port Salé, Cap Bleu, Maguru.

Her heart sank.

Outside, the weather was worse than ever, the wind squalling in wild gusts from a dull, grey sea. She set her body against the driving rain as her borrowed waterproof flapped around her. The instructor was kneeling by the wheel, his wet hair plastered against his head. He screwed in the last of the wheel bolts and jacked down the car, squinting up with a smile. Raindrops ran in rivulets down his face. Dolly noticed his eyes, deep green against the steel colour of the landscape.

'Done,' he said. 'Come on, let's get out of the rain.'

'Look, thanks, but I better not,' Dolly said. She felt uneasy. The map couldn't be a coincidence, could it? But she was wet, and cold. She found herself following the instructor up to the office, despite her suspicions. Inside, she clasped her hands around a mug of tea, shivering, as he switched on a heater and sat down, fashioning a rollie with big fingers. But when he offered her one, she shook her head. They sat in parallel at either side of the desk, looking out at the torrent of drops smashing against the windows.

'Good wet,' he said.

'Sorry?'

'More Marines' slang.' He grinned. 'It means brew, cuppa, tea... I'm Evan, by the way, but everyone calls me Cakey.'

'I much prefer Evan.' She returned a small smile, deciding not to enquire about the nickname because from what her brother had told her, male nicknames had their own infuriating logic. 'I take it from the tea towel that you're Scottish?'

'Through and through.'

She took a sip of the tea, said casually, after a second or two, 'That map up there – have you been to Lusenka?'

'I served there in 2005, when Kilomi was running for another term. One of the toughest wee tours I've done.'

'You said you were in the Marines?'

'Platoon Weapons Instructor for twenty-two years.'

'You must have seen some terrible things.'

'No more terrible than Iraq, or Afghan, but yes, I must admit, Lusenka left its mark on me. Some places do that.' He went over to the map, pointing at the arrows and lines. 'These are our operational marks. It was a dangerous mission. Didn't think I'd get out of there alive.'

'My mother was Lusenkan,' Dolly said after a minute, watching for his reaction. 'I've never been there though.' She paused, with a quizzical expression. 'Anyway, it's a coincidence.'

'Or fate.' The instructor winked across the top of his cup. 'Messed up place, if you don't mind me saying.'

'Sure.' She shrugged. 'Sometimes messed up is interesting though, don't you think?'

He gave a low chuckle. 'Exactly.'

By the time they finished the tea, the rain was subsiding. She handed the empty mug over and made her way to the door, but as she went to walk away down the track, the instructor caught up.

'Hey, where can I find you again?'

'Do you *want* to find me?'

The instructor grinned, locking Dolly's eyes. 'I don't change tyres for just anyone, you know.'

She observed him standing there, shoulders square against the rain-washed beach, and told herself she must be careful. He seemed a nice bloke, certainly, but all too easily in the past, she'd fallen for such charms, such gallantry and heroism, and she would not willingly do so again. That he'd been to Lusenka raised red flags in her mind, too, and a gut instinct warned her to be cautious. It seemed too convenient, too coincidental. Something was off, and she couldn't shake a feeling of unease.

'Well, I'm only down the road,' she said firmly after a moment, shooting him a nonchalant smile, and getting into the car. 'I'm sure with all your commando training you can locate me, if you really want to.'

Driving away, she pressed the button of the car tape machine, just to check. To her surprise, Gloria's voice immediately filled the car, continuing the instalment where it had left off the day before. The tape had paused, not ended. Dolly whooped, turned out onto the main road, and began to listen.

CHAPTER TWENTY-FOUR

Gloria

I was dropped on the moor at midnight. The night was clear, the moon a waning silver crescent in a sky wild with stars. Even so, it was too dark to read my map, too difficult to move anywhere now in the dead of night. I'd stop and rest, I decided, and resume my trek at dawn. The deep silence was broken only by the wind howling across the tors. I'd never felt so perfectly alone in my entire life.

I ducked down behind the bank of a hill, out of the wind, wrapped my coat around me and lay back against my rucksack, listening to a cacophony of rustlings and stirrings in the undergrowth. Small animals perhaps, and birds I recognised from my survival training; an owl hooting, the rising pitch of a nightjar, the curious drumming of a snipe in flight. I understood suddenly that Seal was testing my reaction to this consummate dark, this bitter cold and isolation, away from other humans in an unfamiliar wilderness. Out here, I was no better than any other wild animal roaming the land, a fox or a boar, driven by sheer primal instinct to find the necessities for life, to stay warm and fed and alive. So, like an animal, I'd survive.

In the wake of this thought came a flood of memories, of Lusenka, of Chilembé and my childhood, of fleeing from the militia that terrible day when our parents were killed. Running for our lives, we had waded through swamps and cut our way through the dense forest. In the heavy heat, we slept on the hard ground, surrounded by wild creatures and insects. And now, here I was on a heathery moor in England in springtime – positively benign in comparison – preparing to embark on a mission to seek justice for my parents, for Chilembé, for all those who'd suffered at the hands of President Baptiste Lourenco.

As I lay hidden there, waiting for the sun to break, I thought of Sunstar orchestrating my journey into this shady undercover world, and how he must have recognised something in me – a fire burning, I suppose. A single-minded resolve to make things right, no matter the cost, for the sake of Chilembé. I wondered if my brother would have wanted this life for me and I knew for certain that he wouldn't: he would have only wanted me safe. But perhaps if I'd stayed with him all those years ago, our lives would have turned out differently. I recalled Sunstar's words when we first met: *He was a good agent, one of my best, and he knew of my plans to meet with you, too.* So it seemed that in the end, my brother had given his blessing for my recruitment. Sunstar was right – this was not just my chance at retribution, but at redemption, too. If Chilembé were here, he would have reminded me that things could always be worse, and that we were the lucky ones, Sis...

Dawn came, heralded by a chorus of birds, a skylark, stonechats, a pheasant. I delved in my rucksack for breakfast, a foil-wrapped Cornish pasty, and sat eating and watching the sky turn purple and pink, streaked with glorious burnt orange as the sun came up. Soon, I checked my watch, calculating the time I had to make it back to Gwynarthen – exactly two hours – and climbed the summit of the hill. There I pulled out my map and looked around, getting my bearings and feeling a sudden sense of exhilaration. Here I was, with the wind and the sun against my skin, surveying the wild moor, released from all the usual boundaries of civilisation, free of people and rules and the strictures of daily life. Here I was, waking with the sun, adapting to the elements, perfectly safe. There were no militia here, no crowds or eager audiences, no reporters hunting me with their cameras and their microphones. Here, I had only to exist.

Over the next half hour, I located the landmarks I needed – a set of twin tors in the distance, a bridge, an unusual boulder formation

– and triangulated my way across the course that zigzagged down a narrow path towards the tors. From there, I hiked the rest of the way beneath a light spring sun, eating the remainder of my pasty as I walked, appreciating the taste – heightened after the long night in the cold – and the sight of the hawthorns' early blossom, and the wild drifts of daffodils and primroses peppering the moorland paths. I finally arrived back at Gwynarthen for elevenses, just as it began to rain, exhausted and sore, but mildly euphoric. I knew Chilembé would have been proud of me, and I smiled to myself, because I could almost picture him cheering me on. *Right on, Sis!*

When I opened the heavy front door, Sunstar was standing in the hallway, the first time I'd seen him for a while. He had a small smile on his face as he gestured me into the hallway.

'Well, well, Miss Fontaine, you've more than made the deadline.'

'Thank you,' I replied.

He seemed pleased, to see me, or by my performance, I wasn't quite sure, though I knew which I was secretly hoping for. We shook hands and I went to my room to change, only to find him a little while later downstairs in the dining room. I sat down, and he called for the kitchen staff to bring us the lunch.

'Does this mean I've passed?' I asked once we'd eaten heartily, and the plates had been cleared away.

'With flying colours, I'm told. Gregory Seal speaks very highly of you – says you have pluck, which is the highest of compliments coming from him, I can assure you.'

Sunstar ordered a whisky and offered me a cigarette, which I declined, wanting to prolong the sense of physical wellbeing I felt after my time outdoors. He seemed impressed, and stashed the box in his jacket pocket with a raised eyebrow and a flicker of approval in his eyes – or was it affection? I thought how different he seemed now compared to that first time I met him, the shadowy stranger in the back row of the theatre. Still shadowy, but no stranger.

'What happens now?' I asked after we'd talked some more.

'Well now, let's see. Tomorrow morning you'll get up, eat your breakfast, and without telling anyone, take the car that will arrive here to the airport.'

'And then?'

'And then I fear we're all very much in your hands, Miss Fontaine.'

Sunstar listed the details for the airport and the flight, instructing me to memorise them. I would be met in Port Salé, he informed me, where a junior diplomat at the British High Commission would be my primary contact.

'Remember there *is* a British High Commission in Port Salé. If for any reason you need a place to bunker down, head there.'

'Will I see you again?'

Sunstar furrowed his brows and extinguished his cigarette in the ashtray, circumventing my question, as usual.

'I wish you luck, Gloria. And remember one thing. The principles of fair play, of honesty, which you have in abundance, must be put away when you do this job. Use everything you've learned here to avoid capture. There's nothing more important.'

With that he clasped my hand again, lingering there for a split second – a mere fraction of a moment – so that we stood facing each other with our hands interlocked. I could feel the warmth of his dry palm pressed against mine. Once again, his glance flared with an unmistakable tenderness.

'Don't get caught, Gloria,' he murmured, his eyes on mine. 'For God's sake, don't get caught.'

With a barely perceptible squeeze, he released my hand and wordlessly turned to go. Minutes later, I stood by the window of the dining room, watching through the rain-washed glass as he disappeared into the back seat of a mustard yellow Ford Grenada waiting outside. All at once, in his customary way, Sunstar was gone. I was on my own.

CHAPTER TWENTY-FIVE

Dolly

Some time in the afternoon, Dolly found Gracie at the beach house, cooking at the stove in the kitchen, dicing pepper, courgette, and aubergine, singing along to Erykah Badu.

'Yo,' called Dolly, wandering in, pinching a piece of pepper from the chopping board. She sat down at the table, crunching it slowly.

'Hey, sweetheart.' Gracie looked up, flashing a grin. 'Heard you and Rich had a good time the other night. He's only just recovered from the hangover.'

'It was a blast.' Dolly flicked the kettle on, fetched two mugs from the cupboard. 'Tea?'

'Thanks, love.'

Dolly prised the top from a metal tin, chose a tea bag called 'Womankind' flavoured with rose and camomile, and watched the boiling water turn the liquid a healthy-looking green colour. She glanced over to where her sister-in-law was adding sliced onions to a cast iron cooking pot with a loud sizzling sound. The vegetables sent up a delicious, drifting smell. In her own mug, Dolly brewed a cup of Yorkshire, golden-coloured, bitter and strong; hearty builders' tea.

'Gracie,' she asked as casually as she could, 'did you ever work on Lusenka when you were at Human Rights Watch?'

'Ye-es, a little.' Gracie gave her a swift look as she poured a tin of tomatoes into the frying pan. She reached and turned down the music. 'Why do you ask?'

'I thought I might write something new, as I haven't got anything else to do.'

'Sounds like a good idea.'

'I know Human Rights Watch does annual country reports, and I thought there might be something...'

Gracie frowned, opening a cupboard for a pot of spice. 'On Lusenka?' She sprinkled cumin into the pan and glanced up with a questioning expression. 'Is that a good idea?'

'I've got to do *something* down here.'

'I thought you were lying low. Not stirring the pot etcetera.'

The girls came in chattering, only to wander out again. Gracie was too clever to fob off with a story, Dolly thought. Better to come clean, at risk of causing more trouble with Rich. 'Okay,' she said. 'So apparently Pev Greyson does some work in Lusenka. With the government. I thought I'd—'

'Do some research? I'd expect nothing less, love.' Gracie stirred the pot with a wooden spoon. 'But, for God's sake, don't tell Rich. He's very touchy about all this at the moment. He and Pev, well...' She stopped stirring and crossed her fingers, holding them up. 'They're like that. Ugh, I don't like the guy at all, to be honest. All money, no class if you ask me, and I don't trust him.'

Dolly raised an eyebrow. Why did women always get the measure of people better than men? A woman's intuition, they called it. Over the years, she'd learned to trust this flaring gut instinct, a night beacon in the depths of her subconscious, though, she realised now with a flush of embarrassment, not with Shaun Kingsley – about Shaun she was totally and utterly wrong.

'Why don't you trust him?' she asked.

'Pev's a smooth talker, he's got the local community eating out of his hand. But look, I really shouldn't talk about it. It's none of my business.'

'Because of Rich?'

Gracie concentrated on the cooking pot. 'I promised him I wouldn't talk about his work with Pev. It's confidential.'

'You don't agree with it?'

Gracie tapped the wooden spoon on the side of the pot and turned, leaving the spoon in the pot. She picked up her mug, cradling her hands around it.

'It really doesn't matter very much if I agree or not. It's still going to happen. He'll be furious if he knows I've discussed it with you.'

'I reckon there's something dodgy about Pev. I wouldn't tell Rich, you know.'

Gracie didn't answer, but as Dolly went to leave the room, her sister-in-law called her back. Reaching for a pen and a piece of paper, she jotted down an email address.

'Try my friend, Anakin. Anakin Awadi. We speak from time to time. He was a programme expert at Human Rights Watch, responsible for Lusenka. Now he lives in Truro and heads up a small INGO with an office in Port Salé. He's a bit intense, but he should be able to help. Just don't breathe a word, okay?'

'I think I might have emailed him once from London,' said Dolly musingly, taking the slip of paper, 'before everything happened.'

'Well, maybe don't mention that, just say you're my sister- in-law.' Gracie replaced the heavy lid on the pan, turned the heat down and shot Dolly an awkward smile. 'He might not want to talk to *the* Dolly Fontaine. I'm just glad you're feeling a bit better, to be honest. That brain of yours is too good to lay to waste in the depths of Cornwall. But for goodness sake don't tell your brother, or I'll be in big trouble.'

From her phone, Dolly sent an email to Gracie's contact:

Dear Anakin, I've been put in touch with you by my sister-in-law, Gracie Fontaine. I wondered if we could meet?

With a feeling she was finally making progress, she watched the email swoosh away into the void of the internet.

After sunset, Dolly strolled past the terrace of the Blue Bar, where a cluster of locals were drinking and talking outside. Their light-hearted banter jarred a little after the conversation with Gracie, and Dolly turned away, feeling unsettled.

'Dolly Fontaine, is that you?' It was Evan the shooting instructor sitting on the wall, pint in hand. Another pint glass stood full, next to him. 'Can I buy you a drink?' Then, with a grin: 'Told you I'd find you.'

He was wearing jeans and a Scottish rugby shirt. Close to, in the luminous evening light, Dolly could discern a small scar on his left cheek.

'It's a lovely night,' he remarked, pulling on a rollie with a smile.

'Sure is, but I'm just off home.'

'Just the one? Go on, live a little…'

She nodded at the pint. 'You're not with someone?'

'No, I'm alone.'

'Okay then. A lime squash please.'

Evan extinguished the rollie and went inside, still holding the cigarette in his fingers. While he was in the bar, Dolly told herself that she should leave, abandon this man's mysterious extra pint on the wall and go home, because she couldn't trust him: she couldn't trust anyone.

Yet despite her better instincts she stayed put until, after a few minutes, the instructor returned bearing a pint glass full of lurid green fizzy pop and a packet of crisps. They shared the crisps, talking about his military tours in Liberia and Lusenka, and twice to Iraq. The extra pint, he told her, was for an old colleague, killed there in 2003; a Marine's tribute to a fallen colleague.

'Married?' Dolly asked, determined not to flirt.

'Married, then divorced.'

He had no children, he explained; had set up the adventure centre after leaving the Marines as a leap of faith to make civvy life more bearable. As the conversation drifted and deepened into other topics, Dolly reluctantly had to admit to herself that he seemed genuine, a good-hearted soul, a man of tolerance and bravery. A man of honour, even. More importantly he was not in the least like Shaun Kingsley or any of her other arrogant ex-boyfriends. How strange that he should turn up here in this Godforsaken place where she didn't intend to stay.

Still, she caught herself. She ought to be careful. She couldn't risk someone else screwing her over, and the map she'd seen in Evan's office worried her. Could he have some connection to Peverell Greyson?

'You have bonnie eyes,' Evan said. 'Your parents must have been beautiful people.'

'My father's a mystery,' she replied truthfully, finding herself

167

sparkling inwardly at the clichéd compliment, unimaginative but welcome. It had been a long time... 'My mother was rather fierce, a force to be reckoned with.'

'I can only imagine.'

'The other day you said that guy at the range is a wrong'un,' she said to change the subject. If nothing else, she wanted to see if Evan was hiding anything. 'What did you mean by that?'

'Peverell Greyson?' Munching a crisp, the instructor thought for a minute. 'I've heard rumours, let's put it that way. There's big money floating around in these parts, and it's not always clean.'

'What do you mean?'

'He was bidding for the lease for my place in Godrevy. When I got it, it put his nose right out of joint.'

'I know Pev a little,' Dolly lied. 'A friend's married to him.'

'Well, he's a tit, if you'll excuse my French.'

'I've been trying to find out more about him.'

'Have you, indeed?'

'I have a feeling he's mixed up in something in Lusenka, and I want to know what it is.'

'Lusenka, eh?'

Evan let out a low whistle and fished a tin of tobacco from his pocket. The tin was decorated with an image of a woman in vintage lingerie and a slogan: *Lucky Lady*. Dolly watched the ex-soldier fashion another rollie and light up, the end glowing in the darkness.

'Look, I've still got some mates in the mob.' He exhaled out of the side of his mouth, sending the smoke twisting upwards in clouds. 'Why don't I make a few phone calls?'

'The mob?'

'It's a slang name for the Navy.'

'Would you do that?'

'Of course.' He exhaled. 'For you, anyway. I'll see what I can dig up.'

'Thanks.'

In the rising darkness, Evan's expression was indiscernible, but Dolly could sense his eyes on her, that soft look men got when they wanted to kiss you. She sighed and glanced away, balling the empty crisp packet with her fingers, pressing it into her empty glass. He might be helping her out, she told herself cynically, but whether he had an agenda or not, remained to be seen.

The earthy smell of the tobacco filled her nostrils, oddly soothing, as Evan took a last drag of his cigarette and extinguished the butt on the stone wall. He stood up, still holding the butt between his fingers.

Any minute now, she thought...

'Have this,' he said, taking off his coat and placing it gently around her shoulders, where it hung, far too big. He grinned. 'It's icers out here.'

CHAPTER TWENTY-SIX

Dolly

The interior of the café in the centre of Truro was warm, too warm, and Dolly pulled off her jumper, fanning her face with her hand, and caught the waitress's eye to request a glass of water. A text arrived on her phone: *I'm really sorry,* it said. *I've just put 2 & 2 together and realised you're THE Dolly Fontaine!! I can't talk to you. It's nothing personal. Say hi to Gracie for me. AA :)*

Dolly downed the rest of her coffee, wondering what to do. When the water came, she took a sip of the cool liquid and typed Anakin Awadi's name into her phone's internet search engine, where his former staff portrait was easy to find: he was forty-something, it seemed, with receding hair and spectacles.

There was no point waiting any longer, Dolly decided. She abandoned the drink and set off around the corner, where she hovered outside the revolving doors of Anakin's office building, pretending to check her phone. Presumably Anakin would take a lunch break. It could only be a matter of time before he came out.

Sure enough, after half an hour, Anakin emerged dressed in jeans and flip flops, a beanie hat pulled low over his forehead. Without his glasses, he looked like an off-duty surfer. He was holding a phone to one ear and didn't look very approachable.

Dolly moved into his eyeline, offering a smile and a wave. 'Anakin, I know you don't want to speak to me, but…'

'Dolly?' Anakin muttered something into the phone and ended the call. 'It is Dolly, isn't it?' he added stiffly. 'Sorry. I can't talk to you.'

'I just want to talk.' She fell into step alongside as he made to walk past. 'It won't go any further. I promise.'

Anakin swore under his breath. 'Look, you need to leave me alone. I'm not allowed to talk to journalists unless authorised, and you – you of all people!'

'I don't understand.'

'I was doing a favour for Gracie, but I didn't realise… You're trouble for me. On so many levels it puts my work at risk.'

'Just a couple of questions.'

'I'm serious.' Anakin turned around with a hostile look. 'Leave me alone.'

But Dolly continued to shadow him from afar along the narrow streets, feeling ridiculous as she slowed her steps, trailing him past the cathedral, down a crowded side street lined with places to eat. From a distance she watched him enter a restaurant and sit down at a table in the dingy section near the back, seemingly immersed in thought. In his hunched shoulders she could sense a tension, as if he were aware he was being followed.

Inside the restaurant, she bought a coffee and sauntered over, reminded of such audacious behaviour from other assignments.

'For fuck's sake.' Anakin muttered under his breath. A bowl of tomato soup steamed in front of him. He stopped eating, looking annoyed. 'I take it you *are* Dolly Fontaine? I thought I said—'

'Look, I'm not technically a journalist anymore. I mean, I'm sacked from Cloud, and banned from Westminster – I mean, literally barred from the door. You'd only be talking to some random loser sister of a friend.'

A smile twitched on Anakin's face. He spooned soup slowly into his mouth, eyes turned away.

'I'm just interested in the humanitarian situation in Lusenka,' Dolly insisted, brazen now. 'I'd be grateful for anything you know, even a small nugget.'

Anakin sighed and glanced around surreptitiously, as though checking to see if the two of them were being observed. 'Honestly, you journalists. You guys would sell your own grandmother for a story.'

'Are you in the market for a grandmother?'

The joke raised a brief snort. Still, he wouldn't meet her eyes.

'It's personal for me,' she added. 'I'm half-Lusenkan. My mother was from there. You're one of the only people who can help.'

Anakin observed her with a curious look, then sighed. 'You better sit down. But I *literally* have five minutes, and we need to be careful.'

'Careful of what?'

'Just careful. Anyway, do you think it's a good idea to investigate the very story you've been sacked for?'

'You have a point, of course.' Dolly paused, wondering whether to tell Anakin about Sunstar, then deciding against an all-out confession. 'You reckon it's all connected, then?' she bluffed.

'Probably,' replied Anakin. She listened in silence as he talked. The situation in Lusenka was deteriorating, he told her – and had been for months. Rebel groups backed by incumbent President Florian Kilomi, were targeting the minority Balaika population, and Kilomi was spending cash on guns. The British Government, ostensibly a Kilomi backer, was scrambling to get its foreign policy in order, and didn't want a scandal, so they were trying to block a Human Rights Watch report about foreign arms supplies to the president's rebel groups.

'The situation's got so hot, they don't want people nosing around,' Anakin continued. 'This report's being shut down, big time.'

'Can I see a copy?'

'Christ, you don't ask a lot, do you...' A small laugh.

'Sorry.'

Dolly smiled apologetically and watched him blow on the soup.

'That memo you uncovered,' Anakin said. 'There's something dodgy going on, and Human Rights Watch is onto it, as were you...'

'Yes, but then I got screwed over.'

With careful movements Dolly folded a napkin into smaller and smaller triangles, remembering the rumours she'd been investigating at work about UK weapons turning up in the hands of Lusenkan rebels. There were so many threads and pieces to this story, seemingly random, yet she couldn't shake the feeling that they all fit together, somehow. Was it possible that Shaun was acting out of cold-blooded

172

malice? If so, why would he do such a thing, and what could that have to do with Peverell Greyson?

'From what I know of the political situation in Lusenka,' she said eventually, 'everything's falling apart.'

Anakin chewed, nodded, then spoke. 'Florian Kilomi announced his bid for a fourth term last year, and Lusenka's security services and members of the secret police carried out executions, rapes, abductions, beatings, and intimidation of suspected political opponents, to quash any opposition.'

'Will anyone ever oust him?'

Anakin shook his head. 'Kilomi changes the constitution each time, to allow himself to win another term. The UN has introduced sanctions, but they're not working. We suspect that militia groups, government-funded, are targeting the Balaika ethnic group because their indigenous lands are rich with oil and diamonds. In the seventies, Lusenka was one of the largest oil suppliers in the world – same old story, a rich country filled with poor people. Now NGOs have had their right to operate suspended by the government. The government, police and intelligence services are operating in a climate of complete impunity.'

'So, who's financing the regime? What about the arms – you said the report reveals who's supplying them?'

Anakin looked around with a cautious look, but the café was busy, loud with the buzz of lunchtime diners. He lowered his voice and leaned in. 'That's the thing. It's pretty interesting.'

'In what way, interesting?'

Anakin looked uncomfortable. 'I can't say much. Honestly, if they found out I'd talked to a journalist...'

'Ex-journalist.'

'Right.' Anakin took a bite of his sandwich. When he'd finished the mouthful, he continued to talk. 'Human Rights Watch has found concrete evidence that the arms being used by rebels are coming from the UK.'

From the café kitchen, a dish clattered to the floor with a crash. There followed a burst of laughter and activity over the chill-out beats of Nitin Sawney drifting from a speaker. *Of course,* thought Dolly, taking this piece of information in. *The missing link.*

'You mean the government militia?' she probed, after a moment.

'Right, or at least the so-called rebel groups it's supporting.' Anakin finished off the soup. 'Someone's brokering the deals over here, someone high up. Westminster's involved. We're in all sorts of hot water about it. We're being told we can't publish anything.'

'Why does that not surprise me? So, it's British companies supplying the arms?'

Anakin nodded slowly. 'Or a single company, a massive contract, worth millions.' He screwed up the brown paper sandwich wrapping, only to slam the makeshift ball emphatically on the table. 'Heads will roll if people find out.'

'Do you have evidence?' asked Dolly.

'Only the report, but if I let that out...' He spread his hands wide, mimicking an explosion. 'Boom.'

Dolly nodded, frowning, assembling the fragments of information. 'If I were cynical, I'd say the powers-that-be are closing ranks, and Shaun Kingsley's trying to distract matters away from the fact that he's a junior minister and would have influence in such matters... And the whole scandal around me was one big smokescreen.'

'Sure.' Anakin pushed his chair back with a screech and rose to his feet, gathering the debris from the table. 'If anyone awarded this contract, it's the MOD. Why do you think I can't talk to you, of all people?' he added. 'Sorry, I've got to go.'

'Is there someone I *can* talk to?' Dolly said, finding herself desperately clutching at straws. 'I'll get the evidence, Anakin. After what's happened to me, I've got nothing to lose, so let me investigate.'

Anakin shook his head with a hunted look. 'I'm sorry.' A long pause while he rummaged in his bag, and put his glasses on, giving him a studious air. 'My NGO does good work in Lusenka, and we could be expelled if we put a foot wrong.'

'There's nothing you can give me?'

'Sorry, you're on your own. Good luck. You'll need it.'

With brisk movements Anakin made for the door. Dolly watched the door swing behind him, feeling deflated. Her phone buzzed, a message from Sunstar's contact, Lionel Abimbola, with an address, but no explanation: *The Oxenham Arms, Meavy,* followed by a postcode, and a time: midday, on the 24th. On a sudden impulse, she hastened outside and caught up with Anakin near the entrance to his workplace.

'Please,' she gasped, out of breath. 'I'm just looking for one lead, anything I can follow up.'

Anakin sighed and stopped walking, raising an eyebrow.

'Please?'

He frowned, rubbing his forehead with a finger. He looked tired, thought Dolly, noticing the little dusky dents under his eyes.

'This thing is waaaay bigger than me. I can't guarantee—'

'Then help me.'

With another sigh, Anakin narrowed his eyes at her through his glasses. 'Look, you were on the right track with Shaun Kingsley – there's something off about him. And look into a man called Greyson, Peverell Greyson, ex-military, now a businessman around here in Truro. You might find what you're looking for.'

She nodded, feeling at once puzzled and pleased, her brain flying off in several directions at the confirmation that her theories held some truth. 'Why do I keep coming across that name?'

'Well, just watch your back. And look...' Anakin cast his eyes around the busy lunchtime crowds – watching for eavesdroppers, Dolly wondered, just as Sunstar had. 'Someone at the top is pulling strings. Whoever it is, they're at the heart of this thing.'

'Thanks.'

'Don't thank me.'

Meavy turned out to be a fairly desolate village on the outskirts of Dartmoor, wind-whipped and grey. Dolly couldn't help thinking of her mother's descriptions of Gwynarthen, how bleak it must have been out there on the wintry moor, in the seventies. Still, the inn was a charming, timber-framed building nestled in a river valley. A few people were milling around outside, and by the time she pushed open the door, a hazy sun was glinting off the leaded windows. She had to assume it was the right location, because Lionel Abimbola's text had mysteriously disappeared after ten minutes, leaving her with only the random-seeming instruction to meet there, and no way to check. She stepped out of the car and steeled herself for whatever was to come.

Inside, she spotted a middle-aged man, presumably Lionel Abimbola, sitting near the fire. He wore a tartan shirt and corduroys, a russet woollen scarf wrapped around his neck, and small, round spectacles. He was tall, she could tell, and very Lusenkan, here in the setting of the English country pub with its horse brasses dangling either side of the hearth, its garish paisley carpets, and smells of woodsmoke and roast beef and beer. The man raised an arm to greet her, and she strolled over, shaking hands as he motioned for her to sit.

'Thank you for seeing me,' she said as they ordered a pot of tea from the waitress.

'My pleasure.' A small nod of assent, though no smile. With his right hand, Abimbola passed a length of prayer beads through his fingers, one after another in a rhythmic pattern. He seemed worn down, Dolly thought to herself as she watched the chain of beads drop slowly, hypnotically from his fingers. World weary.

'Do you mind if I record this?'

She felt a vague thrill at uttering the familiar journalistic request after so long. Again, Lionel nodded assent, stirring the tea with a spoon with his free hand. She switched on her Dictaphone and took a sip of tea, waiting for him to speak. When he did not, she pressed on. 'When did you leave Lusenka, Mr Abimbola?'

'Please, call me Lionel.' The beads clicked. 'I was deported here to the UK three years ago, after I tried to go public about my father's plight, and what my country's government is doing. Luckily, I had UK citizenship so they couldn't kill me – they had to deport me.'

'And what is it that they're doing?'

Lionel poured more tea from the pot into his cup, adding milk, recounting how the Lusenkan government was targeting the Balaika people, taking her through the story of his father's assassination and his own subsequent deportation. Dolly listened without interruption, occasionally checking the Dictaphone's recording levels.

'First, they reduced jobs for the Balaika,' Lionel explained. 'There was the odd arrest here, the odd disappearance here.' Then things got much worse, he continued, especially in recent months, with fighting intensified due to a big shipment of arms from abroad, providing more weapons for the government forces. Such was the tacit support of foreign nations, Lionel commented as Dolly listened with attention, holding the Dictaphone in one hand, making notes with the other.

'Is it genocide, do you think?'

Always the calm, rhythmic passing of the beads from finger to finger. 'The UN won't classify it officially as such, but yes, to all intents and purposes, yes. The Balaika are being rounded up and there are mass arrests. Last month they turned a village into an execution ground. There were bodies decapitated, chopped up. The government makes up excuses, saying the Balaika are criminals, that they need wiping out.'

Lionel drew a breath, averting his eyes to stare into the fire. One of the logs spat onto the carpet. Outside in the pub garden, a man on a small tractor mowed the grass.

'A pregnant woman was executed,' he went on eventually. 'They stripped her, beat her, then shot her in the back when she tried to escape.'

'It wasn't reported here?'

'It wouldn't be,' Lionel said, turning his gaze back to Dolly. 'I sent the video evidence to Amnesty, hoping they'd make a statement, but it never made the light of day. When I tried to speak out, the killings were hidden. It was all just beginning. But now there's more money, more weapons. They're blatant about it. We have videos of horrifying crimes.'

'Show me,' Dolly said softly.

Lionel put the prayer beads aside and reached for his phone. He tapped quickly through to a video file, before passing it over without preamble, his hand steady, his eyes focused on the fire. On the screen a woman in a pink dress carried a basket of pineapples. The scene was somewhat pleasing; the woman's eyes stared into the camera, catching the light, and the piled-up fruits formed a striking yellow and rattan still-life on top of her head. The next instant, the woman was being beaten to the ground by a group of teenage soldiers.

Dolly couldn't tear her eyes away as one of the men yanked the woman up again and threw her to the ground, again and again. When the soldiers let her go, the woman began to run, but bullets ricocheted into her back before she could escape, crack, crack, crack, until finally, she crumpled.

At the end of the video, dozens of pineapples lay strewn on the ground, marked with red dirt, leaking sweet juice already buzzing with flies. Lionel took back his phone, but the image of the woman remained imprinted in Dolly's thoughts. .

'Jesus Christ,' she murmured.

Lionel held her gaze for a few moments, his expression impassive, but then, slowly, his eyes filled with sorrow.

'This is why I had to fight,' he said in a resigned voice. 'This is why I had to keep going.'

Lionel swiped to another video. This time an air strike hit a gathering – a wedding, a birthday? Dolly watched in horror as tens of people, men, women, and children, ran for their lives from the raining of the bombs. Everywhere was screaming and noise and darkness. She felt a sinking sensation in her stomach as her body tensed, a primal response to the sight of so much bloodshed.

'These are human rights abuses.' Her voice was tight with emotion. 'I mean, they're on as big a scale as Rwanda. Are they on social media? Can I have copies?'

'Yes, and yes – but the sites take them down. I will email them to you. I believe the British Foreign Office is well aware of what is happening, but they don't want to rock the boat.'

Dolly considered this, then spoke: 'A source told me that our government is lending Lusenka money to buy arms. It seems that billions of pounds to buy British weapons are being loaned, and that the same cash comes back to this country in income.'

'Yes.' Lionel nodded. 'The regime is being funded to buy arms – they must be. Last week, a grenade hit a bus carrying civilians and school-children. Twenty-seven dead. Government militias are stockpiling weapons from Europe, and the situation can only escalate if they have more firepower.'

'Jesus.'

Out of his jacket pocket Lionel took a small, crumpled photograph, and handed it to Dolly, who leaned in to look. A youngish woman in a patterned headwrap and dress glared anxiously at the camera. Beside her, a little girl of six or seven was dressed in a frill-collared school dress, white ankle socks, old-fashioned bar sandals. The little girl was smiling, her eyes lit with excitement as she hung on to her mother's hand. Lionel took the photograph back, holding it between his fingers. If he was emotional, he did not show it.

'My wife, and my daughter, Innocence. We are Balaika. My wife was a very successful lawyer.'

'Was?'

'Her name was Precious. After I was deported, the soldiers came to my village. Innocence was six. My wife and I had been married for sixteen years, and for a long while we had been unable to have a child. Innocence was our gift from God. I was going to bring them both here. I'd filled in the forms; they were going to be accepted under refugee status. The lawyer said we had a good chance of success. But the soldiers shot my daughter as she was coming out of school. Then they took my wife, Precious, and tortured her, and raped her, and then they killed her too and sent me the recording.'

For a moment, Dolly found herself unable to speak, her mind caught inescapably in the trauma of this lonely Lusenkan man, this grieving husband and father. Once, for work, she had travelled to Rwanda, had witnessed the population scarred by sadness and trauma and hubris. In Kigali's tranquil memorial museum, she spent a sombre afternoon perusing the photographs of families like Lionel's, reading their testimonies of human suffering spelt out in almost unbearable detail. She could hardly imagine his pain, his grief. How could these horrific things be allowed to happen again?

'When Precious died, I, I...' Lionel coughed, raising a hand to his eyes. 'Well, she is with the good God now.'

Lionel filed the photograph away in his pocket, patting it absently with his hand, and the two of them sat in silence for a short while, after which Dolly said: 'It's so morally repugnant, Britain claiming to be the great democracy, while funding wars around the world. We can't simply ignore what's happening.'

'Of course we can't.' Lionel gave a low, cynical laugh. 'The weapon they used to kill my daughter was probably imported from the UK. The truth is that politicians are the same everywhere, my dear. Rich or poor nations, it doesn't make a difference. I realised many years ago that they act not for our countries, but for their own gain.'

'Not that power corrupts men,' said Dolly musingly, 'but that men corrupt power.'

'William Gaddis,' agreed Lionel.

Dolly switched off the recording, dropping the phone into her bag. 'My mother was Lusenkan,' she remarked as she did so. For some reason, it felt important to tell Lionel Abimbola this. 'Her name was Gloria Fontaine.'

Lionel looked up with a strange expression, observing her in silence for a second or two. In his face Dolly glimpsed something indefinable, whether curiosity or fear, she couldn't tell. Finally, he reached for his prayer beads and resumed his twiddling. Then he spoke:

'*The* Gloria Fontaine?'

'Yes. The actress.'

'I see. So this is very personal for you.'

'You could say that. I think she would have wanted me to do something, ask questions at least. What can we do, Lionel? Surely we must act.'

Tight-lipped, Lionel gripped the beads. 'We must, and yet what can we do? Sometimes I lie awake at night, imagining the thousands being slaughtered, and wondering if it is real. It doesn't seem real. The simple truth is, here we are, two people in a pub in the United Kingdom.' He spread his long fingers out in a defeated gesture. 'I know in my heart that God will find a way to let me help, but today, I must admit I feel overwhelmed by our task.'

He shifted in his chair, then without warning rose and excused himself. Dolly watched him stroll off around the bar to the loo, struck by the change in Lionel's manner; he was suddenly restless, nervous even. After five minutes he returned.

'Look,' he said, sitting down, 'my wife admired your mother very much, she used to say that Gloria Fontaine showed Lusenkan women that they can dance to their own drum.' He hesitated and looked away over at the fire, then back again. 'Back in my father's day, in the seventies that is, Gloria was known to be quite a woman.'

'Yes, she was.'

'But my dear, your mother aside, there's not much I can do to help. I'm in hiding here, in exile. If they find me, they will find a way to kill me, even in this sleepy English town.'

At the door of the pub the two of them clasped hands. Dolly gave Lionel her email address to send over the videos. As they walked over to the car park, he paused, glancing up at the sky, and she followed his gaze to the congregation of rain clouds gathering overhead.

'You are still young, my dear,' he said after a long silence. 'And spirited like your mother. You'll find a way to do something, God willing. Goodbye.'

Exhausted, a leaden feeling in her chest, Dolly watched him walk slowly over to a battered-looking hatchback Volvo parked under the willow tree, and get in. His head was lowered, he had the slight stoop of the tall and the very sad, almost as if he were waiting for someone to come for him, she thought, this lonely man in a country not his own, stricken with grief. As if he were waiting for a gun to be held to his head. And was it any wonder? His wife and daughter were dead. How did a human being find the will to carry on after such a thing? There was untold strength in that.

Without a look back, Lionel started the engine and drove away. Once the Volvo had disappeared, Dolly turned and walked out to the riverside, where the air smelled of mown grass, cool and sharp.

181

CHAPTER TWENTY-SEVEN

Dolly

On the way back from Meavy, Dolly dropped into her brother's house, still pondering Lionel Abimbola's story, and the gruesome videos he'd shown her of Lusenka's bombed-out towns, of the charred remains of buildings and homes, reducing people to refugees in their own land. She wanted to ask her brother more questions – and this time she was determined not to take no for an answer.

But as she unlocked the front door, something made her pause. She heard the sound of unfamiliar footsteps coming from upstairs – the girls' room? – followed by the sound of a door closing softly. She stood frozen for a moment, straining to hear, aware of a burst of adrenaline surging through her body. On the stairs, the landing light was on.

'Hello!' she called out anxiously. 'Rich, is that you?'

A man appeared at the top of the stairs, his eyes oddly bright. Dolly's stomach dropped.

'Well,' said the man. 'Hello there.'

'What the—?' Dolly stood transfixed as Peverell Greyson descended the stairs. 'What on earth are you doing?'

'No need to get your knickers in a twist.' Pev held up his hands innocently. 'I'm not breaking in. Your brother sent me over from the Blue to get the bunting.'

'Bunting?'

'Open house this evening, thought we'd make it look festive. Course, I'm running around like a blue-arsed fly, can't rely on the staff...'

All traces of the menacing thug at the shooting range the other day had disappeared, and he might have been a family friend, all charm, all suave confidence, but Dolly frowned: what the hell was Pev Greyson doing here, and even worse, in the children's room? She knew better than to trust his charming façade; at any moment he would reveal his true self, cold and merciless. She wondered what he'd actually been looking for.

'But the bunting isn't kept up there.'

Pev's manner changed. He grinned extravagantly and moved Dolly out of the way by her shoulders. 'Sorry, Fontaine darling, I got places to be and people to see.'

Dolly shrugged him off in disgust. 'Get off me.'

He paused, keeping his eyes on her. 'Gosh, those are lovely nieces of yours. Fern and Flora. Quite lovely. All those unicorns and fairies. We wouldn't want anything to happen to them, would we?'

'What do you mean?'

'Oh, nothing specific,' he said casually. 'Just a friendly reminder, you know? As I said before, accidents happen all the time. Children can be so unpredictable. Best to stop all this detective work, hey Fontaine.'

'I don't know what you're talking about.'

Pev's eyes narrowed. Something flashed in their depths, menacing and dark and lifeless. He leaned in closer, and his voice dropped to a whisper. 'Oh, don't play dumb, Fontaine. You should know better than to meddle in things that don't concern you.' His lips curled into a smile, revealing straight white teeth. 'Your precious little family won't protect you.'

'Jesus, don't you dare bring my family into this.'

There was a second's silence, during which she felt a crackling electricity run through her bones and her pores, knowing how gravely dangerous Pev was, now that the mask was dropped.

'I'm onto you, Pev,' she burst out, repressing a shiver, lifting her chin slightly, pushing her fear away. 'And I'm not scared. I know about you and Shaun, and I know about foreign arms supplies to Lusenka. I'll find out how you're involved if it's the last thing I do.'

Pev's jaw tightened for a second, but then he seemed to recover himself. 'The last thing you do, hey. Good gracious, Fontaine, how very dramatic.' He stood back with a quiet laugh; the charm was back.

'*Anyhoo*, are you gracing us with your presence at the bar later?'

She shook her head. 'No, no I'm... I'm busy...'

He gave a shrug as he edged past, slipping through the front door. '*Tant pis*,' he called back cheerfully from the end of the path.

In haste, feeling dry-mouthed and shaken, Dolly ran up the stairs, and snatched the bunting from the study, where it had been all along. She let herself out of the house, locking the door with fumbling fingers. Beyond, she could just see Pev's retreating figure walking down towards the village, phone lifted to his ear. She waited a few moments then followed at a distance. He wasn't carrying any bunting – in fact, he wasn't carrying anything at all.

It was spring festival, Flora Day. Crowds filled the village car park, thronging onto the dune for the start of the celebrations. In the hubbub, Dolly lost sight of Pev for a second, only to find that he'd disappeared in the crowd. She circumnavigated the mass of people and desperately scanned the terrace of the Blue, eventually spotting Pev at the far end. She felt her stomach flip as she watched him climb the steps and join her brother, Rich, who stood in sunglasses, pint in hand, at a table of people near the back. The two men proceeded to talk animatedly; about what, Dolly wondered as she surveyed them carefully, wishing she could lip-read.

She turned to go, only to spot Pev's henchman from the shooting range heading for the group. Wills Brown. There was no mistaking his awful pink trousers.

'Ugh,' she groaned out loud. What on earth had Rich got himself into?

And then her throat constricted as she recognised another familiar figure on the terrace. The man was standing apart on the opposite side of the deck, tall and square, facing the sea with a glass of wine in his hand. Surely, it couldn't be? Dolly squinted, focusing as Peverell Greyson broke away from the other men and sauntered over towards him.

What the fuck, Dolly thought, because the man now standing next to Pev, half-turned away, in a navy-blue polo shirt and sunglasses, was

Shaun Kingsley. The two men strolled into the bar, side by side, and Dolly shook her head with a sigh, and shoved the bunting in a bin. This whole situation was turning into a nightmare.

Dolly climbed the path to the summit of the cliff, where she could hear the echoing cries of the sea birds and the crashing of the waves hundreds of metres below. She breathed deeply, trying to gather her thoughts. What on earth was Shaun doing in Kernow? If Rich knew, he wasn't showing it. On the contrary, it seemed as if it might be a sort of private meet-up between Peverell Greyson and Shaun. And why had Pev been in Rich's house? It gave her the shivers to think of him up there in the kids' room, rummaging in the girls' things.

The sun was breaking through the mist, turning the sea every shade of aquamarine, a sheet of blue glass. A cool breeze ruffled Dolly's hair as she watched a blue tit hop across a hillock of sandy grass and take off, fluttering over the edge of the cliff. She followed the bird with her eyes as it soared with tiny yellow and violet wings on a high air current. You're too far up, she wanted to shout. Too brave and curious! You think you're a gull when you're just a little spring bird, suited to the land. And she, too, was in over her head, she thought then, just like the curious little bird.

Dolly closed her eyes, Pev's threats still echoing in her mind. She couldn't take them lightly, but she couldn't allow the man to intimidate her, either. The trouble was that if she told anyone about his behaviour at the petrol station, at the firing range, or just before, at Rich's house, they'd probably brush it off as crazy talk. He's allowed to get petrol, they'd say. He was probably just getting the bunting... She wished Gloria were here, to ask for help.

'Mum,' she found herself whispering. 'What would you do?'

As if on cue, a breeze got up, whipping across the open cliff. By now Dolly was so used to hearing Gloria's voice drifting from the tapes, and she could almost hear her voice now too, drifting on the wind. *Trust your instincts,* her mother seemed to murmur. *Don't let fear consume you, Sugar. Sometimes the biggest barrier we face is in our own head.*

Believe in yourself, my darling Sugar.

Dolly's phone rang: Evan, sounding hopeful. He was in the village,
he said, for the festival, and wondered if she wanted to meet. For some
reason Dolly found herself agreeing to the plan despite her ongoing
suspicions about his motives.

A few minutes later he appeared, panting, and seated himself on
the ground next to her with legs outstretched. She glanced over at him,
wishing she could confide in him about the earlier encounter with Pev,
his threats to her nieces, and how afraid she felt. Surely Evan wouldn't
think her mad? But still her fears lingered: what if he had something
to do with Pev?

'You probably shouldn't get involved with me, you know,' she
remarked with a small smile, still watching the little bird hovering
on the wind.

'Look, I've lived in some of the most messed-up places on the planet.
I can deal with a drama... What's going on?'

'It's a long story.'

'Well, I'm not doing anything else right now.' Evan pushed a hand
through his hair and seemed to think for a moment. 'Look, that Navy
mate got in touch. Seems this Pev Greyson bloke is dead dodgy. I've
said it once, I'll say it again. You really shouldn't touch this, though I
guess it's a wee bit late for that now.'

'It is,' Dolly agreed with a shrug. 'Too late, I mean.'

A millimetre of ash formed on the end of Evan's cigarette. He stubbed
the butt in the sand then picked it up between his fingers.

Dolly raised an eyebrow, recalling Gloria and Sunstar. 'Surely
Marines don't throw fags on the floor,' she said. 'The enemy can tell a
lot from a cigarette. Supplies, morale...'

'The enemy?' Evan laughed. 'Christ, that's old school. What've you
been reading?'

He took out his tobacco tin and fashioned a rollie; he licked the
paper, shaped the tobacco carefully into a cylinder shape. Dolly watched,
sighed, stared at the fine blue line of the horizon, calling out to Gloria
in her mind for the second time that day. Silently, she conjured Gloria,

desperate for a sign, a clue, anything to navigate her conflicting worries about Evan, the trustworthy nice guy versus Evan, the man who might be harbouring terrible secrets.

For a fraction of a second, there was nothing, and then slowly, softly, Gloria's voice came echoing into her thoughts, soothing and familiar. *Trust your instincts, Sugar. You need an ally. You need to trust someone.*

With a feeling of relief, Dolly dug her hands into the front pocket of her hoodie, and talked with hesitancy at first, then in a rush, letting it all out as Evan smoked and listened, nodding occasionally. She recounted the scandal in London and her disgrace over the Lusenka memo, then her brother's behaviour at the building site, and her suspicions about Peverell Greyson. About the part that embarrassed her most – about Shaun Kingsley and the affair – she was clear and unemotional. Finally, she told Evan about her meeting with Lionel Abimbola, and finding Peverell Greyson snooping around the children's bedroom, and the way he had threatened her family.

'My own brother's mixed up with the bad guys,' she finished with a flourish. 'And I don't know what the hell to do about it.'

Evan took a thoughtful drag of his cigarette, the smoke wafting towards the sea. Dolly studied his profile, his brow creased now, with concern, she supposed. There was a depth to him she hadn't anticipated, a quiet strength that moved her in ways she couldn't explain. Perhaps she could trust him after all.

He turned to look at her. 'Seems as though you've got a lot on your plate,' he said decisively. 'I'm going to ring my pal right now.'

On the way to her brother's house for lunch, Dolly stopped at the village shop to buy a bottle of Australian white, resisting the urge to buy a packet of cigarettes. Outside the shop, she began walking up the hill, thinking about Evan and everything she'd told him.

A noise behind her.

'Dolly.'

Her belly lurched. She turned around to find Shaun Kingsley leaning out of the window of a large, black Range Rover. The car had pulled up without a sound: it must be one of those new electric models, she realised, which was typical of Shaun – the new Shaun, anyway – flashy and underhand. His tanned, clean-shaven, square-jawed face, framed by the window, was filled with a suave smile.

'What the hell are you doing here? You can't just turn up after everything. How dare you—'

'Keep your hair on.' Shaun was still smiling, seemingly unperturbed by her fury, which only made her feel worse. 'Annual leave. I'm down for the festival, seeing friends. Spotted you earlier and obviously couldn't resist—'

She raised an eyebrow. 'Friends being Pev Greyson and his crew, I take it. Why do I find it hard to believe this is a coincidence…?'

'Okay, I admit it, I thought I'd check up on you, make sure you're being good, and not getting embroiled in any more trouble.'

Shaun's manner was still puzzlingly, infuriatingly light-hearted, as if the scandal of the memo, the betrayal, never happened.

Dolly turned to go, blood rushing in her ears. 'Thanks for your concern, but I don't need checking up on.'

It had been a long day. She was shattered. The last thing she wanted to do was face Shaun Kingsley and all that past heartbreak. Yet there was so much she wanted to say and ask. Why, she felt like yelling at him; why did you set me up, asshole! Why did you ruin me?!

'Please,' she muttered instead. 'Just leave me alone.'

'Dolly.' A new note in Shaun's voice, without the usual flirting, the flippancy. 'Don't run away.'

She turned back around. 'I'm not running away – I just don't wish to do this right now.'

All of a sudden, Shaun's face was drawn tight, more serious than she'd ever seen him. He frowned, glancing out of the car's front windscreen then the rear-view mirror, as if checking for onlookers. He met her eyes again with a furtive, conflicted expression. When he finally spoke, his voice was low and gruff.

'Look, Dolly, will you just listen to me, for once, and stay away from this. It's too big, too dangerous. I'm saying this because I genuinely care.'

'Care?' Dolly paused, gathering herself. Now was her chance to tell Shaun Kingsley where he could stick his *caring*, his lies and deceit. But she stood tongue-tied, shaking her head, her heart exploding in her chest. 'Bullshit,' she answered eventually. 'Stop spying on me, or I'll report you.'

Shaun sighed and shook his head with a despairing sigh. He shot her a small ambiguous smile. The car window hummed closed. Dolly watched with tears pricking at her eyes as the car took off slowly down the road with a low alien hum, a predator creeping towards its unsuspecting prey.

In the empty kitchen, the news drifted from the radio, followed by the rhythmic bongs of Big Ben from London. Dolly leaned on the kitchen counter feeling drained and tearful. She wished Rich were here, because she was in half a mind to confess her puzzling encounter with Shaun, and everything else, for that matter. But Rich was nowhere to be seen. On her phone, a text message popped up from Morgan: *How was the shooting, babes?* Quickly Dolly tapped back a white lie. *Loved it!*

If only she could ask Morgan about Peverell, but then again, she sensed the difficult dynamics of the marriage, Morgan as the little wife, as her friend had called herself. Was it her imagination, or did Morgan seem intimidated by her own husband, even a little scared? Increasingly, Dolly felt puzzled by her school friend, who seemed so guarded and tense and *different*, somehow, when teenage Morgan was always the life of the party, a mischief-maker, funny and rebellious. At parties it was always Morgan leading the charge, with her infectious laughter and dishevelled hair, pulling Dolly onto the dance floor. Usually, they ended up being the last ones standing, giggling uncontrollably in a corner after Morgan had snogged some boy, Michael Taylor, as she remembered, and once, Jack Davison, the class clown, of all people.

Dolly smiled, sighed, and poured herself a glass of the white wine from the fridge, adding ice cubes from the freezer. In the lounge, she sat on the settee taking large gulps, watching her nieces building a den on the floor from two chairs and a cotton sheet. Their chatter drifted from inside, followed by a song. The chant lingered like a spell in the quiet room.

'What are you two singing in there?' said Dolly.

'We're learning Cornish at school.' Flora poked a head out of the makeshift tent. 'Myttin da, Auntie Dolly.'

'Myttin da, sweetheart,' she replied, turning on the telly.

On screen the weather forecaster was waving a hand towards the south coasts of the British Isles, where little black clouds and cryptic arrows indicated an impending storm. Dolly held the cold wine glass against her cheek, letting the sensation of cool alcohol flow through her body as she watched the animation zoom in on Cornwall. In her chest she still felt a deep, sickening anxiety that was hard to disguise here in the slow day-to-day atmosphere of the family household.

'A storm's coming in.' It was Rich, behind her. 'Storm Imelda,' he added. 'It's supposed to be particularly bad.'

Dolly looked around, feeling a sort of relief, and launched straight in: 'I caught Pev Greyson creeping around here earlier. Any idea why?'

Rich's expression turned to shock. 'Seriously?'

'He was snooping in the girls' room.'

'Christ.' Her brother frowned and ran a palm over his head, rubbing a spot on his left temple. Then he groaned. 'Listen, Doll, you need to lie low and stop meddling, okay.'

'Meddling?' She felt infuriated. All these men telling her not to bother asking questions! Who did they think they were! 'But I found him *right here*, in your house! Then I saw...'

'You saw what?'

'I saw Shaun Kingsley, here, in Porthlowe – *my* Shaun Kingsley'

Rich's face clouded with animosity. 'Like hell you did. Look, this is getting out of hand. Just let it go, will you!'

Dolly followed her brother into the kitchen, where Gracie was laying the table with mats and the best plates. Rich set his laptop on the dresser, turning away with shoulders hunched, forming a wall

190

between them. In turn, Dolly pulled out a chair and sat down with one elbow on the table, resting her cheek on her hand, feeling glum. Rich was supposed to be her ally, her friend, her brother. The thought that he might somehow be in league with Peverell Greyson, not simply working for him but part of the crew, filled her with dismay. If her own brother was somehow her enemy, who did she have to turn to?

For a few minutes, the whole family pottered with the dishes. Dolly helped herself to a small amount of roast meat, then potatoes and vegetables, broccoli, and cauliflower cheese. From a pan she poured gravy over the top, but once her plate was full, she found she wasn't hungry. Whether it was stress or nerves, her mouth was dry, her throat constricted.

'Look, can we talk, Rich?' she ventured in a low voice. 'About all this?'

'No,' he replied. 'Not a chance.'

'Please?'

'Come on, Rich.' Gracie's voice held a warning as she poured wine, deep ruby red in the best crystal glasses. Dolly clenched her jaw with exasperation: did her sister-in-law really expect them to say cheers and all would suddenly be well? In the awkward silence, Rich sliced meat with his knife, spearing it with a fork. Dolly took a bite of potato but tasted nothing. Once they had eaten, the girls raced off into the lounge and Gracie went back into the kitchen, returning with an apple crumble which she placed ceremoniously in the middle of the table. Rich was still determinedly looking away, fiddling with a spoon.

'Will you tell me,' Dolly persisted, ignoring the pudding, 'how your mate Pev is involved with Lusenka?'

'I am not *mates* with Pev Greyson. It's just work.'

'Can you imagine what Mum would have thought of you being mixed up with something dodgy in Lusenka?'

'Don't, for Christ's sake, bring Mum into this.'

'You need to find some morals.'

The room was dead quiet. Dolly registered Gracie's presence. She was spooning crumble into dishes with an oven-gloved hand. A ray of evening sunlight lit up the vestiges of dinner through the window.

Dolly got up and left the room, gathering her belongings from the hallway, but when she looked back, Gracie stood hovering in the doorway of the kitchen, still holding the remains of the crumble dish with the oven glove.

'What about your pudding, love?' Gracie said in a worried voice.

'Thanks,' said Dolly with a small pang of guilt. None of this was Gracie's fault. 'Sorry, Gracie, I'm not hungry.'

CHAPTER TWENTY-EIGHT

Dolly

By the time Dolly arrived home, ominous blue-black clouds were gathering in a blue-black sky, just as the forecast had predicted. A few big drops of rain splotched the ground. The wind bent the trees towards the earth. Inside, Dolly pulled the curtains and lit the fire with the rain tapping on the windows. Half an hour later, her phone rang with an unknown number. She recognised Lionel Abimbola's deep, accented voice at the end of the line, suffused with a new tone of urgency.

'I fear I haven't been entirely honest with you, Dolly. There's something else I need to speak to you about. Can we meet again?'

'Can't you tell me on the phone?'

'No, only in person. It's important, about your mother?'

'About Gloria? Okay, tomorrow.'

'Same place, same time. I look forward to it.' A pause. 'Oh, and there's something coming by courier, something important that it's not safe for me to keep. Make sure you open it immediately.'

On the other end, the line clicked off abruptly, leaving Dolly staring at the screen. A courier? What on earth might Lionel have to tell her about Gloria, and what on earth might he have to send? True, she'd sensed at the pub that he was holding something back, but she put it down to his Lusenkan natural reserve, a dissident's obvious suspicion of strangers. Tonight though, Lionel sounded hurried, frightened even.

With a sigh, Dolly put the phone aside, went upstairs and got in the shower, brooding about the reasons for Lionel's sudden change of heart as she soaped her skin and washed her hair. While she was drying herself, there was a second call, from Evan. He'd spoken again to his Navy friend Thorny, he informed her, who had some new information, and suggested they talk on Skype. Telling herself it was out of a need for more clues, more than anything else, Dolly gave Evan the address of Genévrier, and invited him over.

An hour later, there was a knock at the door. Dolly opened it to a sodden courier in a black motorcycle helmet, rain pouring down the upturned visor, who handed her a plain manila envelope and requested a signature before roaring away down the gravel drive.

Eagerly, Dolly tore open the seal of the envelope to find three tapes marked 'The Mission', 'Meeting the President', and 'Lourenco's Crocodiles' – surely the final tapes, she realised with excitement – accompanied by a handwritten note in black marker pen, which she read quickly, taking short, ragged, anxious breaths:

Dear Dolly,
Your mother and I met just once, here in England. Gloria told me to give you these tapes if ever you found me. Along with this 'little extra', given by my father to your mother for safekeeping. She entrusted them to me, with the understanding that I would pass them on. Please be careful, my dear.
Regards,
Lionel Abimbola

There was something else nestling at the bottom of the package. Reaching in, Dolly pulled out a tiny drawstring bag that lay heavy in her fingers, and peered inside as goosebumps rose on the back of her neck. Her mind flashed to Lionel's fearful voice on the phone, and at last she understood. Once, covering a news story early in her career about a Hollywood actress accused of accepting bribes from a foreign politician on trial for war crimes, she had seen some uncut diamonds. She knew very well what they looked like.

Now, breathlessly, she counted four, five, six tiny, cloudy rocks glimmering in the electric spotlights of the kitchen, yellowish and rough-edged, nothing special to the unaccustomed eye, but she could only imagine what they were worth. Millions, probably. She shivered at the thought. What was this? A bribe? A payment?

Clutching the tiny bag, Dolly went to the kitchen door and peered outside, feeling raindrops skim her face. The storm was blowing up. A gust of wind blustered her sideways, and she clasped her sweatshirt around her with the uneasy thought that anyone could be hiding around the back of the house, in the garden, in the barns or the bushes, watching. Hastily she closed the door and locked it on the double bolt, pulling at the handle a few times to make sure it was shut tight. In the lounge she perched on the settee and tipped the six yellowish stones onto her palm. They were raw and unpolished; she could see that very well – but her instinct told her they were perfect.

Dolly sat back, thinking hard. There by the fire was her mother's record player, the stack of dog-eared records Gloria had collected over the years. Each record traced Gloria's varied moods and tastes, but how many secrets must be jostling beneath the surface, unsaid! And now here in Dolly's own hand was probably the thing at the root of all of it, material evidence as to why Gloria was like she was.

Dolly got up and went outside, needing some fresh air. In her hand she was still holding the tiny cloth bag of jewels. When she examined the bag again, she found another scrappy note inside, scribbled roughly in pencil on a crumpled piece of paper in Lionel's handwriting: *My father's*, it said. *I know you'll do the right thing. L.*

CHAPTER TWENTY-NINE

Gloria

Tape four
The Mission, 1979, Lusenka

After a longish flight on a nearly empty British charter plane, I reached the marbled front desk of the Sheraton Hotel in Port Salé, where a pretty receptionist in a pink sundress handed me a glass of bubbly and placed a garland of hibiscus flowers around my neck. The sweet-scented blooms were cheerfully, maddeningly conspicuous.

The Sheraton was a plush sort of place with an agreeable buzz, the only luxury hotel in the capital, as far as I knew. My arrival seemed to cause a ripple of excitement amongst the staff, and as I took my key and walked through the hotel, adorned with flowers, I could sense their collective gaze upon me. I spoke to no one, and decided that my obvious arrival was all part of Sunstar's plan. Still, I hoped I could remain fairly incognito amid the besuited foreign businessmen and scores of city socialites who came there in the evenings, to drink and mingle around the hotel's poolside cocktail bar.

Night fell with tropical speed compared to England, but I went to bed entirely unable to go to sleep, despite my tiredness. Sunstar and his rainy ocean eyes frequented my dreams. I tossed and turned for hours, long past midnight, only to wake exhausted and jittery just after dawn, as if I hadn't slept at all. With nothing better to do, I checked over the survival kit issued by Seal before my departure, containing a pocket-sized tin filled with matches, a candle, needles and thread, a screwdriver, snare wire, signal flares and a torch. A map of Lusenka. My Walther PPK pistol, naturally. And my make-up bag containing a small, apparently insignificant tube of mascara, cleverly modified by Sunstar's team for my mission. I loaded the gun with bullets, and double-tested the miniscule camera I was to use to gather intelligence.

Later, on a lounger by the swimming pool, I welcomed the honey warm sun on my light-starved skin, but no matter how hard I tried, it was impossible to relax. My brain was churning wildly, and though I flipped through a newspaper to make the time pass, I couldn't help wishing that something would happen. Something, anything, dammit, to break the monotony and ease my tension.

Sooner or later, I couldn't stand it anymore. I hailed a cab from the hotel entrance, instructing the driver to take me straight to the centre of town. Evidently the city, with all its memories, had changed in the time I'd been away. As we navigated the bustling streets through unruly markets and hooting traffic jams, I spotted buildings and restaurants I didn't recognise. A giant new monument of President Lourenco had sprung up near the town hall – in all probability one of those I'd heard about, funded by the Russians to garner favour with the president. As for Le Tropico, I doubted it even existed anymore.

I felt a strange pang of nostalgia, and thought of my journey back to attend Chilembé's funeral a few months earlier, when I'd bypassed Port Salé and gone straight to Cap Bleu, twenty kilometres out of the city on the coast. There, my brother was buried in a little plot of red earth beneath the whispering acacia trees, overlooking the sea, his grave marked with a simple wooden cross. Now, back in the capital where Chilembé and I had once made a new start, where I'd lived and danced and survived, I was a newcomer in my own city. I suppose I'd never considered the fact that I was now part of Lusenka's diaspora, and it struck me that diaspora was, in fact, just a fancy word for outsiders.

It was nearly noon. I paid the taxi driver and got out of the car, pausing for a moment to look up to the fourth floor of the eccentric, ochre-painted building that housed Chilembé's flat. How I wished my brother were there on the balcony, waiting to greet me... I had a vision, then, of my brother waving down with his beautiful smile. *Come on up, Sis!* His flat was mine now, but I couldn't bear the thought of selling the home where my brother lived his last days.

I climbed the stairs, unlocked the front door, and stepped inside. The place was silent and oppressively warm. Bright sunlight through the windows lit a haze of floating dust particles. There were a few wilted potted palms, on the brink of death, and a vaguely sour smell, of old air and unventilated rooms, and sadness. Otherwise, the flat was more or less as my brother would have left it, almost as if he had woken up one day, locked the door and disappeared. There was an eerie domesticity to the still-crumpled sofa, the dining table strewn with newspapers, a half-melted candle, an abandoned teacup. The kitchen too, was untouched. There was even a stained wine glass still standing in the sink, waiting for a dish washer who never arrived.

I had dreaded this day ever since he died, and now, for the first time, I forced myself to face the idea head on – of my precious Chilembé murdered in cold blood by a bullet through the head. Of some hateful government official dragging my brother's lifeless body outside and cleaning up the blood without shedding a tear. Everyone knew what Lourenco's hit men were like. In which room had Chilembé lain dead, I found myself wondering morbidly, and for how long?

The flat was a mausoleum, yet there was no trace of the brutal slaughter that had happened here. But what about justice? What about right and wrong? I knew the answer – justice was a concept that had no place in the twisted world of President Baptiste Lourenco.

How I missed Chilembé! Alone and utterly desolate in the lounge of my brother's flat, I whispered his name over and over, immobilised by my own despair. How did we humans ever dare to love, I wondered?

How did we find the courage to give our hearts to another person, knowing they could be taken away in an instant? What a devastating leap of faith it seemed. With tears streaming down my face, I collapsed on the settee and buried my head in my arms. Face down in the fabric of my brother's worn sofa, I lay and wept, my great aching sobs ringing in the dead silence of the empty flat.

After a time, I stood up and wiped my face with my hands, breathing slowly. In an effort to gather my emotions I wandered the bedrooms, which were equally clean and tranquil, beds made, curtains half-drawn to keep out the sun.

Beside the shelves in the main bedroom, I stopped to peruse my brother's collection of books. Chilembé liked to read widely, and there were volumes of Descartes and Gide, Achebe, and *Les Fleurs du Mal,* as well as a selection of modern literary novels in English and French. I picked up a battered, orange-spined volume of *To Kill a Mockingbird* lying face down on the bedside table, open with its spine splayed. Inside, Chilembé had scribbled notes in the margins, and a few pages were bookmarked with a turned-over corner. Flicking through the pages, I paused. Into the centre page someone – it could only have been my brother – had slipped a smallish greetings card. There was an insipid floral design on the front, and a couple of lines handwritten inside in black ink: *Dear Chilembé, happy birthday 1977, love from Gloria.* Underneath were the words, *Thank you for the roses x.*

I stared at the card for a few seconds, experiencing a stirring of recognition, and remembering an afternoon session with Seal on code-breaking: 'Be alert for signs, don't take anything for granted.' Chilembé too, had been Sunstar's spy, an asset of the British Government engaged in collecting state secrets on President Lourenco before he was discovered and killed. So why else would my brother leave me a coded message?

You see, I never sent that birthday card. I never received roses from my brother. For one thing, the postal service in Lusenka was non-existent, meaning that Chilembé and I were never able to correspond as we would have liked to. For another, I never signed off as Gloria – not to my brother, anyway. To Chilembé, I was always Sis.

The card in my hand was a drop, I guessed, a code to lead me to a specific piece of information that Chilembé needed me to find, if something happened to him. My brother must have known I'd come straight to the apartment and pick up the trail. He knew me well, better than anyone in the world. All I had to do now was crack the code.

Gripped by a rising sense of excitement, I stashed the card in my bag, left the bedroom and proceeded to examine the rest of the apartment more conscientiously. Roses, I wondered, rifling through the cupboards in the kitchen. Roses. I searched the drawers of the chest in the spare bedroom and checked the bathroom cabinet. In the lounge, I investigated a large teak desk where Chilembé used to keep his paperwork, but there was nothing of interest. No, I told myself; too obvious, too damn straightforward.

It was nearly noon. Outside on the balcony, a glaring sun was baking through the plastic awning. I observed the objects there: a wicker lounger, a round plastic table and chairs, some potted plants, two cycads and a medium-sized ponytail palm. I sighed, thinking over what my brother's last moments might have been like. Had he stood here drinking one of his favourite evening cocktails? A last glass of wine? Then his attackers burst in, holding him at gunpoint. I couldn't bear to imagine how frightened he must have been, knowing he was going to die.

I jumped as a car engine revved on the street below. From somewhere downstairs the lively beats of a song drifted from a wireless. I stepped forward. One of the chairs tucked under the table was tied with a cushion of an elegant floral design. The English-style pattern was a little like the birthday card, a swirl of delicate hand-drawn flowers amongst tendrils of leaves and branches, and pale pink blooms like roses...

I untied the cushion from the chair and took it back inside, closing the balcony door behind me, and sat down on the settee. With my pocketknife I carefully slit open the fabric cover and extracted the inner pad. That too, I cut open. With my fingers I felt about in the soft foam, searching for what, I didn't know – for something. After a short while, I felt something rigid, something smooth and papery, resist my touch, and I drew it out.

The miniscule scrap of paper was folded several times into a square about a centimetre across. With trembling hands, I unfolded it. The paper was blank. Moving across the room, I opened the door again and stepped out into the sunlight. The sun was brightest in the far corner of the balcony. There, I knelt so that I couldn't be spotted from the street, and held the piece of paper directly in the sunlight, letting the rays beat down upon it. To my elation, after five minutes or so, the message – Chilembé had used the simplest of methods, I noted, household vinegar of the kind anyone could buy in the market – was exposed by the heat.

FHSXVCA LIHA NQP, it said.

Perhaps a minute passed. I continued to kneel in the same spot for a few seconds with the paper in my hand, conscious of a rush of adrenaline surging through my body. Slowly, I stood up and, with a sudden, paranoid feeling of apprehension, glanced down over the top of the balustrade, surveying the quiet, unpaved street for any signs of watchers.

Down below, a door guard sat beside the gate of the building opposite, apparently absorbed in the process of brewing tea over a camping stove. Otherwise, there was no one around, just the high, looming gates of the residential houses in this wealthy suburban district, and a bright cascade of hot pink bougainvillea tumbling over a high security wall behind the guard. A few cars were parked below in the sandy dust. Nevertheless, I ducked down before the guard could glance upwards, figuring that, despite appearances, one couldn't be too careful. Inside the flat I locked the balcony door. This time, I drew the curtains.

On the settee I sat staring at the cryptic message – a puzzle to any but the keenly trained eye. Something told me it was a Vigenère Cipher, one of the many basic but effective encryption techniques I'd learned at Gwynarthen. There would be a keyword, I knew – because such ciphers always needed a keyword – with each letter of the original code shifting according to that repeated word.

Brilliant, I thought admiringly. My brother would have also learned the code technique under Sunstar's tutelage. He must have hoped that Sunstar would find me, too; that I would follow his clues and discover the birthday card, then the code. But it would need time and perseverance to decipher. I slipped the scrap of paper into my purse, then quickly locked and left the flat.

Downstairs, I walked a little way and crossed the street, turning as I did so at an angle of ninety degrees in order to glance back over at the opposite side, telling myself the whole time that I had no need to worry. I was just out for a stroll, and there was nothing in the least suspicious about that. I walked a little further, purposely blending into a crowd milling around a roadside fruit stall manned by a trader in voluminous mint-green robes. I bought half a kilo of oranges and a large pineapple, taking the opportunity, while the man searched for change, to put on my sunglasses and a large sunhat stashed in my bag.

Again, I crossed the road with a heightened sense of alertness, scanning my surroundings with every step, making more slow checks in each direction. Feeling confident that I wasn't being shadowed, I walked a street or two extra as a precaution, taking alternate turns left and right for good measure, until after what seemed like forever, I finally arrived at an empty street corner, where I hailed a taxi without attracting too much attention.

I hopped into the cab and gave the driver the address of the

Sheraton. By now it was almost one o'clock and the hot sun was high in the sky, adding to my feeling of unease. What if someone from the British Embassy came to find me, for lunch or drinks, and discovered I was gone from the hotel? From the back seat, I willed the taximan to go faster as we wove endlessly through congested streets, every second an eternity, until we finally drew up outside the sprawling Sheraton.

I was safe, for now.

CHAPTER THIRTY

Dolly

Dolly sat drinking a cup of tea in the shelter of the patio arch, savouring the taste in place of a cigarette as she gazed at the clouds sailing across the darkened sky. The pear tree swayed in the wind, its upper branches dancing furiously. Next to the patio, the washing, which she'd stupidly left out, flapped on the line, and, for a second or two she fancied she glimpsed a code in the billowing pattern of clothes and towels and underwear that she couldn't decipher. And this would be no less perplexing, she pondered in frustration, tapping lightly on the table with an index finger, because quite frankly she was mystified by everything right now, by the diamonds, by the tapes, by her mother's so-called treasure hunt.

Clearly Gloria once knew Abimbola Senior, but how did the Abimbolas fit into the puzzle? And how in hell had she, Dolly Fontaine, become embroiled in a story that started decades ago and was never resolved, by the sounds of things. She had so many questions, and no answers in sight.

It was beginning to rain in earnest now, a light bluster of raindrops filling the air with an earthy scent, then a steady drizzle pattering rhythmically on the ground. Dolly sighed and sipped the tea, not minding the rain, wondering if inviting Evan had been premature, because all she wanted to do was listen to the new tapes. *And* she needed to hide the blasted diamonds, she realised, before the former Marine arrived. What was she to do with such precious, illegal jewels? Blood diamonds, doubtless. Should she tell Evan or keep them a secret? And if not Evan, then who?

She drained the mug and set it on the table, watching a seagull float on the wind above the treetops. How alone Gloria must have felt in Port Salé – there alone in Uncle Chilembé's flat, a *mausoleum*. Uncle Chilembé, who in Dolly's childish mind was always a vague, shadowy figure shrouded in silence, like a mute reflection in a mirror, forever unspoken, forever voiceless.

Dolly got up and went back inside, thinking how ridiculous it seemed, now, that she should have assumed Gloria was just a parent and not a woman, first and foremost, a person in her own right, with hopes and dreams and tragedies of her own. Like most children, Dolly had never stopped to consider Gloria as an actual individual, because in her mind she was just her mother, superhuman and inhuman, but never simply human. Now it was only too clear that Gloria had been young once, full of life and passion. Gloria, too, went through heartbreaks and trauma. Dolly wished she'd understood this side of her mother sooner.

An hour later, Evan swept in on the wind, his head bent against the weather. 'Funny how they always name storms after women,' he remarked, taking off his coat, handing her a bottle of New Zealand Sauvignon Blanc, pale and cold, drops trickling down the sides. He plonked a box of cheese and crackers on the kitchen counter. 'I brought snacks,' he added cheerfully.

Dolly put the wine in the fridge and stoked the fire, watching the orange flames lick up the side of the newspaper until they built into a fiery dance. At the big table in the kitchen they ate steak and chips and talked with ease. Tentatively, she told Evan about her life in London before everything went wrong, as she put it, and a little of her childhood, of Gloria and Rich, of growing up in Cornwall at Genévrier. In turn, Evan recounted memories of his childhood, of a council estate in Glasgow, of a violent father, and the escape from poverty and turbulence that military life seemed to offer a rebellious sixteen-year-old.

While they were clearing the plates, Evan leaned in to kiss her, but hastily she untangled herself from his grasp and reached for her laptop.

'We'd better do this Skype call. Your friend'll be waiting.'

'Yes, dammit.' Evan grinned, rolling his eyes.

There was a sketchy video line because of the bad weather. At the other end, Evan's mate Thorny turned out to be a military type with a South African accent, whose sentences waved in and out with the connection. Thorny had heard a buzz, he told Dolly, that a Brit called Pev Greyson had come by a contract to decommission weapons from the UK's Ministry of Defence.

'There's a big shipment going into Port Salé,' Thorny continued as Dolly listened intently. 'I did a little digging for you – check out the Trident Liberty.'

'Is that a ship?'

'Ja, ja, seems that way, packed full of Kilomi's re-supplies. Look, watch your back, girl. This is not the sort of thing you want to be caught sniffing around.'

A woman called out in the background, *Andy, tea's ready!*

'Anything else?' Dolly insisted.

'Sorry – I gotta go.' Thorny hesitated. 'Look, I said it before, and I'll say it again. Don't fuckin' touch this. You'll only get into trouble, real trouble, if ya know what I mean.'

The screen pinged and went dead. Dolly turned to Evan with her mind full of questions, but he was looking at her with a serious expression, and she could tell he was going to try to put her off again, too.

'Thorny's right, you know,' he said, predictably. 'These people are not small fry.'

She frowned, ignoring him. 'Can you tell me about how the MOD deals with weapons?'

Evan sighed, and Dolly could tell he was sympathetic to her cause, if not entirely convinced of its safety. 'Sure', he said, brushing her right hand with his fingers.

Every few years, he told her, the UK Ministry of Defence decommissioned its weapons. It was someone's job, said Evan, to organise the weapons that were going out of use, and make sure they were safely squared away. But sometimes they were sold for parts or to foreign places, no questions asked.

'Basically, it's the government's responsibility to make sure it's

206

properly done, so they don't get into the wrong hands and sold off, or sold for parts,' he concluded. 'But sometimes, those weapons turn up in other countries. Often, in fact, they get everywhere.'

'Countries like Lusenka?' Dolly rejoined. 'So, say Pev got that contract, and instead of taking the weapons out of play, he's shipping them over there?'

'It looks that way.'

Dolly ran over the facts. Rich was so adamant that she mustn't trespass at the building site on the hill, but by the looks of things, there *was* something being loaded into the lorries there. Could the site be where Peverell Greyson was stockpiling arms? It seemed clear that the business of Dolphin Technical Solutions was weapons, and she was quite sure now that somehow Rich was mixed up in it all – and Shaun too, by the looks of the email from Peverell Greyson she'd discovered in his inbox.

'I wonder.'

'What?'

'Shaun Kingsley's high up at the MOD, and I mean really high. He and Pev obviously knew each other, so what if Shaun's helping Pev broker the arms contract by smoothing things out on the British end? I found an email between them, which is odd if Pev is mixed up with arms deals, and Shaun has the power to put British arms into decommission. Pev used to own – or owns – a company called Dolphin Technical Solutions, which was listed as a contractor for the MOD a few years ago. What if the two of them are in this together?'

Evan poured more wine and put the glass in her hand with a meaningful look. 'I know you're bored of me saying it, but Christ, these are dangerous people, you don't want to piss them off.'

Dolly felt a wave of irritation. 'Anyone would think you two were in league.'

Evan got up to fetch more logs from outside, causing a draft which came whistling through the front door. Dolly caught herself up, struck suddenly by the meaning of what she was saying. . Evan and Rich... After all, Evan had this strange connection to Lusenka, and he knew Rich...

Was it possible that the two of them were friends, and in cahoots, and that Rich had tasked Evan with blocking her from finding out about Peverell and his shenanigans?

And hadn't it been Morgan's idea to send her to Evan's shooting range in the first place, a seemingly innocent invitation that now seemed more calculated and sinister, considering Peverell had half threatened her there... Was she being manipulated?

She closed her eyes, calling upon the only person who could offer her guidance, even if from beyond the grave – Gloria. She recalled the tape, and Gloria's words. *Believe in yourself, my darling Sugar, and the mountain will not loom so large.* And the other day, on the hill: *You need an ally. You need to trust someone.* For what it was worth, Gloria seemed to think Evan was bona fide. But surely her own gut feelings were valid. She needed to ask more questions.

When Evan came back, drenched, Dolly narrowed her eyes. 'How well do you know my brother?'

'Who? Rich?'

Evan stood in the doorway, holding an armful of logs. He seemed completely relaxed. 'We have a beer now and again.' His eyes scoured hers with an amused expression. 'Course, if I'd known he had such a beautiful sister, I might have got to know him better.'

Dolly raised an eyebrow, trying to fit the pieces of the puzzle together in her mind. Evan's light-hearted tone did little to ease her suspicions. She watched him carefully as he knelt down to stack the logs by the fireplace.

'How did you and Rich meet?' she pressed, her voice steady.

'I can see why you're a journo...' Evan chuckled softly, his eyes twinkling with amusement as he straightened up, dusting off his hands. 'You know how it is in a backwater like this. Everyone knows everyone. Word travels fast. We crossed paths at the pub one evening, got chatting about surfing...' Dolly studied his face for any sign of deceit but found none. It was infuriating how effortlessly honest Evan appeared to be. But she couldn't shake the feeling that there was more to his connection to Rich than he was letting on.

'And what about Lusenka?' Dolly asked, voicing the fears that had been nagging at her since they met, and testing the waters further. 'It seems such a coincidence, your history there, and my presence here, don't you think...'

A shadow passed over Evan's face, so fleeting that Dolly almost missed it. 'A lucky chance,' he replied smoothly, but there was a guard-edness in his tone that didn't escape her notice. 'You're a damn sight more pleasant than my memories of that place, believe me.'

Dolly decided to drop the issue, but felt grateful when Evan offered to pop out for more wine from the shop in Penrennie. Left alone, she ran Shaun Kingsley through the search engine on her phone, which brought up a few bios, an official government profile, and a lengthy Wikipedia entry, which she scanned for details of Shaun's early life and career. Of course, in the past she'd stalked Shaun on Facebook for entirely non-professional reasons, but now the facts stood out with a new relevance. Why on earth hadn't she paid attention before?

Shaun Kingsley attended Marlborough School in Wiltshire between 1965 and 1971, she found out now, then read history at Cambridge, before joining the Foreign Office. After a short stint in London, he was posted overseas as third secretary at the British High Commission, rising through the ranks between 1975 and 1981, though it didn't say where. Later he became Permanent Under-Secretary for the Foreign & Commonwealth Office in Geneva, before running for parliament.

'I wonder,' Dolly murmured under her breath as she googled 'Marlborough School, Peverell Greyson'. Quickly she scanned the entries, clicking on link after link. After a few moments she discovered a link to a black and white sixth form photo from 1965, where the names 'Shaun Kingsley' and 'Peverell Greyson' appeared together.

After a while, Evan returned, looking windblown, bearing wine and a chocolate bar. He sat back down, throwing an arm across the back of the sofa, and Dolly found herself overcome, once again, with a lingering sense of paranoia. Was she foolish to put her confidence in this man she'd met out of the blue? Or was it just that since the London scandal she was looking at the world in a different way, and always questioning people's integrity? She tried to imagine Evan pulling the wool over her eyes and could not. He was so easy-going, a veritable open book. But, she wondered, would she ever be able to trust anyone properly again?

'Hey, look.' He wanted to show her an app on his phone, a world map of shipping lanes and passage manifests stippled with red, green, and grey dots – almost as if he could read her thoughts, Dolly mused, and was determined to prove his integrity.

'What's this?' she said.

'A satellite tracking map we used in the Marines. You can follow everything that's going on at sea; all the fishing vessels, all the container ships, and look up their manifests. Here, try it.'

Taking the phone in her hands, Dolly typed in the Trident Liberty. After a few seconds the screen showed the Trident's dotted route from the UK around the coasts of France and Spain, across the Gibraltar Strait, past the Canary Islands and along down the western coast of Africa, past the jagged tips of Dakar and Monrovia, down on south to Port Salé.

'Trident Liberty,' she read. 'Scheduled Plymouth to Lusenka, 15th May.'

'That's next week.'

'Yes.'

They sat in silence for a few minutes. Then, 'Can I play you something?' Dolly said, deciding that there was no harm in Evan hearing a snippet of her mother's story. If anything, she told herself, it might prompt him to open up about Lusenka.

'Sure,' said Evan, his eyebrows furrowing. 'Sounds mysterious?'

'It is.'

Dolly went to get the envelope delivered by the courier, containing the fifth tape.

'It's something of my mother's I'd like you to listen with me – if you don't mind?'

'Course not.'

CHAPTER THIRTY-ONE

Gloria

Tape five
Meeting the President, 1979, Port Salé

When I got back to my room, I was met with the unexpected sight of a handsome young man lounging on my veranda. He appeared not much older than me, early twenties at most; a rugged, big-shouldered type, British, presumably, and evidently rather sure of his own charms. He was smoking a cigarette and drinking from a tumbler, gin or water, I couldn't discern. My surprise must have been palpable, because he shot me a spry look that was slightly maddening, as if his presence there was entirely natural, and I should have been used by now to the clandestine workings of the British Foreign Office.

Summoning my composure, I extended a hand. 'Fontaine,' I introduced myself. 'Gloria Fontaine.'

'Name's Kingsley,' he replied with a debonair smile, offering a firm handshake, only to raise his glass in a gesture that felt vaguely teasing, though I carefully hid my rising irritation. 'Shaun Kingsley. British High Commission. Pleasure to meet you, Miss Fontaine.'

CHAPTER THIRTY-TWO

Dolly

Kingsley, *Shaun Kingsley*.

Dolly switched off the Walkman, overcome with a momentary dizziness, a profound sense of shock. She was poleaxed by this new development. She closed her eyes for a moment, trying to make sense of the situation. What the hell was a younger version of Shaun – *her* Shaun – doing in Lusenka, talking to *Gloria* in *1979?* Was it a coincidence or something more? Surely the latter. As a seasoned journalist, she understood the rarity of true coincidences. Only connect... Who was it who'd said that? Lawrence? Forster? She couldn't remember, but in her line of work, there were gossamer threads everywhere, tying humans and events together – and she should have pointed this out to Evan, earlier.

'Dolly?'

When she opened her eyes, Evan was staring at her with a concerned expression.

'You okay?'

Dolly hesitated, her cheeks flushing, wondering if Evan had cottoned on yet. She frowned and took a big gulp of wine. 'That's Shaun Kingsley,' she said carefully. 'I told you about him.'

'He's your government boyfriend?'

'Exactly.' She made a face. 'I mean, he's not mine,' she added quickly, 'and he's not my boyfriend, obviously.'

'Christ, the bloke seems to turn up everywhere.'

'Doesn't he.'

She gave a small laugh at Evan's awkward joke, though for some reason it made her feel better. She rewound the tape and the two of them listened again, while in her head she ran quickly over the dates and the information she'd gathered previously, making rough calculations. If her maths were correct, Shaun Kingsley would have been in his early twenties in 1979 – twenty-two, maybe twenty-three years old – straight out of Oxford, on a fast track into the Diplomatic Service. According to the official bio, Lusenka was Shaun's first overseas post.

Easy to imagine then, that the responsibilities of a junior third secretary in the political section would have far exceeded rank at a small mission in the back of beyond. And from Gloria's story, it seemed Shaun was cleared to deal with classified information. Up to top secret? Dolly knew enough about the workings of MI6 to know what sort of power this would endow. What a great new game it must have been for this savvy private-school kid on his first foreign jaunt, playing conduit for the British Intelligence Services.

She found it odd that Shaun had never mentioned Lusenka to her before, especially considering he knew her background. In fact, it seemed peculiar now, and unsettling, that they had never discussed her ethnicity in any depth, though she'd always assumed it was because her mixed heritage – her foreignness, as Shaun probably thought of it – made him feel awkward, given that he was that particular kind of Englishman, utterly conventional, and set in his ways, professing liberal views to mask an inherent snobbism towards difference of any kind.

Could it be that Shaun was aware of Gloria's history all along; and that this knowledge was the underlying motive for their friendship? Dolly shivered, rearranging her memories, adjusting her old preconceptions to fit the puzzle of these new revelations.

So when Shaun had suggested they go to Cornwall for a dirty weekend, as he'd put it…

'Shit,' she murmured out loud, cringing to herself and quickly dismissing the thought. There was no way she was prepared to tell Evan that particular detail. The fact that Shaun probably had some weaselly ulterior motive for such a romantic gesture was too awful and humiliating to think about. Yet in her heart, she knew it was true, and she needed to find out why. It seemed Sunstar was right: to make the connection, she would need to go to Lusenka.

CHAPTER THIRTY-THREE

Gloria

'Likewise,' I said, sizing up my counterpart as I surreptitiously kicked my bag containing Chilembé's code under the bed. In his old-school tie, cufflinks, gold wristwatch, and impeccably tailored linen suit, with a pair of sunglasses tucked into the top pocket, Shaun Kingsley was every inch the foreign diplomat, though his youthful appearance suggested he might not be as seasoned as one would expect, and the absence of 'junior' from his title seemed deliberate, perhaps to downplay his youthfulness. With Seal's words echoing in my head: *trust no one, even if they seem like one of ours*, I smiled politely.

'Would you like a drink?' I offered, pouring myself a gin and tonic, adding ice and a slice of lemon.

Kingsley lit a cigarette. 'Vodka Martini for me, please.'

We sat down outside on the shaded veranda, out of the glaring light, but still it was too hot. How could I have forgotten the intensity of my country's midday sun?

'You have a brief for me, then?' I asked.

Kingsley nodded assent, only to pause and scrutinise me while he puffed on his cigarette, running his eyes with a leisurely sort of arrogance from my face to my legs and breasts.

'They clearly didn't pick you because you blend into the background,' he remarked, his tone full of admiration. 'They don't normally send us such attractive operatives.'

'Shall we get to the point, Mr Kingsley?'

He drew on his cigarette, sending up small puffs of smoke. 'Besides your looks, you already have a reputation for being absolutely fearless.'

'I'm not sure about that. But I've undergone training, yes.'

'Training!' He let out a loud guffaw, extinguishing his cigarette in the ashtray. 'I'm sure I don't need to tell you that this is not England. Everything you know, everything you expect – out of the window. It's the wild west out here.'

Though in many ways he spoke the truth, I felt a rising sense of outrage. Lusenka was *my* country, I wanted to say, *my* homeland. How dare this over-privileged Englishman try to tell me, a Lusenkan, about its faults. I found Kingsley irritating, with his big square jaw and insinuating manner, his sleazy eyes tracing a path across my breasts every few seconds. He struck me as nothing more than a well-educated kid who was good at playing politics, the sort to trade on his charming accent and old school tie contacts – not to mention his good looks.

'That's not what I've been told,' I replied, trying to keep my cool.

'They only tell you what they think you need to know. Don't forget it.'

'They?'

'Our esteemed Intelligence Services.'

'Well, Mr Kingsley, then there's no point dwelling. As I say, shall we get on with it?'

With slender hands, too delicate for his robust frame, Kingsley deftly lit another cigarette as he briefed me on the details of the mission. More and more, he explained, the socialist policies of Lusenka's Communist-leaning president, Baptiste Lourenco, were antagonising the Americans. As Lourenco solidified ever greater ties with Moscow, European states were growing uneasy. According to Kingsley, the Yanks had invested significant sums funding opposition factions to thwart Lourenco's chances of re-election. Now, in alliance with the British Government, they were orchestrating his removal via an internal coup.

'Your mission is critical,' said Kingsley. 'Lourenco is planning to build a formidable military stronghold in the north, bankrolled by the Soviets. We need you to find and photograph the blueprints for that base.'

'The blueprints are at the presidential palace?'

'Most likely, yes.'

I was also, Kingsley informed me, to plant a surveillance device in Lourenco's study. 'Worth listening in to the bugger,' Kingsley said. 'He's roped in the East Germans to build a wireless transmission tower up there. If we can get ears on before it gets built, it'll make this whole operation a damn sight easier.'

I asked a few more specifics: the location of the blueprints; how much time I would have; would there be any back-up? When we stopped talking, Kingsley extinguished his cigarette and placed his empty glass on the low table. As he rose from his chair and went inside, I stopped him, and he sat down again.

'Do you know what happened to my brother, Mr Kingsley?'

At my question, Kingsley's gaze drifted away across the edge of the balcony, towards the distant horizon, then back again to meet my eyes. In the subdued shadows, his irises gleamed the colour of polished steel. There was an unsettling edge to his features, something almost cruel; the way his lips set in a firm line when challenged, a shutter slamming down. I couldn't help wondering what Sunstar might think of Shaun Kingsley.

'You mean Chilembé Fontaine?'

'Yes.'

'Your brother was what's known as an illegal asset. He did some excellent work; without him our current standing would be far less favourable. But when it all went tits up, I'm afraid we had to wash our hands.'

'You mean you could have helped, but you didn't?'

'The British Government cannot be responsible for non-nationals, I'm afraid. Especially when their cover is compromised. It poses too

217

great a risk.'

'Even if these *non-nationals* put their lives on the line?'

Kingsley's expression darkened. 'Especially then, Miss Fontaine.'

Seeming annoyed by my questions, he got abruptly to his feet, and frustration welled within me for the second time since he'd appeared, an hour ago. I was bewildered by his indifference towards my brother's demise. Silently seething, I escorted him to the door. Pausing there, he pivoted to face me without expression, yet with a sort of intentness – as if he were curious about me, and my motives.

'There'll be an invitation. Watch out for it. Otherwise just lie low, bask in the sun, enjoy the weather.' He raised an eyebrow and glanced over at my bag, now plainly visible just under the bed. 'And please refrain from meddling. I'll see you at the party.'

'Party?'

'Lourenco's fiftieth birthday.'

'Oh, I see. Naturally, I'll be there.'

'Smashing.'

A strange sense of deflation washed over me as I watched the door slam behind him. For all his debonair charm, I reflected, I couldn't shake the feeling that Shaun Kingsley was a shifty character, and not to be trusted, on any account.

My watch said twenty to three. I went outside again and lit a cigarette, surveying the shadowless lawns stretching down to the hotel boundaries, and the sea, smoky blue, a sheet of glass on the horizon. In the shade, a gardener on his knees was fixing a sprinkler, hammering the mechanism with a series of loud bangs. I watched him stand upright and stretch his back luxuriously while the sprinkler whirred into life, its glittering spray landing on the velvet grass.

Inside, I stripped to my underwear and stood in front of the fan, closing my eyes in the rush of cool air. Feeling refreshed, I poured myself a glass of water and retreated to bed, reclining against the soft pillows as I sipped slowly for a few minutes, trying to quell the turmoil stirred in me by Kingsley's words, his arrogance and offhand manner. The wretched man had really got to me.

I snoozed a little, pushing aside thoughts of Kingsley, and pondering President Lourenco instead, the daunting mission ahead, and feeling suddenly emotional. I could see what Sunstar meant about everything being in my hands. There was so much at stake. Baptiste Lourenco used violence and murder as an electoral strategy, rigged elections, sent his personal militia to kill anyone who dared oppose him. This man ran Lusenka as if he was its king and was willing to destroy my entire country just to keep his job. This man had torn apart my family and shattered the lives of countless others. Now, I was the one tasked with bringing him down.

I thought about Chilembé. Why had I failed to twig that my brother was a spy? If only I'd realised, perhaps I could have saved him. His British visa had been on the verge of approval. I was on the point of whisking him away to England. It seemed all my fault. If I'd acted sooner, he wouldn't be dead. The idea evoked so many strong emotions that I groaned out loud. There was nothing for it now, I resolved, than to avenge my brother's death by bringing down Baptiste Lourenco.

Summoning all my willpower, I heaved myself out of bed and forced myself to concentrate. I retrieved my bag and the small slip of paper bearing the cryptic code, and for a few minutes stared unreflectingly at the cursive loops and curls of my brother's handwriting, picturing him writing out the code, his brow furrowed in concentration. No doubt, he was aware that someone was hunting him, closing in with every passing second. The thought made my stomach churn.

I took a notebook from my suitcase and set to work, remembering my codebreaking lessons with the indefatigable Lavender at Gwynarthen. Chilembé's message held a pattern, I knew. Pondering my brother's favourite things – books, places, writers – I began scanning for repeating letters, replacing 'a's with 'k's and 'i's with 'e's, letter after letter, twisting the combinations around with a dogged persistence I knew would pay off in the end.

Hours passed. Beyond the window's mosquito netting, the boiling afternoon faded into evening. Jazz melodies drifted from below, cutting through the stillness, first a saxophonist, then a trumpet and a female singer, velvet voiced and funky. The music stopped and started and stopped again; the band seemed to be rehearsing. The low grooves of the music interrupted my train of thought, and I paused to pour myself more water, gulping it down, overcome with sudden thirst. I poured myself another glass, and finished that, too.

All at once the fan came to a whirring halt. A power cut. In the background, the jazz singer reached an explosive peak and ended the song on a high note. I returned to my seat on the bed and jotted down a final combination: THINGSFALLAPART as the rotating keyword, shift each letter of the code, match it to the keyword...

Think.

And there it was. In the way of a camouflaged creature emerging from the forest, my brother's ingenious message revealed itself: *Talk to Abimbola.*

For a few seconds, I sat staring at it with a mixture of surprise and disbelief, because the name – Abimbola – was as familiar to me as any prominent figure regularly gracing the news headlines.

In Lusenka at least, Hervé Abimbola was well-known; an easily recognisable figure with his neat, puffy Afro, Lennonish spectacles and flamboyant style of dressing. He was one of Lourenco's inner circle; a youngish, free-thinking politician who'd been Lourenco's right hand man since 1965. He'd started off as a lawyer like my brother, had risen through national politics as a minister of foreign affairs, then secretary of state. A dangerous man, by all accounts, a man who had the president's ear like no other. So why, I wondered, would Chilembé want me to speak to him, of all people? And why now?

Preoccupied, I made my way downstairs to the hotel restaurant for dinner, where I chose a table near an open window and glanced around the room as I waited to be served, wondering what stories the other diners might have to tell.

Near the buffet, a man was drinking wine on his own. He had the tousled look of an expat, thin-faced in a crumpled cotton shirt, chino slacks, pockmarked skin flushed with the effects of alcohol. All of a sudden, I was reminded of Sidney Dunn, my so-called rescuer. Had he stayed here at The Sheraton a decade ago when he found me? How curious that I was sitting here now in this plush restaurant, a woman not a girl, living a life that would have seemed unimaginable to me back then. How could I have foretold what was coming? If once I was grateful to Sidney, now I felt enraged – I had left Chilembé because of him, and I would never forgive myself for that.

It was nearly nine o'clock by the time I finished my meal. I lit a cigarette and wandered back through the front lobby, feeling strangely jittery. I must have sensed something was about to happen, because a young receptionist at the desk called me over as I made my way past.

'A letter for you, Mademoiselle.'

Nervously, I took the long envelope of thick, cream paper from her outstretched hand, and saw the presidential crest stamped in wax, sealing it closed.

Without hesitation, I tore it open. Inside was an invitation card: *You are cordially invited to the President's birthday party,* it said. *Friday 23rd April 1979. 8pm. The Sheraton Hotel.*

Dress code: Black tie

Carriages: 1am

The party was tomorrow. A shiver of anticipation crept slowly up my spine. Well then, I thought to myself. Here we go at last.

CHAPTER THIRTY-FOUR

Dolly

Dolly slowly sipped her wine, thinking of Chilembé's coded message, of the ominous invitation to the president's birthday party. Gloria's story was the shape of a dream upon waking, slipping out of reach, no matter how tightly she tried to hold on. After all, it made sense that Gloria should mention Hervé Abimbola in her diary, given what Lionel had told her about his father the other day. In the note accompanying the diamonds, Lionel said Hervé met Gloria – and so it all seemed tied up in some way. How, though, was another matter. Whatever the answer, every thread seemed to lead directly to Lusenka, just as Sunstar had suggested.

'So that's your mum?' Evan cut into her thoughts. 'On the tape?'

Dolly dragged her mind from the puzzle. 'Her name was Gloria. She went to Lusenka in 1979 on some sort of mission. It's the first time I've listened to these tapes.'

'Did you get on with her?'

'Sort of.' Thoughtfully, Dolly watched the flames of the fire flicker and rise. 'Not really. She was so famous, and a bit of a mystery. She was a cool mum, I guess, but distant. I used to long for her attention. I suppose I idolised her.'

Evan asked if Dolly knew what Gloria was doing in Lusenka, and she pondered this, walking over to the mantelpiece, bending to stoke the fire. 'It was something to do with Baptiste Lourenco, who was the president at the time.' She threw a log onto the glowing embers. 'Gloria was sent to get intelligence on him for the British.'

'At least you have the tapes to remember her by.' Evan got up, disappearing into the kitchen. When he came back, he was holding the nearly empty bottle of wine. Dolly watched him refill the glasses, shaking out the dregs of the bottle. 'Who's the guy she mentions, Sunstar?'

'He was the British intelligence agent Gloria worked for. He gave me some of the tapes my mum left.'

There was a long silence.

'Funny,' said Evan, eventually. 'Me being in Lusenka years later, after your mum. The bloke who came after Lourenco, Florian Kilomi – Killer, we called him – was supposed to be the Brits' darling, but he was already a wee dictator even by then. The power went straight to his head. It was a mess out there. People executing each other bare-handed, murdering women and children.'

Dolly listened as Evan spoke on, about war, about killing, about death. Quietly, he described the gruesome aftermath of an ambush, how he saw limbs hacked off like raw pieces of meat. For months afterwards, even back home in England, he would wake in the night imagining a man holding a machete to his neck. She was beginning to understand that Evan's connection to Lusenka was probably exactly what she'd thought originally – just a coincidence – and that, quite simply, he didn't want to remember the bloodshed and the terror of that terrible military tour.

'It must have been a major backfire for the Brits,' she said, bringing the conversation back to politics.

'It was. We were meant to guard some oilfields for most of the time, up in the north. I always wondered if we were really there as peace-keepers, or just to make sure the oil didn't get nicked...'

'I wonder.' Dolly took the refilled glass of wine and settled next to Evan on the sofa. 'Look, do you mind listening to some more?' she added, deciding to put her earlier suspicions aside, for now anyway. Talking about war brought a heightened atmosphere of closeness between them. Perhaps her previous worries were unfounded. Evan was so straightforward, nothing seemed to faze him. In his company she felt peaceful, calm and almost – almost - happy, as though everything would be all right.

'I just need to know what happens,' she added, resolving not to tell him about the diamonds, even so. She ought still to be careful.

'Sure,' Evan said, taking her hand. 'Why not?'

CHAPTER THIRTY-FIVE

Gloria

The following afternoon, I counted down the hours until the President's birthday party. My stomach was in knots. Gone was the sturdy resolve I'd felt at Gwynarthen, because this was a completely different kettle of fish: a psychopathic dictator to be seduced, for God's sake!

I cloistered myself in my hotel room, locked the door, poured myself a stiff gin and tonic and stared at my reflection in the mirror, willing myself to be brave, and remembering Sunstar's words: *You have no idea how important this is.* I had one shot at getting Lourenco to invite me to a private meeting. What's more, another, new motive preyed on my mind. If Hervé Abimbola happened to be at the function, I intended to find him.

From my suitcase I pulled out the gown I'd been issued with at the end of my training at Gwynarthen. Someone at HQ possessed very good taste, because it was a flawless fit, of a delicate rippling indigo silk that shimmered in the light, backless with a plunging neckline, and hand-stitched with tiny, starry sequins. On further examination, I discovered the garment had a secret pocket sewn into the right hip, unlike any evening gown I'd ever worn. The HQ fashion person really was ingenious.

Naturally, I added my own touches: a pair of diamond earrings with blue accents, which reminded me of a Lusenkan sky in the hot season. A pretty pair of silver heels gifted to me by a friendly costume designer on my first Mirrorball film. I fashioned my hair into a voluminous Afro, fluffy and full. As a finishing touch, I chose a bold, strawberry-red lipstick called Day of Danger, by Dior. The dramatic irony wasn't lost on me.

I planned to arrive late to the party, late enough to make an entrance, late enough for the president to notice me arrive. I needed to make an impression. As the setting sun pitched slanting shadows through the bamboo window blinds of the room, I paced the floor, checking the clock over and over again, touching up my make-up, impatient for the evening – and thus my mission – to begin. I kept one eye on the television, too, where a newsreader was reporting latest developments in the Middle Eastern oil crisis. Prices of oil were up nearly two hundred per cent, she was saying, with European nations scrabbling to meet demand in the face of their embargo of Iran. Interesting, I thought to myself. Lusenka was, and always had been, one of the most oil-rich countries in the world. What a coincidence, then, that the British and Americans should be so keen to acquire a footing here.

At last, at a quarter to nine on the dot, I downed a neat, fortifying shot of gin, locked my room, and descended the main staircase. The moment I entered the ballroom, all eyes turned towards me, but I ignored them, and took a minute to get the measure of the place, quickly noting the details. A gigantic crystal chandelier suspended from the ceiling, casting geometric patterns across a golden hardwood dance floor. Tall windows draped with voluminous blue-silk curtains. Gold mirrors on the walls, which doubled the size of the room and the crowd. A six-piece band was playing jazz, the singer already in full swing, and I recognised the song, the musicians I'd heard practising the day before.

There were three entrances and exits, I noted: all guarded by security men, and another pair of huge doors without a guard, flung open to the gardens. I took note of the guests, who were VIPs and dignitaries, some of them people I'd been briefed about by Seal. The men wore black dinner jackets and bow ties. The women fluttered and shimmered like a flight of butterflies, a rainbow of glittering cocktail gowns.

I crossed the floor and stepped out onto the terrace.

More guests were gathered in groups, talking, laughing, and drinking. The air was hot and breezeless, full of jazz and laughter. I could hear the racket of the crickets chanting rhythmically in the undergrowth. A waiter in white tie was putting on a show, shaking cocktails along to the beat of the music drifting from the ballroom. I could see people whispering to each other, trying to work out who I was, then figuring it out with small exclamations.

I scanned the terrace until I spotted Baptiste Lourenco commanding a small group of admirers near the borders of an underlit swimming pool. In sleek black tie, the president wasn't much over five foot seven, yet somehow he still managed to command everyone's attention. The men and women semi-circled around him appeared to be in stitches of laughter at something he was saying.

I watched surreptitiously. True, he was handsome and charming, but beneath the surface lay a corrupt, tyrannical man who used his charisma to attract and control people. It was no secret that he used our country as his own personal bank account. The sight of the guests laughing and joking with this murderer made me shiver with rage.

Letting my eyes run over the other guests, I scanned the crowd for Abimbola – but there was no one yet present who fitted his description.

'Gloria!'

In impeccable black tie, Shaun Kingsley made a beeline for me. He executed a small bow, full of smiles and buttery charm. 'Wonderful to see you again.'

'And you too, Mr Kingsley.'

'Please be assured that the Foreign Office is exceedingly glad you're here. Come, let me find you a drink.'

From that moment on, the evening seemed to take on a life of its own. Kingsley acquired me a flute of pink champagne, and there followed a whirl of introductions. Whatever else the man was, he was jolly good at socialising. He plied me with drinks which I pretended to enjoy, only to pour my glass at intervals into the potted palms dotted about the ballroom. The band transitioned to a medley of European pop hits – Fleetwood Mac, Shirley Bassey, The Eagles, and The Bee Gees. People began dancing, sedately at first and then with abandon. Men and women gyrated against one other, waving their arms in the air, and kissing. All of them seemed caught up in the same drunken spell.

I remained purposefully apart, watching the arrival of new guests. I had an inkling that Abimbola would turn up at some point, and for this reason I kept a close eye on the people leaving and entering the ballroom. Once or twice, I caught President Lourenco looking over at me, and I willed him to come and talk.

It was midnight though, before he did. Out of the corner of my eye I watched him advance. As if on cue, Kingsley appeared by my side and ushered me towards him, issuing an effusive introduction.

'Miss Fontaine, may I introduce His Excellency, President Baptiste Lourenco, who's a great friend of the British, I might add.'

Lourenco fixed me with eyes dark as midnight, cloudy with drink, and inscrutable. Close-to, there was something unsettling about their depths, a hunger of sorts, as though he were sizing me up for his next meal. I had the disquieting feeling that I was the prey – and he, the hunter.

'Absolutely, absolutely,' he said, with a bow, kissing my hand with a flourish. 'It's an honour, Miss Fontaine.'

Frighteningly, there was no mistaking the unspoken desire that shone in his hunter's eyes, but I tried to pretend I hadn't noticed.

'I must say,' he added, 'I don't think I've ever had the pleasure of hosting such a beautiful lady before.'

'Happy birthday, your Excellency,' I said. To the side of us, three security men in military uniform melted into the background. 'I trust you're enjoying your party?'

'I am,' he beamed. 'We've met before, have we not?'

'Indeed, we have, Your Excellency.'

I reminded the president of our meeting at the party in London in 1976, explaining that I was born in Lusenka, had left for England when I was a teenager – though I suspected he already knew this. All the time he watched me with a mixture of interest and undisguised attraction, occasionally and without embarrassment running his eyes down from my face to my breasts, then to my legs and back up again.

'So, Miss Fontaine,' he interrupted. 'Is it good to be home?'

'Lusenka's map is etched on my heart, Your Excellency,' I replied. It was a line I'd practised over and over at Gwynarthen.

Lourenco's eyes lit up. He was the sort of man who was easily bored, as fickle as a bird. Naturally, it was my job to fascinate him. I couldn't help noticing the cut-glass correctness of his Queen's English, which nearly perfectly hid a faint Lusenkan accent. He'd attended a boys' school in England – or so I'd been briefed – had played rugby for the county of Hertfordshire before returning to his home country to pursue a career in politics. The shadow of brutality in the man's eyes alongside his public schoolboy accent and polished manners made for an unsettling combination.

'You seem more British than the British, Miss Fontaine,' he said, as if reading my thoughts. 'Your accent is impeccable, and I mean that as a compliment. Please, walk with me.'

'Of course.'

At the bar Lourenco ordered me another drink, which I sipped carefully while he regaled me with stories about his military experience, his three wives and numerous children, his love for his country and countrymen. Nodding, agreeing, I made a show of listening to his rhetoric.

'I suppose,' he finished up, 'my people love me because in so many ways, I'm their father.'

I regarded him steadily, not allowing my eyes to fall from his. 'Ultimately, you hold their fate in your hands, Your Excellency.'

If he sensed that my statement was a criticism, he did not show it. On purpose I turned my mind to Chilembé, reminding myself that this man – this man! – had ordered my brother's death, personally. Did Lourenco himself make the connection? Would he even care that I was Chilembé's sister, or even remember Chilembé's name? I breathed deeply and took a sip of my drink. I got the impression that in this tyrant's own head, he really believed he was loved.

'Do you smoke, Gloria? May I call you Gloria?'

'Of course.'

Lourenco reached into his pocket and brought out a gold cigarette case encrusted with a presidential coat of arms. He offered me a Virginia Slim, which I accepted graciously, leaning towards him for a light. The smoke was sweet and faintly aromatic. I was suddenly reminded of a voice-over job I'd done, years ago, and the slogan I'd been asked to read out countless times: *Tailored slim for today's woman; for your hands, for your lips*. Did the president know these were women's cigarettes? I fought back a smile.

'Tell me, where do your loyalties lie, Gloria? With the British, or with your own homeland? You've been in the United Kingdom for many years. Perhaps it's time to come back?'

Lourenco's nationalism was well-known. He had radical views on liberalising Lusenka from foreign influence, despite his English education. Like most extreme stances, there was an underlying post-colonial rationale that I wholeheartedly agreed with – who didn't? – though his arguments quickly descended into the absurd. He had long blamed Lusenka's economic problems on a plot by Western countries, led by the British, to oust him from the presidency. Now I stared at his face and felt the terrible, unnerving insanity of the man. It occurred to me that his opinions seemed ironic, now, considering his fantasy was about to come true. Thankfully, I'd been coached by my Gwynarthen teachers how to respond appropriately. I knew my lines by heart.

'I believe Lusenka must revert to what it was before the colonialists divided it,' I replied coolly, repeating more learnt lines. 'I'm afraid it will be a long journey for our continent. We are bound by artificial divisions. The Europeans are our real enemy, of course.'

'Our enemy,' Lourenco replied with a smile, 'and our oppressor.'

We continued to talk pleasantly, easily, yet I was struck by how many conflicting facets there were to Lourenco's personality. On the one hand, he seemed a normal man, with a genuine interest in the people he was leading and the causes he believed he was fighting for. On the other, there was a terrifying air of ruthlessness about him, a sense of a darker side kept carefully concealed. He was a snake at rest, always ready to strike. In the course of our conversation, I kept glimpsing this lurking menace in his eyes, belied by his genteel English manners.

More and more, I found myself struggling to equate the reality of Lourenco, the president, with the man, the human, standing before me; a caricature of a dictator, a personality cult in the flesh. Yet here he was, one arm leant casually on the bar, as articulate and charming as any capable diplomat. The clash between Lourenco's opposite sides, both of them true, tangled my brain in knots. Now I understood what Sunstar had meant when he said that only I – Gloria Fontaine – could do this. None of those fuddy-duddies at the British Foreign Office would have had the gall to seduce a president.

He took a sip of champagne, seeming to observe me closely over the top of the glass. Then without warning, his eyes swerved to my left, and I heard another voice, highish with a lilting Lusenkan accent. My heart fluttered with excitement as I turned to find Hervé Abimbola by my side. In person, he was a beanpole, tall and slightly built with spidery limbs and a studious looking face.

'Gloria Fontaine. What a surprise to see you again!'

I hesitated. Had we met before? Surely not. Then the penny dropped. Whatever Abimbola's game, it dawned on me that I should play along as best I could.

'Hervé,' I said with warmth, feigning a friendly familiarity. 'How wonderful to see you again too.'

Hervé Abimbola lifted my hand and bent to kiss it with exaggerated pomp. In the minutes that followed, I tried to concentrate on the small talk that ensued between the three of us – the president, Abimbola and me – but my mind was spinning in all directions. Could it be that Abimbola was one of Sunstar's men? An agent also, a double agent at that – what Seal referred to as a mole? But Abimbola was a strange sort; skittish, intelligent, difficult to pin down. I couldn't see myself trusting him anymore than Kingsley.

Another guest came towards us across the room, or two guests, a man and a woman, holding glasses of champagne, big smiles turned on Lourenco. The president revolved around to greet them, exchanging air kisses. At that moment Abimbola deliberately rotated his body so that he was, to the extent that was possible, anyway, obscuring the president's view. He shot me a hard look.

'I must go and work the room,' he said. 'It's been good to see you again.'

A slight emphasis on the last phrase. An intense look in his eyes, which bored into mine. He lifted my hand and dropped a kiss on the back of it. As he did so I felt something pass from his fingers into mine, in the manner of a baton in a relay race. Like a magician, he pushed whatever it was into my hand. In turn, I closed my fingers around the object, smallish, hard, metal. In a flash, I realised it was a key.

The whole thing was over in a split second. Without a word or a change in expression, Abimbola stood back, bowed, and swooped away at the exact moment that Lourenco turned back to me. I felt my mouth go dry and clutched the key hidden in my palm, telling myself to remain calm. With a bright smile that hid my inner discomposure, I fixed my eyes on the president, who was drunk, I registered to my profound relief, and in an amicable mood. There was no reason to be nervous.

'My God,' Lourenco remarked. 'I can see why they say you're a woman of such beauty and intelligence. You are truly exquisite.'

'I don't like to disappoint, Your Excellency.'

'Not at all.' He gulped his drink. 'Your beauty is enough. But your sharp mind makes you...' he swirled the glass, 'captivating.' He took a sip. 'Please, call me Baptiste.'

'Baptiste,' I repeated, rolling the consonants around in my mouth. Keeping my eyes on his, as a distraction, I stashed the key in the secret pocket of my evening gown and shot him a wide smile, teasing him a little. 'And you can call me Gloria, just Gloria.'

'Gloria, would you like to have dinner with me tomorrow? I would be honoured to take you on a tour of my palace.'

'I'd be delighted,' I replied.

It must have been two a.m. by the time I got back to my room, with the mysterious key hidden in the secret pocket of my gown. I was intending to examine it straight away, but to my annoyance, I found Shaun Kingsley sitting on my veranda again, deliberately placed in a dark corner, incognito, a loosened bow tie draped around his neck. God knows how he got in.

'Cheers.' Kingsley raised his glass – apparently he'd already served himself a vodka Martini. It occurred to me that he was drunk, too. Very drunk. 'You did well tonight, Gloria.'

'Thank you, Mr Kingsley.'

'No, thank you.'

I kicked off my heels, poured myself a drink and lit a cigarette, then drew up a chair next to Kingsley, my eyes on the full moon suspended

233

in the night sky. The flowery scent of frangipani and night-blooming jasmine drifted up from the gardens. The dark expanse of the Atlantic loomed invisible beyond the hotel boundary. I could hear the last of the party guests making their way to bed, their strands of laughter catching on the breeze, twirling upwards in the warm night air.

'Tomorrow's an important day,' Kingsley said. 'Ensure you handle it with finesse, won't you.'

'Word travels fast, then?'

'The president's amorous advances were the talk of the party. It seems he has you lined up as his fourth wife.'

'Lucky me.'

I inhaled deeply, observing the inky sea, watching the trajectory of a lone oil tanker in the dark, its lights edging at a snail's pace towards the pitch black shoreline.

'You know Lourenco's nationalist views are unbending,' I said, stretching out my legs, and circling my ankles. 'He wants the British out of his hair. I think in an ideal world he'd banish all foreign diplomats. Don't you think he might suspect I'm a plant?'

'Sunstar believes you're up to it. There's a lot at stake.'

'You've spoken to him?'

Kingsley nodded. 'If things go south, ask the palace housekeeper for a gin fizz.'

'Did Sunstar say that?'

'Any trouble, you hear?' Kingsley narrowed his eyes. 'With Lourenco. Request that cocktail.'

He extinguished his half-smoked cigarette in the ashtray and got to his feet. Without speaking I accompanied him to the door of the hotel room. For the briefest instant, I sensed a hesitation in him, as if he wanted to say more, but in the end, he kept silent, merely nodding to me impassively as he stepped out into the deserted corridor. The door closed behind him with a click. I went to the veranda, picked up our cigarette stubs, deposited them in my purse.

CHAPTER THIRTY-SIX

Dolly

Late now, past eleven, and Dolly walked Evan to his van in the pitch black, trying not to think that she didn't want to be left alone here tonight, not with so many looming dangers that seemed suddenly so tangible. What if something happened and Peverell Greyson found out about the tapes – or Shaun, for that matter? Bloody Shaun. What if Pev came here, to find her at Genévrier? Were her nieces safe, and Gracie? And if Rich really was involved in all this, could he be trusted at all, on anything? The thought was horrifying.

She glanced up at the dim half-moon obscured by clouds. The sky was huge, vast and starless. Down here in the deep country there was no invasion from city lights, and the air had a profound stillness; no people, no cars, just the fields and the open sea stretching out to nowhere. She could quite see why Gloria would have hidden down here, after the mission.

Near the driver's side of the van, Dolly stumbled on a pothole and reached out for something to hold on to, only to feel Evan's arm around her. She found herself tilting into his comfortable bulk. She wasn't surprised when he leaned in and kissed her gently on the lips, just once, before climbing into the van and driving away, leaving her alone in the darkness.

The following morning, Dolly awoke just after sunrise. When she opened her eyes, she could see the leafy crown of the pear tree through the wide-open bedroom window, green branches against a cloudless sky beyond. Sun shadows dappled the yellowing anaglypta walls of the bedroom. She listened to the crickets scratching away in the grass; a distant chirp of a thrush; some sort of farm machine in the distance – country sounds in the dead quiet air – and thought about Evan, the way he seemed to want her with an uncomplicated sort of passion. For the first time, last night, seeing another side to him, she'd almost begun to trust him. The feeling was annoying. Such a quiet sort of happiness – being treated well – was new, unexpected, and disconcerting. What if Evan changed, just as Shaun had? Perhaps she was ready to trust him, perhaps not. So far, she had no idea.

She turned over with a groan and pulled the duvet up to her chin, wondering not for the first time if she was afraid of commitment – a commitment-phobe, as the popular women's magazine writers liked to put it. Was she the sort of person who didn't value other human beings who treated them well? Was she so used to drama or complete solitude that the calm, unassuming surety of someone like Evan seemed alien, boring even.

'Ugh,' she exclaimed out loud. Her phone lit up. A text from Shaun – talk of the devil – was previewed on the screen: *Hey, you okay? Can I ring you?*

She stared at it for a few seconds before pressing delete, because she didn't want to think about Shaun right now, though doubtless he had answers that would help. Instead, she got up and opened the top drawer of the dressing table, then the jewellery box sent by Sunstar. Carefully, she twisted the tiny jewels into her earlobes, turning her head this way and that in the mirror, admiring the effect of the pretty blue centres sparkling against her skin. She cast her mind back to Gloria wearing the very same earrings at President Lourenco's birthday party, and turned to the bedside table.

The folder of newspaper cuttings from the editor in Truro was lying open there. Dolly picked it up as a line caught her eye, from *Vogue*, July 1995: 'I'm very conscious of the fact that people see me as an oddity," says Fontaine, "and I admit, I'm a recluse. I'm getting old, and a little eccentric in my ways.'

The writer, someone called Cary Morgan, must have visited Gloria at

Genévrier, because she described the house, 'rambling and wisteria-clad', and Gloria, to a T: 'Fontaine is not the easiest woman to interview. Evasive, and at times a little cagey, she seems to me a complex woman, at once charming and closed off, a hint of suspicion in her gaze as I ask her questions.'

Dolly smiled to herself – go Mum – and scanned the clipping's headline: Decades of Bombshell, and a photograph of Gloria posing just right-of-centre in the doorway of the greenhouse at Genévrier, next to a line of bushy courgette plants. She looked beautiful, elegant and rather wistful in wide, expensive-looking woollen trousers, a frilly cream blouse and lavender cardigan, and gardening gloves, secateurs in hand. The blue diamonds sparkled in her earlobes. Dolly brushed the picture gently with her fingers. She wished her mother had given her the earrings in person.

Dolly put the article away but kept the earrings on, put on a T-shirt and shorts, and wandered down the stairs to prepare breakfast. Poached eggs with a round of toast, ground pepper, a dollop of ketchup. More coffee. Eventually Evan rang, and she answered after a few rings with a strange, pleased feeling in her chest.

'I'm still thinking about your mum's tape,' Evan said on the other end after a brief preamble. 'The conflict in Lusenka has been going on for years. We were sent in when Kilomi started cracking down on the Balaika, driving them out of their villages, taking away their ancestral lands – which just happened to be those oilfields I told you about, that we were sent to guard on behalf of the government, if you can believe it. But people said there were diamonds too, though it was only ever a rumour. Peacekeeping, they called it. There were mass executions going on. We could see it all coming, but it didn't even make the news.'

'So the president was committing genocide,' Dolly replied, frowning as she held the phone to her ear and took another sip of coffee, 'because he wanted the Balaika's land, too.'

'Too right,' said Evan. 'Even then, everyone wanted the oil and whatever else was in that rich Lusenkan earth. It was so valuable.

And people turned a blind eye to the killings. They *are* still turning a blind eye.'

Later that morning, Dolly switched on the news, glancing absently at the screen before stopping in her tracks. The headline ticker running across the bottom of the screen made her stomach drop: EXILED LUSENKAN DISSIDENT LIONEL ABIMBOLA, SON OF ASSASSINATED 1970s ACTIVIST, HERVÉ ABIMBOLA, FOUND DEAD IN HOME.

She grabbed the remote, turned up the sound as the screen flashed to a live report: a local journalist standing outside a house, microphone in hand, in a rural-looking street, that could have been any English country village, but was, Dolly knew immediately, in Meavy, South Devon.

'Lionel Abimbola was found dead this morning,' the correspondent was saying, 'at the house near Plymouth where he was in hiding. His father was once a prominent ally of Lusenkan dictator, Baptiste Lourenco.'

The report went on to detail Lionel Abimbola's background, his path from activist to exile in the UK, and the fact that he had probably been assassinated by Lusenkan agents following the 'bully-boy' tactics of Florian Kilomi, the current president, to quash all opposition.

Dolly flicked the television off and sank down on the couch, head in hands, feeling devastated, struggling to make sense of this new development. Lionel's urgent phone call had hinted at something important relating to his father, Hervé, and their work against Lourenco in the seventies, and Hervé's encounter with Gloria, the night of the birthday party. And now Lionel was dead. He must have known that his life was in danger, and that was why he changed his mind so abruptly, and why he telephoned yesterday in such a panic.

Dolly was reeling. She took a deep breath, staring at the blank television screen. Whatever information Lionel had to reveal, the clue was in the tapes. He knew someone was coming to kill him, and knew he had to get them to her, urgently. Hence the courier.

With quick steps, Dolly went over to her bag, retrieving the last of the tapes from Lionel: Tape Six. It was no longer a question of curiosity, she told herself. Lionel was dead. Her family was in danger. Now more than ever, she needed to pay attention to what Gloria was saying.

CHAPTER THIRTY-SEVEN

Gloria

Tape six
Lourenco's crocodiles, 1979, Mo Kana

I stood rooted to the spot, listening to the heavy tread of Kingsley's footsteps trail away down the hotel corridor. Once I was sure he was gone, I fumbled in the secret pocket of my gown for Abimbola's key, which turned out to be a small, silver object with a number engraved on its uppermost side: 65. With a feeling of trepidation, I turned it over in my fingers as I weighed up the risks of what came next. Should I trust Abimbola's word and use the key, or was it a trap? For the next half hour, I paced the room in a fever of indecision.

Abimbola wanted me to find him, that much was clear. If I trusted him, I'd be one step closer to solving the mystery of Chilembé's coded message, but if the key turned out to be a trap, I'd have nowhere to turn. I'd be a dead woman.

I fingered the key, hesitating.

Eventually, I slipped off my evening dress, tied my dressing gown around me, and went over to the drinks tray, key in hand. Telling myself that a cover story of fetching water from the kitchen was as good as any, I emptied the water jug into the bathroom sink and carried the jug in my arms, slipping the key into the pocket of the dressing gown.

Outside the room, I made my way along the vast, empty corridors of the hotel and down the stairs to the lobby, where a night receptionist sat nodding off behind the desk. Quickly, I turned right past the entrance to the now deserted ballroom and walked along the adjoining corridor, following my nose until I saw a sign I'd noticed earlier in the day: an arrow pointing to rooms fifty-six to seventy-nine.

There was a long, unlit corridor, then an exterior path with one side open to an area of tropical greenery. I stashed the water jug under a sprawling forest fern and carried on into the night, eventually finding myself on another long path edged with lush banana palms that meandered through the hotel complex. At last, I heard a man's voice coming from inside one of the rooms. The sign on the door said number 65 – matching the key. I slowed my pace to listen.

Whoever the first man was, he spoke English, a well-spoken accent, I discerned as I drew closer, with the distinctively genteel intonations of an English public schoolboy.

Kingsley?

I slowed my footsteps, silent as a cat, and tiptoed closer to the room where the sound was coming from.

'Don't be an idiot. You know we'll look after you.'

Without a doubt the voice was Shaun Kingsley's, but what was he still doing here at this time? Presumably he'd come straight from my room. I glanced at my watch. It was twenty-five past four in the morning. The person he was talking to uttered a small laugh.

'Lourenco's never been more powerful, and he hates the British,' said the other voice in a Lusenkan accent. 'After the election, which he'll rig, he'll close the High Commission and cut all ties. You must know that.'

I sidled up to the exterior wall of the room and backed myself up under the open window. Cautiously, I manoeuvred so that I could peer inside the window without revealing myself. From that angle I could make out two men: Shaun Kingsley and... Hervé Abimbola, I saw with surprise, who was sitting upright in a leather armchair while Kingsley stood before him, with his hands clasped behind his back.

'To hell with Lourenco and his paint-by-numbers dictatorship,' Kingsley was saying. 'We can't afford for the Soviets to get a foothold. Lusenka needs to be back in sane hands.'

'So what's the plan?' said Abimbola.

'For you to continue.' Kingsley hovered over his counterpart. 'HQ wants you to stay with us.'

'I'm married, I've got a son. I don't want to die.'

Kingsley gave a small nod of assent. 'We'll make sure you're duly compensated. A hefty sum of cash for you to keep your wife in style, and, ultimately, a visa for both of you.'

A long silence. Abimbola stared back at Kingsley. From the garden, the sharp trills of a thousand night insects cut through the darkness. Soon it would be dawn, I thought, and these nocturnal gatherings impossible.

Kingsley spoke: 'But we also need the deeds.'

'No.'

Kingsley shook his head in exasperation. 'Just imagine the consequences if the Soviets beat us to the punch. Do you really want Lourenco cosying up with Volkov before we manage to pull off this coup? He's already wooing the bugger with the idea of the oil pipeline, and mark my words, Volkov will be all too keen to jump into bed forever and a day, if Lourenco dangles the diamonds.'

I pricked up my ears. Diamonds?

Abimbola chuckled knowingly. 'We both know the reason you want that dossier is not in the name of democracy. For God's sake, man, with that land in your hands, you'd be a millionaire overnight. I wouldn't be surprised if your superiors in England don't even know about the deeds.'

'Then I suggest you have a think about how much your wife wants her visa.'

In the heavy silence, I watched Abimbola sit still, too still, while Kingsley stood upright, staring at him without expression. My head was beginning to ache. I fought the urge to flee my hiding place, all too aware that I must remember every detail of this conversation, no matter what. Thank God I was used to learning lines, because as the two men spoke, I found I was able to commit their conversation to memory. They were talking about the coup and plans to oust Lourenco, but the diamonds made no sense to me. Afterwards, I promised myself, I'd piece together the puzzle of their words.

After a tense silence, Abimbola spoke up. 'If your people go poking around, Lourenco will know it's come from me. Only he and I know those deeds exist. And he won't hesitate to have me killed.'

'But by that time, Florian Kilomi will be president,' said Kingsley. 'We'll get you out, along with your wife and child.'

Abimbola let out a weary sigh. 'It sounds so simple when you put it like that.'

'Look, we British stand for democracy. You're doing this for the greater good.'

'Greater good.' Abimbola gave an incredulous laugh. 'Forgive me for being sceptical, but I lost faith in that notion long ago.' He sighed deeply, miserably, shaking his head. 'Give me a few days. I need to make sure the coast is clear.'

'As you wish. Two days, Hervé. That's all we can afford.'

'I'll be in touch then if all goes well. God willing.'

As Abimbola got to his feet, I crept across the pathway and hid behind one of the banana palms, feeling a strange mix of cold courage and awful, stomach-wrenching fear. There I waited, monitoring Shaun Kingsley's footsteps as he exited the hotel room and walked the other way. Then came Abimbola. I watched him turn left, gave him a couple of seconds, took a deep breath, and emerged from my hiding place.

'Hervé?' I hissed in a loud whisper.

He turned. If he was startled, he didn't show it. 'Miss Fontaine.' His eyes seemed to search my face. 'You were watching all that?'

I nodded, holding up the key. 'Presumably you wanted me to

find you.'

'Yes.' He nodded, indicating for me to follow him. 'Absolutely. Please come in here.'

Back inside the hotel room, he closed the door and poured himself a large glass of neat whisky at the drinks tray, but when he offered me a drink, I shook my head. Double agent or not, I still didn't know if I could trust him. I could only hope he wasn't going to lock me up in the damn room and report me as a traitor.

'So,' I said, 'I take it you're working with the British?'

Abimbola frowned, looking troubled, as if deliberating whether to carry on. Slowly, he sat down in the armchair.

'You're known,' I persevered, 'as one of Lourenco's closest men. It's a dangerous position to be in.'

'Lourenco is becoming more and more unpredictable. His decisions are... flawed.'

I raised my eyebrows.

'I own an area of land, a thousand acres or so out near Cap Bleu. Hell of a place, hot and lawless. I'm Balaika, and those lands have been in my family for years.' He hesitated, glancing over at the door as if to check no one was eavesdropping. 'Look, there are diamonds there, Miss Fontaine. A man, a friend, found some stones. I've had them checked by a geologist and they're real, some of the purest white diamonds ever found.'

'What happens if word gets out?'

'There'll be chaos, a diamond rush. Without proper management, the Balaika people will go treasure hunting and get picked off by government troops sent by Lourenco. The Soviets will want access. Everyone will want a finger in the pie.'

Abimbola got up and went over to the other side of the bed, where he leaned down from his great height and re-emerged with a slim leather briefcase. Laying it open on the bedcover, he rummaged inside and brought out a tiny cloth bag.

'Hold out your hand.'

I held out my right hand. Opening the bag, he dropped a few small, dirty-looking stones onto my palm.

I stifled a gasp. 'These are the diamonds?'

He nodded. 'Yes, Miss Fontaine. Millions of francs, right there in your palm. Please, put them back.'

In haste, I grabbed the little cloth bag from his hand, poured the stones back in, and tossed it away from me onto the bed. I didn't want to touch the wretched jewels. I didn't want anything to do with them. At that moment, I felt absolutely terrified.

'What the hell does this mean for the British?'

'The British authorities don't know about the land, but Kingsley does. When I agreed to work as a British agent, I made the mistake of trusting him, thinking it would keep my family safe. Now, he wants to get his hands on the diamonds. The title deeds would make him rich, once Florian Kilomi gets put in power – especially as the new president will be no more than a puppet in British and American hands.'

'What are you going to do?'

Abimbola stared at me through his round spectacles. His thin shoulders were slumped, his expression defeated. I could see him struggling to hide his emotions. With a sudden air of resignation, he shrugged. 'They'll kill me – either Lourenco or the British. It doesn't really matter anymore, I'm in too deep on both sides.'

'But if Kingsley gets you a visa, you'll get out, and your family.'

'Only if I'm in time. But there's still the matter of the diamonds.' Abimbola opened up the briefcase and brought out a paper folder.

It was A3 sized, I noted, about an inch thick. On the front there was a stamp: 'Top Secret'.

'I want you to take this dossier and guard it well. Take it back to England. Don't tell a soul.'

Abimbola tried to press it into my hands, but I hesitated, thinking fast.

245

'Not on your life!' I exclaimed, stepping backwards, thinking of Sunstar. I had to keep focused on my mission. 'I'm sorry, Mr Abimbola, but I can't help you, whatever this is.'

We stood like that for a moment or two, wrestling the folder between the two of us, until I broke free and went to stand by the window, where I stared out at the empty hotel gardens for a minute or two, then turned back to face Abimbola.

'What's inside?' I asked, relenting a little. I couldn't help but feel curious.

'The title deeds to the lands, the coordinates, the lot. There's only one copy. Hide it. Guard it with your life.'

'Why me?'

'I studied law with your brother. We were good friends. Great friends.'

With an ambiguous smile, Abimbola came over and pushed the folder into my hands again. The air in the room was thick with tension, the stakes suddenly too high for me to handle. My mind was reeling. If Chilembé was a friend of Abimbola, didn't that change things? This time I held on to the folder as Abimbola spoke: 'Chilembé was a good man doing good work, standing up for what is right. He told me about you, how much you meant to him. Call it an act of love. One day, you must return the deeds to the Balaika.'

'For heaven's sake,' I murmured. 'It's a hell of a responsibility.'

I didn't want this information, regardless of any historic pacts my brother might have forged with this man. I didn't want to know about the diamonds or the land deeds, let alone have them in my possession. I understood all too well that possessing such knowledge could very well get me killed.

But Abimbola wasn't taking no for an answer. He said nothing more, merely taking hold of my shoulders and pulling me into an awkward embrace that lasted a few seconds.

'I trust you,' he murmured in my ear.

With a nod of his head and a muttered goodbye, he turned away, gathering up his briefcase. Before I knew it, he'd disappeared out of the door, leaving me alone in the empty hotel room, shaking slightly, full of dismay, holding the folder of title deeds in my hands. I turned to go, but paused, noticing a heaviness in my left pocket, and cursed to myself. Surely Abimbola couldn't be that devious?

With another curse, I drew out the little cloth bag containing the half-dozen stones, miniscule, dusty, not at all sparkling – but diamonds, nonetheless. Abimbola must have slipped them into my pocket when he embraced me, a calculated move on his part that made me groan at my own stupidity. He must have known I wouldn't consent to take the jewels, so he'd forced the issue. And I'd let down my guard.

I cursed again, loudly this time, at the sight of the dangerous little bag in my hand. Having contentious title deeds in my possession was bad enough, let alone diamonds. For the moment, I had no idea what to do next.

When I stepped outside, the sun was just beginning to rise, and a chorus of little, chirruping birds in the fronds of the palms celebrated the commencement of dawn. For an instant, thinking I heard footsteps coming down the pathway, I ducked back into the hotel room in a panic. But when no one appeared, I re-emerged, anxiously scanned the grounds for onlookers, and retrieved the hidden jug of water, tucking the folder under my dressing gown. I hastened back up to my room, closed the door, and turned the key in the lock with an exhausted gasp.

I slumped on the bed, groaning, and closed my eyes, thinking hard. I knew I ought to contact Sunstar straight away and tell him of this dangerous new development, but there was no way to get in touch apart from via Kingsley's silly password – and that was only for use at the presidential palace. I supposed this was deliberate, a way to protect me from capture.

I considered my options. I could go back and try to return the folder and the diamonds to Abimbola, though that seemed a terrible idea, considering the risks. I could hide them somewhere in the hotel, but that too, was far too risky. Suddenly I felt enraged at Abimbola, at the British Government, even at Sunstar, for landing me in this wretched, godawful mess. I felt exhausted, with no idea what to do.

On the balcony, I lit a cigarette and stood smoking for five minutes, collecting my thoughts as the eastward sun turned the sky a dusty pale pink. The scene was inapt, in stark contrast with my own perilous early morning predicament. If only the world could follow the classical rules of poetry, I mused, the sky would be red, the colour of flames, the colour of fire and fear.

With a sigh, I finished my cigarette and went back inside, where I fished my pocketknife from my survival kit, along with a sharp embroidery needle and some brown cotton thread. I turned to the deeds and the little bag of diamonds.

At the end of my training, Seal had issued me with a large, leather travelling bag designed especially for my mission, he informed me, by Vivienne Westwood herself. I rather loved that bag, and now I loved it even more, because hidden inside, beneath a stitched-in double layer of silky material lining the bottom, was a piece of solid material separating the outside shell from the silk. Inside this: a secret leather compartment which screwed closed, invisible to the naked eye, invisible to anyone searching the case.

Gingerly, I slit open the silk material with my knife, lifted the cardboard, and unscrewed the cover of the leather wallet. I stashed the folder of deeds and the little bag of diamonds inside, and spent the next half hour sewing up the lining material using neat, careful stitches. Once I'd finished, I placed the bag, as good as new, in the bottom of the wardrobe.

I took a step back, surveying my work with a certain sense of pride. I'd been meticulous in my craft, and I was confident no one would ever be able to find the dangerous contents of the bag unless I personally let them know where they were.

Feeling safe, for now at least, I closed the wardrobe.

Down in the breakfast room, I served myself a strong coffee and sat on the terrace, lighting one cigarette after another, trying to calm my nerves. Something told me Abimbola's gift, the burden of it, was something I'd have to live with for a very long time.

CHAPTER THIRTY-EIGHT

Gloria

The following afternoon, a handwritten note was delivered to my room: *The forecast for Tuesday is good,* it said. Signed, *S. Kingsley*. I stared at the note, caught between relief and dread, then pocketed the message, and went back up to my room.

After some deliberation, I put on a knitted catsuit in a pale shade of gold which hugged my figure in all the right places. I wound a canary yellow silk scarf around my hair and chose flat leather sandals – flat, I reasoned, in case I had to run – along with a dash of mascara, lipstick in a pale shade of rose, and a spritz of Chanel No 5. In the mirror I turned sideways, considering the effect: just carefree enough, summery and chic and alluring, or so I hoped, though it seemed no amount of breezy summer fashion could ease my rising nerves.

With shaking hands, I poured myself a double gin and tonic and smoked two cigarettes, trying to summon my courage and quell my growing misgivings about the coming hours. In my head I found myself running endlessly through Seal's briefings: *be charming, distract him with your conversation, don't let him sense you're intimidated.*

Should I be afraid, I wondered? Should I be saying a prayer or making a will? I was still shaken from my encounter with Abimbola the night before, and cross about the deeds he'd so unexpectedly burdened me with. Still, there was nothing for it, I supposed, but to proceed with my mission as instructed. The show must go on.

Late in the afternoon, the telephone shrilled next to my bed. When I answered, the receptionist's voice on the other end registered no emotion. 'Miss Fontaine, a car will pick you at a quarter to four,' she said.

Hurriedly, I gathered up my travelling bag, checking I had everything else I might need in case of – what, I paused to wonder to myself. An emergency? Capture? A shudder ran through me. Along with the hidden folder and diamonds, the bag contained my gun, a flask of water, and my survival kit. In a side pocket, a tube of military-issue sleeping tablets. I clipped it shut and stared around the room, satisfied that only the remainder of my clothes were left there. Only the possessions I could safely leave behind.

Half an hour later, I arrived downstairs in the lobby, carrying my bag on my arm, to find a silver convertible Rolls Royce drawing up to the Sheraton's marble steps, attracting awestruck looks from the pair of uniformed doormen and a cluster of Israeli tourists arriving from the airport. The Lusenkan flag waved on the driver's side, the president's flag on the other. I noted the number plate: Lourenco1. With a ceremonial bow the driver flung open the back passenger door, revealing creamy leather seats, carpeted footrests, and a radio set into the wood veneer.

'Miss Fontaine, welcome to President Lourenco's car.'

The driver shut the door with a click. We drew noiselessly away as the amazed hotel guests stared after us.

We left the city and drove for an hour through urban slums dwindling gradually into a familiar forest terrain, traversed by a single highway. The four o'clock sun was dipping behind the trees, casting the glow of late day in the tropics; luminous gold, like honey being poured over the landscape. I leaned my head against the backseat of the car, thinking how, after so many years in England, I must have forgotten the sheer knock-out beauty of my home country. The shadows flaring with the passing of the sun on the red earth. Crown berries, tall and spiky, forming black lace silhouettes against the sky. A woman and a child with baskets of fruit balanced on their heads, who smiled and waved on the side of the road as our shiny, silver Rolls Royce sped past. And always the deep, primordial beat of the ink-green forest, pulsating with life.

Soon after, we passed through a small village where a band of children were playing football in the road. There was a commotion as they ran along in our wake, eyes lit with laughter, dust rising in smoky clouds, their joyous shouts carrying softly through the heavy golden air. I turned in my seat and waved back at them with a tightness in my chest. It wasn't so long since Chilembé and I were just as poor and as hungry.

Chilembé.

At the thought of my brother, I sat up straighter, forcing myself to focus. I put a hand on my bag on the seat next to me, feeling for my gun, and peered out of the car window, remembering how, when Chilembé and I were children, President Lourenco had flattened a massive section of jungle a few miles out of Port Salé to build his palace, Mo Kana, roping in local men like my father – your grandfather, Sugar – as labourers on the construction.

I suppose, at the time, we were too innocent to understand that Lourenco was shamelessly plundering our national economy to build his opulent home. I just recall seeing the lorries and bulldozers trundling past our village in a trail of dust, and imagining with an awed sort of wonder what it must be like to live in an actual palace, like a king. Since then, I'd heard countless stories about Mo Kana, but I'd never laid eyes on it until now. Even as an adult, I wasn't immune to that appalled sense of wonder we humans usually feel at a dictator's madness and extravagance. Despite everything, I was intrigued to see Mo Kana firsthand.

The sun was low, the air full of heat and green shadows, traced with the lingering scent of forest flowers, jasmine and orange blossom. As we turned through high wrought-iron gates into a sweep of drive lined with tall, blood-red oleander bushes, beautiful and deadly poisonous,

I clasped my bag to my chest, aware of a dull ache in the pit of my stomach, and my hands trembling.

Half a minute later, we came to the end of the drive, and I let out an audible gasp of surprise. If I close my eyes, I can still see it now, the towering palace of pink and white marble rising against the light-drained sky, the corkscrew turrets, the minarets topped with coned spires, and up high, perched atop the spires, what looked, bizarrely, like ostrich eggs. Up a wide flight of steps, the palace was fronted by an elaborate colonnade straight out of a Greek play, and several incongruous balconies that seemed dreamt up by an eccentric Shakespearean set designer. It was a wild flight of fancy, a sugary confection, flamboyant and unreal, like something out of a children's fairy tale.

I was reminded, then, of all those stories of evil queens and kings, of desperate anti-heroes lurking in their palaces, plotting the world's downfall, and I felt a strange feeling of foreboding that turned the ache in my stomach into a sharp, persistent pain. A huge swimming pool lay beyond, surrounded by empty loungers and parasols, and a moat horseshoed around the palace, veiled by dense foliage – the home of Lourenco's pet crocodiles, I realised with a shudder as the chauffeur came around to open my door, and I climbed out of the Rolls Royce. The whole thing was artificial, mesmerisingly bizarre.

The car disappeared. Curious, I went over and peered into the moat water, which was still and murky, glazed with swarms of mosquitoes. To my horror, I saw the gleam of a pair of eyes through the gloom, then another. Scaly bodies basked in the shadows. I gasped out loud and took a step back. Just as the rumours said, these crocodile pools were not just part of some extravagant display. They were a weapon – a means of disposing of anyone who posed a threat to Lourenco and his regime. I shivered despite the heat. There was so much beauty here – the light, the forest, the flowers – yet within the palace walls there existed unimaginable depths of depravity.

I tore myself away and walked up the steps to the entrance, where I was greeted by a pretty, dumpy little woman in traditional dress – the housekeeper, I wondered? – who reached to put a kika garland around my neck, soothingly sweet-scented, though the crimson flowers could do nothing to calm my mood. The little woman gave a faint smile and led me through to a covered veranda overlooking the hills, then disappeared. There was silence. The crickets chirped. Some forest creature cackled hoarsely in the undergrowth. President Lourenco was nowhere to be seen.

Oh, Sugar, sometimes years later, I look back on that moment, and see myself as I must have been, standing on that terrace, a straight-backed, swashbuckling figure in my gaudy catsuit and chichi yellow headscarf, holding my head high as I determinedly played the diva – and I'm filled with a sense of disbelief and awe at my own audacity. I was in such acute danger. Now... now, as a mother – as *your* mother, Sugar – I shudder at the thought. God knows, when you were children, I was so paranoid about you both, so fearful for your safety. Sometimes while you were out at school, my mind would run away with grim scenarios; you wandering alone, falling off a cliff, being taken by a stranger. I would find myself drowning in a sea of fear. Perhaps all parents experience this sort of irrational, existential dread about their children, but I've come to believe that for me it was far worse, because of my audacious past, and that dreadful, heart-stopping night at President Lourenco's palace, when capture seemed all but inevitable.

God knows, I'd never put myself so close to the edge ever again, not for anything in the world. But I see now that, back then, as I stood there on that darkening veranda with everything on the line, my fear made me strong. It was unthinkable to fail. I had to carry on, no matter what.

Ten minutes later, the little woman returned carrying a silver tray with a gin and tonic in a crystal glass.

'Please, Miss Fontaine,' she remarked in heavily accented English, casting me an odd look. 'Don't hesitate, if you need anything at all... Another drink, perhaps.'

I nodded back, acknowledging her words. She *was* the housekeeper then, mentioned by Kingsley when he'd told me to *request that cocktail.*

I stood by the balustrade taking slow sips of the gin, hoping the alcohol might still my shaking hands. A low setting sun cracked the sky with threads of red and fuchsia. Below, an acre of bristly lawns descended towards a dense ribbon of green-gold forest stretching as far as the eye could see. The capital Port Salé, a sprawl of slums and skyscrapers, glowed silver in the far distance. And as night fell, a chorus of crickets rose up, as if nature was assembling an audience for the night's events – with me the reluctant actress poised at the side of the stage, ready to play my part, jittery before the performance.

'Miss Fontaine, you look glorious.'

Lourenco was behind me.

'Please, do call me Gloria,' I said, turning to greet him. My mind was dead calm. If it was the effect of the gin, then I was grateful. I'd never felt so focused.

Lourenco wore traditional Lusenkan dress: a pure white robe with an embroidered silver collar, matching trousers, leather sandals. Against the pristine white cotton of the robe, his skin shone like polished ebony wood. Around his neck tonight were numerous gris-gris – amulets, I knew, designed according to Lusenkan traditions to give him strength and sexual prowess and protect him from evil. And he wore a flower garland too, of bright yellow hibiscus blossoms strung with dried shells and bird feathers. He was the epitome – such a dangerous epitome – of charm and cunning.

'Gloria, then.' Lourenco smiled and took my hand, bowing slightly to kiss the top of it. One by one, with a creepy sort of tenderness, languorous and fawning, he took off our garlands and put them aside on the marble balustrade. 'Come, you must want to see my place, as you say in English. It will be my pleasure to show you around.'

As the sun fell quickly in the sky, Lourenco escorted me on a tour of his garages, where a sable-coloured Jaguar, two Rolls Royce Silver Shadows – including the one we'd travelled in earlier – and a poppy-red Corvette were all neatly parked in their own sections. In the corner, near the entrance, was a worn-looking old Land Rover, presumably for the use of the palace staff – exactly the same, I noted with interest, as the vehicle I'd learned to drive at Gwynarthen.

As we strolled around, I couldn't help thinking of the villages in the forest a few miles away, and the straggles of dusty children who'd followed our car that afternoon. Recalling their hungry eyes and thin limbs, I found it difficult to meet Lourenco's eyes. Look, I wanted to say: look at what your greed has done to our country. Here you are, Your Excellency, with cars nestled in garages like precious jewels in boxes, and the children of your country are starving.

But I kept my mouth shut, nodding, agreeing, admiring.

Presently, Lourenco led me on a tour of his gigantic outdoor swimming pools, before showing me the crocodile river, where he seemed highly amused by my unease.

'Impressive, aren't they, my babies?' he said with a smirk, brushing his hand across my bottom. I felt a light shiver of revulsion as he told me the creatures' names: Empress, Caesar, Nefertiti, and King.

Someone back in England had done their homework, thank God, because back inside, with a thrill of relief, I recognised the rooms and corridors I'd committed to memory during my training at Gwynarthen, and found I was able to follow my own mental map of the labyrinthine palace interior.

When we came to the presidential study, there was the mahogany desk, familiar from photographs I'd studied, surrounded by national flags and towering bookshelves. A noisy air-conditioning unit emitted a stream of icy air, and I shivered in my flimsy catsuit, feeling goosebumps rise. Somewhere here, I thought to myself, were the blueprints I'd come for.

Concentrating my mind, I fashioned a mental photograph of the room, exactly as I'd been trained to do. I noted the position of the entrance, exits and windows, the layout of the furniture, and the room's various storage cabinets and ornaments, all the time making polite small talk with Lourenco – who was becoming more and more amorous, squeezing my bottom, running his beastly fingers down my spine with that light, spidery, sickening touch of his, barely there, always there.

After the grand tour was finished, we strolled over to the veranda again, where someone had laid a table for two with glasses and dinner plates. Darkness had fallen, the lamps were lit. Candles adorned the balustrade, attracting squadrons of flying insects who batted through the air, their spindly shadows dancing grotesquely across the marble floor where they met the candlelight.

With a low bow, Lourenco pulled out my chair and invited me to sit. 'Now, Gloria,' he murmured with a slow smile, narrowing his eyes, a tiger teasing his prey. 'First we eat. Then we talk.'

CHAPTER THIRTY-NINE

Gloria

All through dinner, Lourenco and I talked easily of politics, international affairs, history – even opera. As expected, he was intelligent and amusing, educated, widely read, and charming. But there was no disguising the mixture of arrogance and *froideur* lurking beneath the constant stream of intelligent banter. He was a cold fish, and a killer.

The food was good; a Lusenkan meal, rich and tasty, accompanied by a copious quantity of expensive French wine which Lourenco drank freely from a large, stemmed, crystal goblet. I allowed myself only small sips, refusing a refill, making a show of enjoying myself. At one point Lourenco excused himself, and hastily, I took my chance. I pulled the packet of sleeping tablets out of my bag, dropped two tablets into his glass, and checked my watch. Eleven o'clock. The powerful drugs would take exactly thirty minutes to take effect.

The meal ended. A waitress came to clear the table. Predictably, my dining companion was becoming steadily drunker and more insistent, making insinuating comments about my looks and my body. Once or twice, he reached across to take my hand with that dreadful tigerish look, as if he intended to eat me.

Silently, I willed the sleeping tablets to work.

Eventually, Lourenco got to his feet, arrow-straight, and wandered to the edge of the terrace, sipping at a cognac and looking out at the view.

Beside him, I contemplated the wall of dark forest and the lights of the city beyond, aware of a tense current of expectation coming off my companion. He seemed suddenly out of sorts; moody and a little short, presumably because the sleeping tablet was starting to work. I glanced surreptitiously at my watch – quarter past eleven – and felt my belly flip with nerves. For all their 'field experience', I don't think either Seal or Sunstar ever realised how hard it would be to dupe Lourenco, the wiliest of men. How *did* they expect me to lure him without sex? Naturally, Lourenco wanted to screw me – excuse my French – and I needed him to go to sleep before that happened.

He turned his dark eyes on mine, expressionless. My heart leapt a fraction when he pulled me towards him and embraced me roughly, pushing his tongue in my mouth. All the charm and decorum of earlier had disappeared. I felt sick, scared, disgusted. I'm not sure what was more awful or terrifying: Lourenco's persistent hands, or the fact that one wrong step could cost me my life. I wasn't prepared to let my mind dwell on the moral complexities of the situation. For the sake of my mission, I needed to take a cold-eyed view of any physical contact between us. Even so, standing there, willing the sleeping tablet to kick in, with that ghastly man groping my breasts and muttering sweet nothings into my ear, I've never felt so far away from safety.

Lourenco took my hand and led me into the bedroom, where he continued to kiss and fondle me with intensifying passion. When he began to undress me, I knew I had to act fast. Thank goodness, with his shoes off, he was about three inches shorter than me, meaning I had to crane my neck at an awkward angle to kiss him. Naked, in the guise of an embrace, I reached my right arm around his neck, bent my elbow and – just as I'd been trained – applied pressure to both sides of his neck with my bicep and forearm, so as to briefly cut off his air supply. Immediately, he lost consciousness.

My watch said eleven twenty-nine. I stood for ten seconds, then released him, only for him to regain consciousness with a groan, but his eyes were sleepy, his breathing slow. He pulled me onto the bed, fumbling to undress me.

And then, thank God, the tablet finally took its effect.

Lourenco rolled off me and fell dead asleep, one leg splayed out to the side, emitting loud, grunting snores. I checked his breathing, which was mercifully slow and deep, and then I stood for a few moments watching the rise and fall of his chest, a man-eating tiger at rest. Here was a monster who'd killed thousands, and I could easily become his next victim if things went wrong. Would I even get out of this alive?

I wrapped a towel around myself, grabbed my bag, and made my way out of the bedroom, closing the door softly behind me. Crossing the corridor, I glanced around, but if there were servants working nearby, they did not show themselves.

The door to the study was not locked. Inside, I turned on the light, and looked around. The atmosphere was quiet and cool, heavy curtains drawn across a French window. In the corner the air conditioning unit emitted a low, juddering sound. I went to the desk, which displayed a large white telephone, an encased notepad planner, and a carved, teak bust of a woman with her arms around her lover. On the right hand wall, a Lusenkan flag hung in a neat rectangle. Opposite, hung up on a wall overlooking the desk, a large oil painting showed fruit arranged around a woven drum, a run-of-the-mill sort of still life, presumably gifted to the president by some foreign dignitary or another. I recalled the painting from my briefings.

I lifted the desk chair over to the wall and climbed up. Leaning upwards to the painting, I inserted the listening device firmly behind the frame, and switched it on.

In haste, I searched through the drawers of the desk for the blueprints, to no avail. I approached a filing cabinet near the window and examined the lock. Thank God, it was a simple sort of mechanism, one I was well-used to handling during training. From my bag I took a couple of bobby pins, straightened one out and inserted the flat end into the keyhole of the cabinet to about a third of an inch, just as Seal had shown me. The other pin I inserted an inch deep, bending it to an angle of 90 degrees.

It took ten seconds of moving the two pins back and forth, and a few more precise circular motions, to click open the lock. I breathed a small sigh of relief and triumph at having got this far, registering the absurdity of the scene: me, Gloria Fontaine, actress turned spy, standing there naked in my towel, ransacking a cabinet of top secret documents in the study of an insane dictator. Honestly, Sugar, you couldn't have made it up…

I rifled quickly through the files, but there was nothing of interest in the top drawer. I did the same for the other three drawers, fruitlessly. Eventually, in the bottom drawer, I discovered a brown folder labelled: FORT KOLDA. I noted it with satisfaction: according to my brief, this was the name of the military base. When I turned the folder over, this was confirmed by a stamp on the cover – Top Secret, EYES ONLY.

'Take your time, take it easy,' I whispered quietly, reminding myself that Lourenco was asleep, and there was no need to panic. Time was accuracy, time was exactness. There was no point rushing this. Deliberately, I slowed my breathing, counting in and out to a count of four. With each breath I felt my heartbeat slacken and my movements become steadier and more precise.

From my bag, I extracted my tiny camera disguised as a cigarette lighter. One by one, I photographed all the blueprints in the folder, about fifty pages of documents and a handful of pencil-drawn plans, maps, and drawings. With hands that shook only moderately, I replaced the file in the cabinet. The whole thing took no more than ten minutes. Carefully, I rolled the film into a miniscule cylinder. From my make-up bag, I extracted the hollow mascara tube that, under the meticulous tutelage of Lavender Campbell, I'd practised using many times during my training.

Now I rolled the cylinder of film in plastic and deposited the roll into the mascara tube. Once everything was safely in place, I hid the camera back in the lining of my bag. On my way back from the study, I nipped into the bathroom, flushed the loo, and returned to the president's bedroom.

Minutes later, Lourenco groaned and sat up in bed, looking groggy. He rubbed his forehead with another groan and collapsed back against the pillows, following me with his eyes. Something was up, I could sense it. I needed to distract him, fast. With an air of studied nonchalance, I let my towel fall and prowled the room, teasing him with my nakedness. I picked up a trinket, asking questions, flirting. But though Lourenco answered my vacuous enquiries, his expression was inscrutable. I couldn't tell what he was thinking, but instinctively I knew something was wrong.

'So what really brings you out here, Gloria?' he asked eventually, propping himself up on the pillows, his bare feet resting atop the sheets. 'Tell me the truth.'

His words made my blood run cold, even though he was slurring them. Otherwise, he seemed to have recovered surprisingly well from the sleeping tablet, which seemed typical of this man, this wily dictator, who apparently had a remarkable ability to duck out of trouble.

An eerie sort of emptiness hung about the palace, now. There was no sense of real life there, you see – no hustle and bustle of servants, no sign of a human existing there at all. Disconcerted, I cleared my throat and tried to regulate my breathing, willing myself to be calm.

'Out where?' I replied in a casual tone. 'Here in Lusenka, you mean?'

'Here with me, for dinner and sex.'

'I suppose life leads us on new paths.'

'An interesting theory. But it doesn't answer my question. I don't believe you came here simply to enjoy my company.'

I felt my insides turn to ice.

'Then you would be wrong, Your Excellency,' I answered coolly. 'I am here purely for your pleasure.'

Nursing an erection, Lourenco observed me from the bed with a steady gaze, cold and analytical, as if he were a surgeon who'd just operated on me, and was carefully weighing up his next clinical decision. Something told me he had something up his sleeve, and I suddenly felt all too conscious of my own body, of my heart pumping and the blood pulsing through my veins, my forehead, the tips of my fingers. Most of all, I was hyper-aware of the cylinder of micro-film inside my bag.

I stood frozen, conscious of the bedroom door behind me, shut tight. Could Lourenco hear my heart flying in my chest? Could he see in my eyes that I was lying? At that moment I felt certain that this cruel man could detect all the thoughts in my head. Time slowed, my mind raced. I needed to find a way to leave, right now.

There was a knock on the door. It was the housekeeper, bearing the tray from earlier with two cups and a silver jug on it. She must have been in her forties, short and homely looking, with that pretty, pleasant, shiny face above her immaculate wax cloth outfit. She didn't seem fazed by the fact I was naked. In fact, she barely looked at me at all, until she turned slightly to her right as she approached the bed and gave me an almost imperceptible nod. A second late and I'd have missed it. Thank God I didn't. It was a sign; I knew that for sure.

'Good evening, Your Excellency,' said the little woman in a low, calm voice. 'Your nightcap, sir.'

Gin fizz, I thought with a flash of realisation. The password. As I'd suspected earlier, this housekeeper – though not at all the sort of person you'd have expected to be caught up with a load of British spies – was my ally, my get-out route. A foreign agent, just like me. How I admired her courage! She must have been listening, somehow, and was reacting according to her own mission instructions. In turn, I knew my part.

'Excuse me,' I remarked casually. 'Could I trouble you to bring me a gin fizz?'

The woman turned. 'Of course.' She registered no expression at all. 'Two minutes, Miss.'

With unhurried movements, the woman set down the tray and left the room. I could feel the president's eyes on me as he rose from the bed and put on a dressing gown. He crossed to the bathroom and closed the door.

Once I could hear him pissing into the bowl, I took the opportunity to put my clothes back on. As an afterthought, I stowed my sandals hastily in my bag and tucked my pistol into the side of my custom designed bra, where it fitted neatly, completely hidden.

Lourenco returned. From somewhere came the sound of a telephone ringing. A minute passed and I told myself to keep calm, to breathe, to think, to trust my instincts and concentrate. I kept smiling.

Another knock. The woman opened the door, bearing my cocktail on a tray. She placed the drink on a side table and addressed Lourenco. 'I'm sorry to trouble you, Your Excellency, but there's a telephone call for you in the office.'

'Oh? At this hour? Did they say who it is?'

The little woman shook her head. 'No name, sir.'

I watched Lourenco leave the room. Half a minute later, I heard the office door click closed. With a strange, portentous sense of calm, as if everything in my brain was at that moment clarified in the most microscopic detail, I picked up my bag, opened the bedroom door, and made my way briskly, barefoot, along the passageway, around the corner and down the main stairs. At the bottom, a burly, heavy-set guard in uniform stood with his back to me. I went to walk past but he turned, spotting me, and stepped sideways, blocking my path.

'Excuse me, Miss,' the guard said. 'You are?'

'A visitor,' I said, making eyes. 'Just looking for the loo.'

'Oh, I see.' He gave a sleazy smile, running his gaze suggestively up and down my body. 'It's back up the stairs, Miss, near the bedrooms. You're in the wrong place.'

I gave a small flirtatious laugh, bit my lip, and looked up at the man from behind my lashes, remembering the American actress's advice. *Tilt your head, Honey.* 'I just need to pop outside,' I said. 'I'm desperate for a cigarette.'

'Go on,' the guard bowed with an insinuating grin, 'as you're so beautiful. *Mon Dieu,* the president's a lucky man.'

I gave a jaunty wave and backed towards the front door, already planning my next move. Time was of the essence. I was running for my life.

Barefoot, I sprinted down the path, remembering the route Lourenco had taken us on earlier in the evening, recalling every twist and turn through the heavy tropical darkness, thick and fragrant, mercifully swallowing me whole. A cacophony of insects cheered me on. I tried not to think about the crocodiles lurking in the river beyond, somewhere in the blackness, the many pairs of treacherous eyes I'd seen glinting in the inky depths.

Sweating, gasping, I reached the garage, remembering the large doors left ajar by Lourenco earlier, and let myself in. I ran past the row of sports cars to the old Land Rover. Whether by chance or design – the housekeeper perhaps? – the driver's side of the car was unlocked, and someone had left the windows open. I chucked my gun onto the passenger seat and yanked open the door.

I had a few minutes, I estimated, before the president would realise I was gone and gather the other palace guards. With my screwdriver, I tore open the small plastic panel under the car's steering column and sorted the wires with my fingers, remembering Crispy's sturdy, Northern accent: 'Battery, starter, ignition; it'll look intimidating at first, but they'll always be grouped into these bundles.'

Sure enough, the wires were classified red for battery, blue for ignition. I cut away an inch of the insulation from the ends of both wires with my pocketknife and twisted the two together. Suddenly, music came pouring from the wireless. I frantically turned it off. Next, I stripped the starter wire and placed this on the ends of the two other wires, which caused a spark or two. To my relief, the engine kicked into life.

I could have hugged that car, I was so happy to hear it start!

I revved the engine twice, turned on the headlights and yanked off the handbrake, twisting the steering wheel hard to break the lock from its parking position. As a precaution, I tore off a piece of my dress and tossed it over the live wire ends to protect myself from electric shocks. Finally, I hit the accelerator hard with my foot and launched the Land Rover forward out of the garage.

A gun shot behind me, then another. I gasped as a bullet ricocheted off the car's metalwork. Ducking, I veered the car towards the front gates of the Mo Kana estate as shouts echoed in the darkness behind me. Another shot was fired. At the gates, I turned right and slammed my foot on the accelerator, speeding flat out along the empty highway through the forest, flooring the decrepit car to its maximum speed. I had no thoughts, no emotions, no fear to cloud my judgement, just a concentrated focus on what I needed to do: escape.

I must have driven for an hour or two. After what felt like an eternity, I slowed the car and searched for somewhere to pull over along the pitch black forest road. Sooner or later, I spotted a track leading down to an opening in the trees. Breathing hard, I turned the steering wheel, bumped onto the track, and pulled up on the edge of a deserted section of forest. I killed the engine, then the headlights.

The moment I stepped out of the Land Rover, my body turned to jelly. My teeth were chattering uncontrollably. In the pitch darkness, I lit a cigarette and sat against the bonnet of the car, dragging deeply, desperately, as I tried to calm down. For the first time that evening, there was no plan.

I took more deep, soothing drags on the cigarette, until at last a strange feeling of déjà vu came over me. I listened to the hullabaloo of thousands of creatures in the silence, birds and mammals of every size, a clamour of hoots and shrieks coming from the undergrowth. An insect bumped my cheek, and I swatted it away. Usually, this midnight forest anarchy would have frightened me, but tonight I was more focused on other fears, of the unseen presidential soldiers who would soon be hot on my heels. How close was I to my own demise, I wondered. An hour? A few minutes?

I reminded myself that I'd been here before, running with Chilembé from the gunmen who murdered our parents. We'd stayed in this forest for days, hiding out like animals escaping hunters. With this realisation, I felt myself relax a little, and a bizarre sense of calm drifted over me. I should have been dead years ago, slashed by a machete, a bullet through my head, but somehow, I'd been lucky enough to survive. Now, running from Lourenco, an even more dangerous hunter, I could only hope that luck would be on my side this time, as well.

I exhaled slowly and tried to pull myself together. My mission was far from over, and it wouldn't be over, I knew, until I was safely back in London. I needed to get back and rendezvous with Sunstar in Port Salé.

Above all, Sunstar.

Not far from here, I knew, the dense equatorial forest dwindled into a coastal road and a series of small settlements carved out of the bush that formed the outskirts of Port Salé. One of them was the Balaika village of Cap Bleu, where I was born and lived as a child. Therefore, though it certainly didn't feel that way, I wasn't too far from the city boundaries of Port Salé.

Likely as not, Lourenco's men would be here soon. The Land Rover, though formidable, and well-adapted to jungle terrain, was far too recognisable. No one in Lusenka owned such a distinctive vehicle but the President himself. I needed to ditch it quick sharp and find my way back to the capital on my own steam. Navigating on foot was the best chance of avoiding capture, because I could hide if necessary. From this point onwards, my survival relied on using the cover of the forest and my own ingenuity.

I got out my torch, spread out my map on the bonnet of the car and plotted the shortest route through the jungle with my finger, circumventing the outskirts of Port Salé to an area a few miles north of the city, along the unpopulated coastal corniche. There, I knew, I'd be able to hail a moto taxi. As the crow flew it wasn't far, a hike of two or three hours at most. I would head to the airfield marked in red on the map, I told myself, where presumably a plane would be waiting to airlift me out.

Sugar, I needed to get rid of the car, right away. My watch said four a.m. According to my mission schedule, I was exactly on time. There in the guts of the forest, I stood listening to the shrieks and scratches of a thousand nocturnal creatures, as my heart thudded in my chest, my skin poured with sweat. I was shivering slightly. Lourenco's men would be here soon, but I told myself there was nothing to be afraid of. After all, wasn't this once my world? Trying not to panic, I groped for my flask through the rear window of the Land Rover and took a long swig of lukewarm water.

Think, I told myself, think.

It was just getting light; luminous gold streaks slashed the deep indigo of dawn. I could see a dense tangle of vegetation organised in tiers, from a towering canopy of mahogany and teak trees through to the lower palms and fruits – paw paws, mangoes and sops, bananas and bread fruit – to the fungi and rotting leaves of the forest floor. A little way ahead, through the trees, I thought I could make out a small dip, and, as the sun rose further, I made out a meandering stream, then a hill sloping downwards to a deep ravine.

From the passenger seat of the car, I grabbed the rest of my belongings: the map and torch, my gun, and the leather travelling bag containing the deeds and the photographed blueprints. I wound down the window of the driver's side and leaned in, releasing the hand brake, then shoved the car as hard as I could in the direction of the ravine. But the wretched thing was large and heavy, and the more I pushed, the more the tyres caught. I looked down to see a creeping, red-blossomed orchid, metres wide, whose tendrils were entwined vice-like around the chassis. I drank more water and set about cutting it away with my pocketknife. I'd been ambushed by a damn plant.

Then, mustering all my strength, I pushed and rocked, pushed and rocked, until at last the car caught the momentum of my movements, and with a final heave, began to roll in silence across the dip, towards the ravine. I watched it teeter on the edge, then jackknife theatrically downwards, generating a commotion of breaking branches and a flock of parrots which took off with a great deal of noise, flapping and shrieking as the car crashed to the ground.

Amid the pandemonium, I could have sworn I heard the thud of footsteps through the trees, and voices calling over and over, the voices – or so I imagined – of all the men who'd ever pursued me. Baptiste Lourenco, Sidney Dunn, Mr Adalao.

Oh, Sugar, it must have been my paranoia speaking! Even so, I understood with a flash of fear that I was only hours away from being captured, and from nowhere Sunstar's voice came echoing: *Don't get caught, Gloria. For God's sake, don't get caught.*

CHAPTER FORTY

Gloria

Now that the Land Rover was gone, I forced myself to focus. At least it was daylight, I told myself, the sun warm on my skin, the air coolish now, at the beginning of the day. Everything was bearable. I consulted my compass and began trekking southwards through the forest.

I walked briskly, compass in hand, tense as a prowling wolf, keeping to the edges of the forest near the road, and cutting my way through the vegetation when necessary. A couple of times I paused to pick wild fruits recognisable from my childhood – paw paws, mangoes, guavas. I ate them as I walked, sucking out the juice, replaying in my mind the evening before; the president's clammy hands on my body, the frightening chill of the presidential study, and the folder of blueprints, swiftly captured. With any luck, the miniscule bug I'd planted in the study was even now transmitting intelligence back to the UK. Perhaps Lourenco would discover the bug, perhaps not. Perhaps in the end my work would all be for nothing. Still, all that seemed strangely disconnected from my current situation.

The sun beat down hotter and hotter. I must have trekked for hours. After a while I stopped thinking, stopped feeling. Quite simply, I put one foot in front of the other, taking tiny sips of water from the amount remaining in the flask of water in my bag, until eventually I reached a small town rising from the red dust, situated along the sides of a road. The place seemed composed of low buildings and parked motorbikes, and a jumble of alfresco market stalls shaded by ragged parasols waving in the breeze.

Checking the map, I realised with a start that it must be the neighbouring village to Cap Bleu – where my brother was buried - or at least, a new version of the old village that had been so brutally destroyed a decade ago by the militia. I looked around with curiosity, wondering for a brief, delirious instant if there might be someone I knew here, who might help me. But of course, that was nonsense. Those days were gone; the houses burnt; the people murdered. History erased.

I suppressed my rising sadness and walked on.

Along the road was a tailor's shop, very Lusenkan, easily recognisable from the dusty, headless, plastic mannequin outside, wearing a green wax dress with a geometric design – evidently an advertisement for the tailor's skills. Feigning a relaxed manner, I entered the shop, where a young seamstress emerged without a word from behind a sewing machine table. Holding out a note and some coins, I pointed at the dress outside. The woman nodded with raised eyebrows and went to take the handmade dress from the mannequin.

When she came back, I wasted no time, changing there and then in the shop's curtained changing area, tipping her with more coins. I added the matching headwrap and rubber flip flops to the outfit for a small additional sum and abandoned my old clothes.

The seamstress stared after me open-mouthed as I left the shop in my new attire. Naturally, I counted on looking like any other Lusenkan woman off to market, and I believe I carried it off as I tripped along in the sunlight with my precious travelling bag perched neatly on my arm. Little would anyone have guessed that I was a spy for the British Government, carrying dangerous documents in that very bag!

The sun was hot now, the town suddenly busy. A band of thin-looking sheep were tethered to a post, and someone was herding a small flock down the street, kicking up dust and causing the stationary traffic to hoot and growl – horse carts and the noisy Chinese motorbikes that were all the rage by then, ridden by men in helmets, and women in high heels, engines buzzing loudly; a swarm of angry insects.

Meanwhile, a throng of children circulated with plates of assorted wares on their heads. Without turning a hair at the fracas, pedestrians browsed the market stalls buying fruit and groceries. I purchased a bottle of water and some biscuits and purposefully blended into the crowd, until in the corner of my eye I spotted a cluster of motorbikes parked in the shade of a mango tree. Beside the bikes, a teenage boy stood eating a baguette from a fold of newspaper. He must have been about twelve or thirteen.

I called over to him in the local dialect, which felt rusty after so many years away. 'Hey, you ride these things?'

'Yeah, Miss?' the kid replied in French, pausing his chewing to stare. 'You wanna buy one?'

'I need a lift. I can pay well.'

'No problem,' he said, shrugging. 'At your service, Miss.'

The boy stopped eating and stood up straighter, all attention, as I pulled out my map and showed him the location of the airfield. He kicked one of the bikes off its stand and wheeled it out from beneath the tree. With a small smile, he nodded at me to get on.

It was a long time since I'd ridden a moto-taxi. I gamely hitched up my dress, slung my bag over my shoulder, and settled myself on the back seat, trying not to hold onto the boy's skinny teenage frame for fear I might pull the poor child off. Instead, I clung to the edges of the seat, clutching my bag as if my life depended on it – which I suppose you could say it did.

The kid revved the engine and, after a few false starts and a wobble or two, we set about negotiating the traffic out of town. Like that, we buzzed past the lush, tropical vegetation of the outer forest, then on along the coast road, past glittering beaches where creamy breakers rolled onto pale sand fringed with groves of coconut palms. The scenery was beautiful, the road relatively smooth. I began to feel a growing sense of elation at the apparent ease of my escape thus far.

But as we approached the outskirts of Port Salé, something unusual in the distance caught my eye. On drawing nearer, I saw that the main road was blocked by a wide jam of motorbikes reaching several bikes across, and nearly a mile long. The air was filled with the smell of diesel fumes and the disgruntled hollers and hoots of riders and their passengers stranded in the hot sun.

We drew to a halt at the roadside, where I hopped off the bike to peer along the verge down the queue. In the distance I could see an army truck and several soldiers wearing the distinctive and much-feared uniform of the government militia – the president's army. My stomach turned over. They appeared to be patrolling the road, stopping each vehicle as it passed, presumably because Lourenco had already issued orders to find me.

In a flash, I felt my elation subside. For the first time in nearly twenty-four hours, I felt truly frightened at the thought of what the soldiers would do to me if I was captured. I'd been naïve, stupid even, to imagine I might escape a dictator like Lourenco without consequences.

'What's your name, kid?' I asked the boy.

'Momo,' he said. 'Why, Miss?'

'Momo, I need you to get past this, okay?'

'They're looking for you?'

I shrugged, and he contemplated this piece of information with an impassive expression. Then his eyes darted around, across me and the traffic and the soldiers. He frowned, making a cut-throat gesture with his right hand.

'Soldiers. No good.'

'No good at all,' I agreed.

Out of the corner of my eye, I spied an outlying group of militia making their way on foot along the ranks of bikes, checking each rider's identity documents. By my estimations they were a hundred metres or so from us, five or six men working quickly through the regiments of bikes. At that speed it wouldn't take them long to reach us, I calculated with a dry-mouthed sort of panic.

'I'm afraid we might have to get a move on,' I said smoothly.

'Yeah, Miss, let's go.'

Revving hard, Momo swerved the bike out of the queue and zipped away from the line of traffic in the direction of the city centre, but not before the soldiers spotted us. I glanced behind and saw a few of them running up the road, flailing their hands and shouting. One raised his gun. I craned my neck just in time to see the soldier hustle a rider from his bike, jump on and set off in pursuit.

Momo sped up, dodging across the opposite lane into a dusty side street, not three metres wide, making the turn so abruptly that the bike lay almost flat. We zigzagged through more narrow streets as I clung on for dear life, my right foot grazing the red earth.

'Go, for God's sake, go!' I gasped.

There was a shot behind us. I could hear the sputter of another engine as the soldier on the bike drew closer. I looked behind me and glimpsed the whites of the man's eyes. He was bent low over the handlebar, grimacing with determination, and nearly upon us; it was time for drastic measures. I pulled my pistol out of my bra and fired three shots at his front tyre, only for the bike to swerve off course and skid to a stop, sending the soldier tumbling onto the road.

'Good one, Miss!' shouted Momo.

Half a minute later, we left that soldier behind, but there were more soon enough. Dozens of them in military vans, leaning out of the windows. The slow wail of sirens as a stream of police cars followed in hot pursuit. But we were smaller and nimbler than those cumbersome official vehicles, and we hurtled this way and that along hidden side streets, with me yelling directions as Momo dipped and ducked the bike through impossible gaps. After a time, our pursuers seemed to fall off our trail. Finally, Momo slowed the bike, and we motored on in relative peace through towards the airfield to the east of the city. After a tense half hour, Momo turned a corner, and we came to an abrupt halt.

'C'est ici, Miss.'

He killed the engine and I groaned, my whole body trembling with fear and adrenaline. I was acutely aware that, in time, Lourenco's men would catch us up – and if not those men, then others, other soldiers, more ruthless and determined than the last. There would be roadblocks and house searches. I wasn't naïve enough to imagine that Lourenco would ever give up looking for me.

The sun was high in the sky. It must have been nearly half past one. I shaded my face with my hand, squinting. The bright rays of light hurt my eyes. Unnervingly, there was no plane waiting as I had expected, just a stretch of rough ground and a bumpy-looking runway stretching towards the horizon beneath an intense white sky. I stumbled across the reddish soil towards a low wooden building, with Momo following behind.

'What next, Miss?' he said as we approached the door of the building.

I squeezed the child's shoulder. 'I wish I knew, darling,' I said. 'You're a plucky boy. Well done.'

Aching with exhaustion, I pushed open the door with Momo beside me, not entirely sure what I was going to do next. I couldn't just hole up at the airfield forever.

Oddly enough, when I spotted Sunstar lounging inside the hut on a beaten-up old settee, casually sipping a large whisky as though it were any other run-of-the-mill afternoon, I wasn't altogether surprised. At that moment, as my mind scrambled to make sense of the sheer, surreal madness of the last few days, even Sunstar turning up in Lusenka couldn't shock me.

'You?' I said, struggling to catch my breath. 'You're here?'

'Indeed,' he replied coolly with a slight nod. 'You got the intel, placed the device?'

I nodded in the affirmative and introduced Momo. Sunstar got up and fetched the boy a glass of water, before discreetly guiding him to the bathroom.

'Mission accomplished,' Sunstar said, handing me a neat Scotch. I accepted it gratefully, despite my usual aversion to whisky. 'Now it's time to make a quick exit.'

'How did you know I'd come here?'

'That was always the plan. You really don't want to mess with Lourenco's army.'

I half-smiled. 'It's unnerving how you always seemed to know me better than I know myself.'

I lit a cigarette, savouring the sweet, drowsy taste of nicotine as I noticed the unmistakable weariness displayed on Sunstar's face, despite his air of calm. He looked worn out.

'But thank goodness you're here,' I added. 'I swear they'll kill me if they find me.'

A roar filled the air, becoming louder and louder until it was almost unbearable. When I peered out of the tiny window, I saw a plane coming into land.

'Thank God,' I murmured.

Sunstar rose to his feet and thanked Momo, handing him some notes which the boy slipped quietly into his pocket. Sunstar enquired his name and where he lived, clearly impressed, because he also handed Momo what looked like a business card, and in characteristic low-key fashion, urged him to get in touch, 'When this has all blown over, you hear?'

'Bye, Miss,' Momo whispered softly, clasping my hand, then enveloping me in a hug. Returning the embrace, I felt my heart break a little. This was our final farewell, I knew, and it was hard to let the boy go. A shiny official car drew up outside the shack, and I stood waving, tears pricking at my eyes at the sight of his small face peering back at me through the car window. I felt suddenly terrified for him, this sweet child on the threshold of life's journey. I couldn't help wondering if he'd be okay. Would life treat him well? Would he find the love and kindness he deserved? As quickly as he'd come, Momo was whisked away into the hot afternoon.

'The plane's waiting,' Sunstar announced briskly. He patted my arm, as if he knew what I was thinking. 'We need to go, Gloria. The pilot won't wait. We've no time to lose.'

'Back to London?' I asked in surprise.

'Via Brussels,' Sunstar confirmed with a nod. 'We'll make a brief stop to change planes, then on to London. I can assure you that diplomatic immunity proves invaluable at times like these.'

It was a quarter to two, and the heat of the day was giving way to a golden haze of late afternoon. Outside, on a patch of badly maintained tarmac, a medium-sized silver jet stood in the reddish dust. A yellow-suited stewardess in heels and a jaunty cap stood at the bottom of the steps, looking as if she'd walked straight out of the flicks. With a big smile, she welcomed us with no sense of urgency whatsoever.

Sunstar too, appeared only mildly hurried, though I felt the gentle push of his hand on the small on my back, encouraging me up the flight of steps into the aircraft. Clutching my bag containing the deeds, the diamonds, and the blueprints, I found my seat, gazing out of the plane window as the jet engines roared to life. With a jolt, the wheels began to roll along the bumpy runway, and the plane ascended into the sky, banking northward towards safety, towards home.

Amid the whirring of the engines and the levelling out of the aircraft, I found myself feeling strange – caught between relief and exhaustion and happiness – and utterly disbelieving that my mission was accomplished. The moment felt like the falling of a stage curtain, the end of the performance, though not quite the grand finale. And to think that I, Gloria Fontaine, the timid girl from Lusenka, had managed to pull it off!

All at once, it came to me, a final truth. The act was over. Somewhere along the way, I'd ceased to be an actress playing a spy and become the real thing: a fully-fledged British secret agent. Here I was sitting in this aeroplane, poised between my past and my future – a future which I no longer feared. How could I? My world would never be the same, now, and this was an entirely new sort of theatre, but I didn't mind. Not one bit.

I glanced out of the plane window and saw a convoy of military trucks trailing clouds of swirling dust as they rolled onto the airfield below, just a few short minutes too late. Soldiers spilled out, ants onto the red earth, waving their fists and peering up as our jet pointed into the sun. But we were already airborne, and I'll never forget the music that came playing through the onboard sound system as the jet gained height, lifting its nose to the cloudless skies towards Europe. It was Shirley, of course: Shirley Bassey, *What I Did For Love*, a song that spoke to me of all the loves and dreams I'd lost, and all the battles I'd won along the way.

Perhaps the pilot cranked up the music, because as the engines throbbed and we flew higher into the clouds, the singer's voice filled the plane. At first, I hummed along to the melody, but as the altitude increased, a euphoric sense of happiness washed over me. Before long, I was singing at the top of my voice. Sunstar smiled broadly, and when the melody changed, he continued to smile and stare at me with a funny look, all soft around the eyes. Lost in his expression, I hardly touched the lunch brought by the waitress, nor the coffee that followed. Instead, I found myself staring at Sunstar, trying to decipher his thoughts.

Somewhere over the Sahara, the waitress served us each a gin fizz. In a gentle Lusenkan accent, she shyly asked for my autograph on a napkin. Later on, alone with Sunstar as we cruised the skies above southern France, I recounted the events at Lourenco's palace and my subsequent escape. Sunstar listened intently and made occasional notes.

'You've handled yourself remarkably, Gloria,' he said, once I had finished talking. 'Few can claim to have achieved so much.'

'When Lourenco confronted me, I thought I was done for. But I'd nothing to lose. It's all for my brother.'

'That's the spirit.'

'So, what happens now?' I asked, my curiosity piqued. 'What of Lusenka, and Lourenco?'

'That's classified information, I'm afraid. Rest assured you've played your part.' Sunstar smiled cryptically and raised his glass of gin fizz. 'To Chilembé.'

A smile tugged at the corners of my lips. 'To Chilembé,' I echoed, raising my glass in turn.

CHAPTER FORTY-ONE

Dolly

Dolly was woken by her mobile phone buzzing with a message from Sunstar: *If you can get to Lusenka, you'll need to meet a man called Momo. He knows you're coming. S.* Then a phone number with a Lusenkan country code. She stared at the message for a few moments, letting it sink in that Momo must be the same boy who'd helped Gloria escape all those years ago.

She felt her chest tighten at the thought. This was it, then; this was really happening, and she didn't know whether to feel excited or just downright scared at what seemed a hare-brained mission, at best. She cursed herself for getting embroiled after everything that had happened in London. Nevertheless, she texted a thank you back to Sunstar, and the reply pinged back immediately: 'Take care, my dear. If anything goes wrong, don't hesitate to ring me.'

If anything goes wrong. Dolly sat up in bed, trying to bury the ominous thought. She had to do this – her nieces were in danger; she was in danger. She had no choice.

After breakfast, she opened her laptop, and using her savings, she booked a single airfare from London to Port Salé before she had time to change her mind.. In a rucksack she packed summer clothes and toiletries, including a quantity of pens in her hand luggage, a back-up Dictaphone and spare batteries, a couple of notepads, and her British and Lusenkan passports. Finally, her digital camera with portrait and zoom lenses, a microphone, and spare SD cards. To Evan she sent a text, then relented, and called to say goodbye.

'I'm not telling anyone I'm going,' she told him. 'So keep it under your hat.'

'I don't have a hat,' Evan joked.

For some reason she found herself confiding Sunstar's phone number, though she referred to the former spy as Robert Montgomery, unwilling for Evan to make the connection without an explanation. 'This man will help if I get into trouble,' she explained, adding hurriedly. 'Not that I will, but just in case.'

Just in case.

'Call me, any problems.'

'Don't forget about me,' she concluded in a jokey tone, struck by a sudden deep-held anxiety, but Evan's voice at the end of the phone was dead serious.

'I'm not going anywhere, Dolly. I'm right here if you need me. And I'll keep an eye on your family.'

Finally, she hid the bag of illicit diamonds carefully in a drawer of the old pine chest up in the attic, under a pile of Gloria's clothes. She would just have to cross that bridge later, she decided. The first step was to solve the mystery of her mother's illicit spy mission, once and for all. By lunchtime the following day she was purchasing mosquito repellent in the departure hall of Heathrow Airport and downloading a newly released geo-tracker app which she set to track her movements. On a last-minute impulse, she sent the link to the tracker and the map to Evan and Sunstar.

While she waited in the departures lounge, another text arrived from Shaun: *Hey, we need to talk. Where are you? There's some stuff I need to tell you about x*

She stared at the kiss, mystified. Surely, he couldn't be imagining a reconciliation after everything that had happened? Or was he making contact to work out her next move?

Dolly's thoughts were interrupted by a flight attendant calling for passengers to board. She turned off the phone, dropping it in her hand luggage, telling herself to forget about Shaun for now. On the plane, she read a guidebook bought in departures, and studied the map of Lusenka, trying to memorise the marked edges of dense forest stretching inland from the coast, the lush stretches of vanilla plantations in the east, and the undulating line of the River Ciel running towards the country borders, then the towns and villages marked with dots and stars: Cap Bleu, Maguru, Port Salé, recalling them from Gloria's story.

Afterwards she stared out at the clouds for a while, then closed her eyes and slept. Hours later, she found herself peering down at the sun-white roofs of Port Salé as the pilot circled above a glittering bay – with unnecessary slowness, Dolly thought to herself impatiently – in preparation for landing.

It was nearly midday when Dolly disembarked in Port Salé. On the face of it, Kilomi International Airport was modern and well-run, with only a short queue through the kiosks at immigration control. Scents of dried fish and damp earth filled the air, warm and swampy, reminding Dolly of a summer rainstorm. She stood at a creaky carousel along with the other passengers from the half-full flight – American peace corps and aid workers, presumably, from their suntanned, world-weary appearance. After all, Lusenka was hardly the sort of place you came for a holiday, though hadn't Anakin Awadi said that all the NGOs were being shut down?

It was her first time here, and everything was new. Why hadn't she visited sooner? She hauled her rucksack off the revolving belt and thought of Gloria, of how her mother would have shown her around, in a different life, and how much she would have liked that. The thought brought a small, aching sadness.

The centre of Port Salé was some miles from the airport, so she hailed a taxi, was dropped off in a quiet residential district where the midday sun cast steep shadows across the unpaved streets. She paid the driver, swigging water, and walked the rest of the way. Everything was dry, everything scorching, save the bursts of orange and red bougainvillea tumbling over brickwork. After the long flight, the sunlight made her eyes ache. The only backpacker's hostel listed in the guidebook was down a side street: a peaceful, gated compound contained by white-washed walls with hammocks set beneath a wide, sloping sunshade.

No other guests were discernible, just the manager, a European man with oak-tanned skin and tousled grey hair who emerged, yawning, in flip flops and a batik shirt.

Afterwards, Dolly followed the map through a maze of sleepy streets lined with private homes, embassies, and NGO headquarters. The Sheraton stood majestically on the coastal peninsula flanked by a sweeping drive and landscaped gardens, where regiments of tallish date palms flanked satiny lawns reaching all the way down to the sea. The marble steps were buzzing with activity: a few arriving foreigners, well-dressed men and women – diplomats or businesspeople – and one or two aid workers Dolly recognised from the flight.

She wiped the sweat from her forehead, observing from afar. She'd been to similar places on foreign reporting trips before, and was all too familiar with the peaceful colonial rhythms governing such luxurious hotel chains – rhythms of afternoon tea and tranquil poolside cocktails, of leisurely dips in crystal blue waters and long, languid evening suppers, that were utterly disconnected from the jostling dog-eat-dog worlds playing out just beyond the plush hotel boundaries. She was uneasily aware of how one's accent, one's clothes and gender, one's foreignness, was usually a ticket to enter unquestioned, while locals were stopped at the door. Nevertheless, she decided, she would have to use this unspoken class system to her advantage now.

At the marbled entranceway, she affected a relaxed air, nodding to the doorman, who sent her a broad smile in return. She walked through reception, scanning for signs to the swimming pool, which was easy to find, down a corridor and through a fire door, from where she emerged into the light and blue of a predictably vast infinity pool, whose iridescent water seemed to melt into the deeper indigo of the ocean beyond.

Dolly stood, taking in the scene. Wooden sun loungers were arranged at discreet distances beneath red parasols on a patio running the perimeter of the pool. To one side, on an elevated terrace shaded with a stripy cloth canopy, an array of well-to-do people were dining in groups. More well-heeled diners hovered around an arrow sign advertising a lunchtime seafood buffet.

Dolly selected a towel from the pool house and strolled over to a lounger on the far side of the pool, in the shade. There weren't many people sunbathing; presumably everyone was at lunch or napping in their rooms. She stripped off to her bikini and put on her sunglasses, surveying the pool, and ordered a drink from a hovering waiter who returned within minutes, bearing a tray. She lay back against the headrest of the lounger and sucked the cold fizz through a straw, enjoying the sweet, sugary hit of cola.

Half an hour later, someone threw a towel onto the next-door lounger. A man in his mid fifties, Dolly estimated, with a round, well-proportioned face. Momo? He stripped off to swimming shorts, displaying a muscular chest scattered with grey hairs, and nodded to her behind sunglasses. He left the lounger and dived into the pool with a splash, before executing two energetic lengths of crawl and breast stroking across to the far side where the water line and the sea dissolved into one other. There he hung, chin on arms, surveying the view.

Dolly slid into the pool, swam a few lengths of breaststroke. No one was paying much attention. All the diners were busy talking and eating. A languid atmosphere reigned, doubtless brought on by lunch and the intense heat. With lazy motions, she swam over to the side of the pool, next to Momo.

'You look just like her.'

His voice was low, his English pleasantly accented with the cadence of Lusenka. He continued to stare at the sea as he spoke, but shifted an imperceptible distance closer, so that Dolly could hear him more easily. With a sudden feeling of tension, she willed herself not to look round, aware that their meeting must not be obvious – that she must do everything not to jeopardise Momo's safety for her own sake.

'Who do you mean?' She squinted in the direction of the sea. 'I'm like who?'

'Gloria Fontaine.'

'She was my mother.'

284

'I know. Your ma was very famous here in her day. I helped her once, and now Robert has asked me to help you.'

'And will you?'

'I will try, for the sake of my oldest friend.'

Momo leant back with arms straight, as if he was about to do a racing start. In turn, Dolly dropped under the surface of the water, breathed out, popped back up with a splash. They could have been two random guests having a chat, she thought to herself. Flirting perhaps. It happened all the time.

'The Trident will dock tomorrow at 11 p.m.,' said Momo. 'I have a car. Where are you staying?'

He nodded when she told him the name of the hostel, all calm, all surety. 'I'll pick you up there tomorrow night. Be ready at half past nine. You'll need your camera.'

'I've a Canon, and my phone.'

He shot her a sideways look of curiosity. 'Are you sure you want to do this? If these people catch wind we're onto them…'

Again, Dolly submerged herself beneath the water, resurfacing with a deep breath, thinking of a saying – what was it? – something about how true bravery was not the absence of fear, but the conquering of it? That was Gloria all over. Her mother wouldn't have shied away from taking action, that much was certain – and nor would she.

'Yes,' she replied in a firm voice. 'I'm absolutely sure.'

With a splash, Momo shot away, backstroking athletically across to the other side of the pool. Dolly watched him pull himself out, water dripping from his limbs, gleaming in the sun, forming little puddles on the smooth concrete poolside. He stalked around the patio and dried off, rubbing the towel over his face, staring not at her but at the restaurant, or somewhere far off to the side of it.

In turn, she swam twenty lengths of slow crawl, trod water for a few minutes, and emerged from the pool. At the sun loungers, Momo was gone. In his place, a middle Eastern woman in her forties was sunbathing in a black swimsuit and dark sunglasses. The woman cast Dolly an incurious glance and looked back to her phone. As quickly

285

as she could, without drawing attention to herself, Dolly gathered up her belongings, and left.

Hours later, evening fell. Dolly sat upright in a hammock on the hostel veranda as five minutes, then ten minutes went by. To pass the time she checked her phone, her camera, her sound recording equipment and spare HD cards. She watched two tiny hummingbirds flicker in and out of the greenery, her mind wandering to home. British summertime was two hours behind, and Flora and Fern would be getting ready for bed, she knew, running around in their pyjamas, begging to stay up a little later. Evan would be cooking his tea. She felt a small stab of longing in her chest for the glorious mundanity of it all, realising with a start, a sudden moment of revelation, that she loved Cornwall, loved being near her family. She didn't want to be lonely anymore, and she would like to see her nieces grow up.

Seconds later, Momo's car drew up, a maroon Peugeot with fluffy beige seat covers. From the rear-view mirror, an air freshener disguised as a religious emblem dangled alongside a length of prayer beads. She snapped her mind back to the present with a feeling of resolve. Focus, she told herself; there was no going back now.

'Hey.' He leaned through the driver's window, munching a large baguette sandwich. 'You got your phone, your camera?'

'Yes, I have everything I need.'

'Good.' He swigged Coke from a can. 'Let's go, then.'

Momo switched on the radio, eating with one hand, driving with the other. From the speaker came a stream of afro-pop fusion, sabar drums, rumba, pop, and Mbalax. Then the excitable tones of the presenter. *This is Star Radio, bringing you the tunes of the late night in the city...*

Dolly watched out of the windscreen as Momo expertly navigated the dark city streets, through the centre onto a corniche, along the coast past a nightclub with beacons strobing, along a road that snaked through scrubby slums on the other side of the peninsula towards the fishing port, until they came to the industrial district of Port Salé.

Dolly rolled down the passenger window and closed her eyes, lifting her face to the coolish flow of air. Drops of perspiration trickled down her back under her t-shirt; she waved it about to generate a breeze. Eventually the streets dwindled into the port limits, where high-rise cranes and containers were stacked like Lego bricks, then the high chimneys of the fish canning factories towering above the fishing port, the ship repair facility, the container terminal. Dolly knew from the manifests on Evan's phone app that Lusenka's ships transported their goods to and fro from here, along the international sea lanes to Europe and America.

Momo wended the car between the lines of containers into an unlit outer section of the port, where a couple of smaller cranes were lined up on the dark quayside. The place was deserted. Bits of rubbish floated in the oily water of the harbour, which glimmered in the moonlight, its thick sea walls opening out to the dark Atlantic Ocean.

'The Trident's due at eleven, God willing,' he said. 'I'm going to park up here in the shadows.'

'What happens now?'

'We watch, we wait.'

Momo munched the last of his sandwich. After a moment he produced a plastic bag of weed from the glove compartment and rolled a large joint, licking the paper, pinching the end. He lit, puffed, offered Dolly the joint, but she shook her head.

'You sure?' Momo checked half a minute later, breathing out with an open mouth, leaving the odour of marijuana heavy in the air. 'We might be here a while.'

Midnight. The car was sweltering hot. Though Momo had stopped smoking, the festering smell of ham salad, sweat and weed lingered in the air. Dolly swigged water, flapping her sweaty t-shirt around herself and watching the tiny red dot of the tanker edge across the tracker app on her phone.

She wanted to ask Momo about Sunstar, about her mother and the past, but whether he was shy or just stoned, the man was evidently not a talker. He too, seemed engrossed in his phone, lost in his own world, and they sat without speaking, as if they were family members who knew each other well, thought Dolly, waiting for a bus or an aeroplane in a comfortable, resigned sort of silence.

Seconds later, Momo spoke. 'It's here,' he murmured. 'Get your camera out.'

Dolly followed his gaze to the water, where the shadowy bulk of a tanker was gliding in silence through the pitch black towards the landing quay. The vessel was a rusty red colour, stacked with dozens of containers.

'Is that it?'

Momo simply nodded.

The vessel came alongside the wharf with engines growling. Wordlessly, Dolly watched, transfixed, straining her eyes to see better through the dark.

From nowhere, two men leapt like feline creatures onto the deck of the tanker, then back again onto the wharf. Ropes were thrown. The tanker was tied up to the bulwarks, and without delay two cranes began to move in sync, their noisy clangs ringing out as the men hoisted container after container onto the portside.

'But this isn't the right ship?' Dolly said, noting the name of the tanker in large painted white letters: CORALI. 'We want the Trident Liberty, don't we?'

'They've changed it en route.' Unperturbed, Momo reached again to the glove compartment and brought out a pair of small binoculars. With casual movements he raised them to his eyes, peering through. 'There must have been a customs boat nosing about. They'll have repainted it to put them off, a quick paint job over the top.'

'Is that usual?'

Momo shrugged, and kissed his teeth with the binoculars still held to his eyes. 'Sure. These guys can navigate around arms embargoes, customs, Interpol. They're up to all sorts, like mislabelling shipments as farm machinery or radioactive waste.' He lowered the binoculars and sent Dolly a small smile. 'Or there's the old trick with week-old potatoes in tropical heat. You might have seen it in the films.'

He stopped talking.

Then, 'Get your camera ready,' he added with sudden urgency. 'You'll want to see this.'

From behind the stack of containers on the port side, Dolly spied a large, open-backed articulated truck approaching the wharf. When it rolled up beside the tanker, two more men jumped out of the cabin and climbed aboard the boat, nimble as cats. Another dockworker wrenched open the metal doors of one of the containers. The three men appeared to be inspecting the contents.

Momo handed Dolly the binoculars. She peered through before swapping them for her camera, adjusting to focus the lens on the tanker.

Momo kissed his teeth again. 'You want guns,' he murmured under his breath. 'You got guns.'

CHAPTER FORTY-TWO

Dolly

Morning broke. The air was still, the sky slowly lightening with delicate streaks of lavender as the fully loaded truck rolled out of the port. Momo followed the vehicle at a distance, headlights turned off, through the crisscrossing streets of Port Salé until they reached a potholed highway leading out of the main city. A fireball sun slowly rose ahead of them through the low-lit forest. In the passenger seat, Dolly's gaze fixed on the road ahead.

'Lourenco's palace,' Momo said suddenly, nodding at the roadside, slowing the car as they passed a dilapidated gate and half-a-dozen zinc-roofed huts, evidently abandoned long ago. The remains of a tiered marble fountain were falling into the red dust, and the forest beyond was reclaiming the space; long grass, bushes and small trees poked through the cracks of the road. A thick-set vine straggled through the crevices of a tumbling stone wall.

Odd that her mother too had made this same journey, years before, Dolly reflected, allowing her mind to drift to Gloria in the silver Rolls Royce, being driven through that very gateway and up to the palace where Lourenco – *Baptiste Lourenco,* one of the world's most renowned dictators – was waiting. How petrified Gloria must have been, how daunted yet determined, just as Dolly felt now.

Momo drove on in silence, chewing on a tooth stick. They passed scattered villages, most of them abandoned, into the deep jungle. In the passenger seat, Dolly scratched at a mosquito bite, stifling a stomach rumble of hunger. She regretted now not bringing malaria tablets, more water. When she shook her bottle there was only a centimetre of liquid left, and she drank it thirstily. She was woefully unprepared – in, as usual, out of her depth.

Light now; six thirty-five a.m. They turned onto a red dirt track past small villages carved into the bush, though there were no people here, only more desolate-looking huts, some pitted with bullet holes. Others were blackened wrecks, entirely destroyed by flames. The residents must have fled from the militia into the forest, Dolly realised, just like Gloria and Uncle Chilembé had years ago, preferring to take their chances in the wilderness than face the horrors inflicted by government forces.

Dolly felt a low jolt of fear somewhere deep down in her stomach. She and Momo too, could be ambushed at any moment. Her hunger pangs disappeared. This was a no man's land shattered by decades of brutal civil war and the chaotic aftermath of Baptiste Lourenco's twenty-five years in charge. There was nowhere more dangerous than this.

In the village, a strange, sickly stench hung in the air, like out-of-date meat left in the sun. At once, she knew something was wrong. When they got out of the car, a young man in shorts and t-shirt with a festive logo, *Happy Holidays Delaware 2002!*, lay near a ditch, recently dead. The side of the man's face was completely ripped out by a gunshot. Nearby, a young woman lay by a stream with her arms stretched above her mangled face, serene in death. Next to her, a dead boy of five or six reached for his mother.

It was hot, so hot. The dawn light seemed strangely cruel above the dozens of dead bodies illuminated by its fresh, unrelenting glow; not so much human beings as a collection of bloodied limbs belonging to men and women and children. Some of their arms and legs had been hacked off, as if the soldiers weren't satisfied with simply shooting their fellow men and decided to use their machetes to finish the job. Yet, Dolly couldn't tear her eyes away from the scene, the cold, golden eye of the sun and the harrowing cruelty of the bloodshed. She longed for some alternative explanation, some glimmer of hope to counteract the bleak notion of humanity's inherent penchant for conflict. But amidst the chaos and the carnage, she couldn't see it now.

'Jesus,' she murmured eventually. 'It's an execution ground.'

'For the Balaika, everywhere it is like this,' said Momo flatly. 'Every village, every town. They use guns, grenades, machetes. There is nowhere to hide anymore, and we don't have the firepower to defend ourselves.'

'You're Balaika?'

Momo gave a short nod. 'Like your Ma. Now I think every day is the day I am going to die. It's only by God's grace that I'm still alive.'

She watched Momo roll another joint, understanding, now, why he was helping her, not just because of Gloria, but because the ins and outs of Lusenka's bloody civil war barely got a mention on the British news, though the papers seemed fixated on other conflicts: the uprising in Syria, ongoing tensions with the Russians, and the aftermath of war in Iraq and Afghanistan.

It was why she'd wanted to cover this story in the first place, knowing only too well how the foreign editors of the British newspapers were largely indifferent to forgotten wars in forgotten countries; places Angus usually dismissed as 'God-forsaken backwaters'. These were conflicts that dragged on for decades with no resolution in sight. It didn't matter if you mentioned horrific human rights violations, daily attacks by gunmen, gender-based violence, or children out of school. Only when Lusenka concerned the Brits and their fuck-ups, their government scandals – as with her original story, which seemed a lifetime away now – did the headlines fly, though dramatic pictures or videos of killings in action might just pique an editor's interest.

It was why Angus had been so reluctant, in the first place, to let her cover the Balaika story: 'War-torn Lusenka? That's old news,' he'd said at first. 'We need some bang bang, Dolly, to make it fly.'

When Prime Minister Ed Pickering messed things up, overspending the defence budget on a country no one cared about, it had almost seemed a gift: her scoop, and thus Lusenka, had hit the headlines.

Momo puffed on the joint, watching her in silence, as if waiting for the next question.

'Government forces did this?' she asked.

'Most likely,' said Momo. 'They're systematically wiping out Balaika villages. It's a free-for-all.'

Dolly did not press him.

Droplets of sweat rolled down his face, and he wiped an arm across his forehead, seeming exhausted. After a pause, he added, 'Now the rebels are violent too. Both sides at fault, regardless of who started it. Nobody wins. The day they came to kill my family was a Friday, prayer day, though it is hard to imagine that God was there.'

He paused to pull on his joint, the next words emerging with the smoke:

'On the weekend I was leaving for the city to try to find work. There was practically no food in the house because people had been bribing the militia with food and sex to let them live a few days longer. My wife brought me beans and passion fruit to eat, because there were no more bags of rice.'

The scratchy drone of insects in the stillness. Momo crushed the joint into the dust with the toe of his flip flop and checked his phone.

'Passion fruit,' he added in a low voice, as if talking to himself. 'The last meal my wife gave me.'

There was a long silence. They both stared at the bodies.

'I'm going to take photographs,' Dolly said in a low voice, 'and some video, as evidence. We need to document this.'

'I understand.'

Attempting to render her mind blank, in the face of the horror, she snapped photographs to record the bodies in high-resolution film. The sun beat down on her head, unrelenting as she moved from one corpse to the next, pausing at each body to lean close, taking video recordings of the people's faces, intact or mutilated, and the swathes of glistening black flies humming on their rotting flesh, clear evidence of the massacre. A heavy, sickly smell settled on her nostrils and skin. Each body had been a living person once, she thought; a human being with dreams and hopes and loves, and now this – for the sake of power, for the sake of money. By the time she was finished, her head was spinning, she was dripping with sweat. She went to the side of the road and stood with her hands on her knees, then knelt on the ground, vomiting over and over on to the dry red dirt.

CHAPTER FORTY-THREE

Dolly

The lorry was parked up on the edge of the forest. The driver, in dirty jeans and a t-shirt, leaned against the side, smoking a cigarette. A little way along the track were half a dozen low kiosks where stacks of water had been left out in the sun, and oranges, bananas, and fat green and pink watermelons were piled in symmetrical triangles under parasols. A handful of children were playing footie in the street; the football faintly tinged with red dust. Women traders sold biscuits from trays on their heads. Despite the horrors a mile earlier, it was an oddly mundane scene, thought Dolly, as if the killings down the road were just another part of ordinary life here, these days.

Momo parked the car behind a pile of teetering mineral water bottles as Dolly forced herself not to worry. She flicked through the photographs she'd captured, then the videos with their terrible close-ups of dead people's faces; the scenes of killing made all too real by the instant cinematic technicolour. Feeling queasy, she turned off the camera and transferred the footage from the camera's SD card onto her mobile phone, attaching everything to a WeTransfer link. Quickly, she despatched it to Evan and Sunstar's email addresses, holding her breath as the upload circle span slowly and the files transferred in excruciating slow motion across the slow 3G connection: 10 per cent, twenty-five per cent, then finally, 100 per cent.

Sent.

Dolly breathed again.

She could feel Momo beside her, straight-backed and alert. He checked his watch, staring out of the windscreen. With a jittery, anxious feeling in her chest, she used the geo-app to pinpoint her location with coordinates, noticing the low battery sign on her phone. Five minutes later, it went dead, and with a lurching feeling of panic, she kicked herself for not bringing a remote battery pack.

Out of the blue there was a loudening pump of rap music. The open-air military trucks came up fast, slamming on the brakes, the soldiers sitting randomly beneath canvas canopies with legs hanging off the open sides, gun tips in the air. They were dressed in the military uniform of the Lusenkan army: camo fatigues and red berets with lines of bullets slung around their necks. Some wore flip flops, others, Wellington boots. Suddenly the town grew still and empty. Even the children dissolved into the bush, leaving just the deep jolt of the rap music in the heavy stillness matched by the explosive hammering of Dolly's own heart, the heavy pulse of the hot sun on the metal car roof, and the soldiers' sweating faces. She stilled her breathing, squinting against the sunlight, willing herself to concentrate.

One after another, six or seven men jumped out of the back of a truck, Kalashnikovs slung around shoulders. They were mostly young teenagers; thin, and rangy, hungry looking. They swaggered over to the other vehicle, where an older-looking commander in a scarf and wrap-around sunglasses was conferring with the driver. The rest of the soldiers began to pass guns down the line from one truck to the other. Some of them headed off into the bush carrying a grenade launcher. Dolly sank low in her seat, taking picture after picture of the machine guns and grenade launchers, of the rifles and RPGs, of the dozens of boxes which the soldiers ripped open, revealing piles and piles of ammo and grenades.

Through the camera lens, in the glow of the sun, Dolly saw Peverell Greyson standing by the back end of one of the trucks. He was utterly still, his gaze resting on Dolly with an unsurprised expression, as if he'd known all along that he would find her here. There was a barely perceptible smile on his face, of pleasure or of triumph, Dolly couldn't be sure, and she felt a chill of fear and dread creep sickeningly up and down her spine as she set her camera down in her lap and met his eyes.

They seemed to look at each other for an eternity. Through the trees, behind Pev, Dolly could see the sun glimmering softly, its pinkish rays illuminating the tips of the outer forest vegetation. It was too idyllic, too green; a picturesque postcard. She should be here as a tourist, she thought in a panic, not some sort of doomed action heroine.

Pev did not move, did not approach the car, did not attempt to speak. He simply stood centre-frame, staring across with the placidity of a big cat who had finally found its prey. How naturally he seemed to fit here, Dolly thought, in this tangle of forest and soldiers, rather than in England, Cornwall, where he must make a pretence of being civilised. As it turned out, Peverell Greyson was just an amoral Army man turned mercenary in a bush jacket and combat fatigues, his face smeared with camouflage paint, a gun slung across his chest. Of course he'd been this all along, thought Dolly.

Out of nowhere a bullet sliced past the car window, followed by an ear-splitting bang and the sound of shattering glass. Momo slumped forward. In that infinitesimal moment, time slowed, stretched and fell away, sweeping Dolly into the steady rotational pull of the universe. She could hear nothing but the blood rushing in her ears and the thump of her own heartbeat marking each passing second, metronomic, everlasting, while the earth continued its slow, predictable spin.

All was still. All was silent.

After a few seconds, minutes, hours – time stretching limitlessly – there was nothing but the deep green forest glowing in the morning light, the scratching cacophony of insects and the rising, deadening, all-encompassing heat. Everything went black.

When Dolly regained consciousness, she was lying on a wooden floor in the dark, her wrists tied in front of her with rope. There was a faint smell of marijuana mixed with cigar smoke, and the acrid whiff of male body odour. Other smells too; of engine oil and the briny odours of the ocean, and an off-balance feeling indicating that she might indeed be somewhere at sea, or at the very least on a moored boat. Her suspicion was confirmed by the gentle sound of water rippling nearby. How long, for God's sake, had she been here?

In the dark, Dolly groaned and tried to sit up, but there came a sharp shot of pain in her thigh followed by a dull ache that brought tears to her eyes. She was not in control anymore, she realised with a sudden acute awareness of the fragility of her own body, her slender, shatterable limbs, her soft, penetrable skin. With a sudden, wild lucidity, all clarity, all calm, she contemplated the marvel of existence, the preciousness of human life that was so delicate and fleeting and miraculous. People were not supposed to die in this way. This was not how she'd ever imagined the situation playing out.

She lay back down again, methodically appraising the rest of her body limb by limb, in the way she'd learned on various hostile environment courses through the years, for work. Airway, Breathing, Circulation, Disability, Exposure. She was surprised to remember the details of the mnemonic. But miraculously, it seemed her thigh was the only major injury she'd sustained, though it hurt like hell.

'Help,' she whispered weakly into the dark. When she moved her legs, there came another sharp shot of pain. 'Is anyone there?'

Gradually, through a small porthole to Dolly's left hand side, the space filled with a greyish half-light. Morning, she supposed, another morning – though she had no clue how many hours or days had passed since her capture. When her eyes adjusted, she made out some bundles of ropes hanging from the walls and a quantity of shipping equipment stashed at either end of the bunker. She let out a frustrated groan and jiggled her hands about in the rope, but the hessian was thick and strong.

With a loud groan she suddenly remembered Momo's lifeless body, the blood and the glass, the horrible sickening suddenness with which her ally – her mother's friend and saviour – was gone. She'd never seen anyone die before. Now her head reeled, and nausea rose, stealing her breath. She vomited bile on to the floor, her stomach heaving with nothingness.

Once she had finished, she clambered to her knees and staggered forward. With a great effort she shuffled painfully to the door. Predictably, it was locked.

She recalled being shot at, the truck chasing them and Pev, Pev...

Peverell Greyson who was brokering arms deals between Lusenka and Britain with Shaun's help. Was this Pev's boat, then? Were they still in Lusenka, or another place? Where had they brought her to? If Pev's men had indeed captured her, there was no reason for them to keep her alive, nor a way for anyone to find her.

'Help!' Dolly called. 'If anyone can hear me, help!'

Immediately there was a movement on the other side of the door, and she felt a cold shot of terror in her throat and stomach. She pushed against the rope with no noticeable effect and cried out. Someone slid the bolt across. She shuffled back, watching helplessly as the door opened.

The Lusenkan guard, gigantic and moody looking, had a Kalashnikov slung around his chest. He stared at her with bloodshot eyes that harboured a familiar faraway look, unfocused from marijuana. To imagine this man in charge of a gun made Dolly nervous, more than nervous.

'Get back,' the guard said in French. Roughly he pulled open the door and came in, locking it behind him. *'Restez-là!'*

The guard pulled out a mobile phone from the pocket of his combats. Dolly watched him speak animatedly in some sort of dialect to someone at the other end. She followed his gaze to the doorway. Footsteps outside. She braced her muscles, ready to run though she was incapacitated, responding to the danger with her whole body. Blood pumped in her ears; her heart flew wildly in her chest. Fight and flight. Fight and run.

The door opened, and Pev Greyson came in.

'Fontaine!' he exclaimed facetiously with a mock expression of joy. 'Fancy seeing you here.'

He was bigger and squarer than Dolly remembered, armed to the teeth; a machine gun slung across army fatigues. His eyes were glistening in the half-light; in them she glimpsed a frightening coldness. He gestured for the guard to stand to one side and closed the door at a leisurely pace. He lit a cigar, filling the room with gusts of pungent smoke that made her cough.

'Well, well, well, Fontaine, how delightful,' he said, eyes lit with cold enjoyment. 'But I'm forgetting my manners. Please, do have a seat.'

Pev waved an arm at the guard, who brought over a chair with languid movements. More gently than she expected, the guard picked Dolly up and hauled her onto it, causing her legs to spasm with pain.

'Hey,' she protested, still coughing. 'Let go of me!'

'Well now, that's better, isn't it?' Pev took another long draw on the cigar. 'Now, what are we going to do with you, Fontaine, eh, with all this naughty investigating of yours? It's really not on, you know.' He crossed his arms, pursing his lips with a babyish expression and making mock tutting sounds.

'What do you want?' Dolly said.

'The title deeds, *obviously.*'

'I don't know what you're talking about.'

'Your mother, Gloria Fontaine, has documents containing information that we want.'

'My mother is dead.'

'Past tense then,' Pev said. 'Your mother *had* the documents, and you know where they are. Don't pretend, Fontaine. You're a very bad liar.'

Dolly stared back at him, and for a second or two their eyes locked, a pair of combatants readying for a fight, and neither of them were willing to yield. Curious that it should come to this, she thought. It struck her that perhaps she wasn't so helpless after all. As long as she had something Peverell wanted, she could bargain. Wasn't that the way it always worked?

'I've uploaded information to the cloud,' she bluffed. 'Videos, photos, it's all recorded there, so if you kill me, they'll find you. There are people who know exactly where I am, and what I'm up to.' She shifted in the chair, holding Pev's eye and wiggling her fingers in the rope tie. 'So free my hands and maybe I'll agree to talk to you.'

Silence. But after a moment Pev gestured at the guard, who came over and undid the rope. With a gasp, Dolly stretched her arms, rotating her aching wrists.

'I don't know anything about any deeds,' she said.

'*Putain.*' Pev shot her a cold, sardonic smile. 'Just answer the question, will you?'

Dolly touched the wound on her thigh with her gaze fixed on Pev. With her fingers she felt a sticky mass of drying blood. The pain was intense, low and throbbing.

'I need a doctor. I'm losing blood.'

'God knows, the woman's demanding.' Pev shot her a cold, sardonic smile. 'Just answer the question, will you?'

'I don't care what you and your henchmen want. I need treatment first.'

Ignoring her pleas, Pev left the room followed by the guard. The door clanged shut. Dolly hauled herself over and leant her ear against it, listening to two men were talking urgently in English, in low voices. 'She's the only one who can tell us where they are.' The voice was familiar, too familiar.

'My days,' said Pev. 'That woman has been a pain in the ass for too fucking long. Get her some antiseptic, will you, Lobster. Anything to shut the bitch up.'

Dolly tracked the men's footsteps as they descended the corridor and disappeared up a flight of stairs.

CHAPTER FORTY-FOUR

Dolly

Hours, maybe days later, bright pinpricks of light seeped through the porthole of the cabin. Footsteps, then the clank of the door opening. Dolly was dragged outside, brought up through the bowels of the boat to the deck. She couldn't think, couldn't breathe.

Cautiously, Dolly peered out, wincing in the searing midday light. As her eyes adjusted, she realised that she was being taken, in the cabin of a dinghy or a fishing boat, across water to the shore. Grains of sand beneath her feet. All thoughts of escape disappeared from her mind; she was too fragile to stand up, let alone run. Thanks to the antiseptic delivered by the now-familiar guard – who, to Dolly's surprise, was not unkind – her injury had not become infected but the wound was still painful, bleeding often; a continuous dull ache in her thigh.

'Drink,' someone commanded.

Dolly drank a pint of water and ate the food she was offered greedily with her fingers, rice with some sort of spiced fish sauce, the most perfect food she had ever tasted in her life. She cleared the plate, licking her fingertips. Afterwards she slept on a soft bed, or was it a sofa? She did not dream. Was she there for minutes, hours, days?

Dolly sat up and gazed around. She was sitting on a rattan chair in an open-sided hut with palm-wood pillars facing the beach. Here, out of the sun, a pleasant breeze cooled her skin, and she could feel some sort of woven matting against her bare toes. In a daze she took in woven bamboo sofas upholstered in wax prints, with patterns of palm fronds and colourful parrots. On a side table, a drinks tray with straws, cocktail umbrellas, jugs of juice, and spirits: tequila, vodka, vanilla rum, Pastis and Curaçao. Little tweeting parakeets fluttered in and out of the thatched roof like bright pieces of silk. Beyond the shade, a deserted beach of bone-white sand, waving palm trees, and a smooth indigo sea. Everything was so bright it made her eyes throb, reviving her headache.

'Dolly.'

He was sitting at an oval bamboo table, finishing lunch. Flies buzzed around a fish carcass on his plate. A packet of cigarettes and a lighter lay on the tablecloth. She observed him take a piece of bread from the basket and chew thoughtfully.

'Gorgeous, isn't it?' He nodded at the view, waving away a fly. 'A proper holiday paradise.'

Dolly stared, speechless. 'What on earth are you doing here?' she managed to say.

Shaun Kingsley smiled over with a look bordering on... could it be affection, she wondered, incredulously.

'Christ, Dolly, I always did fantasise about seeing you on the beach in a bikini.'

Dolly snorted with disgust. 'Are you *actually* trying to flirt with me? You do realise I'm a *hostage*.'

'Oh, even better.'

'Asshole.'

Shaun gave another smile and brushed away another fly. In his eyes, Dolly recognised the familiar cheekiness, the wry humour that had attracted her a lifetime ago.

She shook her head. 'I don't understand, Shaun. All this. I thought...' She winced, rubbing at her temple. 'Jesus, I don't know what I thought anymore.'

'Look, I had to get you out of the way, Dolly. You were sniffing around with your usual vigour, getting too close for comfort. Our operations would have been ruined. It was nothing personal.'

'*Nothing personal?* You got me sacked on purpose, you set the whole thing up, and it's nothing personal? Jesus, it was always you, wasn't it, from the beginning?'

'Of course,' Shaun said between bites of bread. 'Collateral and all that.'

'You tried to contact me. Those texts?'

'Call me soft.' A shrug, a half-smile. 'I wanted to warn you, for old times' sake, then thought better of it. It would have also been useful to know what you were up to.'

'Nice,' Dolly said dryly, meeting his eyes, and for a moment the old spark passed between them. She looked away, out to sea, then back again. Another insect hovered near Shaun's ear, and she watched its trajectory past his head, up and away through the open doors of the hut. 'What are your operations, anyway?' she said evenly. 'You and Pev are working together, right?'

A nod. 'He owns a company, Dolphin Technical Solutions, which brokers deals for arms and ammo discarded by the British at a cheap price, the usual thing. Lucrative, obviously.'

'No wonder you come in useful then.'

'Plus, he does security work.'

'Security work?'

'As in private security contracts.' Shaun set down his fork, wiping the sweat from his forehead with the palm of his hand. 'Mercenaries, I think some people like to call them. Pev's running a private army for Kilomi, to defeat Balaika rebels threatening to overrun Port Salé. It's known as a "regime survival package" on the paperwork, would you believe it?'

'Except they're not rebels are they, they're just normal civilians? People trying to go about their lives. So Peverell Greyson – and therefore you – the two of you are assisting a genocide. And all because of oil and diamonds. My guessing is that the cost of the' – Dolly made inverted commas in the air – 'regime survival package is the rights to Lusenka's natural resources?'

Silence. Shaun took a gulp of water and went back to his lunch, eyes down.

'And am I right,' Dolly continued purposefully, 'that you deliberately targeted me, right from the start, because you wanted those land deeds from years ago, given to my mother by Hervé Abimbola, so you can claim the land as your own?'

Shaun shrugged, still chewing. 'What do you think?'

There was a long silence.

'And sleeping with me? Was it always the plan?'

Shaun flashed a grin. 'Trouble was, you were too attractive. You made me feel alive. What's a man to do?'

'Asshole.'

'Oh come on. It was a great plan – I'd seduce you, lucky me – and get the deeds in the process. What could possibly go wrong? Trouble was, you were just too intelligent for your own good. When you told me about your new lead, I knew you'd dig deeper, and discover the arms contract eventually, and then follow the trail to us. I had to do something, and quickly.'

Shaun pushed his plate away and leaned back in his chair, staring out to sea. He looked older, thought Dolly, the rosacea on his cheeks florid and raw-looking, from stress, she wondered, or just the sun? A day or two's stubble shadowed his chin. His face looked gaunt, yet he'd put on weight since she'd seen him last. She felt almost sorry, the old feelings bubbling up, but she reminded herself that the two of them were never meant to be together. It wasn't love – just a dangerous flame fuelled by chemistry. She knew now that true happiness was about safety and reality and belonging, not reckless passion. And Shaun could go to hell...

'You really took the wrong track, didn't you, Shaun?' she said, musingly. 'You once told me how you never felt good enough, how you were the hardworking state school boy from inner Birmingham, mixed up with all those posh boys at Marlborough. Teased because you were on a scholarship. Is this your way of proving yourself? You just never struck me as the type to get involved with something like this.' She paused, her voice softening. 'I thought you were *nice*, kind even. I thought we had something together, something special. Did I really get you so wrong?'

There was a long silence before Shaun gave a deep sigh, his face suffused with something resembling regret – or was it sadness? Somehow, Dolly could tell she'd got to him.

Shaun took another gulp of water and stared at her impassively. 'Look, my mother was a cashier in Sainsbury's, my father a hospital porter.' He didn't take his eyes off hers. 'Neither of my parents believed I'd amount to anything. How could I ever feel good enough compared to rich boys like Peverell Greyson. They had it all, this golden life that came from nowhere, loads of money, the proverbial fucking silver spoon. After A Levels they went straight to Sandhurst for officer training, and there was always money to back them up if life took a wrong turn. Whereas I had to make a success of my life, just to survive. Those boys never had to face hardship like I did – I dare say they couldn't even imagine what my life was like.'

'So you were dazzled, and you still are? You wanted to impress him, even at school?'

'Sure. Pevvers bullied me, until I became useful to him. Lobster the Mobster, as he liked to say.'

'Jesus, Shaun, are you schoolboys or grown men?'

'Call us childish. Anyway, my position and power were valuable, very valuable, which was very satisfying. At last, I had a purpose, and power over Peverell Greyson, of a kind, and it felt good.'

Shaun grimaced and fell silent, and Dolly could tell he was upset. But then he gave an embarrassed laugh, and the moment was gone. A shadow seemed to pass over him, covering any softness that might have existed there. He lit a cigarette and puffed slowly.

'Anyway, Dolly, enough of the counselling. Shame it came to this, eh. To get to the point, I need those deeds. You must know that.'

There was a pause, and Dolly registered, with interest, Shaun's use of the first person pronoun. Pev also knew about the deeds, she was well aware of that – so was this Shaun's single-handed bid to get his hands on the deeds for himself?

'The land's still worth a fortune,' Shaun continued. 'There's enough oil there to make Lusenka the third largest exporter in the world, just as it was in the seventies, despite the ruins of Kilomi's rule. Let alone the diamond mines. Look, don't be stupid. Pevvers is a violent motherfucker, and he'll stop at nothing. Just tell me where the deeds are, for fuck's sake, Dolly.'

Dolly reached over for the packet of cigarettes and helped herself. She lit up and took a long drag, feeling the strength drain back into her limbs from the food and the nicotine.

'So Pev wants to get his hands on the deeds too, as if the arms money isn't enough?' she asked on a hunch. 'You're fighting over these deeds, right?'

'Yeah.' Shaun looked sheepish. 'But it was my idea, the plan with you. I don't see why Pevvers, of all people, should reap the benefits.'

Dolly continued to smoke, turning her gaze to the sea and the huge tanker floating just offshore. It seemed she was a prisoner on The Trident or The Corali, whatever its name was, in a place so remote it might be the end of the world. Were they even still in Lusenkan waters, or somewhere further down the coast, somewhere grim in the back end of this place where the rule of law didn't apply anymore? Perhaps no one would ever find her, and her lifeless body would wash up one day on a distant foreign shore, unrecognisable. She took a drag of her cigarette. No. No, she refused to believe that.

'Look.' As if reading her thoughts, Shaun spoke, not unkindly: 'No one's coming, you know.'

'People *are* coming for me.' Dolly took long, gulping draws on the cigarette, as if the tobacco would somehow bolster her courage. 'Believe me, they are.'

But she could feel her certainty slipping away, replaced by a profound sense of exhaustion engulfing her body and mind. In truth she couldn't imagine, now, how anyone might rescue her. After all, there was no record of her journey and no way to get in touch. Only luck could save her now.

'Surely you're not going to let Peverell Greyson kill me?' she added with a note of panic. 'Do you not even care *at all* what happens to me? Jesus...'

He gave no answer, but narrowed his eyes and met hers, lingering there. Suddenly she felt a deluge of hurt wash over her, knowing for certain that the man she'd once loved – she could admit it now – had never been what he seemed. This awful moment, seeing him for what he truly was, broke her heart. How could she have got him so wrong? It saddened her to think of the man Shaun Kingsley could have been, with all his potential, and the man he actually was – a fraud, a charlatan, a lying shit. Oh, the list of appropriate synonyms went on… It was a sobering reminder of the masks people wore, concealing their true selves. How little anyone truly understood of another's inner life…

'I do know about the deeds,' she ploughed on, pushing her emotions aside and trying to concentrate. 'When did you realise Gloria had them?'

Shaun gave a low laugh. 'Christ. No need to go all investigative journo on me.' With slow movements, he lit up another cigarette. She watched him rise to his feet with a creak of the chair's bamboo frame and wander over to the drinks tray, where he stood smoking with luxuriant puffs. 'Have a drink, Dolly, for Christ's sake. You look like you could do with a strong whisky.'

'Jesus, I hate fucking whisky, surely you know that.' She wiped away the sheen of sweat on her forehead, shifting on her rattan chair to face him on. 'Alright,' she relented. 'I'll have a rum.'

Cigarette in one hand, Shaun poured with the other, handing her a tumbler of the dark alcohol. The rum was warm and fiery, stealing her breath, burning away her fear.

'I met your mother,' Shaun continued, smoking: 'in '79, during her mission to Lusenka. Brave woman, difficult as hell.'

Dolly laughed loudly. 'By difficult, do you by any chance mean she was outspoken and feisty and not willing to do exactly what you, a man, told her to do?'

'Quite,' said Shaun. 'I knew she wasn't going to give me the bloody deeds. The mission was a big thing for the Brits at the time. I knew Abimbola must have passed them to her, somehow.' Shaun downed his whisky and drew on the cigarette, puffing smoke. 'When she died, I came up with a plan to find you, because you were the one person who could help me get those deeds back.'

307

'That was why you hooked up with me?'

'As I say, it wasn't a hardship.'

'And when you suggested coming down to Cornwall, it was to look for the deeds?'

'Sure. I was planning to have a good look around your mother's house. All it would have taken was a little forget-me tablet in your wine glass...'

He trailed off with a snigger, and Dolly made a disgusted expression. 'But then,' she took up the story, 'I got too close to your shady dealings with Pev and the arms. I became a nuisance, all that nosing about. You thought you'd get me out of the picture by trashing my story – and manipulate the deeds out of me later.'

Shaun was staring at her, frowning. 'As I say, it was business, politics, nothing personal, nothing to do with how I felt about you. A man's got to live.'

'Except,' she continued, ignoring him, 'then I started investigating Peverell Greyson, which was the last thing you expected. And so, well, here we are.' Then with a sudden, dawning realisation, she added: 'It was you, wasn't it, who had Lionel killed. You and Pev! You total fucking bastards.'

A long silence. For a second, she thought she glimpsed genuine remorse on Shaun's face.

'Sorry, Dolly,' he said eventually. 'I never thought it would get to this. Honestly, I never meant...'

Peverell Greyson came around the side of the hut, up the steps, bare-chested in swimming shorts, dripping wet and panting slightly, a vision of rippling muscles and tanned skin. He wiped a towel across his face and wandered over to the drinks tray, where he mixed up a concoction of vodka and yellow juice, humming The Beach Boys under his breath, *Kokomo*. In a daze, Dolly listened to the humming and the light ripple of the liquids, the ice cubes rattling down into the glass. A sunset-hued cocktail took shape. The effects of the rum had worn off, she felt her fear flood back. She blinked and looked away towards the sea.

'For Christ's sake, Dolly,' murmured Shaun. 'Just go along with him. You've no choice now. I can't protect you.'

Pev's pinkish lips, cupid-pretty, wore a half-smile as he crossed to the table. Still humming the song, he jiggled his hips, mouthing the words at her. 'Oh, I do love a hula dancer, Fontaine, don't you?' He gave an insinuating laugh. 'Lobster does too, don't you, mate... Evidently. Mmm, Fontaine, you'd make a splendid hula dancer, dressed up in a pretty little straw skirt. Yummy.'

Pev lowered himself onto a chair and swung his long legs up on the settee, appraising Dolly as he sucked at the cocktail through a coral-coloured plastic straw. After the sea swim, his blonde hair was drying into angelic little curls.

'Cracking spot, *n'est ce pas? Le vrai paradis.* Enjoy it while you can.' He jiggled the straw noisily in the glass. 'Decided to cooperate yet, have we, Fontaine darling?'

'Fuck you.'

'Now, now, that's a bit uncalled for, nice girl like you. Look, last thing I want is to get heavy-handed but...' A sigh. 'I do love a diamond ring.' Pev twirled a pink-patterned cocktail umbrella in slender fingers, shaking his head with mock despair, though there was no apparent menace in his voice, no interruption to his tranquil facial expression. 'Needs must, hey. The thing is, you have something that isn't yours, Fontaine, do you see my point? The blasted deeds *elude* us every time, despite the most *assiduous* efforts on our behalf to find them. And *my, my,* Fontaine, your Ma really did leave you a lovely pile, didn't she, you dark horse, you—'

'What do you mean?' Dolly blurted out, trailing off as she watched Shaun's face turn from neutral to a surprised frown. She remembered the records strewn mysteriously about the living room floor when she'd first arrived at Genévrier, as if someone had been rummaging through them.

'So it was you,' she said. 'Your so-called cleaners looking through the house?'

'*Mea culpa.*' Pev wiggled the straw in his cocktail glass. 'Quiet and tidy as mice, my boys. You'd never know they visited.'

Clearly Shaun wasn't in on it, Dolly realised. If he'd been planning to search Gloria's house, he'd never gone through with it. No, it was Pev who'd had Genévrier searched off his own bat. The 'cleaners' probably thought the deeds might be stashed with Gloria's LPs – which explained the mess.

'It strikes me as rather lovely,' continued Pev, 'rather poetic even, that you should die here, in your home country, Fontaine. *Retracing your roots,* finding *your people,* and all that.' Pev sucked loudly at the drink with the same sardonic half-smile. 'Lobster, my dude,' he added, glancing over in Shaun's direction. 'Can you call Yves, get the lady back on-board? Thanks. Terrific.'

The guard appeared, heaving Dolly up by her arms. With surprising gentleness, he guided her out of the hut as she struggled in his large arms, mustering her strength, ignoring the pain in her leg.

'You're nothing but bloody thugs,' she called back. 'You're just gangsters! Shame on you!'

'Don't be fucking stupid, Dolly,' she heard Shaun call, and she noted in his voice a new and unmistakable tone of fear. 'Just fucking well do what he says, will you?'

CHAPTER FORTY-FIVE

Dolly

During daylight hours, Dolly could hear the splashing sounds of the crew joking about, diving and swimming. From somewhere, the scent of barbecuing fish drifted in, sounds and smells of parties and alcohol and laughter that seemed cruel, at best. Were Pev and his gang choosing to holiday, she wondered in a daze, while she, their prisoner, slowly expired in the dark hold.

Occasionally, the engine revved and idled, and she had an inkling that the tanker was on the move from one bay to the next. Days passed. She drifted in and out of sleep and consciousness. When she slept, restlessly, painfully, she dreamt of home and Gloria and Genévrier in August, over and over, its windows flung open to let in the summer light. In the dream, she wandered the uninhabited rooms pulling at flaps of yellowing anaglypta paper hanging from the walls like dead skin. Outside, hydrangeas mushroomed into gigantic balls of palest pink blossoms, and she pricked her finger on a thorn, watching it spring sticky and scarlet with blood. When she woke, she was disorientated and thirsty, calling out for someone, anyone, to come and help.

One day, when the guard appeared, she mustered enough energy to offer a series of gory charades indicating sea sickness. Hastily, the man disappeared, returning with tablets and more water. From that moment on there was more food, enough water, more time unsurveyed. Fortified, ignoring the agony of dull throbbing in her thigh, Dolly forced herself to do one hundred sit-ups every hour; then laps of the hold, walking until she was exhausted, press-ups, and air punches.

With her renewed strength came a plan. In the guard's absence she examined a pile of shipping equipment dumped in the corner of the hold, consisting mostly of dirty oilcloths, coiled ropes, and a handful of deck brushes and empty fuel cans. Even so, she identified a piece of rope of a useful size and length, and a heavy fire extinguisher that could feasibly be used as a weapon. She clutched at the cold metal, its weight a tangible promise of action, of possible salvation. Then – with a blooming optimism, the first time for days – she found two hand-held emergency flares. Her mind veered back to Gloria in Mirrorball, of her gutsy mother setting off those flaming beauties to get help, and her stomach contracted at the thought. Suddenly, the dimness of the ship's hold seemed less oppressive. What were the odds the flares might work? This wasn't a film, and it was highly unlikely she would have her mother's good fortune. Still, it was something. She needed to become Gloria, Dolly resolved staunchly, and fight back.

One afternoon, Pev opened the door, though Shaun was nowhere to be seen. He was barefoot in a t-shirt and board shorts, his face darkly tanned from so many days under the sun. She could see why no one would ever believe he was a criminal. He looked more like a champion surfer than an assassin or an arms smuggler.

'I'm afraid we're close to the last laugh, Fontaine, darling,' he said, pulling out a cigar and lighting it up. Gentle puffs of smoke hung suspended in the boiling atmosphere of the hold.

Dolly coughed, head bowed, making a show of weakness. 'Oh?'

'Yes.' He dragged on the cigar, exhaling with a popping sound. 'Someone will have to kill you soon. Might be me. Might be your Shaun, might be a stranger. Still. Got to be done, eh.'

'For fuck's sake,' she muttered.

Pev shot her a look of mock sorrow. 'Holiday's over, Fontaine, darling, and oh, what a damn shame. Better get your act together...'

Dolly stared after him. 'What about Morgan? Does she know about this? She'll ask about me, you can't get away with it. You've got a daughter. You're having a *baby*, for God's sake.'

Pev made for the door, cigar held delicately between long fingers. When he turned back with a wave, 'Bye Fontaine', his face registered no real expression; a blank, Dolly thought to herself, Oscar Wilde's Dorian Grey. His true soul must be hidden somewhere else, withered and decaying back in Cornwall. And in his eyes, what? Disgust? Hatred? Or simply annoyance that she was still in the way, unyielding about the location of the deeds.

She watched the door slam heavily behind him, and listened to the sound of his footsteps as he climbed back on deck.

'This is total bullshit!' she shouted. 'Total, fucking bullshit!' Then she sank, still swearing, onto the hard teak floor of the hold.

It was early evening, and Dolly could hear the swish and slap of waves against the boat, indicating calm seas. The sun glowed gold through the porthole; these were ideal conditions for swimming. Sure enough, after half an hour or so, the ship's crew could be heard splashing about to the portside of the ship. She could hear Pev's braying laugh rising above the rest, and after an hour or two the festivities on the dock grew louder and more raucous. By the sounds of it everyone was drunk, probably high. Usually, after these high shenanigans, the whole boat slept in a stupor. She had already manoeuvred her stash of found equipment, so it was reachable. Now she positioned herself behind the heavy door to wait for the guard. Ten minutes later, she heard the key in the lock, then the man's familiar deep voice. *Allô.* A smell of fish drifted through the hold.

'*Ton dîner,*' the guard muttered in heavily accented French. '*Ici. Putain, où es-tu?*'

With all her force, and quite a lot of guilt, Dolly brought the fire extinguisher down on the man's head. He emitted a low groan and fell immediately. She tied his hands and feet with the rope.

Hours passed, until the hold was pitch black, the party over. The whole boat slept. Only then did Dolly dare to slip out, carrying the flares, and lock the door behind her.

The yacht was not so large, she registered as she moved slowly along the corridor, and it was conveniently laid out for her purposes with the bedrooms below and living areas upstairs.

All was quiet.

313

She made her way up some steps, searching for a deck open to the sky while committing the route to memory. At a carpeted area with staircases leading up and down, she surveyed the layout in a panic: *where now?* On the left was a narrow passageway that must lead to other areas of the ship, she told herself. She jogged down the passageway.

To her relief, she came to a glass door, through which she could see a metal railing with a lifeboat suspended on it, and the open sea. She took a deep breath, pushed the door. Locked. Again, she inhaled, once, twice, trying to calm her rising panic. She looked around for something to break the glass. Nothing.

She turned back and sprinted up the second staircase, figuring that, from her limited knowledge of boats, the layout would be mirrored on each deck. Voices now, too close. Taking the same route as below, she swerved around to the left and into the passageway. Sweat was pouring down her back. Her body shook, her breaths came shallow and coarse. There was a heavy glass door. She pushed the metal bar, and the door opened.

She gasped at the shock of the fresh air and grappled with the flare whose instructions she'd scrutinised so many times, she knew them by heart. After a few seconds she was able to wrench off the cover and point the flare at the sky. Of course, the flare might be spotted by people on the other side of the yacht, she reasoned, but she had to take that risk. With a quiet hiss, a plume of red smoke rose into the darkness. Then another.

Jesus. Jesus. She held her breath. Now, the wait. She had not accounted for the paralysing fear; the rising doubt that her half-conceived plan, slapdash at best, would work. After all, everything depended on the geo-tracker and the drunkenness of the crew, on their complacency and inattention to the skies above. On fate. On luck.

She strained to hear any shouts or other sounds of pursuit, any evidence the crew had spotted the flare. But all was quiet, just the sounds of the sea slapping against the side of the boat and the scarlet plume of fire falling from the sky.

CHAPTER FORTY-SIX

Dolly

Dolly couldn't stay on deck: it was too exposed, too risky. She crept back to the hold where the guard was still tied up. For a moment, the man protested, but the walls of the hold were thick, and Dolly gagged him with her t-shirt despite her misgivings about the moral niceties of such a measure. He settled down, staring at her dolefully. She almost felt sorry for him.

She settled down to wait, her body trembling, full of adrenaline, her mind shooting in all directions. She noticed that her thigh was bleeding again, a dull, excruciating ache, the wound doubtless aggravated by all the movement of the past hour. It must have been past midnight. Finally, unbelievably, there came unexpected movements in the dark, and the sound of the door opening quietly. She braced, ready to fight if necessary. Please God let it be them…

'Over here,' she whispered, taking a gamble. 'In the corner.'

Through the darkness came the barely audible murmur of a male voice, very British, very Northern. 'You're safe. Don't make a sound, please.'

'You saw my flare,' she gasped. 'You came?'

Footsteps and someone leaning close, so close Dolly could smell the not-unpleasant whiff of male sweat. The voice was whispering: 'What's your name and where you from?' He was lifting her up now, supporting her with capable arms to her feet.

'Dolly,' she said. 'Dolly Fontaine, from England.'

'Tell me the name of your brother.'

'Rich.' She took in the electronic tablet strapped to the man's arm with her picture on it, remembering something Evan had said once, about how the military identified hostages when they found them, by asking the names of close relatives. 'Richard Robert Fontaine.' She gulped for air and breath. 'That man, in the corner,' she added hurriedly, 'he'll need medical help. He was just following orders.'

'Good. Don't worry. Let's go.'

Quickly, silently, she found herself propelled out of the yacht's hold and up through the galley to the decks. From above came the loud whirr and crack of a helicopter, then other voices, yells from the waking crew, the quick crackle of gunshots being exchanged. There were other men too, other commando soldiers with low British accents and berets silhouetted in the dark who seemed to move as one with smooth efficiency, through the darkness. As she was handed from one soldier to the next, Dolly had the feeling that there was no apparent danger, no panic, just the expert, systematic flow of a well-practised master plan.

Go, go, go!

With a strong sea breeze whipping her hair, she took in a cluster of dark figures securing lines to a helicopter hovering above. A soldier on the deck making hand signals. A winchman descending. Before she knew it, a sling was slipped over her head and she was borne aloft, borne away, into the noisy interior of the helicopter. The relief was so overwhelming that Dolly could hardly catch her breath. As the helicopter lifted with stomach-dropping speed and whisked her away, fluently, effortlessly, a feather in the warm tropical night, she closed her eyes with tears streaming down her face, unable to believe she was safe.

Dolly woke in a hospital bed, a tube snaking from her arm to an IV drip. As she opened her eyes, she saw that the curtains were drawn around the unit, but to her surprise there was an elderly man rearranging flowers on the nightstand. When he noticed she was stirring, he turned and beamed at her.

'Sunstar?' she managed to say. 'What on earth are you doing here?'

'You should call me Robert, my dear.' He smiled even more widely. 'Those old spy games were a very long time ago, though you seem to have single-handedly wrenched me from retirement.'

He looked down at her with twinkly eyes, and Dolly recalled what Gloria had said, *a lifetime of figuring things out.*

'Where on earth am I?'

'The Royal Cornwall. You were air-lifted out of Lusenka, my dear girl, thanks solely to your ingenious scheme – very risky, I might add – and the fortunate fact that you were geo-tracking yourself to a certain point. Remarkably clever, if I may say so – such technology was unheard of in my day, I can assure you. Nevertheless, with the assistance of your chap, Evan – fine fellow, I'd say, hold on to him – and Rich, of course, we managed to find you. Just in the nick of time, dare I say it, although we lost Momo, poor chap.' Sunstar paused, adding, 'A true hero, without a doubt.'

The tribute was characteristically matter of fact, though Sunstar's eyes looked watery. He cleared his throat and briskly turned away, giving his attention to the flowers which he proceeded to rearrange, tulips then daffodils, cheerful yellow against the hospital blue of the curtains.

'Poor Momo,' Dolly murmured, feeling her throat constrict at the memory of Momo's lifeless body slumped against the steering wheel, the suddenness and tragedy of his death. 'He was incredible,' she added, fiddling with the frayed edge of the hospital blanket.

Sunstar gazed at the flowers and murmured, as if to himself, 'Indeed he was, indeed he was.'

A minute later, she said, 'And Peverell Greyson? Shaun Kingsley? What happened?'

'Mercenaries are unsavoury chaps to be mixed up with, my dear girl.' Sunstar turned to look at her, seemingly recovered, tut-tutting as he explained that the network was dismantled, and Shaun Kingsley and Peverell Greyson apprehended by Interpol when the British Navy intervened in the arms operation. 'Which had been going on for years,' he added.

Shaun, *arrested,* came Dolly's fleeting thought. Then: Fuck Shaun. Whatever had existed between them was over, long ago.

'It seems,' continued Sunstar, 'that certain members of the British Government have been funnelling aid payments to Lusenka, and knowingly facilitating the purchase of arms from Greyson and his associates, who struck a deal with Kilomi. The scandal broke in the papers yesterday, along with the report from Anakin Awadi's lot. Undoubtedly our government will be facing significant embarrassment – they'll have to take corrective action on the situation. Here, I'll put these ready for you to read.'

Sunstar reached across to a side table, where several thick weekend newspapers all carried similar headlines. Some featured Dolly's photo, others a by-line credit – 'field reporting by Dolly Fontaine'. She picked up *The Sunday Times,* unable to believe what she was seeing.

'You arranged this?'

'I still have contacts up there in Legoland,' Sunstar chuckled softly. 'Friends in high places can occasionally prove very advantageous, my dear, and I couldn't let the story go without your name attached to it. Rest assured: Whitehall was very averse to the notion of a scandal.'

'What about the diamonds?'

'Diamonds?'

'Yes. Lionel Abimbola sent me a bag of diamonds. When my mother was on the mission in Lusenka, at the Sheraton, his father Hervé Abimbola slipped them into her pocket, without her permission. Years later, Gloria must have given them to Lionel for safekeeping.'

'I see.'

There was a long pause, and Dolly waited for an answer as Sunstar fiddled with the flowers with a frown, looking thoughtful.

'I fear Gloria got herself in a bit of a pickle,' he said after a moment or two. 'She never told me about any deeds, let alone diamonds. You'll have to update me.'

Briefly, Dolly told him of the deeds to the Balaika's ancestral lands which were handed to Gloria by Hervé Abimbola. Then she recounted how Hervé's son, Lionel, had sent her a bag of diamonds by courier, evidently the ones Gloria talked about in her diary.

'There must be a way to return the lands to the Balaika?' Dolly added. 'And the jewels?'

'Yes, indeed. May I suggest we talk to the ambassador. Nice chap, owes me a favour.'

'That sounds good.' Dolly smiled, turning her gaze to a bandage on Sunstar's arm. 'You got injured too?'

'Not at all. You were in a bad way, you needed blood urgently. It was touch-and-go for a while there.' He peered at her with an expression halfway between worry and relief. 'The very least I could do.'

Dolly considered this, feeling puzzled, then shook her head emphatically. 'No, no, that couldn't happen. I'm RH negative. It's a very rare blood-type—'

'And as a matter of fact, so am I.' Sunstar recommended arranging the flowers on the bedside table. A few seconds later, he stood back to survey his handywork. 'AB negative, that is. We're the lucky nought point five per cent, my dear girl.'

Before she could ask more questions, a male nurse appeared wheeling a blood pressure machine, and proceeded to place the fabric band around her arm with practised ease, noting her readings, before nodding in satisfaction and jotting some more notes on his clipboard. Without a word, he wheeled the machine away and disappeared into the hallway.

'I can't believe you've got the same blood type as me,' Dolly remarked speculatively when the nurse had gone. 'What a lucky coincidence. Imagine if you hadn't been there...'

There was a short silence, during which she could hear the sounds of the hospital; a machine bleeping from another ward, footsteps down the Lino corridor, the gentle shush shush of a coffee machine from somewhere. A text from Morgan buzzed on her phone: *'Congratulations, babe,'* she read, the words accompanied by several red hearts and a smiley face. *'You killed it! Me and the kids'll be fine, my EX-husband was an asshole x.'*

Then a triumphant PS: *'we're getting a divorce!'*

Dolly glanced up as Sunstar broke the silence. 'My dear Dolly.' He cleared his throat, then fixed her with an earnest look, containing a burgeoning smile. 'There's one final tape that your mother recorded. It may well be the most important. Once you're feeling better, you must give it a listen.' He paused and sighed heavily. 'I was a foolish young man, to sacrifice everything for my career. They took too much of me and I should have stood my ground. But perhaps there's a chance for me to make up for things now.'

'Make up for things?'

Sunstar reached out, patted her hand. 'My dear girl,' he repeated in a soft voice. 'My dear, dear girl.'

CHAPTER FORTY-SEVEN

Dolly

Dolly and Rich sat together at the table in the garden. It was a Sunday, crisp and lazy beneath a watery sun. Rich's face had grown thinner, Dolly noticed, and there were bruise-like shadows under his eyes as if he hadn't slept properly for weeks. After a few moments, Sunstar came out of the house through the French windows, carrying two mugs of tea. He handed them over with a smile. 'Here you go, kids.'

'Thanks, Dad,' they chorused as Sunstar excused himself and disappeared.

'I'm just relieved you're okay,' Rich said, taking a sip of his tea. 'Things got a bit wild back there, didn't they.'

'I still don't really understand.'

Rich ran a hand across his head with a sigh. 'I don't blame you.' He gave a low laugh. 'Sometimes I've had to wonder what's legit and what's just in my head.'

'So, you never actually left the Met at all?' said Dolly.

'Never. It was all a front. I've been in deep cover here for the last few years, tracking Greyson and his pals. Not even Gracie knew. When you came poking about, it caused a whole load of problems for me and the operation. I had to throw you off, for everyone's safety – not least yours.'

'If only I'd known, I wouldn't have been such a bloody pain, trying to be Miss Marple.'

They both laughed.

'How did you know to find me?' she asked.

'Cakey called; we'd met a couple of times over the years, nice guy.'

'Cakey? Oh, you mean Evan? I didn't know whether to trust him at first. I was suspicious of everybody.'

'Turns out he had your back the whole time. He got in touch with Sunstar the minute you gave him the number, thank God. I already had a tracer on Greyson – we knew some major shit was going down over in Lusenka. Greyson and his boys had been prepping for months, guns and drugs, dirty fingers in lots of different pies.'

'Then Cakey told me you'd gone, and we were both bricking it, to be quite honest. So we teamed up to follow your tracker, up to the point when your phone went dead, and we were able to nail down the intel we had, and Greyson's tracer. Plus we knew you'd come up with something badass.' Rich grinned broadly. 'Dolly Fontaine, the ultimate nightmare hostage. Shit, I wouldn't like to mess with you, Doll.'

Dolly laughed, listening as Rich told her about the doctored manifest logged by The Trident, which had changed its registered passage to pick up and drop off arms and drugs along the way. A Navy frigate had been patrolling off Lusenka, Rich explained, with a unit of Royal Marines commandoes on board.

'Lucky for us, the commander's a pal of Cakey's, so he had a chat,' continued Rich. 'Asked if they'd keep an eye out for the ship – and when we said it might be narcos on board, it set off all sorts of alarm bells. We pulled a few pretty tough strings and got clearance to board. Honestly, without Sunstar – sorry, Robert, sorry, *Dad* – whatever – tapping up his contacts at Whitehall, we would have been screwed. But thanks to him we got the green light. So, when the unit saw your flare, they were already geared up to go. Lucky break, Doll.'

'Right. The gods were on my side, weren't they?'

'Definitely were.'

She stared out at a chaffinch hopping along a branch of the pear tree, then beyond to a plane crossing the sky, its trail fluffy white against the gentle pale blue. The garden was still, windless and unseasonably warm. In the foreground the little bird sat on the branch, chirping and ruffling its rust-coloured feathers.

'They were going to kill me. Pev was, I mean. A few more hours, and...'

'I did tell you to quit being such a busybody.'

'I should have listened.'

Rich shrugged. 'It all worked out in the end. Without you, we wouldn't have wrapped up the op so quickly.' There was a pause. After a short while, he spoke again. 'What are you going to do now?'

The chaffinch flew off, landing on a higher branch.

'Get a local job,' Dolly replied decisively, shooting her brother a sideways smile. 'I might write that novel. I was thinking a crime thriller, actually, maybe a gripping, white-knuckle plot about a reckless journalist and a ruthless arms-dealing mercenary.'

Rich groaned, hiding his face with a hand in mock despair, and Dolly found herself smiling with the sun in her eyes, laughing along with her brother.

'So, you'll be hassling me again for your research.'

She grinned. 'Of course.'

'Here...' Rich fished into his bag, brought out a parcel. 'For you. Sunstar – sorry – *Robert* – sorry, *Dad* – shit, I've no idea what to call him these days – anyway, he told me to give this to you, very hush hush. Seems like he's still got that spy vibe going. Once a spook, always a spook, I s'pose.'

Dolly shook her head with a laugh. 'I can't get used to Robert, or Dad. I *have* to call him Sunstar.' She took the parcel and tore open the sellotaped seal. Inside was a single tape. 'Wow, this is—?'

'Mum's last tape, apparently,' Rich finished her sentence, and looked at her pensively. 'She told me about the tapes and Dad, before she died, you know. But she wanted you to listen to them yourself – your journey, she said. I think she knew you'd go crazy and start being nosy. That's what she wanted, I think, for you to know how much she loved us.'

'Jesus, talk about melodramatic,' said Dolly softly, gazing at the parcel. 'She was right though – it *was* my journey to go on, wasn't it. I'm just sorry I got to have all the fun.'

'Don't be. You needed this to make peace with her.'

'You sound like Gracie.' She laughed, and there followed a long pause. Then she spoke, contemplatively: 'Our mum, she was a legend back then, wasn't she, Rich? Gloria Fontaine, the baddest spy around.

323

I never realised how cool she was back in the day.'

'No doubt about it. Funny how you two never got on, but you're basically two peas in a pod.' He reached for Dolly's hand and gave it a tight squeeze. 'You're just like her, Doll, in so many ways. I'm glad you finally saw that.'

CHAPTER FORTY-EIGHT

Gloria

Tape seven
Conclusions! Love, Mum x

I can picture you listening to this, Sugar, wondering why on earth I never told you. Believe me, there were so many times I nearly confessed. How you must have wondered about your annoying mother and her refusal to discuss the past! Even now you think I'm shutting you out, keeping secrets. I can imagine you grumbling behind my back: 'Mum's so difficult, so cantankerous.' Now you've heard my recordings, chances are you'll say I pulled the wool over your eyes.

The truth is, I never intended to hide my past from you – or from anyone, for that matter. It was never about pulling wool over eyes, but rather about letting old ghosts sleep. I believed that silence could exorcise what happened long ago. I feared those events would come to spoil the present, like milk souring in a storm. I was caught between wanting to unburden my soul and my instinctual need to protect you, my child, my darling, from the harsh realities of my past.

There was too much pain there, you see, and too much loss. Fear too, in those difficult years that followed the mission. Let me tell you, there was always a looming threat of discovery by the Lusenkan Secret Services, not to mention exposure in the British press, which would have been disastrous for all concerned.

You could say my life has unfolded in two acts, and act one and act two are as different as night and day. Looking back, I've come to understand that the old Gloria, the other Gloria, was left behind that day, there in the whispering half-light of the forest, a silhouette taken captive by the sunlight through the trees. A different woman emerged that morning, who wanted different things, and it was this new version of me who set off through the jungle ready to embark on act two. And so do you see? There are two parts of me – the same Gloria, of two halves.

Life has a way of surprising you, Sugar. It comes along and changes your course when you least expect it. Sometimes, it takes a shock to make you realise what you really want. Other times, we have to push ourselves beyond our own limits to really know what we're capable of. It took me many years to understand that the woman who escaped Lourenco was the truest version of myself I had ever known.

Let me tell you about Sunstar.

It turned out his real name was Robert, Robert Montgomery, though I never did get used to that. To me, Sunstar would always be Sunstar.

He told me his real name during those rainy, dreamlike days afterwards in London, when we debriefed in a warm room on the top floor of a nondescript mansion flat – a Civil Service safe house somewhere in Chelsea. There, I handed over the photographed blueprints I'd stolen from Lourenco to a rather mousy woman wearing glasses and a brown tweed skirt suit, who exactly fitted my previous imaginings of the shadowy figures at HQ. She seemed friendly enough, serious and polite. It turned out she was head of the whole operation. The microfilm would be taken and turned into Polaroid by HQ, she informed me, for British Intelligence teams to beaver away at.

According to Sunstar, everyone was pleased. That following September, a coup took place in Lusenka, as planned. President Baptiste Lourenco was overthrown. In his place, President Florian Kilomi became an ally of the Americans and the British – or so their governments thought at the time. Soon afterwards, the oil crisis ended for Europe, with a new foreign source of oil undermining the Iranians and causing prices to plummet to normal levels.

Naturally, I had mixed opinions about all that. If you ask me, one politician is as bad as the next, and weaponising Kilomi to access Lusenka's oil was one of the worst mistakes our Western nations ever made. But who was I to make judgments about such things?

After the mission, it was no longer feasible for me to return to acting. The British Intelligence Services were jumpy about reprisals from Lourenco or his allies, and HQ moved me to a safe house in remote Cornwall. They paid for everything, though they didn't need to, and I liked the house very much, so I decided to buy it. As you know, I'd made an enormous amount of money from the films, and royalties continued to roll in. I would be financially comfortable for the rest of my life, thank God. I christened the house Genévrier, after the word for 'juniper' in native Lusenkan – a fact I'm not sure I ever mentioned to you before. For obvious reasons, gin was more than just a favourite cocktail to me by then: it had jolly well saved my life. The name Genévrier remained a constant reminder to cherish the safe haven and tranquillity of my home.

Before long, Sunstar moved in, and in many ways, those were the happiest years of my life. Our existence was simple and sheltered, some would say boring, but for the first time since Chilembé's death, I learned what it was to be close to another human being. We both knew that our life together was finite, a fleeting glimpse of normality amid an existence that for Sunstar – and increasingly for me too – seemed cocooned from the real world, crisscrossed as it was by the complex fictions of Sunstar's work life. I couldn't complain. I loved him, whatever that entailed. Besides, I was well-used by that time to the transient nature of happiness in my own life.

Our domestic idyll lasted long enough for you, Sugar, to come along the following year, then Rich, two years later. I'll never forget the night you were born, precisely at one minute before midnight. You were a tiny little girl with a full head of hair and bright, watchful eyes that shone like newborn stars. For some reason, you didn't cry, you just lay on my chest without a sound, gazing up at me, and I was overcome with love for you – my baby daughter – a love like I've never felt for anyone before.

When Sunstar lifted you up, you fitted perfectly into the palm of his hand. 'She's no bigger than a sugar bag,' he exclaimed, completely enthralled by you.

Now you know where your nickname came from. God knows, he was besotted. I've never seen such adoration in anyone's eyes. Let me tell you, Sugar: your father was wild about you from the minute you entered this world.

In the background, things were heating up. The Intelligence Services were drawing in their horns, the Soviets were at large. One night, there was a frightening incident here at the house; we found a man with a gun downstairs. It became clear that being associated with Sunstar was dangerous for me, and for you and your brother. Your father knew it too – he was increasingly worried for our safety, and it seemed HQ were putting pressure on him to make a decision. I couldn't help thinking of the brown tweed woman back in that London safehouse, turning her thumb down like a Roman empress at the Colosseum games, pronouncing the fate of the gladiators. In the end we faced a devastating choice. Those shadowy figures in Whitehall forced our hands. Sunstar and I decided he would have to leave.

That day, that day... Oh, how painful it is to go back there in my mind, and yet how sweet. A sunlit evening in late September, gusty and cloudless, nostalgic and imperceptibly chilly, the lazy final days of an Indian summer. The lawn was scattered with leaves and windfallen pears, ripe and golden, thrumming with wasps. An early sunset streaked the sky tangerine, lavender and crimson. Together, we put you and your brother to bed. Through the open window, a church bell sounded in the distance, and the swallows played in the dying sunlight. Sunstar read you both a bedtime story, planting kisses on your foreheads before you went to sleep.

Downstairs, Sunstar opened a bottle of wine and put the record player on. Joni Mitchell's *Both Sides Now* meandered out through the open doors to the garden. My dress caught the wind like a ribbon, and he caught my hand.

'Dance with me, my love,' he said.

I'll never forget the sound of the music, low and rich and sad, and the grainy quality of the vinyl, and the occasional scratch of the needle on the record. There in the spellbound amber twilight; there beneath the last, fierce rays of the setting sun, I pressed my cheek against his and listened to the tendrils of the song drifting across the shadowy garden. Like that we danced, just the two of us, Gloria Fontaine and her spy, until the light was completely gone.

That night I fell asleep in his arms. The next day, he was gone.

I fell into a lonely existence. If it hadn't been for the two of you, I would certainly have fallen into a depression. Inevitably, I dwelt on the fact that, one after another, I seemed to lose the people I loved – first my parents, then Chilembé, then Sunstar. I used to think about the time we lived together, short but so intense, with a longing that almost destroyed me. Moreover, it dawned on me that my mission for British Intelligence had meant very little in the end. The Cold War rolled on with no sign of stopping. What had really changed, I questioned? What was it all for?

Left alone, I became unreasonably fearful about you and your brother's safety. My dreams at night were vivid and frightening. I'd wake drenched in sweat, crying out Sunstar's name. Sometimes I'd sit bolt upright in bed, my heart racing violently, my whole body alert for sounds – from the hallway, from the garden, from downstairs. Quietly, I'd get up and tiptoe to your bedrooms, listening for the sweet sound of your childish breathing, checking you were both safe. How could I have known that becoming a mother would exaggerate all my worst fears, or that the demons of my past lives could loom quite so vividly from the dark, invading my dreams, threatening everything I loved.

Naturally, you were always sleeping soundly in your beds, arms and legs flung across the sheets, undisturbed by intruders real or imagined. Later, when you straggled in, sleepy-eyed, still in your pyjamas, I'd be sure to show nothing of the night's skirmishes. As you chit-chatted away with all the eagerness of your younger years, I'd allow myself a glance at your little face. The sweet, childish curve of your cheek lit by fragments of sunshine through the window. That single curlicue of hair, loosened from its pale pink bobble, curling just above your earlobe. My sweetest of girls, I would think, filled with an aching tenderness that was so physical it tightened my chest with love and pure terror. Wordlessly, I'd bring breakfast to the table, as if the banal mechanics of this simple, domestic act could somehow transform me into just another mother, as ordinary as the next.

Do you see how I had no wish for you to fathom the dramas of your mother's past life? You and your brother were innocents; you brought so much light, so much joy. As you grew, I felt, if anything, a greater determination to protect you at all costs from everything to do with my secrets. One day, I promised myself. One day I would tell you my story, but only when you were grown and you saw life for yourself, for what would be the point of burdening a child?

There's a photograph here on the mantelpiece – you know the one? An August afternoon, hot and breezeless beneath a ferocious blue sky. I suppose you must have set up the automatic frame on your camera, because all three of us are in the picture: you stretched out on a rug in the shade of the parasol, wearing that flowery, Dorothy Perkins swimming costume you begged me for, do you remember?

You're reading a book, so beautiful already, and so clever. Rich is tending the barbecue; he was always in charge of that. And there I am carrying out a tray, ketchup and cutlery and dinner plates. I remember the smell of sizzling sausages in the air, and freshly mown grass. The glow of the sun on your faces. Do you know why I love that photograph so much, Sugar? Because I look like any other mother from any other family, making you two happy for once.

God knows, I've been a terrible mother, distracted and selfish, too critical and hard on you both, too reliant on alcohol to soothe my pain. I'm sorry I disappointed you. The truth is that you and your brother made my life worthwhile. You were the reason I woke up every morning with a smile, though you didn't know it, and your presence illuminated even my darkest days. I saw the same fire in you as in your Uncle Chilembé, who would have adored you...

To practical matters. Look in the attic. Rummage for the travelling bag in all my junk. I wasn't rambling or mad when I told you I would leave a box of secrets. You must have thought me such a crazy, messy person, but there was method to my madness, and I've every confidence you'll find Abimbola's deeds amid my purposeful clutter. As you will know by now, I arranged for those wretched diamonds he slipped into my pocket that night to reach you another way.

I'm proud of you, Sugar, I always have been. I want you to know that I've loved you from the very moment you were born into this world, from the very depths of my being, as powerfully as any human heart could ever love another. You are my greatest treasure, my greatest blessing, the sunshine in my day.

When I'm gone, Sugar – my darling Sugar – remember that.

CHAPTER FORTY-NINE

Dolly

A late afternoon, the landline ringing. Dolly answered to Angus Cunningham, offering her job back with a smile in his voice. 'It's yours, Dolly,' he enthused. 'Bloody awful business, but what a story! Our bestselling front page for a long bloody time!'

She put the receiver down, expecting to feel a rush of joy at such a complete vindication, but found instead that she was overcome by a new serenity, mingling with a tinge of anger that Angus hadn't stuck up for her in the first place. How quick, how glad he was to take the credit now. *And* he hadn't apologised properly. But perhaps the old longing to prove everyone wrong had disappeared because, she realised, not for the first time, the city was no longer her home, and she belonged in Cornwall with her family. She would gladly accept the job offer from Peter Lowen at the *Cornish Guardian,* she decided, with its interesting brief, heading up a new digital platform for West Country news and politics, and she would finally write a novel. Not forgetting Evan, too, whom Gracie had issued with an official green card: 'Looks like you've found a keeper, Doll,' her sister-in-law had pronounced, delightedly, on meeting the ex-Marine. 'Finally!'

Dolly recalled her mother's words. *Sometimes it takes a shock to make you realise what you really want.* Gloria was right, of course. Looking back at her past self, she saw nothing but a lonely, power-hungry journalist. How could she ever regret leaving that woman behind?

For a few days after leaving hospital, she'd racked her brains about Gloria's last clue, *rummage for the bag,* because she'd sorted through everything in the attic while looking for the tapes, or so she thought, and still she hadn't found the title deeds.

Then all at once, it hit her. In the darkest, furthest corner of the attic, she discovered her mother's travelling bag slung with apparent carelessness near the bottom of a box of clothes. The bag turned out to be rather Bohemian, of supple tan leather with seventies-style fringing and a long, slender strap, as well as a number of well-designed pockets imprinted with the Vivienne Westwood logo. Sure enough, beneath a double layer of silk lining the bottom, Dolly found a secret compartment locked shut with rusty screws. With a bit of effort and a screwdriver, she was able to open it up and retrieve the deeds.

The three of them, Dolly, Rich and Sunstar, went up to the Lusenkan Embassy on a sunny Tuesday morning the following week. A last mission, Dolly called it, and she was especially excited when Sunstar suggested they travel in his car, a sought-after 2+2 Jaguar E-type, which Rich nearly had kittens over.

'Jesus, it's a V12,' he exclaimed, diving boyishly into the beige leather driving seat, gushing about its engine as Dolly looked on, giggling.

'What, this old thing?' Sunstar's voice was nonchalant, though he had a wide grin on his face. 'I had it restored a couple of years ago.' He handed Rich the keys. 'You kids might as well have a ride.'

Now, the ex-spy sat in the front passenger seat, reminiscing about the past; about Gloria and MI6, not rambling exactly – though Dolly couldn't help feeling there was still a lifetime to catch up on. In the back she looked out the window, half-listening, humming to herself and feeling a deep-rooted sense of contentment at this newfound family life, at having a father, finally, which felt as if she'd been handed the missing piece of a complex puzzle.

Of late, Dolly and Sunstar had been engaging in some long conversations. He'd followed her career over the years, he confessed: a silent observer, always concerned for her safety. Now he showed a gentle paternal interest she found both odd and comforting. She only wished he'd been present in her life sooner. Yesterday, they had shared a gin fizz in honour of Gloria, outside in the garden at Genévrier as a low sun dropped over the fields beyond the garden. Their conversation turned to her life, and the future.

'Tell me, my dear, what do you really want?' Sunstar enquired. 'Is it success or happiness?'

'I'm not sure,' Dolly replied truthfully. 'Are the two mutually exclusive?'

'Sometimes.' He observed her with a shrewd smile over the top of his teacup, a statement not a question. 'It depends how you classify success. Isn't life about being happy, in the end? I always feel that's the mistake your mother and I made.'

'You regret letting her go?'

'Always. I should never have left her, or you.'

The consulate was not at all what Dolly expected. After the long drive up from Cornwall, they turned off the M25 and followed the sat nav, puttering through the Surrey Hills, dreamy and sun-baked after the long summer; grassy yellow hills and ploughed fields rolling into the distance.

'Are you sure this is the right place?' said Rich dubiously, glancing at Dolly in the rear mirror. She assured him that this was indeed the correct address – 3 Lilac's Lane, Witting Green – but still, it hardly seemed a typical location for an embassy. In the distance, a church steeple rose against a pastel-coloured sky, straight out of a Monet. The gentle sound of birdsong carried through the open car windows. They could be out for the day, Dolly thought with amusement, imagining a picnic hamper strapped to the back of the car, complete with ginger ale and cucumber sandwiches.

Half an hour later they came to a picturesque village a few miles west of Dorking, where Rich parked the Jaguar outside a graceful red-brick house with sash windows, tall chimneys, and a frill of holly-hocks running along the outside wall. An elderly man with a kindly face and a shock of white hair emerged. He wore a yellow jumper over a shirt collar, a pair of reading glasses perched on his head. When he saw Sunstar, he let out a hearty chuckle.

'Robert.' His voice was from another time, jocular and well-spoken, fifties newsreader mixed with old-school diplomat. 'My word, after all this time.'

'Ned,' declared Sunstar. 'It's been years, my dear fellow.'

The two men embraced, patting each other on the back for quite some time. Dolly noticed that Sunstar looked a little misty-eyed.

The Ambassador turned to Dolly, then Rich, and shook their hands formally, one by one. 'Edward Gilligan, Honorary Consulate of Lusenka. A pleasure to meet you both.' Then he clasped his hands behind his back, rocking on his heels with a jaunty look. 'Now, I understand we have the small matter of some diamonds and land deeds to discuss. Please, do come inside.'

At the end of the garden, in an airy, elegant metal-framed greenhouse with a desk and several chairs inside, they sat down without ceremony. A bench was covered with potted orchids displaying waxy flowers in showy colours. There was a wispy Areca Palm in a terracotta pot, some tall, cartoon cacti, a cheese plant, and a towering banana palm with wide, flat leaves. The windowsill was lined with small gourds in all shades of orange. On a side table was a kettle and some mugs. Ned went over to it and switched the kettle on.

'Shall we begin with you telling me all about it?' he said. 'And then we can attend to the paperwork.'

While Ned Gilligan sipped tea and listened intently, Dolly told him everything: about Gloria's classified mission; about the Abimbolas' involvement; about Peverell Greyson and the illegal arms dealing. An hour or two later, once the folder of deeds and the bag of diamonds were locked in a government safe, and an official agreement was signed and stamped, witnessed by Sunstar and Rich, Ned shook Dolly's hand with a warm smile, and congratulated her. The deeds, he said, would serve as solid proof of the indigenous Balaika's right to their ancestral lands, and could pave the way for eventual negotiations towards peace.

'We can use the diamonds to raise funds, provided we can verify their source,' he said. 'Outstanding work, my dear. Positive developments like these are rare, I can assure you.'

It wasn't until they'd said their goodbyes and were back in the car, being driven home by Rich, that Dolly allowed herself to feel all the emotions bubbling up inside her. Gloria would have been filled with pride; she knew that now for certain. Her mother was convinced her mission had been in vain, just a flashy display of heroism, a victory for the British Intelligence services but a misfortune for Lusenka. At last, Dolly was glad to prove her wrong. Even thirty years later, the deeds her mother risked her life for were an important weapon of justice for the Balaika. If only Gloria were here to witness it all.

Dolly's train of thought was interrupted by Anakin Awadi phoning with his congratulations, telling her that the contentious Human Rights Watch report on UK arms involvement in Lusenka, so long hidden, would now finally be released. 'Thanks to you, Dolly,' he exclaimed, and she could hear the delight in his voice echoing down the line as she stared out at the motorway traffic.

'It's all because of my mum, actually,' she replied with a smile. 'My mum, Gloria. She was a spy. It's a long story. I'll tell you sometime.'

Now, barefoot, Dolly put a record on and wandered into the windy garden where Sunstar was busy tidying up, with Lucy by his side. He'd mown the lawn and now he was engaged in pulling weeds from the overgrown borders while the sheepdog dawdled in the undergrowth. The garden smelled of freshly cut grass, high and sweet, a summer smell lingering in the first throes of autumn. Dolly watched the old man potter and bend to empty the contents of the wheelbarrow into the compost bin with a clatter. So this was happiness, she was thinking. Not starry, high-powered success but life success. Sunstar was right: what was life if you couldn't simply be content?

'Autumn's coming,' she called out as the deep velvet tones of Shirley Bassey, *What I Did For Love,* swelled and drifted from the record player through the French doors, a song about love and dreams and seizing the future, without regrets.

'It certainly is.' Sunstar stood upright in the middle of the border, tugging off his gardening gloves and stretching his back. A fresh breeze whipped in from the sea, sending fallen leaves and cloud shadows scudding across the lawn. He brushed a hand across his eyes, chuckling softly. 'Your mother loved this song.'

'I remember.'

They stood in silence for a moment as the music and the wind danced around them, both caught in the melodies of the past.

Finally, Dolly broke the silence: 'Shall I put the kettle on?'

'Absolutely.' Sunstar grinned, his face crinkling and twinkling in the sunlight. 'One sugar, please, my dear,' he added. 'And if there's any cake, I'd kill for a slice.'

ACKNOWLEDGEMENTS

I'm hugely indebted to my publishers, Aleksandra Markovic and Goran Baba Ali at Afsana Press. To be published by Afsana is to become part of a literary movement and a family. Thank you for believing in me. I am forever grateful.

A special acknowledgment to my editor, Laura Joyce, whose thoughtful edits elevated this story to new heights. Also, to Anne Hamilton, whose insights during the writing process have been instrumental in shaping this novel. And the most enormous thank you to Goran for his meticulous editing, and his endless dedication to making *Oh, Sugar* as perfect as possible.

Thanks to Andy Bridge for the lovely cover illustration. And especially to designer Ben Aitchison, who took such care, at the last minute, to make this book truly shine.

I am hugely indebted to David Snoxell, former British Ambassador to Senegal, former British High Commissioner to Mauritius, and father of my dearest friend, Laura Snoxell, for generously sharing his anecdotes about life in the British Foreign Office during the 1970s and '80s. Our telephone conversations transported me to another era in quite the best way, and inspired a number of scenes in this book.

As ever, my greatest thanks are due to my beloved parents, Paul and Jennifer, who unfailingly love and support me in all my endeavours. To Daddy, for being my biggest, smiliest fan, and for carrying my books on the back shelf of the car, at all times, just in case someone asks. And to my lovely Mummy, for the cups of tea when I most need them, and for everything you do for us, every single day.

Special extra thanks to the mums: Jennifer Labous and Jane Teverson, for their heroic, last minute proofreading. As ever, mums rock.

To my little brother, The Dood: the only person with whom I can both argue and snort out loud with laughter in the space of five minutes. Thanks for being the best (and funniest) sibling ever :)

To Adam, for always being there, so steadfastly. You are my hero.

Last, to my precious daughter, Bella, without whom all this would mean nothing. As ever, this book is dedicated to you, my darling girl. You are my greatest treasure, my greatest blessing, the sunshine in my day. I love you so, so, so, so, so, sooooooo much. With all my love, Mummy x

Also by Afsana Press:

Past Participle

A novel by Jane Labous

Dakar, Senegal, 1987: On a rainy night after a wild party, the British Ambassador's wife, Vivienne Hughes, is involved in a car crash. Her vehicle hits the motorbike of a young Senegalese doctor, Aimé Tunkara, killing him. Three decades later, Aimé's little sister, Lily Tunkara, now a high-flying lawyer in Dakar, finds a photograph that compels her to investigate what really happened that rainy night.

'*Past Participle* is a captivating story of murder and imperialist corruption, of friendship and motherhood and of the past haunting the present, told through the interlinking stories of two women. The novel tackles an important subject matter, but in a way that doesn't feel hectoring or didactic. It recognises the nuances of power dynamics, personal desires and social and political realities in framing how people act and why. The novel offers a strong critique of western imperialism, attentive to the macro and micro applications of that, alongside a dynamic and moving story.'
Kieran Devaney, Author & Literary Editor

Release date: September 2023 / 352 pages
Paperback: £ 10.99 / ISBN: 9781739982478

Also by Afsana Press:

Whispering Walls

A novel by Choman Hardi

The US invasion of Iraq is looming. Three siblings – two in London, one in Slemany – recall their troubled past. Stories of war, displacement, and coming to terms with the tragedies of a Kurdish family, all told from their different perspectives. Torn between two countries and various life stories, the siblings find themselves dealing with complex life choices, and the mystery of their sister's suicide twenty-two years ago.

Whispering Walls is a story of love, relationships, affection, and hope, with a cautious view of the future.

'A book that is written with the same sharp observation, fresh language and moral imagination of Hardi's award-winning poetry, it asks a question we all must consider: how can we grapple with the tragedies of the past as we try to fashion a better future? Not only is Choman Hardi a brilliant poet, she is also a great novelist. I want everyone I know to read her book!'

Catherine Davidson, Poet & Novelist

Release date: September 2023 / 304 pages
Paperback: £ 10.99 / ISBN: 9781739982454

Also by Afsana Press:

Winter Sun

A novel by Miki Lentin

A spiky father-son relationship is tested to its limits on their last holiday together. A nine-day winter break in Tenerife. Nothing is quite good enough. A son tries in vain to ask his ailing, elderly Irish Jewish father questions about their past before it's too late. The absurdity and hilarity of family holidays in the sun are brought to life in this sharp and fiercely honest novel that crosses borders, carrying the reader on a tide of childhood pain, a search for identity, and growth.

'Bittersweet, funny and tender, Winter Sun is about the mysterious relationship between parent and adult child, the fragility of the ageing body, the strangeness of family holidays and the comforts of alcohol and literature. You can't help falling in love with Miki and Abba, willing them on to find a common language—and ideally a whiskey they can both agree on.'
Viv Groskop, author of The Anna Karenina Fix

'Written from the heart, with skill and honesty, this is a warm, highly intelligent novel. Just beautiful. I was thoroughly moved by *Winter Sun*. A page turner!'
Niamh Boyce, author of *The Herbalist* and *Her Kind*

Release date: 13 March 2024 / 208 pages
Paperback: £ 11.99 / ISBN: 9781739982492
Hardback: £ 19.99/ ISBN: 9781738555277
e-Book: £ 7.99 / ISBN: 9781738555208

Also by Afsana Press:

The Glass Wall

A novel by Goran Baba Ali

The tale of a teenage refugee who must re-live the pain of his past to enter a land waiting behind a glass wall. Will his story be convincing enough to guarantee his safety? A story of struggle and persecution, yet abundant in hope, *The Glass Wall* is a clear-eyed, emotionally honest account of displaced people, illustrating the true hardship that refugees experience.

'An unforgettable novel, made cruelly relevant by what has been taking place in Europe ... Goran Baba Ali has seen and felt the worst of the exile condition. But he has turned it into an almost Kafkan allegory which runs all through the book, the sustained image of a glass wall.'
Neal Ascherson, Writer & Journalist

'Poetic and beautifully rendered, it probes the boundaries between those who have and those who seek.'
Isabel Hilton OBE, Journalist & Broadcaster

Release date: November 2021 / 352 pages
Hardback: £ 14.99 / ISBN: 9781739982409
Paperback: £ 12.99 / ISBN: 9781739982416 (April 2024)

Also by Afsana Press:

The Good, the Bad and the Gringo

A novel by Kae Bahar

At the age of ten Merywan Rashaba's life is shattered when the local Mullah declares him a neuter, neither a boy nor a girl, and therefore a doomed child. Merywan is terrified. If his father gets to know about his gender ambiguity, he will put a knife to his throat. Growing up as a Kurd in Saddam's Iraq, he feels he doesn't belong to this twisted society, but finds inspiration and comfort in the magic world of cinema. He secretly writes letters to his hero, Clint Eastwood, whom he calls Gringo, begging him to help him escape to America. As his plans are disrupted, Merywan is drawn deeper into a dark roller-coaster ride of savagery, passion, betrayal and heroism, which makes the movies he adores almost seem trivial by comparison.

'It makes me laugh out loud and gasp in horror, too. I think it's really, really special and I feel very excited about it and honoured to read it.'
Barbara Marsh, writer, poet and musician

'Intriguing and informative, a page-turner, very absorbing, and difficult to put dow.'
Audrey Swindells, MBE

Release date: October 2024 / 416 pages
Paperback: £ 14.99 / ISBN: 9781738555239